A Secret in Singapore

An Elspeth Duff Mystery

Ann Crew

D1738183

Cover photographs of Singapore Skyline and High Tea at Raffles Hotel by Ann Crew © 2007

Author's photograph by Ian Crew

ACE/AC Editions
All rights reserved.
ISBN-10: 1500932175
ISBN-13: 9781500932176

Library of Congress Control Number: 2014920321
CreateSpace Independent Publishing Platform
North Charleston, South Carolina

anncrew.com

elspethduffmysteries.com

To Gim with love and thanks for the exquisite Chinese banquet in Singapore

Also by Ann Crew

A Murder in Malta

A Scandal in Stresa

Praise for *A Murder in Malta*:

"Each main character has a rich backstory with enough skeletons in closets to provide grist for a number of future novels.

An often compelling. . .excursion through exotic locales featuring unusual, complex characters." —*Kirkus Review*

Prologue

In the unusual act of rising unsettled from her mid-afternoon rest, Magdelena Cassar crossed the cavernous room at the center of her home, a resplendent converted farmhouse on the island of Gozo in the Republic of Malta. She approached Elspeth Duff. Elspeth was one of the few people in the world who merited any disruption of Magdelena's normal daily routine. When Magdelena retired to her room an hour earlier, Elspeth was sitting on an ornate baroque settee covered in intricate needlepoint that was one of the few pieces of furniture in the great room other than the two back-to-back grand pianos. Magdelena looked at Elspeth with the deep love a mother might have for a child, although Elspeth was not hers.

Always sensitive to her niece's moods, Magdelena spoke to Elspeth. "Even with the warm breeze coming in my window, I couldn't sleep. I tried to study the Chopin nocturne for tomorrow's soirée, but I couldn't lift it because I could feel the weight of your sadness a room away."

She sat down next to Elspeth with the effort of an aging woman, oversized by modern standards in London and New York although acceptable as venerable in Malta. Magdelena still had the grace of the long-famous but blew her breath through her eagle's nose at the effort of sitting down. She put her hands on Elspeth's.

Elspeth had not moved over the last hour. The set of her sculptured Gaelic jaw, the stiffness of her backbone pushed against the hardness of her chosen seat, and the tightness of her lips had not altered. Although her eyes were open, they did not take in her current surroundings but were focused on another place than this, a place of pain rather than beauty. As she often did as a child, Elspeth laid her head on Magdelena's ample chest and smiled weakly as she negotiated a spot free of the strands of amber beads.

"Elspeth, *cara,* where are your thoughts?"

Elspeth turned a sad stare toward Magdelena as if puzzled at her presence and the warmth of her caress. "Sorry, I was far away."

"And not in a good place." Magdelena's rich voice whispered in Elspeth's ear.

"No, not in a good place. Richard says I'm still haunted by those days in Cambridge when Malcolm died. Did you know Richard was there afterwards, after they found Malcolm's body?"

Magdelena remembered those times, when Elspeth had come here to Gozo after Malcolm Buchanan had died. Three decades had long passed, but Magdelena could recall each heart-rending day Elspeth spent in Gozo at the end of the summer of nineteen sixty-nine, acting as if she were unalive herself. Elspeth stayed under Magdelena's wing for a month. Only at the end of that time could she raise her head and get through a day with the normal gestures of the living. Finally she was able to return to Girton College at Cambridge to complete her studies. Caressing Elspeth now, Magdelena knew her niece was back in that old place of sorrow.

"My dearest, do you revisit that time often?"

"Dear Aunt Mag, you'd think after all these years I'd have more sense."

Magdelena rose from the settee, to the protest of the aged piece of furniture, and retreated to one of the piano benches, which bore her weight with more fortitude.

Despite her artistic temperament, and often passionate rather than rational way of dealing with difficult situations, Magdelena Cassar offered a solution to Elspeth.

"Have you ever gone back, *cara*, with all your great skills and looked for the person who shot Malcolm?"

Magdelena's suggestion roused Elspeth from her torpor. "Go back? But you know the police searched for years and never found anything."

"If you went back now, could you find out what happened?" Magdelena asked.

"Of course I couldn't. How many years has it been? Thirty-five? Trying to find the murderer at this point would be hopeless."

"Would it?"

Elspeth set her jaw stubbornly, "How could I? Lord Kennington relies on me to provide security at his hotels, and I rely on him for my livelihood. I simply can't ring him in London and say, 'Sorry, Eric, I have some old ghosts to exorcise.'"

Magdelena had heard her niece expostulate about her employer often enough to know Lord Kennington was a demanding boss. "Doesn't that scoundrel give you any time off? It seems to me you have worked for the last year with no break at all."

"That always happens when there are urgent security issues at his hotels. Things have become worse since the recent rise of terrorism."

"Does he ever compensate you for all your time?"

Elspeth avoided the question and posed one of her own.

"What good would it do to go dredging it all up again? Can you imagine me going back to Cambridge and delving into a murder that happened a over a third of a century ago?"

"I can imagine it very well. Elspeth, you must put Malcolm to rest. Surely you have the ability to find the murderer."

"Should I go dig up the old police records, if they still exist?"

"No, not at all. I think you should go back to Cambridge as a mature woman and skilled investigator and find Malcolm's murderer on your own."

"How?" Elspeth challenged.

"I do not know, *cara*, I play the piano; I do not investigate crimes. That is what you do."

Elspeth smiled at this.

Magdelena thought of her own past. In her heyday, she was one of the most celebrated pianists in Europe. Even now those visiting Gozo who remembered her performances, which had filled concert halls and recital rooms throughout Europe for several decades, sought an invitation to her monthly soirées. Magdelena had retired to Gozo, where she had lived since before the Second World War, to be with Elspeth's uncle as he grew older, and she had remained on after he died. Although Magdelena never married Frederick Duff, she had been Elspeth's beloved "aunt" for many years.

"Are you suggesting this ridiculous idea as therapy, Aunt Mag?"

"Of course! You still love Malcolm and won't let go of him. You haven't let him die, *cara*. I'm suggesting you find his murderer. Then you can bury Malcolm and get on with marrying Richard."

Elspeth's face contorted the way it did when she was a child and was considering whether to be rebellious or not. "I've no intention of marrying Richard," she said. "Where did you get that idea?"

During Elspeth's several visits to Malta over the last eight months, Magdelena had watched Elspeth change and sensed the alteration had not come about because of the successful conclusion of the case at the Kennington Valletta hotel but rather because of her re-acquaintance with Sir Richard Munro, KCMG, British High Commissioner to the Republic of Malta.

"I suggest you don't close yourself off to those who might help you," Magdelena said.

Elspeth looked up at her with the expression a petulant child.

"Ask Richard," Magdelena persisted. "You said he was there shortly after Malcolm was shot."

"That was a long time ago."

"Richard's in love with you, Elspeth."

"With me? No, Aunt Mag, he only thinks of me as a friend." Elspeth flushed slightly and avoided her aunt's eyes, the way she did as a child when she was not telling the truth.

"If you say so, *cara*."

"He's a high-muck-a-muck in the FCO and at the European Commission in Brussels. He wouldn't have time to pander to the pathological obsession of a childhood friend."

"Why don't you ask him? I believe Richard could be of more help than you think."

"Aunt Mag, you are a hopeless romantic. No, I must get back to London tomorrow. I often feel a bit morose after a case is done. The last one in Stresa was terribly complex, but my involvement's over."

"I've invited Richard for dinner tomorrow. You cannot refuse to be here."

"But he was here two evenings ago," Elspeth protested.

"I told him I would play Chopin for him if he promised not to stay too late. I said you would be here. Surely, *cara*, you would not mind seeing him again before you go back to London."

"As my children would say, you are quite wicked, Aunt Mag."

"At my age one is allowed to be."

*

Not only did Magdelena Cassar contrive to invite Sir Richard to dinner, she also found a way to leave Elspeth alone with him after she made excuses to see to the preparations for the dinner. Elspeth knew Magdelena's cook and housekeeper, Teresa, was perfectly capable of preparing and serving a meal without Magdelena's oversight, but Elspeth was grateful to have a chance to speak alone with Richard.

The two of them strolled out to the balcony, which, in the distance, afforded them a view of the sun setting over the terraced fields of Gozo and the Mediterranean beyond. They stood quietly for a moment, comfortable in watching the sun and sea without needing to comment on their beauty.

Finally Richard spoke. "You seem distracted," he said softly.

Elspeth turned away from the view and toward him. "I'm still unwinding after Stresa," she said. "Cases like that are never easy."

"Where are you off to next, dearest Elspeth? I will miss you."

Since the case at the Kennington Valletta, she had seen Richard many times, both in London and Malta and most recently in Stresa, but she always had mixed feelings about him. He tempted her emotional sensibilities, but she did not trust herself to give into them. Still, she enjoyed his company and attentiveness and did not send him away.

"Magdelena wants me to go back to the past," she said.

"Has she figured out a way for you to do so? Such a task seems the purview of science fiction." His voice was filled with humor.

"It's about Malcolm Buchanan. Like you, she wants me to find out what really happened. Our conversation about Malcolm the other night has made me moody." Elspeth tried to brush off the extent of her feelings with this evasion, but she wondered if Richard believed her.

Richard reached out and turned her to face him. "She and I are both right, you know."

"Oh, don't be silly, Dickie. I'm a grown woman now. Malcolm was a. . .was something that happened when I was eighteen years old. What good would it do to go back?" She looked up into his hazel eyes, which bordered on green, and which held hers for a long time.

"All the good in the world."

"Why?" She did not drop her gaze. She hoped he would lower his, as it churned up emotions inside of her that had nothing to do with Malcolm and everything to do with Richard.

"Because you never have accepted his death."

"Yes. . .no. Oh, I don't know," Elspeth said, her thoughts going back to Malcolm's murder. "It stays with me and has since he died. It nags and nags. I think the memories have gone, that I'm rid of them for good, and then suddenly there they are all over again, filled with pain and loss and anger at his death. After he was killed, things were never the same again. I've never forgotten him, not when I was married to Alistair, not afterwards, not with the children. Malcolm comes back when least expected, when I am on a plane, or in a place we visited in London, or when I'm driving up the coastline in California, where he and I never went together. There seems no reason to it."

"Could it be that he comes back like all ghosts because his murder was not solved," Richard suggested.

"What good would it do now to find the murderer? His family seems to have disappeared and probably few people remember him."

"You do and so do I, and he is standing between us."

"This is foolish!"

"Is it? I've already told you I think not." He sounded pompous.

"Don't bully me, Dickie," she said clenching her jaw so hard that it tightened the muscles in her cheeks.

"Elspeth, I don't want to bully you. I just want you free of Malcolm." His voice was tender.

Elspeth chose to ignore his remark. "Then let's get back to the original question. What can I possibly do about it?"

He came closer to her but did not touch her again. Nonetheless she could feel his nearness.

"Do what Magdelena suggested. Go back to the past, find his murderer and then lay Malcolm to rest. If you remember," he continued, "last April you asked if I would help you. You know I will. I told you two nights ago, my dearest one, my motives are completely selfish. I cannot ask for your heart if it still belongs to Malcolm."

A Secret in Singapore

He took her in his arms and kissed her hair. She rested her head against his shoulder but did not respond to his endearment for fear of doing something she might later regret.

1

Elspeth stood by the window of the room across from the porter's lodge. She had stood there thirty-five years before and watched Malcolm Buchanan peddle through the gateway out of Girton College. He turned round to see if she were there, grinned widely and waved to her in his silliest manner. He took his hands off the handlebars of his bicycle, and its front wheel careened back and forth insanely. He turned the corner and disappeared from sight. Minutes later he was dead. One shot entered his heart and the other his head, both with deadly accuracy. They never told her which one killed him.

The image was as clear in her mind as if it had happened moments before. She had lived through the same scene often enough that the details had no chance to fade.

In Malta, Richard Munro said to her, "Don't try to forget any more. You must try to remember. Not just the haunting thoughts but every small thing. Not only what happened that night but also anything Malcolm said or did during the time you knew him. An ordinary Cambridge graduate student doesn't die the way Malcolm did."

Now she had three months to make the journey back, to bring up all the memories latent in her mind and to try to dig out any new information that would lead to the person who murdered Malcolm Buchanan.

Lord Kennington was unusually kind after she walked into the Kennington Organisation two days before. His reaction to her entering his glass-walled office looking out over the City of London was one of welcome. Elspeth suspected his warm greeting was a precursor to another difficult assignment.

He looked at her and cleared his throat not once but twice. "Elspeth, I have known you a long time, and you have helped solve many devilish problems in my hotels, but you don't look like a woman who is ready to take on a new job for me."

Elspeth acknowledged his concern by lowering her eyes, a most uncharacteristic gesture. "It's nothing," she said untruthfully.

"I think it is something. Let me call Pamela." He picked up his phone and rang through to Pamela Crumm, his business partner. She appeared instantly through the connecting door that separated their offices.

Elspeth evaded Pamela's eyes, hoping Pamela would not question her. Pamela took her by the arm and led her to one of the chairs Eric Kennington kept for visitors. Elspeth followed docilely. She was trying to compose her words.

"I'll get us all a cup of tea, only you prefer coffee don't you?" Pamela said.

Elspeth's voice broke, "Tea will be fine, Pamela"

"Brandy!" Lord Kennington bawled. "I don't give a damn if it is only ten o'clock in the morning."

"Thank you, Eric. No, brandy won't help," Elspeth said.

"Then what will?" Eric roared.

Elspeth took her courage in hand. "I want three months off," she said flatly.

"What? I can't do without you for three months. What put that misguided notion in your head? Are you running off and getting married to Sir Richard Munro?"

Elspeth flushed. "No, Eric" she replied softly, her throat dry and hurting. "Nothing like that. I need three months to find the murderer of Malcolm Buchanan."

"Never heard of him!"

"Let Elspeth speak, Eric," Pamela said.

Elspeth had once shared the pain of Malcolm's death with Pamela and knew she remembered.

"All right, speak." Eric Kennington said.

"Malcolm Buchanan was murdered when I was a student at Cambridge. An unknown sniper assassinated him," Elspeth said, wishing afterwards she had said things spoken less emotionally.

"And why is that more important now than the problem that came up yesterday at the hotel in Bali?" Eric demanded.

Elspeth did not realize her request would be so hard for her. "Malcolm Buchanan was my fiancé. He died the night he proposed to me. His murderer was never caught."

"And?" Eric challenged.

"I want to go and find his killer."

"Now? Haven't you put this off rather long?"

"Yes. . .to both questions. I just want three months off." She set her jaw.

"Who put you up to this?" asked his lordship.

"If you must know, my aunt, Magdelena Cassar."

"Does she think you'll find the assassin after all this time?"

"No, but Richard Munro and she think I need to, as Richard says, 'put Malcolm's ghost to rest'."

"So Sir Richard is involved, as well as your aunt. I should have suspected! You Scots!"

Elspeth smiled at this. "Although Richard may be Scottish," she said, "I think you have just offended Magdelena and Malta in two words. As much as she loved my uncle, Magdalena Cassar is intensely Maltese."

"Damn Malta and damn Malcolm and most of all damn Sir Richard, who seems to meddle in your life on every possible occasion. The situation in Bali is becoming acute."

"Eric, I must do this. If necessary I will resign."

"No you won't. Take your three months." He turned his back to her and paced up and down. He went over to the glass wall and surveyed the traffic twenty stories below. He stood there several minutes, during which time his mood slowly softened. "Find your murderer, Elspeth. I need you back and, until you find him, your best efforts won't be here. Call Pamela if you need any help."

Elspeth deliberated where to begin her quest and decided to return to Cambridge first. At eighteen Elspeth entered Girton College at the University of Cambridge filled with seriousness and devoted herself to completing a law tripos. Because the college was outside the bounds of town, Elspeth could sink into her studies without the distraction of the men's colleges, except on the days she went into Cambridge for lectures. On occasion, she saw fellow male students socially but could not force herself to conceal from them her excitement about her studies or the world of ideas. None of her would-be suitors ever asked her to join him again. For the most part, Elspeth was relieved because she found all of them insufferably dull. She remembered her summers with her cousin Johnnie and his serious friend from Oxford named Richard Munro and the laughter, lightheartedness, and outrageous ideas they shared together. The young men from Cambridge's colleges could not compare.

Then came Malcolm Buchanan. They collided in the doorway of King's College Chapel or rather their umbrellas did, while they both were trying to extricate themselves from the accouterment that Cambridge students carried on days of heavy rain. The boys' choir was rehearsing for their Christmas concert, and their silvery voices had drawn Elspeth and also Malcolm. Both were trying to enter the vestibule of the chapel, along with their umbrellas, books, mackintoshes, and gowns.

Elspeth was perturbed at the clumsiness of such a confrontation, until she looked up at Malcolm, who was completely amused at their entanglement. She began to laugh, the kind of laugh one gets that will not turn itself off. She turned away, not wanting to seem impolite, and tried to suppress the gulps of hilarity shaking her body.

"Aha! Fair maid, have I done thee in?"

"*Snerk*, gasp."

"I see I have. Then I must apologize profusely and offer you my assistance and name, which is Malcolm Andrew Bartolomeo Buchanan."

"I am Elspeth *snerk* Duff."

"*Snerk* is an unusual Christian name, but I'll accept your word for it."

"Bartolomeo is an unusual Scottish Christian name since your other names appear to be from north of the border. Is it truly your names?"

"True it is, sworn on the soul of my Italian grandfather, although I doubt *Snerk* is really yours."

"So, *snerk*, you should."

"Well, Elspeth *Snerk*, let us leave our egregious weapons against the rain here in the provided racks at the door and proceed into the innards of this chapel, built under the patronage of Plantagenet kings, so that we may listen to the purest form of the human voice."

For the next five months they became inseparable. They sparred irreverently, which they code-named *snerking,* they sat quietly and listened to music together, ate boisterously together, walked hand in hand together, and studied tenaciously together.

Malcolm was a graduate student at King's College. He read art and archaeology as an undergraduate but always had a fascination for the law. Unable to decide on a graduate course that required him to choose between his two disciplines, he had opted for a degree in art history with a concentration in the theft of historical art and artifacts. He spoke with such enthusiasm about this issue that Elspeth was entranced. Britain was emerging from the world of imperialism. The rightful home of the Elgin marbles was beginning to be questioned. Revelations of Nazi art theft had become an enflamed issue, as Holocaust victims began to assert their rights. In the East, claims were being made against the Japanese, Nationalist Chinese, and Chinese Communists. Art was plundered and stored against future changes in the political landscape.

Malcolm dragged Elspeth to museums, and she learned about the arts of the world. He introduced her to ancient as well as modern artists. She became fascinated with the role of the law in the possession of art and devoted one of her papers to the topic.

Outside of Malcolm and her studies the world ceased to exist, until one day in May, just after she had finished her end of the year examinations, Malcolm turned and looked at her standing in the window across from the porter's lodge. He then disappeared from her view and died several moments later with bullet wounds to his brain and heart.

She could recall each solemn word the police detective sergeant spoke to her and even the way he knotted and unknotted his hands. Elspeth had hardly slept the night before because her heart was filled with joy and merriment. Her tutor came to her on the afternoon after she became engaged to Malcolm and led her into Girton's chapel, which was empty save for one man. A policeman, whom she now knew as Detective Superintendent Tony Ketcham of the Anti-Terrorist Bureau at Scotland Yard, was waiting there.

"It is my sad duty to inform you, Miss Duff, that Malcolm Buchanan was shot last evening and must have died instantly," Tony said. Tony's words killed a part of her as much as the assassin's bullets had killed all of Malcolm, and Elspeth never recovered that part of her self.

It being after the end of Michaelmas term, in early December two thousand and four, the room where Elspeth stood, lined by the photographs of the great women of Girton and the college's generous male donors, was empty save for her. She did not hear the woman come into the room and did not know how long she had been standing there. Elspeth finally became aware of her and turned.

"Girton has changed since I was here," Elspeth said smiling sadly.

"Are you all right, Elspeth?" the woman asked, using the familiarity. Elspeth did not notice because she was absorbed in her own thoughts.

"Yes, I will be." She put her hand to her cheek and felt the wetness of her tears, which she wiped away. "An old memory, I'm afraid and not a pleasant one."

"I was here then as a student. I remember it all well."

Elspeth addressed the woman. "The night when. . ."

"Yes. Afterwards we all mourned for you, although Malcolm charmed many of the girls here and was sorely missed."

"You knew him?" Elspeth's tone was filled with a sad joy. She looked up at the woman whom she did not recognize.

"May I help in some way? I feel you have come back here with a purpose," the woman ventured. "Will you to come to my rooms and have a cup of tea or something stronger if you prefer"

A few moments earlier Elspeth would have resented the intrusion but now meeting someone who had known Malcolm, and who had been at Girton with her, seemed calming and reassuring.

"I would like that," Elspeth replied. "I really would."

The college had changed, not physically but socially. Male students were now admitted, and the old protective feeling of the brick walls no longer remained. The hallways were the same and the Victorian brick architecture. The two women wound through familiar passageways and up to the fellows' rooms.

The sitting room they entered was filled with book-lined walls, academic curiosities, brightly colored Moroccan carpets, and a smell of dampness. The woman bent to the fire and turned on the gas.

"I haven't properly introduced myself. I'm Jean Henderson. You may not remember me."

"Jean Henderson? Let me see." Elspeth hesitated and then said with a smile, "Lemon biscuits from Shropshire."

Jean grinned. "Yes, my mother's favorite recipe. I always loathed them, probably because I once ate too many and was thoroughly sick. Mummy sent them anyway, and I always felt it made me popular with the others. I see the impression was a lasting one."

"I was always envious. My mother was a terrible cook and still is, and she never sent anything other than scripts of one-act plays she was fond of writing. I never read a single one."

"Tea or sherry?"

"Sherry if it is not sweet."

"I have a favorite amontillado sent directly from Jerez."

Elspeth accepted the glass of amber liquid gratefully and looked up. "Jean, I'm sorry to be so maudlin. I never quite recovered from Malcolm's death. Life went on of course. I had a bit of a career, married, emigrated to California, had two children, divorced and now have a career again. A textbook early twenty-first century middle-aged woman." Elspeth was not exactly sure why she shared so much, but she felt a strange affinity with Jean.

Jean raised her glass to Elspeth. "Your life sounds like mine," she said, "except for Yorkshire not California and one child not two. I came back here two years ago when I was given a fellowship to pursue my life-long dream of burying myself in the past. I'm fascinated by our mother's lives, lemon biscuits or not, and what it was like for women before the Second World War, not only here in England, but also across the world. My topic has allowed me to travel across Europe, Asia, Africa, Australia and the Americas and talk with women who lived at that time. So often historians try to reach too far back and don't consider the immediate past, while there is still time to interview people who were alive then. But now I'm standing on my soap box."

Elspeth sipped the sherry, glad of a respite from her morose thoughts. "No, please go on. I'm enjoying getting to know you again. I don't suppose you have resurrected your mother's old recipe."

"Some things deserve to disappear from posterity."

Jean produced some cheese and biscuits, savory not sweet. The two women settled into a pair of comfortable chairs. The warmth of the gas fire rose around them. Time slipped cordially by as they chatted about their student days. The early evening darkened into the December night.

Finally Elspeth rose from her chair and was on the verge of saying her goodbyes, when she changed her mind and turned toward Jean. "Jean, will you help me?" The words were a quiet plea.

"If I can, certainly," Jean said. "In what way?"

"I came here not just to remember Malcolm but also to lay his ghost to rest. The killer was never found, which has bothered me over the years. After leaving Girton, rather than joining my father in his law practice in Perthshire, I went to work for Scotland Yard mainly because I wanted to understand how someone could harm another person with malicious intent. I wanted to play a part in bringing resolution to situations caused by these people. It being so long ago, my cases were ones 'not threatening to a woman.' I moved on, of course, and the world changed. Now I work for Lord Kennington of the Kennington hotel chain as one of his roving security advisors. Generally my assignments at the hotels involve seeing to the needs of well-to-do people who want a presentable person to assure their safety and peace of mind. Sometimes it's more. One of my cases involved the murder of a prominent writer who was staying in our hotel in Malta. But, like a *basso profondo,* there's continually the memory of Malcolm's murder, unsolved and finally abandoned. The case won't go away in my mind. Two very dear people in my life have urged me to go back to that time, to try to reconstruct everything I can about what happened and to try to solve the murder. When I returned to Girton I didn't expect to meet someone who was here at the time. What do I want to say?" She shook her head to clear it. "Will you help me reconstruct that time? Can we meet and together try to remember everything we can about those days? Not here this evening, but perhaps tomorrow when I have collected myself. I know this must seem a terrible imposition." Elspeth finished, blew out her breath and felt depleted.

Jean looked at Elspeth, but Elspeth could not read her expression. Finally Jean said, "I have business in the morning I must attend to. Tomorrow afternoon, say at teatime? Where shall we meet?"

"One real advantage of working for a hotel chain is that one's hotel accommodations are arranged from the top. I'm staying in a very luxurious suite at the Queen's Arms. Come round at four. I can't promise such good sherry, but I'm sure they'll have a presentable tea."

"I suspect the occasion may be less social."

"If you don't mind."

"No, not in the least. I hope you won't be sorry you asked me," Jean said.

When Elspeth returned to her hotel, she thought back over to those days thirty-five years ago. Jean had not been one of the "set" at Girton, but Elspeth was not either. Jean desperately wished to be; Elspeth did not care. The "set" had accepted Elspeth and left Jean to try to win approval with the overly sweet and crumbly lemon biscuits. Elspeth knew her unwanted attention by the set was in part because of Magdelena Cassar's intervention. Aunt Mag was insistent

Elspeth did not enter Girton in the tweed skirts and Highland jumpers her mother bought for her in Perth. Magdelena took Elspeth to Paris and purchased a new wardrobe for her that was understatedly trendy. Magdelena had a *comtesse* of her acquaintance teach Elspeth to walk like a French noblewoman. Elspeth's unruly hair was cut by the best French hairstylist in London. Elspeth never forgot those lessons. Despite Elspeth's proclivity toward studiousness, the girls at the college did take notice of her.

Jean laughed at the sweet biscuits now, but she must have been bitter at the time. Elspeth was kind to Jean at Girton. Whenever they crossed paths Elspeth gave her a wave, a nod, a smile. Jean obviously adored Elspeth for this, which Elspeth acknowledged in a remote way.

The "set" now had dispersed to the Counties and were of little consequence to the whole of humanity and only slightly to themselves. Elspeth could recall only a few of their names, but she had kept a special place for Jean in her memories of Girton and sometimes wondered what had become of her.

A sorrowful Elspeth had returned to Girton the term after Malcolm's death. Elspeth never again spoke of Malcolm to anyone at Girton, and everyone there politely avoided mention of his death. For this Elspeth was grateful. She plunged into her studies and completed her law tripos with a first, an accomplishment few of the male students at Cambridge could match. Richard Munro came and went from her life, but she took little notice of him other than his kindness to her.

2

Elspeth rose early. She ordered a full English breakfast to be served in her room and asked for a pot of strong coffee in place of tea, but she found the coffee was not up to Kennington hotel standards. Her meeting with Jean Henderson the evening before had changed Elspeth's mood from melancholia to thoughts of action. During the upcoming morning, following Richard's instruction, she would immerse herself in her memories of Malcolm and Cambridge by walking among their favorite places.

The morning was clear and crisp, the late rising sun casting long December shadows outside the hotel. The streets of old Cambridge had changed little. Malcolm and she wandered through them all, often looking upward, finding odd gargoyles, twisted rainwater leaders, curious corbelling, and irregular rooftops. They named each strange object, sometimes lovingly, sometimes sarcastically, but in the process each one became etched on Elspeth's mind. Most of these relics of the past were still there. She found Timon of Athens and the Ogre of Takreet and Suzie the Hooker and Wilma the Washerwoman. Evil Quentin was missing but George the Gorger was still in place. She smiled as she walked, remembering the comfort of Malcolm's arm casually wrapped around her shoulders.

She noticed a coffee shop on the corner, which brought her back to the twenty-first century and a drinkable cup of coffee. Fortified with strong caffeine, a biodegradable cup and paper lid, she strolled along the Backs. This was their playground, the two of them. Here they walked hand in hand, flew kites, basked in the winter and spring sun, ate cleverly devised picnics and brought their books to study for tutorials and exams. From here they took punts and glided down the Cam.

Remember everything, Richard had said to her, not only the good but also the bad, and, most importantly, the incongruous. When he suggested this, she brushed it off, but the word "incongruous" came back to her. What exactly did he mean? She must pay better attention to her thoughts.

She sat down on a bench, still cold from the previous night. During a particularly intense period of study for them both, filled with the stress of deadlines and papers to be written, Malcolm said he never wanted to leave the "haven" of Cambridge. Elspeth challenged the word "haven," and Malcolm retorted that no exam or paper or academic requirement meant anything when a person's life was at stake. She recalled it so clearly because Malcolm spoke with more seriousness and concern than usual. He took in his breath and blew it out, his nostrils flaring slightly.

Another time in late February he suddenly volunteered, "I must go up to London for a day or two. Family business. The mater and pater being out in the colonies is such a bore. The other MABB and I have to deal with family matters here in England."

The other MABB was his sister Mary Anne Buchanan Berkeley, who was older, married, and a denizen of Chelsea. Elspeth met Mary Anne fleetingly one day when Malcolm invited Elspeth to view some Turner watercolors at a small gallery close to Mary Anne's home. She joined them for tea at a small restaurant nearby.

Family business kept Malcolm away for a week, which seemed an eternity to Elspeth. He dropped her a note every day from London, sending all his love and assuring her that she had grown more precious to him during their forced separation.

Elspeth passed the police station and thought of Detective Sergeant Tony Ketcham, who came to Girton to tell her of Malcolm's murder. She remembered his shoes, stout black ones, neatly tied with the bows exactly the same length. She stared at them and responded to him in monosyllables when he asked her several simple questions. Her whole inner being became frozen, but she had always been imbued with the common sense her father had taught her. "Elspeth," he had advised her, "when you are in trouble, seek out an old friend. Someone you have known for a long time and whose calmness and good sense you can trust." After the policeman left, she contacted Richard Munro, who was in London. He came immediately to Cambridge and took her home to Scotland.

Elspeth never saw the record of the investigation. Emotionally she could not cope with the details. When she returned to her home in Perthshire, she spent the long summer days crossing the hills above Loch Rannoch and Loch Tay with her family's two gamboling Labrador retrievers, Frolic and Froth, in tow. Numbness filled her. She spent the evenings bolstered by the loving, fey qualities of her mother and the quiet reassurance of her father, who believed she would heal with time. After six weeks of abject loneliness, she went to Gozo and her Aunt Magdelena. In the autumn she returned to Girton and hid her grief from the rest of the world by burying herself in study.

She must ask Richard and Tony Ketcham what transpired in Cambridge after the murder. She never had done this.

She also needed to read the police reports and speak with Inspector Garth Llewellyn of the Cambridge Constabulary, who was in charge of the case. She wondered if he still was alive. He was a youngish man at the time with the serious air of a policeman who had been given responsibility that reached to the upper levels of his capability.

In order to access the police records, she would probably have to recruit the help of Tony Ketcham, who was involved during the case at the Kennington Valletta the previous May. In the meantime, she could go through the newspaper accounts of the time. She returned to the hotel and went online to find the website of *The Cambridge Evening News.*

Jean Henderson entered Elspeth's hotel suite not as Elspeth's devotee as she was during their student days but as a confident equal. Time had treated Jean well. She now was established in her field and comfortable with herself, and her demeanor conveyed these qualities.

Elspeth looked forward to talking with Jean. When Elspeth walked along the banks of the Cam that morning, most of her thoughts were of Malcolm, but her thoughts occasionally wandered in and out of life at Girton, and she recalled more about Jean than she had the night before.

Jean Henderson was a tall and awkward girl, who was short-sighted and in need of thick spectacles. Her clothes were unfortunate, although they were obviously expensive. The spectacles and out-of-date wardrobe branded her an outsider from the very beginning. Jean arrived at Girton each term in a long, liveried Rolls but emerged from it in an ungainly fashion and sent it away immediately, clearly embarrassed by its ostentation. There was no crest on the side of the car, which led to speculation that Jean's parents were among the nouveau riche. No one vaguely connected with Shropshire had heard of the Hendersons, or so they claimed. Jean was as shy about her background as she was about her intellect, which was good, and a secret talent, which was devastating. Jean had an uncanny ability at drawing caricatures. She did this quietly, away from view. Many were cruel, but all were unmistakable. Today one might call it a form of art therapy.

Elspeth once came across Jean when she was sketching in the corner of the Junior Common Room on an afternoon when no one was about. Elspeth watched Jean's pen glide across the paper and saw the intent look on her face. Suddenly Jean had looked up and blushed.

"I won't ask to see what you are drawing. I hated it when my mother or father asked to see what I was doing, or, worse, one of my nosey cousins," Elspeth said.

Jean initially turned the page away but then turned it back and let Elspeth see. Elspeth tried to suppress her smile but could not help but make merry eye contact with Jean. The skilled drawing showed the Honourable Victoria Smythe-Welton as a princess trying to allure her tutor, portrayed as a handsome wolf, into the bushes. Both were rendered convincingly, their poses unflattering. Their relationship had been sniggered about behind many of the girls' doors.

"Jean, you have a cruel pen!" Elspeth cried.

"I shouldn't have let you see it, but I thought this one was particularly. . .well drawn," Jean ended up saying. Elspeth wondered what the first adjective was going to be. Truthful?

After that, Elspeth took an interest in Jean. Some evenings Elspeth would drop by her room, and they would exchange pleasantries about the weather or gossip about the latest items in the news. Elspeth saw more of Jean's sketches and came to appreciate their biting wit.

The Jean Henderson who Elspeth met the night before had only the slightest resemblance to the awkward girl. She now was self-assured and graceful. Her clothes were still a bit old fashioned, but they suited her. Elspeth had been privy to fashion for many years and could recognize the well-cut and expensive cloth and exquisitely understated jewelry. The thick glasses had disappeared either through laser surgery or contact lens. Something about Jean radiated comfortable wealth and independence from trendiness.

Elspeth ordered tea and cakes, which were brought on a silver tray with a small vase of flowers. She put the tray aside and arranged the suite's two chairs around the coffee table by the sofa. She noticed Jean had a portfolio under her arm.

"Do you still draw?" Elspeth asked after they seated themselves.

Jean chuckled. "Not so viciously. Caricatures were an outlet when I was a student. I resented the girls who had so much self-confidence. I never wanted to admit to my own background. My father was an impoverished baronet, Sir Hugo Paisley-Henderson, and consequently married my mother, who was an American whose grandfather had made his fortune in oil in the state of Oklahoma. Mummy loved her title and the show, although she lived in Tulsa and Daddy stayed at home in Shropshire. I was always humiliated my parents didn't live together and my mother was a brash American with a dreadful accent. My dark secret was that my mother never sent biscuits. In fact, she had nothing to do with us after we were young, except to insist we arrive at school in expensive cars. The only real favor she did for me was to hire a 'drawing master' in the manner of romance novels. The biscuits came from my old nanny, who also dressed me in those terrible clothes. I also hated being short sighted. My mother died twenty years ago and left half of her wealth to my brother and me and half to Daddy. He revived after that and married a nice woman, and they still live in Shropshire. But I'm rambling. Please forgive me. I always wanted to tell you this when we were students."

"I'm glad you did now. I always wanted to know, although asking would have been terribly rude in those days."

"Yes, we weren't as open as the students are now. Most of my students would consider it archaic not to divulge every detail of their lives, however sordid, and analyze each to death."

"How things have changed," Elspeth said, thinking of her own children.

Jean settled into her chair and sipped her tea. "Many people keep a written journal, but I prefer a pictorial one. I've found my ability to capture someone on paper has opened people's doors and mouths in invaluable ways. As a student of oral history, I find my drawings serve me incredibly well. I save them all."

"Are you going to tell me you still have drawings from our time at Girton?"

"Most of them. That's why I brought this." Jean indicated to the portfolio at her side. "There're drawings of Malcolm and you among others including Detective Inspector Llewellyn, and several other people whose name I don't know but who came to Girton after Malcolm died. If I was quietly sketching in a corner, no one paid any attention to me, so I was able to hear quite a lot of what was happening."

"Will you show the sketches to me?"

"That's why I brought them." Jean took out several drawings.

"Here you are," Jean grinned and pointed to one of them. "I treated you better than most because I liked you."

Elspeth looked at the drawing and was startled that Jean could have captured her so completely and was pleased to see no undertone of meanness in Jean's portrayal.

"Here's Malcolm. It's not as flattering."

Elspeth took the drawing and looked at it closely. Jean was right; it was not nice. It depicted a large-headed young man, with a wicked expression that was more than a mere twinkle in the eye. The scene was at a Chinese restaurant called Ming Palace, which Malcolm and Elspeth frequented often. Malcolm had his arm around an adoring Elspeth, but he was looking hungrily at the Honourable Victoria Smythe-Welton. A scowling waitress wearing a tight Chinese dress with shockingly high slits at each side looked through a beaded curtain at the side.

Elspeth winced. "That one's not particularly kind, is it?" she said.

"No, it isn't. Nor was I in those days. It was envy on my part. You had Malcolm, Victoria had good looks and status, and the waitress, whose name I remember was something like Jing, seemed so exotic and evil."

Elspeth bit her lip.

"Here's Inspector Llewellyn," Jean continued.

Jean handed Elspeth another drawing, but Elspeth closed her eyes for a brief moment before she examined it closely. It showed a man in a mackintosh and heavy shoes who was pointing his binoculars up to a window of a building, obviously Girton, at a group of girls. Near a bush close by and unobserved, someone was being shot.

"You didn't have much faith in the inspector, I see," Elspeth said.

"He was a bit of a nosy parker who asked questions that hardly seemed relevant to a murder committed outside of the college."

"I shudder at asking to see the other drawings."

"They're rather horrid. Until I dug them out last night, I didn't realize how harsh they were." She drew the last two out.

"I don't know who these people were, but they came on your behalf, I think. I treated them much more gently."

Elspeth looked at them both and was startled. One was of Richard Munro and the other of Tony Ketcham. The likeness to Richard, even today, was uncanny. The drawing made no statement. Instead, it showed a young man, dressed in a morning coat and looking down an aristocratic nose that was far longer than his real nose, but he was nonetheless recognizable. Tony Ketcham was dressed in an ordinary suit and fedora with its brim turned down and slanted over one eye. He looked like Sam Spade.

"Do you know them?"

Elspeth laughed. "Yes. I know them both even today. They haven't changed much."

Elspeth served the cakes and dispensed more tea as Jean returned the drawings to her portfolio.

"From what you have shown me, you must have been close to the police investigation after I left Girton to return home. No one ever told me exactly what happened."

Jean nodded.

"I remember coming around to your room and seeing you sitting and staring at the wall. I knocked, but you didn't turn around, so I left you alone. I watched from the window where you were standing yesterday and saw the young man I showed here in the morning coat hand you into a taxi. You had no expression on your face, but his eyes could not leave it. After that I thought about you frequently, wondering how you were coping and if you would come back to Girton the following term."

"What happened during the investigation? From your drawings I assume the police came to the college to investigate?"

"Detective Inspector Llewellyn from the Cambridge police came every day for the next week. He questioned all of us who'd been there the night of Malcolm's death. He asked again and again about Malcolm's and your friends, where you spent your time together and with whom, and for every detail any of us could remember about the night Malcolm was killed."

"Was he satisfied?"

"I don't think so. Afterwards the plainclothes policeman from Scotland Yard came. He asked the same questions Inspector Llewellyn had, but one felt he listened more closely to the answers. None of us knew anything really. Malcolm and you were always so intertwined with each other and so apart from the rest of us. Victoria Smythe-Welton claimed she was close to Malcolm, but no one believed her. She said her father knew Malcolm's father in Malaya during the war."

"How like Victoria," Elspeth said.

Jean laughed. "Several times the man in the morning coat came with the inspector. The man was extremely polite to us all but said little. Afterwards we all dispersed for the summer vacation. In the autumn we were glad you came back."

Elspeth thought she owed Jean a brief account of the long days in Scotland that followed Malcolm's death.

"The man in the morning coat is Richard Munro. He took me back to my family in Perthshire after the murder. At first I didn't think I could go on living, but the care of my family and the deep sense of belonging I have with the Highlands around my home saved me. When I was feeling grounded enough to travel, I went to Malta and stayed with my uncle and aunt. She is the most loving person in the world and restored me to the feeling of being alive. You must meet her someday. She's very special."

Jean smiled, acknowledging the compliment. "I should be delighted. I've always loved Malta. Who is Richard Munro?"

"He's an old and dear friend." Elspeth realized she flushed when she said this. "In fact it was he who urged me to try to find out who killed Malcolm."

"Is he still in the picture? I always thought he had a thing for you."

Elspeth felt herself redden more deeply. "He did rather, but he went on to marry the daughter of the Earl of Glenborough and had a successful diplomatic career." Elspeth set her jaw and decided to share no more information on this topic with Jean.

3

The Honourable Sir Richard Munro, Knight Commander of the Order of Saint Michael and Saint George, British High Commissioner to the Republic of Malta, traveled frequently between Valletta and London, but this trip had a purpose other than diplomatic affairs. As soon as he deplaned at Gatwick and settled in the car that he had ordered, he picked up the car phone and rang Elspeth's flat. A crisp message answered his call and asked him to leave his name and number. Disappointed not to have reached her, he gave his name and the number of his club. Then he phoned Pamela Crumm at the Kennington Organisation's offices in the City of London.

"Sir Richard, what a pleasure." From her tone Pamela's sentiment was genuine. "Yes, Lord Kennington gave her three months to go settle the mystery of Malcolm's death. She was quite determined, you know, and said she would resign if not given the time. She's the only one in Eric's employ who would threaten that because she knows he won't let her go. I booked a room for her at the Queen's Arms in Cambridge and made arrangements for a hired car. Let me give you a contact at the hotel." Pamela's voice had the sweet sonority and depth that is common to women without outward beauty. On the phone they became goddesses.

Richard rang the Queen's Arms and was told Mrs. Duff had checked out several hours before. They did not say where she was going.

During the long ride into London through the crush of traffic, he thought back to the day Elspeth rang him and told him of Malcolm Buchanan's death.

Richard had met Malcolm with Elspeth several times and disliked him instantly. Looking back now, he wondered if his feelings were merely jealousy or if there was something more. Malcolm was possessive of Elspeth, and she seemed completely in his thrall. She had lost the independence of spirit she had during the rambunctious summers that Richard had spent in Perthshire with Elspeth's cousin, Johnnie, and the three of them had explored the Highlands and life together. Richard found Malcolm self-centered and did not like the changes he saw in Elspeth when she was with him. Richard felt Malcolm was using Elspeth and was showcasing her to the world as his conquest. Elspeth did not seem to mind. Richard shared his feelings with Elspeth, and she became irritated with him for doing so.

"Dickie, why can't you like Malcolm?"

"He's far too free-spirited, Elspeth, and you have become less so," he replied. "It all seems quite fun now, but it's not the sort of thing to plan a lifetime around."

"He's quite serious at times. His college finds him quite brilliant on the subject of art theft," she had retorted.

"And, how will that qualify him for gainful employment? His topic is insubstantial at best. Is his family sufficiently well off that he needn't be serious about finding a solid profession? Certainly you don't have enough money to support him without help from your family, and I doubt they will be happy with that arrangement."

"Dickie, you sound like a stern uncle rather than a friend. I've no idea if his family is well off, but they must be because Malcolm never seems short of money."

Richard would not be placated. "If you are serious about Malcolm, you must get to know more about him. Despite the fact that class lines are blurring these days, serious relationships must be based on more than flights of brilliant conversation."

He remembered the teasing grin that crossed Elspeth's face. "Don't be dreary, Dickie. It is quite annoying the way you get so stuffy at times."

Richard and Elspeth had argued this way almost from the first time they met, not just about Malcolm but also about conduct in general.

"I prefer to be cautious. It's not a bad trait." He knew he sounded severe.

"Let's not quarrel," she said. She smiled radiantly at him, and his heart softened.

The call from Elspeth from Cambridge came the morning after a long, tiring day at his job at the Foreign and Commonwealth Office. Richard was given the task of escorting a tribal chief from West Africa through Harrods, Harvey Nichols, and Fortnum and Mason. The chief's accent was difficult to understand, his taste noisy, and his laugh too loud. Richard returned to his small bed-sitting room and opened a tin of stew he bought at Waitrose on the way home. The meal was overly salty and had more gravy than substance. He wished he had bought a small bottle of wine, but his budget was strained that week, and he did not want to dip into the small inheritance from his family. He was saving that for a walking holiday between historic inns along the Cornish coast in the summer. He had just dozed off when his landlady knocked rapidly on his door. "Oh, Mr. Munro, Mr. Munro, do open up! There's a miss on the line, and she is very upset, crying like. She wants to talk to you."

The phone was in a niche down the hall, and despite the lack of privacy Richard asked Elspeth to repeat what had occurred several times. His heart was aching with love for her. He promised to come at once.

When he arrived in Cambridge, he comforted her as best he could. She clung to him in a way that required him to exert the greatest of will power not to embrace her and tell her how much she mattered to him. As a defense against his feelings, he assumed his most avuncular manner. For once Elspeth seemed to find this a great strength.

After accompanying Elspeth on the train to Scotland and putting her in her parents' good care, Richard returned to Cambridge and sought out the police. Richard's training in diplomacy served him well with Detective Inspector Garth Llewellyn. At first the inspector seemed uncomfortable at with Richard's involvement. Richard understood this reaction, which men frequently had toward him because he was tall and aristocratic. The inspector was of average height and squarely built. The inspector represented the workingman, and Richard, despite his upbringing in Scotland, represented London and the Establishment. Richard was by habit well dressed; the inspector looked slightly uncomfortable out of uniform.

Richard thought of ways to put the policeman at ease. "Inspector Llewellyn," he said pronouncing the name in the Welsh way, "it's not my intention to push in where not wanted. I, like you, am a civil servant, and I want to respect proper boundaries here. Miss Elspeth Duff, Malcolm's Buchanan's fiancée, is a friend of mine, and I'm close to her family in

Scotland. My only concern is to keep them informed about your investigation because Miss Duff's emotions were too ragged to stay in Cambridge even for a few days to answer questions. I suspect she is so emotionally damaged right now that she cannot share much with anyone."

They were sitting in the inspector's office, which was cramped but orderly. The inspector adjusted his National Health Service glasses and drew his hand through his dark hair. He cleared his throat but did not respond to Richard.

"Have they done a post-mortem yet, inspector?" Richard asked in order to break the lingering silence. The question seemed to relax the inspector.

"This morning. He must have died instantly. There were two bullets. One went through his left temple to his brain and the other directly into the heart. Very neat and tidy." Richard could hear the resonant tones of Garth Llewellyn's Welsh homeland.

"Did the pathologist determine which bullet killed him?"

"No. The two shots must have been fired in rapid order, so it would be impossible to know."

"But wasn't Malcolm on a bicycle? It seems strange that anyone could hit a chap on one with such precision. Most cyclists wobble a bit. It must have been done by a practiced gunman."

"A bloody good pair of shots." The inspector's tone seemed admiring.

"Have they determined what sort of the weapon was used?"

"Not yet. No one here recognized the bullets extracted from the body. We've sent them to London to the ballistics department at Scotland Yard for examination."

Richard felt a certain respect for the inspector. Garth Llewellyn was not a sophisticate, but Richard sensed he possessed an intelligence that would make him a success with both the townspeople and scholars at the university. Richard tipped a figurative hat to the young Welshman.

Richard took out his card and carefully wrote his office telephone number on it. "I accompanied Miss Duff to her parents' home in Scotland before coming back to Cambridge. She's in a state of shock. Right now she won't want to know the details of Malcolm Buchanan's murder, but there will be a time when she does. Please let me know how the investigation progresses. I find it disturbing that the murder of Malcolm imitates the recent sniper killings in America. I'd be particularly interested in the type weapon used. I'm not an expert, but the weapon itself may be important."

"Mr. Munro," the inspector said, his voice warming to Richard, "would you be willing to help me and Miss Duff as well?"

"Certainly."

"Will you assist me when I question the girls at the college? I think they would be more comfortable answering questions in front of you rather than me."

Despite Girton's bluestocking reputation, Richard knew the students there might respond more easily to one of his class and background. "Of course," Richard said. "Just let me know how I can help."

Not finding Elspeth at her flat gave Richard the afternoon to pursue other things. He decided to ring Detective Superintendent Tony Ketcham at Scotland Yard, whom Elspeth and Richard had assisted during the FitzRoy affair in Malta.

Richard entered the detective superintendent's office and extended his hand. "Thank you for seeing me. We actually never met last spring. I am glad to see you again."

Tony Ketcham took his hand firmly. "The pleasure is mine. I was grateful to have Elspeth Duff and you on our side in Valletta. Do you ever see Elspeth? If so, give her my regards. She's such a capable person and a handsome one as well, an excellent combination, of which I'm sure the Kennington Organisation takes full advantage. It was she and not I who uncovered the truth in Valletta. But why do you say you are glad to meet me again when I don't recall meeting you in person before."

"Detective Superintendent, you may not remember, but we met a long time ago, in nineteen sixty-nine, and then only briefly and under less than happy circumstances. That's why I'm here."

Tony looked puzzled and gestured Richard toward a heavy wooden chair, which Richard presumed had held many others in less comfortable moments.

"Did we meet on a case?" Tony asked.

"Yes, the murder of Malcolm Buchanan at Cambridge. Do you remember it?"

Tony rounded his large, government-issue desk and lowered his body into an ergonomic chair. Richard saw weariness both in Tony's face and his bearing.

"Far too well. The murder was never solved. I was new at the Metropolitan Police and thought I could crack any case. I've learned better over the years." Tony smiled wryly.

"Elspeth Duff is a childhood friend," Richard explained.

Tony Ketcham leaned back, raised his hunched shoulders, stretched his neck and let out a small tired grunt. "Yes, she said so when I told her you would be involved in Malta."

Richard wondered how Elspeth had described him. The detective superintendent gave no hint.

Richard realized Tony was about the same age as he was, but the responsibility of heading an anti-terrorist branch at Scotland Yard had taken its toll on him. His hair had grayed and dark circles ringed his eyes. Although he was still lean, his face was washed out in the manner caused by poor food quickly eaten and too little sleep.

"I'll try to be brief," Richard said. "It's an old crime, and perhaps its urgency exists only in the minds of those who cannot forget. At the time of Malcolm Buchanan's death, Elspeth was in a state of denial, but recently she confided in me that she has never resolved her feelings about Malcolm's murder. That's why I'm here today. I hope I'm not interrupting something more pressing."

"No, not at all. They do allow me an occasional bit of time away from the current crisis of the moment. That's one of the privileges of rank. Besides, I owe a debt of gratitude to Elspeth after Malta."

"I hope I'm not abusing that time or presuming on that debt," Richard said. "I remember you were involved in the murder at Cambridge, and I thought at the time you simply represented Scotland Yard. I didn't know then, and don't know even now, if you were from Special Branch."

"I was there as more than an ordinary policeman. I'd recently begun at Special Branch and was working mainly with the troubles in Ireland. They put me on the case because my superiors thought Special Branch should be involved, and I had studied at Cambridge. Not that those connections did any good. I enjoyed going back and staying at my old college, but I never was able to find any hint of who the murderer might have been. We kept the file open for several years, although after the first month of dead ends, the case was put on inactive status. Inspector Garth Llewellyn of the Cambridge Constabulary worked on it long after that, but the trail went cold. He might remember more than I."

"I am curious why Special Branch was involved. Can you tell me without breaching security?" Richard asked.

"I'll tell you as much as I'm allowed to. The Cambridge police contacted the Met when Malcolm's body was found. The incredible marksmanship required to kill a person on a bicycle with two perfect shots was highly unusual. They thought it might be an assassination."

"Was it?"

Tony shook his head in a way that made Richard think it was not a denial.

"After the post-mortem, our ballistics department analyzed the bullets found in Malcolm Buchanan's body. They were from a Soviet semiautomatic pistol, one favored by the communist rebels all over the world after the Second World War. This was one of the very rare instances when that type of gun was used in the UK. We never could trace its origins or discover why it was used."

"What about his family?" Richard asked. "Would there be any clue there?"

Tony hesitated before replying. Richard suspected he was weighing his answer carefully. "His mother and father emigrated to Australia or New Zealand, I don't remember which, when Malcolm was at boarding school here in England. Llewellyn may have traced them. Malcolm had a married sister who lived in London, but she was as perplexed by the murder as the police."

Richard found Tony's answer more evasive than informative.

"Do you know where his sister is now?"

The detective superintendent took a deep breath, as if he wanted to skirt a sensitive issue. He exhaled slowly. "Until I met Elspeth Duff at Lord Kennington's office last April, I'd put the case out of my mind. As I said, we left the final investigation to the Cambridge police."

"Then would it be best to contact Inspector Llewellyn, if he is still alive?"

"He may be. Let me see what I can find out, and I'll let you know."

"Thank you, Tony. I'm staying at my club. If you think of anything more, you can leave a message for me there. I won't be returning to Malta until day after tomorrow."

Tony shook Richard's hand and left him with the distinct impression that Tony knew more about the case than he was telling.

"Richard, a pleasure," Tony said. "Call me if you need anything else. Again regards to Elspeth. She's a fine woman indeed."

Richard fully agreed.

After leaving New Scotland Yard, Richard rang Elspeth's flat but once again reached her voice mail. Disappointment filled him.

4

Elspeth discovered the whereabouts of Chief Inspector Garth Llewellyn, lately retired from the Cambridge Constabulary, by asking at the police station. Elspeth rang him from her mobile. The voice that answered held the eagerness of someone who had few calls but savored each one.

"Llewellyn here," he chirped.

"Chief Inspector Llewellyn?"

"Yes."

"The police in Cambridge gave me your name, and I shamelessly used the internet to find your number. My name is Elspeth Duff. You investigated the murder of my fiancé, Malcolm Buchanan, many years ago. I'd like to come and speak to you about it, if it would be convenient."

There was silence on the other end of the line. Elspeth hoped he would still remember.

Finally he spoke. "No, I've not forgotten. It has been a long time."

"I'm coming to the New Forest to see friends," Elspeth prevaricated. "I wonder if we might meet."

"Yes, I have a small cottage on the Beaulieu River. It would be best if you came here where we can talk without being interrupted. When do you plan to be here?"

They set up an appointment for two o'clock two days later.

Elspeth had little recollection of the policeman who in the summer of nineteen sixty-nine had come to Scotland to her family's home on Loch Rannoch to question her. She remembered he was a tidy, square-built man but little else. Her father sat next to her on one of the sofas in the drawing room and held her hand. The only things in the interview she remembered were his questions about the gun and about Malcolm's family.

"Do you know how to shoot a gun, Miss Duff?"

"Yes," she had replied. "My uncle taught me how. He thought it was a skill I should have."

"Do you own a gun?"

"No," she said.

"Did Mr. Buchanan ever mention any enemies or anyone who would wish him harm?"

"No, never." She was certain of that.

"How well did you know Mr. Buchanan?"

"We had just become engaged."

"How long had you known him?"

Elspeth swallowed at the use of the past tense. "Since last December."

"Do you know his family?"

"No. I met his sister once. That's all."

"Do you know where he was from?"

"No. I think his family lived abroad." How thin her answer was.

"Did you have any reason to wish him harm?"

Elspeth's father, a solicitor, stepped in at this moment. "Inspector Llewellyn, surely you must have some sense of decency. I think you have asked enough questions."

In retrospect, why had Inspector Llewellyn asked these particular questions?

As Elspeth drove toward the New Forest, the interview in Scotland came back to her, sometimes crisply spoken and sometimes distorted in the way that voices are warped when played too slowly on a voice recording. Much as she had tried to suppress her earlier meeting with Inspector Llewellyn, his words echoed in a loud crescendo while she hastened along the motorways and finally slowed to the sedate pace necessary to negotiate the narrow lanes of Hampshire.

She would be asking now-retired Chief Inspector Llewellyn questions the answers to which she did not necessarily want to know. Malcolm's death was still too close to her. In the past she had been able to keep the horror of the actual murder away because she did not know the details. In this small way Malcolm's loss could be contained. Even now did she really want to know every lurid fact of the murder? When Richard advised her to probe everything, she realized she would have to deal with the forensics of Malcolm's death, not as a professional investigator but as an emotional casualty of the murder. Chief Inspector Llewellyn might tell her most of what she wanted to know, but would he remember? He had been on the Cambridge police force almost forty years. Why would this case stand out in his mind?

She almost picked up her mobile to break off their meeting, but she knew that would be neither helpful nor courageous. Would opening up these old wounds help heal her, as Richard suggested? She considered herself a person of intellect, not one swayed by passions. Strong emotions frightened her because of the intensity they aroused in her. She did not know if her favoring the mind over the heart was a curse or a blessing. For her it was reality.

She had carefully chosen her wardrobe, tailored tweed trousers, a loose fitting cotton blouse accented with a bright woolen scarf she had bought in India, and a soft suede jacket belted in the back. The day was warm for December, so she did not wear an overcoat, although she had one in the boot of the car. She decided against any jewelry except a conservative pair of gold earrings that her aunt had given her many years before, saying, "When you need to be absolutely correct, *cara*, wear these. No one can fault them." Her clothes were familiar ones, and she hoped they would give her comfort when she was feeling none.

He was waiting for her outside of his cottage. She wondered what he would think of her arriving in a small hired car rather than a showy saloon or estate car. The graduates of Girton often drove these large cars. She hoped he wouldn't be disappointed. She unfolded herself from the driver's seat, stood up and straightened her clothing, which had become disarranged during her trip.

Llewellyn seemed unsure of how to greet her. His frame had bent with time, although he could not have been more than ten years her senior. She guessed his retired life was lonely and he had aged more than his actual years would suggest.

As she approached, he spoke to her politely and asked if she would join him for a cup of tea and some biscuits. He led her into a small, tidy sitting room with windows overlooking the river. The room reminded Elspeth of a captain's quarters out of a Horatio Hornblower novel. As Llewellyn dispensed tea, he poured out the story of his retirement, as so many older people do.

Elspeth listened with a sympathetic ear to his rapture with the cottage that he had handcrafted, a boat called *Circe* that he had built, and his love of the Hampshire rivers and coast that he had adopted as his home.

Knowing she no longer could put off the purpose of her visit, she broached the topic of Malcolm's murder.

"Chief inspector," she said, taking a deep breath, "when we spoke on the phone, you seemed to remember who I am. I've come a bit under false pretenses, since I drove down this morning from London purposely to see you and ask you about Malcolm Buchanan's murder."

He smiled an old man's smile. "I remember far too much, as it was my first murder case, and I never could solve it."

"Do you remember the details?" Elspeth asked, still not certain whether she wanted this information or not.

"Of course, because I never had another case as unusual, although there were murders afterwards, usually domestic affairs. None of them brought in Special Branch." He adjusted his steel-rimmed glasses and said, "I always wondered what happened to you and the others. No, I haven't forgotten you, Miss Duff. I'd never seen such sadness and disbelief in a person's eyes when I visited you in Scotland. I always regretted I couldn't find the murderer for your sake alone. I can still see the devastation that my asking questions did to you. I apologize for my roughness. Before then I didn't know a policeman's enquiries could bring out such grief. But why have you come to find me after all these years?"

Elspeth took in a deep breath. "Because after thirty-five years of avoiding the truth, I need to know it, or at least as much as I can find out now." Then, surprising herself, she said, "I have personal reasons to put Malcolm's death to rest." She felt herself redden, although Llewellyn could not have known why.

He rose and crossed the room, where he opened a drawer and drew out a file.

"I've kept this, because I thought someday I'd find someone who would care. When I retired, they allowed me to make copies of the microfiche." The pages were dark and the white text ragged.

"Miss Duff, I'll try to summarize for you and tell you what I remember. I'm an old police officer who never liked unsolved cases, and I'm still bothered by this one particularly. Also I have always wondered why you never came and asked me any questions." He sounded puzzled at her failing to do so.

"Life has a funny way of intervening," she said, "and I didn't want to stir up the past in those days."

"Will you tell me what happened to you? I've often wondered. I cared in my own way."

Elspeth did not expect this. She clamped her teeth together, swallowed and forced the tears away. "I finished at Girton," she said, "and then went to work for Scotland Yard. Because of the horror of that night I hoped I might learn how such things could be prevented."

"Did you ever marry?"

"Oh, yes, eventually. I went to America and had a family, but I never forgot Malcolm. Strange, isn't it?"

"No," he said sympathetically. "Tragedy isn't always wiped out by happiness. What happened to the young man from the Foreign Office who was so obviously in love with you? You didn't marry him, I suppose."

Elspeth stiffened and hoped he did not notice. "No," she said. "He married the daughter of an earl and went on to have a highly successful diplomatic career."

"Then you still know him. What was his name again?"

"Richard Munro," Elspeth said, hoping her voice sounded neutral. "We still meet on occasion. Currently he is the high commissioner in Malta." Why did the assumption that Richard and she might have married make her so defensive? Both Magdelena Cassar and Eric Kennington had mentioned the possibility earlier. Damn you, Dickie, she thought, and unwanted warmth overtook her body.

Llewellyn did not seem to notice her discomfort. "I'll tell you what I know but you might ask Mr. Munro as well. He was able to talk to the students at the college more freely than I could. I know he kept notes. He told me one day you might want to know what happened."

Wanting to turn the conversation away from Richard, Elspeth reached in her handbag and brought out a pad of paper. "I have some questions here. Do you mind if I take notes?"

"It will be an interesting reversal of rolls, you're asking the questions and not me," he said, "but please ask. It will jog my memory."

"Did you work on the case for a long time?"

"Actively for two years. We followed every lead but in the end came up empty-handed. I was determined not to give up, and my superiors were kind enough to give me a great deal of latitude."

"Can you share anything of this with me, chief inspector?"

"I think enough time has passed that anything confidential can no longer be relevant. Yes, perhaps I can."

He sat quietly but said nothing more for a long time. He offered more tea and another biscuit. She accepted gratefully, not only because she was hungry, having skipped lunch, but also because it made them both relax.

When he began his narrative, Elspeth did not interrupt.

"Crimes in Cambridge involving university students were generally consisted of drunkenness and bawdiness, and later to drugs. The students had no real harm in them. They were young and often had to let off pent up emotions. We at the police recognized this and generally tried to frighten them in a way that they would consider their actions more carefully the next time. We seldom kept them for more than a night in jail and put nothing in their records."

Elspeth smiled at this.

"Murder at the university was almost non-existent," he continued. "There were one or two cases earlier in the century—or should I say the last century—but each was because of family issues. What made Malcolm Buchanan's murder extraordinary was that it seemed to be the act of an assassin. In today's world, with Islamic extremism so much in the news, we have become almost inured to acts of terrorism. When Malcolm Buchanan was murdered, assassinations, other than those by the Irish Republican Army and the ones in the States, were much more rare than they are today. One didn't expect a student at Cambridge to be killed in the way Malcolm Buchanan was.

Elspeth nodded her head in understanding.

"I was assigned to Malcolm's murder the night the body was found. I don't know how much Mr. Munro has shared with you about the method of Malcolm's murder. The automatic pistol and ammunition used was the same type preferred by the Soviet and Chinese Communist underground forces at that time. For this reason the murder came to the attention of the Special Branch and is why Detective Sergeant Ketcham came to Cambridge so quickly. Special Branch felt that the assassin might be Chinese. They didn't explain why because subversive Chinese Communist activity in Britain was unheard of in the nineteen sixties. Britain recognized Communist China from the very beginning, unlike the Americans."

Elspeth frowned. She could not connect Malcolm with the regime in China or the Soviet Union.

The chief inspector continued. "Malcolm was born in Malaya in the Second World War before the Japanese surrendered and was only a child when the Chinese Communist Revolution ended, but his parents, or more specifically his father, might have been politically involved with the Chinese in Malaya during that time."

"That seems far-fetched," Elspeth said.

"Not considering the gun. We checked with Malcolm's college at the university. His next of kin was listed as his sister, Mary Anne Buchanan Berkeley, whom we contacted immediately. She was married and living in Chelsea at the time. It was she who led us to you. When we interviewed her later, she was evasive, merely claiming her parents were dead and she could shed no light on Malcolm's murder. She said her brother and she had not been on good terms for quite some time, but before he died she had hoped to make the situation better."

"Malcolm did mentioned he was not on good terms with Mary Anne," Elspeth confirmed.

Llewellyn continued. "We asked her why there was no recording of either Malcolm's or her birth at Somerset House. 'We were born abroad during the war' was her short answer. She went on to say probably the records had been lost in the chaos after the war but they both had British passports, which until now seemed to be all they needed.

"I went next to the Foreign and Commonwealth Office. They confirmed that Malcolm and Mary Anne were indeed

British citizens—subjects as we often called them in those days. They both had been born in Malaya, Malcolm in nineteen forty-five and Mary Anne in nineteen forty-three. We found records at the FCO that their father, James Andrew Malcolm Buchanan, native of Ayrshire, Scotland, had registered both of their births at Government House in Singapore in nineteen fifty-two, nine years after Mary Anne was born and seven years after Malcolm was. Their mother was listed as Anna Maria Cornelia Buchanan. We confirmed the issuance of Malcolm and Mary Anne's passports, but the details of their birth were lost. It's still a mystery how British children could be born in Malaya when it was under Japanese occupation."

Elspeth frowned.

"Afterwards I went to the Imperial War Museum," Llewellyn said. "They had no record of a James Andrew Malcolm Buchanan serving in the military. I suspected he might have been involved in intelligence, but those files couldn't be unsealed even if they were no longer relevant to Britain's security.

"Since I couldn't trace Malcolm's parents, I tried another tactic—any Chinese Communist Party activity in Britain at that time. Tony Ketcham was helpful. He was still new at the Metropolitan Police, and we both had Cambridge connections—I town, he gown.

"Using the help of the Special Branch, I also contacted a number of organizations that might have information on Chinese activity in Malaya or Singapore during the war or afterwards. They tried to be helpful, but the murder of a twenty-four year old Cambridge student had little historical significance for them. I contacted people in Singapore and Kuala Lumpur and advertised in the local newspapers, to no avail."

Inspector Llewellyn had been thorough, Elspeth thought.

"The Cambridge police force had a limited budget, and I was getting nowhere. Finally my supervisor requested that I be reassigned to more urgent and current cases."

"Without resolving anything," Elspeth said.

He took off his glasses and wiped the bridge of his nose. "When I retired, I thought of traveling to Malaysia to see where Malcolm and his sister were born, but where would I start? If Malcolm's father was in intelligence, he might have operated under an assumed name."

Elspeth took notes as she listened. When the chief inspector finished, she knew it was time to ask what was most frightening for her.

"Did you ever reconstruct the night of the murder?" she asked. Her voice broke.

"He must have died instantly, if that is any consolation. Two bullets hit him, one entered through his temple and the other through his chest. Either one could have killed him. They were fired directly at him, not from above or not from below, which made us assume the assassin was waiting for him in the bushes. The shots were clean, and the bullet holes small."

"Thank you for not sparing me," she said in a low voice.

"I thought you would want the truth or you would not have come here."

Elspeth swallowed, her throat painful. "When I last saw Malcolm he was on his bicycle. How could he have been hit so accurately? He must have been moving at some speed. He always rode that way."

"A good marksman could have hit him twice because the first bullet would not have stopped him instantly. That is why we always assumed he was assassinated."

"Can you tell me where you found his body?"

"Behind some bushes at the south end of the fence that surrounds Girton. His bicycle was beside him. There were signs where it had broken through some of the branches as it crashed through them. He was lying on his back and his arms were crossed over his body, almost as if some unknown hand had laid him out for burial. His body was hidden from view from the street, and it took a while before he was found and we were informed. It was about ten o'clock when the call came.

"Who found him?"

"A man from one of the houses nearby, or rather his dog. After discovering the body, the man rushed home and dialed the police. He thought the body was that of a drunken student, because of Malcolm's gown. He didn't know Malcolm was dead."

"I see," Elspeth said, although she wished she did not see so clearly. The spot where Malcolm had fallen was one she passed often frequently in her three years at Girton.

"You said you contacted his family after he was found."

"Yes, his sister. The porter at King's College had her name on file but also knew her. He said she visited the college earlier in the day looking for Malcolm and waited in his rooms for him to return, but he never did. She told the porter she needed to return to London and couldn't wait. When I phoned her about midnight, she confirmed this and said Malcolm probably had gone out to Girton to see you, Miss Duff. That's why DS Ketcham came and found you the next day."

Elspeth drove away from Llewellyn's bungalow in deep thought. Malcolm, the man she had loved above all others, suddenly had become someone she did not know at all well.

Richard had continually warned her about Malcolm and his antecedents. Now she knew she would have to piece together what she really did know about Malcolm. His life might not be what she thought it was.

Fighting traffic back to London through the early darkness of the evening, she began to arrange the pieces, the way one would lay out a jigsaw puzzle, edge pieces in one spot and similar colors in separate piles. The number of pieces that fitted together were few. She would have to find all the missing ones before the picture was complete.

Her heart was filled with the acute pain she knew had to come as she learned the truth, pain that had lain hidden inside her for a long time. Richard told her the truth would be healing. Right now it did not seem to be so.

5

Tired as she was of dealing with the traffic going into London, the descending darkness of evening, and the complexities of what Llewellyn had just told her, Elspeth entered her flat in Gordon Mews in Kensington and instantly felt its comfort.

This was her private place and space. She had crafted it over the last six years to her own liking. She wanted her home to provide sanctuary when she arrived back from assignments, most of which demanded her full-time attention often for weeks at a time. The upstairs flat at the end of the quiet mews had its own garage beneath. She did not keep a car in London, but the convenience of having a parking space for any hired car made her keep the space free. She pulled the small car into the garage, and, with relief, mounted the stairs and opened the door into her place of peace.

Here she dwelled in her own solitude. She seldom invited guests here other than her family and Pamela Crumm, her friend and confederate in dealing with her employer, Lord Kennington.

The light on her answering machine in the kitchen area was blinking, which was rare, because Pamela and her parents and children usually called Elspeth on her mobile phone. No one else knew the flat's number except Magdelena Cassar, who seldom rang. Elspeth pressed the button, expecting a wrong number or a nuisance call, and felt a surge of pleasure when she heard Richard's voice. She had forgotten she had given him the number months ago in Malta.

She did not ring him back immediately. Instead she entered her main room and felt comfort spread through her. Raised on the shores of Loch Rannoch in Scotland, she had lived in many other places, Cambridge, London, Hollywood, northern California, and numerous Kennington hotels in just about every part of the world, but the Kensington flat was now her home.

When she first accepted her job with the Kennington Organisation, Lord Kennington insisted she have a flat in London. He felt this "compensation for employment" gave her a base of operation and a reason to stay in his employ. She agreed only if she could chose the location and furnish it herself. She was offered a generous allowance to do so, and, for the first time in her life, she had imposed her tastes on a space so privately her own.

Her parents' home on Loch Rannoch contained chintz, overflowing bookcases, watercolors of Scotland, playbills from her mother's favorite plays, comfortable but sometimes mismatched sofas and chairs, and a variety of worn but good quality Persian rugs. Her ex-husband, Alistair Craig, set up their homes in Hollywood as altars to the many stars who benefitted from his instruction in weapons and fight choreography. Art deco was his preferred style; she did not question it because she did not care. Lord Kennington's decoration of his hotels was impeccable and, she felt, the subject merited a whole chronicle of its own.

When she looked at her main room, she compared it with Magdelena Cassar's great room in Gozo and smiled at the difference. Both rooms were large, open areas with smaller rooms to the side. Each space was furnished sparingly but in a radically different way. Magdelena Cassar favored the baroque; Elspeth preferred refined simplicity.

She took a long time to furnish the flat and waited to buy pieces until she was satisfied they were compatible with her other furniture. She wanted her hideaway to be unencumbered, physically and emotionally. Her first purchases, after a large bespoke bed, were a long dining table with four chairs, an armchair and a standing lamp. On the table she put her laptop, ate her meals, read the newspaper and studied the papers for her various cases. In her mind, the table was operation central, even now.

The table—her table—was of understated modern design with a polished stainless steel frame topped by heavy glass. The glass was kept spotless under the careful attention of Mrs. Brown, Elspeth's housekeeper.

Later Elspeth added two sofas, a simple coffee table, bookcases, and other small bits of furniture. Their austereness purposely preserved the bareness of the room. She used the side rooms for a small office and a guest bedroom and slept under the skylights in the open loft above.

Returning to her flat after seeing Garth Llewellyn, she threw her handbag in her office and pulled out a notepad from her desk drawer. She poured herself a glass of sherry and sat down at her dining table. For a moment, she stared at the gridded pad. Finally in bold square letters she wrote: MALCOLM'S FAMILY.

In her large hand she made quick notes of the random things she remembered from the snippets of Malcolm's conversational allusions to his family, which she had mentally noted during her drive back to London from Hampshire. She would sort them out later:

His family in the colonies

His Italian grandfather Bartolomeo

At the beginning of the war his mother and father took their wedding trip along the coast of Thailand, although it was not yet the resort it is today.

After Malcolm's childhood years in the heat, he said he enjoyed the briskness of the English weather.

His sister MABB refused to go to the Antipodes even for a family Christmas.

His father was multi-lingual, but neither of his children inherited this skill. (Odd, since Malcolm spoke Chinese to the waitress at Ming Palace. He called it Mandarin baby talk.)

His mother was beautiful in a dark sort of way. (Dark sinister or dark in colouring?)

His father had spent most of his life abroad.

His sister and he were close in childhood because his parents were constantly off and away doing whatever parents do.

During school breaks MABB and he stayed with their aunt Cornelia, Cordelia(?), who was lovingly distant from them.

Elspeth had known Malcolm for five and a half months, and this was all she could remember about his family. The year they met, he spent Christmas day with his sister in London but was in Cambridge for much of the rest of the Christmas break working on his thesis. He refused to come to Perthshire. Elspeth returned to Girton several days early so that they could spend Twelfth Night together.

What did Chief Inspector Llewellyn say? Elspeth went back to her notes. Mary Anne claimed her parents were dead, but that wasn't what Malcolm had implied. He always referred to them in the present tense and said they were abroad. Was it in Australia or New Zealand?

During the time she knew him, Elspeth was only interested in Malcolm, not his parents. Richard chastised her for knowing nothing about them, so Elspeth countered by accusing Richard of class snobbery. She now thought Richard might have had a point. Understanding Malcolm's parents' lives was becoming vitally important in unraveling the reason for Malcolm's death.

She could not remember any more facts about Malcolm's parents. Had they disappeared in the Antipodes or were they dead as Mary Anne had told the inspector? How could she learn the truth?

She looked up and again saw her answering machine. When returning Richard's message, she might have to acknowledge her youthful foolishness, but if anyone could find out the identity of Malcolm's parents it would be Richard. She rang the number of his club and was told that he was out, but she could leave word for him.

She returned to her list. On another sheet she wrote:

What colonies?

If his grandfather named Bartolomeo was Italian, was his mother also?

Why in the early 1940's would a couple spend their wedding trip on the Thai coast, which was in a neutral country strongly affiliated with the Japanese Empire? Or did Malcolm mean the beginning of the European war not the Asian one?

Where was the warm climate he railed against? (Inspector Llewellyn had indicated it might be Singapore or Malaya.)

If MABB had refused to go to the Antipodes for Christmas, did that mean at one time Malcolm's parents did live in Australia or New Zealand and had invited them for Christmas?

What languages did Malcolm's father speak, and what did that say about where he lived?

If Malcolm's mother was dark (Inspector Llewellyn mentioned Italian given names), why were both of her children fair? Malcolm was sandy-haired; his sister's hair was carroty. Both had blue eyes.

Malcolm said he was at school in England by the time he was eight, which might indicate his parents' absence. Was this true?

Who was Aunt Cornelia or Cordelia?

Before transferring the notes to her computer, she added:

When did Malcolm's parents die, assuming they are dead? And where?

Elspeth massaged her temples with the tips of her fingers as she thought, but no answers came to any of the questions. Yet writing them out helped ease the pain she felt earlier in the day. Once again she made her mind dominate her heart.

She felt tired and decided to have a bath. British interior decorators often surpassed their American counterparts in quiet sophistication but sometimes overlooked the delights of a decadently luxurious Californian bathroom. Elspeth entered the bathroom she had designed for herself with the help of a Hollywood set designer, who was grateful when she recovered a briefcase of sketches stolen at the Kennington Beverley Hills. She shed her clothes and turned on the taps of the large spa. She did not answer the phone when it rang but could hear Richard's voice acknowledging her call.

"All in due time, Sir High Commissioner," she murmured, "when I'm ready to face admonishment for being so starry-eyed an innocent thirty-five years ago." She stepped into the large tub and surrendered to the massage of the pulsating water.

When she finished toweling off her warmly glowing skin, she wrapped herself in a large bath sheet and reached for her mobile.

Richard suggested dinner at a fashionable restaurant but Elspeth demurred, pleading fatigue. She invited him to dinner in her flat on the condition he would bring the makings of a salad. After she rang off, she wondered what the protocol office at the FCO might think of this intimate invitation to one of their high commissioners from a half-naked divorced woman, but Richard sounded delighted.

He arrived with three kinds of lettuce, shredded reggiano, fresh garlic, Tuscan olive oil, freshly baked croutons, and a small bottle of specialty balsamic vinegar. He kissed Elspeth's offered cheek, deposited his purchases on her kitchen counter and launched into a discourse on making a proper salad. She smiled at this touch of domesticity and was grateful she could put off telling him what she had learned from Chief Inspector Llewellyn.

Richard became thoroughly engaged in the task of salad making. He rubbed garlic along the sides of the salad bowl and began tearing the lettuces. Elspeth wondered where he had learned to do this because she knew his now-deceased wife, Lady Marjorie, and he never kept a home of their own. They lived most of their married life in the British Commonwealth, where servants would have taken care of duties like this. Somehow Elspeth could not envision Richard watching cooking shows on the television.

Elspeth's housekeeper had stocked some frozen chicken scaloppini, and Elspeth produced the now-thawed fillets and some lemons. Richard supplied a chilled bottle of pinot grigio. The two worked leisurely to produce their supper, sipping the wine, and laughing together as they had done as teenagers. Elspeth felt a strange, warming comfort in their shared activity. They ate at Elspeth's table, sharing memories of their solving the mystery of FitzRoy's death in Malta and the murders and kidnapping in Stresa.

After their meal Elspeth brewed freshly roasted decaffeinated coffee that she had brought to London from her recent trip to California. They took their cups and settled on one of the sofas in the sitting area and, in deference to laws imposed by the City of London, enjoyed the warmth of a gas fire in the fireplace. "I still burn wood at my retreat north of San Francisco despite protests of the strictest environmentalists," Elspeth said. "You must visit someday. It's a place out of time."

Richard looked up at Elspeth and acknowledged her kindness with a quiet smile. "I'd love to."

She wondered what he was thinking and if she ever would follow through with the invitation. She was dreading talking to him about Malcolm. Their easy companionship covered the pain she was feeling, but it would not go away. Although she had never asked Richard to her flat before, she felt he was aware it was a special place for her. Her decision to invite him was a good one. The past hour encapsulated the relationship that had grown between them since they had re-met in Malta in April, old friends who shared common interests and a common history. They made an attractive couple, as many who saw them together noted, and their long acquaintance made their conversation unaffected and their laughter easy.

Elspeth knew Richard cared more for her than she allowed herself to care for him. She could not deny his physical attraction, as her body responded to it whenever they were together. She carefully avoided interpreting this as love or an invitation to further commitment. In that moment she knew she needed him, not just to enjoy dinners and outings together but as someone to tend to her hurting heart. She abhorred dependence on others, but still she wanted Richard to hold her emotionally as she continued on her quest for Malcolm's murderer. During dinner she had tried to push these feelings away but could avoid them no longer.

Her voice constricted. "Oh, Dickie, I feel like such a failure. My search has opened old wounds but has done nothing to close them." She turned away from him so he would not see the nascent tears.

He covered her hand lightly. She wished instead he would reach out and hold her close to him.

"Elspeth, you will hurt until you know the whole truth," he said softly.

Taking herself to task for wishing more from him, Elspeth rose and fetched her two lists, which she handed to him.

"Perhaps I'm still too close to it," she said, regaining her composure. "What do you make of these?"

He took the sheets of paper and read through them quickly. He asked where she obtained the information on the list. She related her interview with Chief Inspector Llewellyn, only leaving out her reactions to it.

"I never thought Malcolm's past would be so important," she admitted shyly, "but its significance is growing in proportions I wouldn't have imagined earlier."

Richard did not chide her, as she feared he would. Instead he read through her notes again and looked up at her with curiosity in his eyes.

"Even the chief inspector, whose knowledge of colonial history may have been limited, recognized that Mary Anne and Malcolm being born in Southeast Asia during the Japanese occupation to a Scots father, and what sounds like an Italian mother, was unusual. As you probably know, at that time European men and women were sent to separate camps. If Malcolm and his sister were born then, his mother and father met at least twice, but, if they lived together, one might conclude that they were not interned. Perhaps because Italy was on the Axis side and Malcolm's mother was Italian, they did." Richard said, clearing his throat.

Elspeth's stomach churned. "Could the Buchanans have been collaborators? The inspector didn't say if the declaration of their children's birth at Government House in Singapore gave her nationality. We don't know for sure that Malcolm's mother was Italian. She may just have had Italian given names."

"True. Her parents may have been British with a passion for Italy."

"Malcolm said his grandfather's name was Bartolomeo and he was Italian," Elspeth said, hiding her memory of this under a half-smile.

"Then perhaps Malcolm's grandmother married an Italian, long enough ago that there might have been some connection to the Fascists. There also is the possibility Malcolm's parents might have been in hiding together. There were Chinese guerrilla bands in the jungles in Malaya all through the war. A few Europeans lived among them, but I don't think there were any women and children with them. I don't know if there is any way to find out. I'd add that question to your list."

Talking to Richard helped calm Elspeth. She found his steady voice, his intelligent and caring hazel-green eyes, and his long serious face reassuring. His eyes caught hers, and she smiled thanks.

He put down the lists, stretched out his long legs and took up his coffee. "Elspeth, tell me more about Jean Henderson and her conversations with you."

Elspeth remembered Jean's drawing of Richard. "Jean still has drawings she did at Girton that tell more than her words. She drew a marvelous caricature of you, Dickie, one of her few flattering ones. She asked who you were. You made quite an impression on her."

"Tell me about the others."

"There was a hideous one of Malcolm with all of us: Victoria, Malcolm, me, and the Asian waitress at the Chinese restaurant where we used to eat." Elspeth blew out her breath and sighed after she described it.

"What do you think it meant? Think carefully. Jean was a keen observer." Richard's serious tone challenged Elspeth.

"She didn't like Victoria Smythe-Welton."

"More than that. What did she see in Malcolm?"

Richard's question pierced Elspeth. She became defensive. "She obviously was jealous."

"No, I don't think so. I think she saw Malcolm more clearly than you did," Richard said.

Elspeth bristled. "Are you suggesting that Malcolm and Victoria had something between them?"

"Jean must have thought so. She also observed something about the Asian waitress. Did you all go to the Chinese restaurant often?"

"It was a bit of a hangout for the students at Girton. The food was cheap and, in those days, we thought it good. Boys from the other colleges often went there to see which girls were about."

"I think you need to talk to Jean again. She may remember what she had in mind when she drew the pictures."

Elspeth wished he had not brought up the topic of the drawings and turned the conversation away from it.

"Do you think if I went to Singapore, I could find out more about Malcolm's parents and where they were during the war?"

"I still have colleagues and friends out there. I could contact them."

"Let me give it some thought, Dickie."

Elspeth wondered if Richard's channels to the British High Commission in Singapore would be helpful. She knew he had been high commissioner there, and Lady Marjorie had been with him. Why did the thought of Lady Marjorie suddenly invade her psyche, and why did it give her unpleasant feelings of jealousy? Turning her mind away from such foolishness, she changed the topic again.

"What about the Antipodes?" she said. "They seem to have come up a number of times with both Malcolm and Mary Anne. Is there any way to see if their parents immigrated to Australia or New Zealand, or do you suppose that the term 'antipodes' simply referred to the other end of the earth?"

"I can make enquiries."

"Official ones?" she asked.

"Semi-official, I suppose. I have FCO friends in Canberra and Wellington, assuming Malcolm and Mary Anne's references were to Australia or New Zealand."

Elspeth put her fingers to her temples. Her head felt heavy. She was not sure if it was the wine or the emotions that had bombarded her all day. She wanted everything to stop, to be finalized, to be resolved with no more pain, but she knew this was impossible.

"My head is swimming. Can we talk about something else and leave the investigation until we both have more time to think about it."

He rose. "I have to return to Valletta shortly. When I'm back there, I'll send some emails and see what I can find out for you. Please come back to Malta soon. I must be gone as it's getting late. Rest well, my dearest Elspeth. I'll let myself out."

When he was gone, Elspeth retired to the loft but could not asleep. She was filled with thoughts not of Malcolm, whose remembrance had exhausted her all day, but of Richard and Lady Marjorie. Elspeth wondered what their marriage had been like and if they ever made dinner together. As Elspeth recollected Marjorie, she thought not. Why did that give her pleasure? Elspeth decided her emotions regarding Richard Munro were getting more complex than she could handle at the moment. She went downstairs and made herself a cup of hot chocolate.

6

After his four-day absence from the high commission in Malta, Richard's inbox was overflowing, despite his PA's careful attention to it, and consequently answering his phone messages occupied most of the afternoon. He attended a formal dinner party at the French Embassy, where he was paired with a woman from the embassy staff who thankfully seemed to have no designs on him. He thought of the night at Elspeth's flat as he ate and politely responded when addressed without hearing his companion's replies. He made his excuses as quickly as was diplomatically correct and returned to the house on Triq It-Torre in Sliema, where he lived.

Cold December winds were blowing down from Sicily. He kept on his overcoat and went up to the terrace on the top floor, where Elspeth and he had breakfasted together several times during the FitzRoy case. At that time he had not seen her for almost seven years, but his heart never forgot her. He loved her more now than ever before but wondered if he would ever fully understand her complexities. Her face was too strong and sharp for beauty, but, as Tony Ketcham had said, she was handsome. She had an easy sophistication, and her intelligence and competence could not be doubted. When relaxed she had a quick wit and an infectious smile. Her dark cobalt blue eyes were startling in their intensity, but in happy moments they became merry and mischievous.

Richard was learning, however, that Elspeth used this overlay to hide deeper vulnerabilities. He loved her and wanted to understand her inner feelings of sadness. That night at her flat she momentarily allowed him to see through a narrow window into this part of her, but he watched her batten it down and resort to her intellect to cope with her grief. Richard wanted to reach out to her, to assure her she would find out the truth and then to hold her when she discovered more than she would want to know, but he knew she would withdraw from him if he did. He could not understand why she kept a distance between them. At times he sensed she was struggling with her feelings toward him, but then she would find an excuse to turn away. What made her so distrustful of him? He could only go on loving her, hoping one day she would open to him and find his love waiting.

The wind from the sea added rain, and he stepped back inside, returning to an uncluttered room where he had a desk, a phone and his laptop computer. He checked his watch, and saw it was after eleven, which would make it past ten in London. He took a chance and called Elspeth's number. As the phone rang, he could see her in her flat and felt deeply moved that she had invited him there.

"Oh, Dickie, it's you," she said, pleasure in her voice. "I'm so glad you rang. I've come to a bit of a dead end about Malcolm's family and need to talk to someone."

Richard smiled. "I'm sure if I go on the internet, I'll be able to turn up some names of people either in Singapore or the Antipodes who might have some recollection of them. Let me see what I can find. I'll get back to you." He did not add what was in his heart.

He phoned her again half an hour later.

"I tried the high commission in Singapore, but the night duty officer told me Mark Collins, whom I mentored when he first entered the diplomatic service, has moved on to New Delhi, but I discovered an old friend is now high commissioner in Canberra. I'll email him tonight and copy you."

She thanked him, and he thought she was about to ring off.

"Elspeth?"

"I'm here, Dickie."

"I wanted to thank you for inviting me to dinner. I can feel how difficult all this is for you."

"Your being here helped. I hope I wasn't too maudlin."

He did not want her to brush him away again. "No, not at all," he said. "I understand."

"Good night, Dickie, and thanks again for all you are doing."

"Good night, my precious one," he said to the emptiness of the room after she disconnected the call.

Richard missed the days when correspondence was an art. He disliked the short missives email had spawned and took great pains to see that his own electronic correspondence was sufficiently dignified. He wrote to Sir Andrew, the high commissioner in Canberra, as if he were handwriting the message rather than pecking it out on his keyboard. He sent it with a blind copy to Elspeth.

> *Dear Andrew,*
>
> *How strange it is for me to be sitting in Malta and 'penning' you a note on a machine resting on my desk. Through my window I can see an unsettled*

Mediterranean and wonder if we are going to have more storms tomorrow.

Last spring I aided Scotland Yard in arresting a terrorist they had been pursuing for quite some time. Even in sleepy Malta, we have some excitement on occasion. It is that event that has prompted me to write you. During the course of the investigation I met an old friend who was involved in an unsolved murder that happened in 1969, when all of us were young and hoped the terrible things that happened the year before in America were only anomalies. Now we know better.

I am rambling a bit, but I would like to ask you a great favour? Does your office have any record of a Scot named James Andrew Malcolm Buchanan or his wife, Anna Maria Cornelia Buchanan, living in Australia in the late sixties? It seems a long shot to ask you, but if you could dig about a bit I would appreciate it.

I know Australia has marvelous beaches, but Malta can offer some of the oldest temples in the world. Why don't Dorothy and you come and visit during one of your home leaves?

I would be most appreciative of any help you can give me. I remember our service in Wellington together and your excellent gin slings.

With best regards,
Richard Munro

The following morning Richard forwarded Elspeth the high commissioner's reply to Elspeth.

Richard— Delightful to hear from you. I will have my drones begin their search immediately and will be back in touch. —Andrew

*

Two days later when Elspeth was out shopping, she received a voice mail message on her mobile from Richard. His tone was constrained. "I've had an email from the consular section of the high commission in Canberra, and I'm forwarding it on to you. After you've read it, ring me. I want you to see it before we talk further."

Elspeth paid hurriedly for the few items she had taken from the shelves and made her way back to her flat. She hastily opened her email and found the message Richard had forwarded on to her.

Dear Sir Richard,

Sir Andrew asked me to research James Andrew Malcolm Buchanan and his wife, who lived in Tasmania from June 1965 until their deaths in February 1969. Both were murdered in Tasmania on 23 February of that year, but no charges were ever brought against their killer or killers. I have assembled a small packet of information on the murders, which I will put in the diplomatic bag this evening and should be in Malta in several days' time. Please feel free to contact me for more information once you have received the packet.

Yours most sincerely,
Lesley Urquhart, Consul

Elspeth read the email over several times and was stunned by its contents. Malcolm's murder happened in mid-May, which would be twelve weeks after his parents had died.

The multiple murders could hardly be a coincidence. Had the same person killed all three?

Taking in gulps of air, she rang Richard.

"Malcolm never said a word about his parents' murders. We were together constantly during that time. He must have known, and surely he would have told me."

Richard cleared his throat before responding. "Elspeth, I think it's important you think back and to try to remember if there was any change in Malcolm's behavior after February twenty-third."

She could not think clearly. Finally she replied. "I first met Malcolm just three weeks before Christmas, and, except my being in Scotland for a fortnight at Christmas, we were inseparable until he died in May. Everything during that time was filled with such. . .energy. I never noticed any change."

Richard's next words sounded careful. Elspeth grimaced, hoping he would not bring up his old prejudice against Malcolm. "Do you suppose he purposely withheld things about his life from you?"

She winced. "We spent so much time together that it seems unfathomable he could have hidden anything from me."

"I can see that, my dear, but obviously other things were going on in his life. Let me propose a plan. The papers from Australia will arrive here shortly. Can you come to Malta in two days' time?"

"Of course. I'm sure I can stay at the Kennington Valletta, or, better, I know Aunt Magdelena will welcome me with great joy. Can you get away to Gozo?"

"No, come and stay here in Sliema. I adore your aunt, but I think we need to talk in private. I'll have my housekeeper prepare one of the bedrooms for you. I've something else to suggest. The name Victoria Smythe-Welton has come up several times. You said Jean drew a vicious caricature of her and also mentioned that Victoria claimed her father had known Malcolm's father in Malaya. Can you follow up on that lead?"

Elspeth smiled. "Dickie, I think you're becoming a far better investigator than I am."

"No, but I think that I'm a bit more objective when it comes to Malcolm," he said.

Elspeth did not agree but did not say so.

7

Elspeth rang Jean Henderson at Girton and found her in.

"Jean, I need your further help. First, do you know what happened to Victoria Smythe-Welton?"

"No, but I certainly can find out if she has kept any ties with Girton. I'll see what I can discover."

Elspeth cleared her throat because the second request was harder to ask. "When you came to my hotel room, you showed me a drawing you did that included Malcolm, Victoria, the Chinese waitress, and me. Do you by any chance recall why you did that drawing?"

Jean chuckled dryly "I'm embarrassed that I do remember. When I drew it, I was intensely jealous of Victoria and you and the Chinese waitress as well."

Despite the pain it cost her, Elspeth pursued the topic. "Why should you feel jealous of the three of us?"

"I always admired you, Elspeth, and still do. My thoughts were hateful then."

Elspeth would not be deterred. "Hateful of whom?"

"Of Victoria and the waitress and you. You all had, how shall I put it, Malcolm's attention."

"Are you saying Malcolm was. . ." Elspeth didn't know how to continue.

"Was sleeping with Victoria? Oh, Elspeth, it shouldn't hurt after all this time. Victoria was such a vamp and had to seduce any man who was seeing someone else at Girton. Malcolm wasn't the only one."

"Victoria and Malcolm had. . .an affair?" Elspeth hoped her voice stayed level, but her stomach roiled.

"Not an affair. Probably just a one night stand."

"Do you know this for sure?"

"Victoria bragged about it to her set. Who knows if it was true?"

"And you heard them."

"Yes, I did creep a bit behind the scenes in those days."

Elspeth drew in her breath. Was Jean still jealous? A wiser and older Elspeth thought not and asked, "What about the Chinese waitress?"

"There was nothing there as overt as Victoria. It's just several times I saw Malcolm talking secretively to her in the alley beside Ming Palace. I've no idea what they were discussing because they were speaking what I assumed was Chinese, but she seemed to have control of the conversation."

Elspeth demanded clarification. "Control? What do you mean, Jean? This may be important."

"He seemed to be asking something of her, but she kept shaking her head angrily, as if refusing to do something for him, and then she seemed to make her own demands."

"Could you hear what they said?"

"I couldn't, but, even if I could, I don't speak Chinese."

"It's all very strange," Elspeth said, hoping her voice did not reveal her inner turmoil, "but if you can get back to me about Victoria's current location, I'd be very appreciative."

Elspeth could hear the contrition in Jean's voice. "I fear, Elspeth, I haven't been a kind friend."

"Jean, it's more important right now that you've been an honest one."

Jean rang back that afternoon. "According to the college records, Victoria has been married three times and has moved about a bit. She's living with number three in Essex. His name is Edgar Brewer, and she uses his name. Do you have something to write with? Here's her address and phone number. She also has email."

Elspeth took down the relevant information and, as a return favor to Jean, promised to ring her after talking with Victoria.

Elspeth debated whether to call or email Victoria and finally decided phoning would get faster results. The most Victoria could do would be to turn Elspeth down. Before taking out her phone, Elspeth pondered her best approach. Experience told her people changed little as they grew older despite how much one hoped they might. She tried to remember what she could about Victoria. At Girton Elspeth found Victoria vain, critical, and arrogant. Victoria also was quite beautiful, Elspeth recalled, and dressed in trendy clothes, sporting the shortest mini-skirts the college would allow. Elspeth wished that she had better memories of Victoria.

The phone rang, and Victoria answered in the same breathless voice she used at Girton.

Elspeth introduced herself, and Victoria instantly proclaimed an undying interest is seeing her "long lost friend." They set up an appointment the following day to meet for lunch in the dining room of the Tate Modern Museum in London.

Elspeth arrived early and arranged with the maître d' for a quiet table in a secluded corner. She sat watching people coming in past the reception counter, wondering if she would recognize Victoria after all this time. Elspeth did, although she was glad Victoria was far enough away that she could not hear Elspeth's intake of breath. Elspeth calculated that the once slender Victoria now weighed about seventeen stone. She was dressed fashionably but flamboyantly, and her makeup was immaculately but heavily applied. Her hair was an unnatural shade of auburn with blond streaks and combed and lacquered in an exaggerated sculpture. Elspeth eschewed hairspray, gel, or scent in her own hair because she expected her stylist to cut her hair well enough to fall into place naturally and be free to move with the air. She blushed to think how often Richard touched her hair and wondered if any man had ever tried to do the same to Victoria's. Victoria's bulging and wrinkled arms were heavy with numerous bracelets. She waddled with the sway that obese people often have. Reaching the table, she grabbed the back of the chair. She gasped for her breath with the desperation of a drowning sailor who was finally thrown a lifeline.

"Elspeth, darling! How divine to see you again. You haven't changed at all." Elspeth did not return the compliment but, because she needed information from Victoria, she replied both with a warm smile, albeit feigned, and courtesy, which was her habit.

It being early, the restaurant was not crowded. The few diners had chosen window seats so that they might watch the activities on the South Bank and the River Thames. Consequently, Elspeth and Victoria were able to talk without restraint at the table in the corner. They exchanged pleasantries and presented life histories in glowing terms. This occupied them through the process of ordering their meal and the arrival of their drinks. Victoria ordered wine, although Elspeth suspected she might have preferred something more robust; Elspeth requested sparkling water.

Elspeth was not surprised when Victoria, characteristically, first broached the purpose for their visit. "So after all these years, you are still wondering what happened to Malcolm." Despite the flat statement of fact, there was a slight sneer in Victoria's voice that Elspeth recognized from the past.

"Yes. You seem to be a person who's able to move on without regret, and I envy you that quality," Elspeth said honestly. "Perhaps that's because I'm a stubborn Scotswoman who needs closure. I never got it after Malcolm's death."

"You still love him, don't you?"

"In a way, I suppose I do."

Victoria then threw her bomb. "He wasn't faithful to you, you know. Many of us can attest to that," she said and laughed.

Elspeth's heart stood still. She hoped her face stayed passive. She smiled sadly. "So I understand. Jean Henderson told me."

"Jean always was a sneak. Horrid girl! Why they let girls like that mix with the rest of us, I never shall know."

Elspeth could not bear this. "Actually her family was terribly wealthy and her father titled, but Jean didn't want anyone to know."

Victoria did not react to her statement other than asking, "Have you seen her recently?"

"Yes, when I was in Cambridge just the other day. She's settled in as a research fellow at Girton and has made quite a success of her career. She also inherited half of her mother's wealth, which was considerable, and enjoys it rather *sotto voce*. Her father, the baronet, is still very much alive and doing well in Shropshire." Elspeth knew it was not kind to compare Jean's success, wealth, and family connections with Victoria's now rather debauched and seemingly idle state. Elspeth inwardly chided herself for becoming petty. Victoria still had that effect on her.

Elspeth continued, trying to tone down her contempt. "And what of yourself, Victoria? You seem to have an interesting life."

At Girton, Victoria liked talking about herself, and over the years this had not changed. She bragged about her three boys, her two grandchildren, and her wonderful husband's thriving businesses. Elspeth had Googled Edgar Brewer in Essex and had discovered he owned two used car dealerships. Victoria rhapsodized about living in the country after so many years in town. She never mentioned what she did all day. She didn't need to; Elspeth assumed it centered on eating and drinking. In the end, Elspeth felt sorry for Victoria, who may have had as wonderful family as she boasted, but whose life seemed vacuous.

Lunch lasted longer than Elspeth wanted, but she found out some things about Malcolm she had not known before. After Victoria's first comments, Elspeth was not sure she wanted to continue to pry, but she did anyway. Her apprehension was rewarded.

"I knew you were friends with Malcolm," Elspeth lied, "but I had no idea you were closer than that."

"We were very close, but it was the late sixties, and everyone was close, if you remember. No inhibitions and all that sort of thing." Victoria spoke between large mouthfuls, demurely finished with a touch of her napkin to her lips.

Elspeth swallowed and went on. "What about the waitress at Ming Palace? Did you know her?"

"I don't think they were lovers, if that's what you mean. He called her his 'evil sister' and argued with her in Chinese.

He grew up in Malaya, you know, and spoke Chinese as a child."

Elspeth was beginning to realize others knew things about Malcolm that she did not. Was her love that blind? Or did Malcolm not want her to know?

"Did you ever meet Malcolm's parents?"

"Heavens, no. You know how much he distrusted them."

Elspeth did not know and wondered if Victoria was making all this up. Victoria had many faults, but Elspeth did not remember lying was one of them, although Victoria did like to exaggerate.

"Did you ever meet Malcolm's sister?" Elspeth asked.

"Many times. Her husband, Edward, was a good friend of my brother, at least before Mary Anne and Edward went to live in Australia."

"When was that?"

"Probably about a year after Malcolm died."

"Do you know where in Australia?"

"I may have known but have long since forgotten. I think I shall have another piece of this delicious chocolate cake."

Elspeth regretted the high cost of the lunch when she reviewed her credit card bill the next month.

8

Elspeth took the Air Malta afternoon flight from Gatwick in London to Malta's Luqa Airport. Her mood was dark and had been since her lunch with Victoria Smythe-Welton Brewer the day before. She spoke to no one on the flight and, when she entered the terminal, she was disappointed Richard had sent a car for her rather than coming himself.

Richard was not home at his borrowed house on Triq It-Torre in Sliema when she arrived there. The housekeeper showed Elspeth into a large, furniture-filled bedroom with a bathroom beyond, which had the most ornate bear-clawed bathtub she had ever seen. Elspeth poured a large hot bath, luxuriated in it and allowed thoughts of the evening ahead to supersede the lingering displeasure of lunch at the Tate Modern and the vileness of the innuendoes with which Victoria had poisoned their conversation. Elspeth dressed carefully, hoping Richard would notice, and made her way to the drawing room below, where she found him. He greeted her with a chaste embrace, nothing more.

"Elspeth, you look magnificent, but I also sense all is not well with you," he said, holding her out from him.

Elspeth accepted the glass of sherry he offered and sat down in one of the fan-backed bamboo chairs that faced the windows looking out to the Mediterranean. A strong wind swept across the sea and chopped at the water forming thousands of small waves. It reminded her of the turmoil in her heart.

"Did you know Victoria too?" Elspeth said without introduction. There could be no doubt about her meaning of the word "know." She sounded gruff and then regretted it. "Oh, Dickie, I am sorry. Things have just become too awful." She put her hands over her face.

He sat across from her without responding. When she removed her hands from her eyes, she found him looking at her, his eyes serious, but he did not reach out to touch her. "I think it would be best if you told me about Victoria," he said stiffly.

Elspeth felt chagrined that she might have considered Richard and Victoria together and dropped her eyes. "She's worse than ever. She insinuated that Malcolm and she were lovers, that she knew all about his past, and that her brother was a friend of Malcolm's brother-in-law. She gushed familiarity. It was disgusting."

Richard set his lips together and nodded, but he did not smile. "I heard gossip about Malcolm and Victoria too, but, Elspeth, gossip is simply that. I'd take no store by things that haven't been proven." He was less discreet about Victoria. "At Girton Victoria was rather forward, I must admit, but she didn't appeal to me at all, despite her money and family connections. How could she compare with you?"

Elspeth relaxed and grinned.

"Thank you for that, Dickie, especially after my rude question."

He smiled in response. "I understand, my dear, but eventually you're going to have to accept that what you hear from others might be true."

Elspeth's throat tightened. "You mean about Malcolm's faithlessness to me."

Richard nodded. "I don't know the truth, but others seem to have seen and heard things you did not."

Elspeth could not read his tone. She wanted to tell him more of what Victoria had said, but she did not. His words stung. She turned from her hurt by changing the topic.

"Chief Inspector Llewellyn told me you kept a journal during the investigation. Do you still have it?" she asked, keeping her voice as even as she could.

"It's probably in an old box somewhere at my brother's home in Aberdeenshire. I haven't poked through those boxes in years. Marjorie was continually at me to throw away all that rubbish, as she called it, but I never could."

Elspeth tried not to react to the casual way he mentioned Marjorie's name. Marjorie must have commented many times on the minutiae of his life during their thirty years of marriage. Obviously he still kept Marjorie in his life without thinking. Why should it matter, Elspeth thought, but it did.

"Could your brother find it?" she asked, trying to still her thoughts.

"Probably not. I'm not certain I could find it myself, but the next time I'm in Scotland, I will try. I doubt it would shed anything new on Malcolm's murder because it merely recounted the day-by-day efforts of Inspector Llewellyn and his frustration at finding nothing that might lead to a solution to the crime."

The honesty of Richard's tone made Elspeth believe him.

"Perhaps I'm being foolish mucking about in past memories the other girls at Girton had of Malcolm. They don't seem to be as fond as my own."

"You loved him, Elspeth, and you didn't know him long enough to find out his faults."

"Are you going to scold me again after all these years?" She looked up at him, defiance in her eyes. She wished she could read his mind.

"You know I am a bit stuffy about people's past histories, but I promise not to scold. It was far too long ago and too many things have happened since. The world and morality have altered as well, and we all have changed with them."

"Where do I go from here, Dickie?" She hated herself for saying this and for her need of him right now. She found his eyes again and felt their coolness.

He cleared his throat and started to speak, and then he stopped. Elspeth wondered what he had planned to say. "There must be a link between Malcolm's murder and the deaths of his parents. After reading the material from the high commission in Canberra, I think you need to go there," he said.

"There meaning Australia?"

He nodded. "Yes."

"To face what happened there?" she asked. "To find the connection?"

"Yes," he said again. "I can arrange with Sir Andrew to get you assistance, and I'm sure the young consul at the high commission in Canberra will help you as well."

"Do high commissioners usually do this sort of thing for each other?"

"It's a bit unusual, I must admit, but long-time members of the diplomatic corps do help each other out on occasion. Come and let me show you what came from Canberra in the diplomatic bag this morning. The packet Lesley Urquhart sent includes the death certificates for Malcolm's parents, but the cause of death had been blacked out by some unknown censor."

They decided to dine at one of the better hotels in St. Julian's, and they ate without mentioning Malcolm. Richard bade her goodnight soon after they returned to Triq It-Torre. He pleaded an early morning appointment at the high commission and left her at her bedroom door.

She lay in bed, staring at the shadows thrown from the multitude of ornate objects in her bedroom. They formed grotesques shapes on the wall in the cold winter moonlight. She could hear the bitter wind off the sea rattling the loose-fitting windows. Her heart considered what she would do if Richard knocked on her door, but she knew he would not. She was not sure if she was regretful or relieved. Her mind replayed the words he had said to her after her arrival. She missed his usual words of endearment and soft touches. Perhaps he did not like her show of weakness or doubt, or perhaps he hated her clinging to dreams of Malcolm. She must try to keep these feelings in check. She felt she was treading into Richard's emotional territory, which she did not understand or know how to handle.

It took Elspeth almost three days to get to Australia. She booked a flight to Rome on Air Malta and a Qantas flight to Hong Kong and on to Sydney. Using frequent flyer miles she upgraded to business class but missed the comfort to which she was accustomed when traveling first class with the Kennington Organisation.

Elspeth was a seasoned international traveler, but everything that could go wrong on her trip did. Weather delayed her in Rome, and she missed her connection in Hong Kong. When she arrived in Sydney, her luggage had been lost. The chaos of the flights reflected the state her mind. What had she set in motion? Why hadn't she accepted Malcolm's death and moved on? Life had given her more than enough opportunities to be happy, but she had chosen this inner sadness. Why did she need to dwell on something that happened so long ago? Why could she not let it go? What was Richard's sudden coolness, and why did that matter so much to her? Stiffening herself, she acknowledged she had lost her usual detachment from personal feelings and was becoming morose. Let's get done with this, a voice inside her said, and quickly. You have other things to occupy your life and your heart.

She had not been in Australia for many years, the last time being with Alistair, her ex-husband, who was directing the fight scenes for an adventure film about a man wrongly transported to Australia in the early nineteenth century. The film had been a harsh representation of the realities of the unfortunates who were sent to the far reaches of the British Empire for as small a crime as stealing a piece of cheese. Elspeth's memories of the Australian people filled her with warmth. She hoped their kindness would soften her mood.

A brief call to Pamela Crumm from Malta was all Elspeth needed to get accommodation at the Kennington Sydney. Pamela, of course, wanted to know why Elspeth was going to Australia. Elspeth shared the reasons without mentioning the involvement of Richard Munro. If she had, Pamela would make assumptions Elspeth did not want her to make.

Elspeth finally arrived at Sydney Airport and, carrying only her overnight bag, found a taxi to take her to the Kennington Sydney. Lord Kennington's minions had found an historic building across from the luxuriant Royal Botanic Gardens in the center of the city and had spent two years converting it from an office building to a Kennington hotel.

The hotel had all the most modern appointments required in all of his lordship's establishments but reeked of history. As an employee, Elspeth was given a less-expensive room, which faced on a bustling side street. Still, she found the room was supplied with all the amenities she usually requested.

Exhausted, she lay down on the bed and rang Richard. He greeted her call warmly. They chatted about the insanity of her flight, and then she bade him goodnight, although it was still morning in Malta. He spoke affectionately to her as he rang off, and everything suddenly seemed better in her world. Savoring the comfort of a Kennington hotel bed, she hoped she would sleep peacefully until early the next morning. She could not imagine what things the next day would bring.

9

Elspeth woke at three in the morning, jarred to consciousness by the ringing of the telephone. Her first hope was that Richard had rung back, but she was disappointed. Eric Kennington's voice came over the line.

"Elspeth, Pamela tells me you are in Sydney, which couldn't be better for me. A situation has come up at the hotel there that needs immediate attention, and I don't have time to send anyone else out. Since you are staying there, I need your help. It shouldn't take long, but it will mean a great deal to me and to the Kennington Organisation."

Elspeth groaned inaudibly. She should not have accepted Pamela's offer of a room at the Kennington Sydney without being fully aware Lord Kennington might use the situation to his advantage.

"Eric, I'm totally jet lagged, very irritable, and bordering on sleep deprivation. May I call you back when it's morning here?" She tried to calculate what time it was in London and vaguely remembered there was eleven hours difference between the time zones. If it was three o'clock in the morning in Sydney, which her bedside clock indicated it was, then it was four in the afternoon the day before in London

"Or rather, have Pamela email me, and we can talk tomorrow at a good time for both of us," she suggested.

She rang off and wondered why she had not reminded Eric she was on sabbatical and did not want to be bothered with his concerns. She knew, however, she was staying at the Kennington Sydney without paying for her room.

She turned over but slept badly until the morning summer sun came in her window. At seven she crawled out from under the duvet and rang room service for her coffee and a simple breakfast, remembering that the Australians outdid the British for hearty breakfasts. She retreated into the magnificent bathroom and half an hour later emerged, feeling more like herself and ready to resume her search for Malcolm.

The phone rang again. This time it was Pamela Crumm, calling from London despite the late hour there. Pamela never seemed fazed by the world's time zones and worked at all hours of the day and night.

"G'day," said Pamela in an accent that would have curdled most Australians' souls. "How are things down under?"

Elspeth grinned at Pamela's enthusiasm.

"I'm not sure. So far I've seen the motorway from the airport to here. It looked very normal." Elspeth yawned audibly to remind Pamela of the travails of international travel. "I'm sure there are many delights the roadway did not reveal, but I'm here in one piece but *sans bagages*. How are you, old friend? What has put his lordship's bustle so much in a twist that he needed to talk to me practically the minute I landed? What's up?"

"He sent Lady Sarah Brixton to Sydney to photograph the new hotel."

"Is that a problem?" Elspeth asked, not seeing any imminent danger in the presence of a photographer, titled or not.

"No, actually she's quite a remarkably good photographer, particularly for a member of the aristocracy."

"There's more to this than you are telling me, Pamela," Elspeth said from experience. "Otherwise Eric would not have called."

"Elspeth, m'friend, sharp as hever you are." Pamela said in an accent Elspeth could not place. Pamela was fond of accents but did not always get them right. "It's not the photography; it's Lady Sarah's family. She has two stepsons. The younger one is a bit of a problem, and so Lady Sarah—at the insistence of her husband, Clyde Brixton, the mining mogul, you know—decided to take the stepson, named Marcus, to Australia with her. They've been staying at the Kennington Sydney. Yesterday Marcus flew to Tasmania to attend a rock concert, but he didn't meet the car sent to fetch him. Qantas says he was on the flight to Hobart, but after that he disappeared.

Clyde rang Eric and asked for help."

"Pamela, I don't have time for this. I'm on leave."

"You can at least see Lady Sarah."

Elspeth sighed. "Give me her room number, or better yet, call the manager and I'll go through him. Who is the manager, by the way?"

"An Australian, who trained at the hotel in Mayfair. His name is Robert Cole. I think you'll like him."

Elspeth knew she had once again been coerced by Lord Kennington's into doing something she did not want to do.

Before leaving her room, Elspeth rang the British high commission in Canberra and asked for Lesley Urquhart. The alto voice of the woman who answered the phone took Elspeth by surprise. Elspeth had assumed Lesley was a man.

"Oh, Ms. Duff, how glad I'm that you rang. Sir Andrew has instructed me to offer any assistance I can," the voice said.

"I'm very grateful. Richard Munro tells me my request is a bit out of the ordinary." Elspeth was sincere in her appreciation. "I'd like to come to Canberra," she continued, "and talk to you about the murder of James and Anna Maria Buchanan. Is today possible?"

"Better yet, I'll be in Sydney late this afternoon on other business," Lesley Urquhart said. "Can we meet there? I can bring along a file with all the information I have." Elspeth was pleased at the businesslike tone of the consul.

"I am staying at the Kennington hotel. What time could you be here?"

"Half past four?"

"Come for tea. If you haven't had tea at a Kennington hotel before, you are in for a treat. Do you know where we are?" Elspeth asked.

"On MacQuarie Street," Lesley Urquhart said, obviously delighted. "There was quite a write-up in the papers here when the hotel opened, with super photographs. I look forward to seeing it in person."

Next Elspeth rang Robert Cole. She expected an Australian accent, but he had only the slightest one, as she should have expected of a Kennington hotel manager. They made arrangements to meet in the hotel offices at half past ten, which gave her time to check her email.

There was a long and affectionate message from Richard, wishing her well and asking her to let him know how things progressed. She tapped out a short reply, including her thanks. She answered notes from her two children and sent a brief note to Pamela, asking her to tell Eric Kennington she was making arrangements to meet Lady Sarah.

Robert Cole had the tall and ruddy good looks of so many of the Australians Elspeth had met in the past. His hands were large and his handshake welcoming. His open manner, overlaid with the polish all managers at Kennington hotels were required to have, made Elspeth feel at ease.

"Tell me about Lady Sarah Brixton. Is she here as a guest or as an employee?" Elspeth asked.

"Ms. Crumm tells me you have worked for Lord Kennington for many years and know him well." Robert Cole said. "It may be improper for me to say so, but I think he has blurred the lines here between guest and employee. Lady Sarah is a charming woman and quite an accomplished photographer from what I have seen of the pictures she has taken here and shown to me. I understand she has many wealthy, well-connected friends, so her assignment here must be well known to them. As a marketing tool, Lady Sarah's promoting our hotels to her friends is quite brilliant, don't you agree?"

Elspeth cocked an eyebrow and smiled. "Just between us, Eric Kennington is an elitist. He knows a word from a prominent or titled person has vast marketing value. He's completely open about that. Do you fault him?"

Robert Cole's face remained stoic. "Not fault him, rather admire him."

Elspeth grinned at his candor. "Now tell me about Lady Sarah and also about her stepson."

"They have been here for a week. Lady Sarah has been diligently at work the whole time while Marcus has spent his time exploring the nightspots of Sydney. I've seldom seen them together, although once or twice I've seen them arguing with each other. Each time Lady Sarah simply throws up her hands and lets him go. She seems to have given up being the wicked stepmother and gives Marcus free rein to do as he pleases."

"Can you introduce her to me?"

"Of course. I'll call her and ask her to join you for lunch. I'll tell her who you are but not why you are here."

"Good. Also, I'll be having tea with a member of the British high commission this afternoon. Teas at all Kennington hotels, I know, are always wonderful, but make this one particularly so."

Elspeth had not anticipated Lady Sarah Brixton. She had expected a snobbish, somewhat disconnected socialite, who used her name to get photographic assignments and produce mediocre work at best. Lady Sarah arrived at the table Robert Cole reserved for them dressed in her working clothes. They were not elegant. She grasped Elspeth's hand warmly and seemed to read her thoughts.

"Pockets. As any serious photographer will tell you, it's all about pockets." Lady Sarah said.

Elspeth laughed out loud. Sarah Brixton was tall, hearty, and fiftyish. Her tanned skin was wrinkled at the corners of her eyes, her graying hair was short and conveniently but not fashionably cut, and her smile was broad.

Sarah looked at Elspeth, who had dressed with her usual stylishness, and Elspeth could sense her curiosity.

"Eric told me I would like you; I hope he's right," Sarah said, "but I can see I already do. You look quite straightforward despite all the finery."

Elspeth was not exactly sure what to make of her remark. "Pamela Crumm and Robert Cole both tell me your work is excellent. I look forward to seeing it, but that's not why we are here, is it?"

"Unfortunately not. Do you have children?" Lady Sarah asked.

Elspeth smiled. "Two. A son and a daughter."

"Are they difficult?"

"Not recently, although there have been times. Both are now adults."

"Have you had any stepchildren?"

"No. Am I blessed in that?"

"You have no idea how difficult they can be."

Elspeth heard genuine angst in Lady Sarah's tone despite her flippancy.

"My husband is a person larger than life, and that's why I married him," Sarah explained. "We meet on a high and exciting plane, although not always on a quiet one. I used to love him unreservedly. We sparred, fought, loved, and laughed. There could be no better way for an adult marriage except for. . ."

Elspeth filled in the blank. "Except for the stepchildren."

"Exactly."

"And most particularly Marcus?" Elspeth raised her eyebrows sympathetically.

"So you know about Marcus."

"Eric Kennington called me about him. Thus our lunch together."

Sarah nodded acknowledgment. "Marcus was the child conceived to put off his parents' divorce. Such children are always a mistake. I think Marcus knows that, and he's gone about all his life to prove it. Frightful child." Sarah plunged into her salmon soufflé.

"Tell me more about him," Elspeth said.

"He just finished his A-Levels, and Clyde promised him that, if he passed them with Bs or above, which was touch and go, he could have a trip to Australia. As ill luck would have it, Eric Kennington had already scheduled my trip here, and Clyde immediately appointed me guardian. Marcus, Clive insisted, could stay with me in Sydney and pursue his own interests, in other words rock music. Marcus is particularly in awe of a punk rock group here called something about Tasmanian quolls, which I understand are small, vicious and nefarious nocturnal catlike creatures that only exists in Tasmania. After listening to one of their CDs, I told Marcus I couldn't abide the noise the group made, but Marcus assures me my ears are too old and insensitive to understand. Clyde arranged for Marcus to meet these human quolls at a concert here and then follow them to Tasmania where they are taking part in a punk rock festival near Hobart. With Clyde's usual attention for detail, he had arranged for a car and driver for Marcus, which in reality was a detective service that would chaperone Marcus while he was in Tasmania. It seems Marcus got wind of this and gave the detectives the slip."

Elspeth bit her lips to suppress her amusement.

"Your Marcus sounds quite clever despite his teenage attitude," Elspeth said.

Sarah snorted. "Unfortunately, I don't consider him my Marcus but rather my burden. This whole issue is causing no small amount of tension between Clyde and me. He thinks I should be loving toward Marcus, which I'm not. Actually, I've tried to relate to Marcus, but he seems incapable of relating to anyone who isn't covered with tattoos, has numerous piercings in unfortunate places and sports multi-colored spiked hair."

Elspeth laughed. "I'm so glad my children are old enough to have missed the current teen fashions. But, Lady Sarah, Eric asked me to help. I'm not too sure what I can do for you."

"Oh, for heaven's sake, call me Sarah. Only Eric likes the title."

"All right then, Sarah, where do we go from here?"

"Eric told me you might be going to Tasmania."

Elspeth felt puzzled, wondering how Lord Kennington would know that. She had not told him about Malcolm's parents' murders, but she had told Pamela Crumm.

Elspeth hedged. "There may be a reason for me to go there, but I won't know until later today."

Sarah looked at Elspeth. "Perhaps Eric made presumptions."

"I think he did, but that's not unusual. I'll call you later and let you know one way or the other. Will you be in your room at around six?"

"I'll plan to be there," Sarah said.

With diplomatic precision Lesley Urquhart arrived exactly on time. Elspeth had arranged to be notified when Lesley came into the hotel. When the call came, Elspeth took the lift down to the lobby. She was expecting a young woman, as Lesley's voice sounded young, but no young woman was standing in the lobby looking expectant. The concierge approached Elspeth and nodded to an older woman, who was matronly and comfortably clothed. Elspeth went to where Lesley was sitting, introduced herself and led them into the tearoom off the lobby. Under Eric Kennington's guidance, the Victorian Federation architectural style of the hotel building was replicated with exactitude. When one entered the tearoom, one felt taken back a hundred and thirty years. Robert Cole had reserved a secluded table for Elspeth and Sarah, one surrounded by potted palms and ornamental screens. They ordered tea and an assortment of cakes.

As their waiter left, Lesley Urquhart let out a chuckle. "How many people in eighteen seventy-five here in the port of Sydney, do you suppose, actually enjoyed luxury like this?"

Elspeth enjoyed Lesley's forthrightness. "Do I detect anti-colonial feelings?"

"Good heavens, no. I chose a career in what used to be called the colonial service, have savored every moment of it and deplore our British arrogance. The Australians, of course, are unique. There're still a few here who would prefer to be British, but the American influence has taken hold, especially with the young. Things have changed radically since I first came here in the late sixties."

Slowly it dawned on Elspeth that Lesley was in Australia at the time of the murders of Malcolm's parents. Elspeth decided to address the issue directly. "Were you assigned here in nineteen sixty-nine?"

"In Melbourne, which was my original posting. I was terribly excited, as it was my first time away from Scotland—where I grew up and went to university—and from London, where I did my FCO training. Melbourne was, and still is, the most British city in Australia and was the headquarters of the Australian government for many years, although by sixty-nine most of the governmental functions had been transferred to Canberra. Other than the secretarial staff, women in the consular service were rare in those days. I was assigned as assistant to one of the older consuls and worked closely with him."

"Do you know anything first-hand about James and Anna Maria Buchanan's murder?"

"Actually I do, which may be one reason why Sir Andrew asked me to help you. The murder wasn't reported widely, except the morning after the bodies were discovered and then only in the Tasmanian press. The powers that be in the high commission and the Australian government quashed the story quickly."

Elspeth frowned. "Do you know why?"

Lesley was candid. "No, not really. When the story broke, the high commissioner called my supervisor and me to his office. It was the first and one of the only times in the two years I was in Melbourne I met him. He assigned the two of us to deal with the Buchanan family."

Elspeth bit her lip, trying to make sense of this information. "How did Sir Andrew know you were in Australia at the time of the murders?"

"He must have checked my record. I've served for thirty-seven years in the FCO and am on the point of retirement. I've been posted to many of the trouble spots in the world, particularly in the Middle East and Southeast Asia. With the recent troubles in Iraq, however, I requested my last posting be a quiet one. I'm truly grateful I was assigned to Canberra. The Australians are such wonderful people, my work is uncomplicated, and I feel as if I have made the circle of my career complete."

"Ms. Urquhart. . ."

"Lesley, please."

"Lesley. Will you help me?"

"That's why Sir Andrew asked me to see you."

Elspeth tried to find a way to be delicate. "I want you, without breaching security, to find out why the news releases about James and Anna Maria Buchanan were. . .suppressed."

"Why do you ask?"

"In nineteen sixty-nine, I was engaged to their son, Malcolm. Twelve weeks after his parents' deaths, a sniper shot him outside Girton College where I was a student. The

Cambridge police and Scotland Yard never found the assassin despite rigorous efforts. Because I've never been able to put the issue to rest, I asked an old friend, Richard Munro, the British high commissioner in Malta, to help me find out everything I can about the Buchanans' murders. I fear the truth will never be known, but even now I want to try to find it."

"I'll do anything within my power." The genuineness of Lesley's response raised Elspeth's hopes.

"I want to go to Tasmania. Do you know whom I might talk to there?" Elspeth asked.

"Give me a day or two. Do you know where you will be staying?"

"My office in London will set something up for me. May I ring you in the morning and let you know?"

"Please, any time. I'll be in Sydney for the next few days. This is the most interesting thing to cross my desk in the last few months. So much for wanting to be retired."

"I have one more request, which may be harder. Will you tell me what happened in nineteen sixty-nine in Tasmania?"

"If we can do so in private, there are some things I can share with you. I've no idea if what I know is important or not."

10

They had retired to Elspeth's room, which had a generous sitting area where they could talk without being overheard. Lesley Urquhart began her story, which she told simply.

"As I mentioned downstairs," Lesley said, "Australia was my first posting. From the very beginning of my career, I wanted to be in the consular section because I like helping people. That has remained true throughout my entire service whether I was assigned to Tehran, Damascus, Djakarta, Kuala Lumpur or Baghdad. My tours in Australia bracket many far more dangerous postings, but people's predicaments are still the same in most places, except in time of revolution or war, when they become heightened.

"In nineteen sixty-nine I was very idealistic. I'd earned my degree at the University of Edinburgh and went on to join the Foreign and Commonwealth Office on a career path. The authorities in London at that time were sure all of us women joined the FCO in order to find a husband in the 'colonies,' but most of us were sincere in our intent. Many did get married; some of us did not. Believe me there were temptations along the way, but the job was always more exciting than a humdrum marriage might have been. I have never regretted my decision to stay single.

"I think what drew me to requesting postings in Islamic countries, at first in Southeast Asia and later in the Middle East, were the murders of James and Anna Maria Buchanan. Piers, the man I worked for in the consular section in Melbourne, was raised in Australia and lived for a good part of his childhood in Tasmania, although he was English. Normally the Hobart consular office would have handled the murder, but Piers asked to be involved. I was still in training, and he took me under his wing.

"The Tasmanian police notified the high commission in Canberra about the Buchanans' deaths. Both were British citizens as attested by their passports, which were found in their home in a small community called Rushmore, where they were murdered. I'm sure there's no harm now to reveal that James Buchanan was probably in the clandestine services during the Second World War and operated behind Japanese enemy lines in Malaya. Beyond that, I know very little of his career, although I assume it went on beyond the end of the war.

"When the murders in Rushmore were reported to the high commission, a clampdown was ordered. I believe this was because the British government feared the deaths were related to James Buchanan's wartime activity and may have been a reprisal for acts he committed then. The Australians were particularly active in Malaya during the war. Australian intelligence and our British Secret Intelligence Service took charge of the investigation into the Buchanans' murders and used the Tasmanian police to do the legwork when necessary. The intelligence apparatus immediately sealed all the details of the deaths, and the press did not receive any information after the first reports. To the public the case simply ceased to exist.

"The high commissioner called on Piers to handle any enquiries by relatives, and consequently I became involved. The Buchanan's daughter, her name was Mary Anne, contacted the FCO in London, who contacted the high commissioner here. She was anxious to get possession of her parents' effects including their wills, keys, and other important documents and personal items. She was not content to have us send these things to her but arrived rather suddenly in Australia five days after her parents' deaths. I don't know who contacted her in London or how she learned of the murders.

"The high commissioner called Piers and me to Canberra and assigned us to accompany Mary Anne during her stay in Australia. The intelligence officers did not want to give Mary Anne the papers and other items she requested. They became quite belligerent in denying Mary Anne's demands. Cables flew between London and Canberra, copied to Melbourne. Finally, with pressure from people in London in high places, presumably known to Mary Anne and her family, the authorities gave her parents' wills and other personal items to Mary Anne. She stayed in Australia for another two days, disappearing every morning from her hotel and returning late into the afternoon. She telephoned me the last night she was in Melbourne and told me that she was angered by her treatment by the British and Australian intelligence services.

"At the time I was incensed by any mistreatment of women by the Authorities with an upper case A. On the spur of the moment, I invited Mary Anne to come to my flat for dinner. In those days I was less compassionate than I am now, so I asked Mary Anne out of a sense of outrage rather than concern.

"As I prepared dinner, she wanted to talk, particularly about her parents' murders. She told me the facts as she knew them.

"Mary Anne and her brother were born in Malaya, behind Japanese lines. After the Japanese surrendered, her parents did not return to Britain but went into the jungle. During the Malayan Emergency, they lived with the insurgents. When it came time for schooling for Mary Anne and her brother, their mother packed them off to England to stay with her cousin. Both children were sent to boarding school at an early age, and they never lived with their parents again. During this time Mary Anne and her brother, I gathered, formed the deep bond that many abandoned or orphaned siblings do. Both children went on to university but kept close ties. Mary Anne married and, when I met her, had a baby daughter whom she called Maudy. I think this was a nickname; Mary Anne never told me her daughter's real name.

"I served some cheap Australian wine with dinner. The wine loosened Mary Anne's tongue. Soon she became quite tipsy and a little self-pitying. She told me her brother and she had lived with the fear all of their lives that their parents were living in harm's way. Mary Anne's first memories were of living in the camp of the guerillas, mainly ethnic Chinese, who spoiled her and gave her tidbits of food from their meager bowls, as she described them. She said she saw the time as an example of what living in an anarchist society might be like. There were no rules, other than guns, and they all lived in great terror for their lives every day. After her mother took them out of the jungle, her brother and she saw little of their parents, because they moved frequently to all parts of the world.

""Later, when Mary Anne was at university, she tried to re-establish some sort of bond with her parents, particularly her mother. She visited them in various places including Peru if I remember correctly, but her mother, although loving, always skirted the issue of her father's and her wartime experience and reason for staying on in Malaya during the Emergency. Her mother said some things about their time in the jungle were too dangerous to disclose.

"The last time Mary Anne saw her parents alive was in the summer of nineteen sixty-eight. She flew to Hobart, hoping to see both her mother and father, but her father did not want to leave Rushmore. When Mary Anne traveled to Rushmore, she was shocked to find that her father had become an old man, bent, forgetful, and in ill health. Mary Anne stayed for only a short time and then excused herself, not able to bear what her father had become. As she left the cottage where her parents were living, her father drew her apart and said, rather cryptically, 'Don't let them get the key. It's a secret and it's worth a great deal of money and possibly someone's life.'

"In parting Mary Anne asked her mother about this. Anna Maria shied, like a deer in headlamps, and said, 'Mary Anne, those are the ravings of an old man. Don't heed them. They're of no importance. Leave it alone, my dear. It all happened a long time ago, and no one can find us here.' But Mary Anne said that her mother was terrified as she spoke.

"After dinner I helped Mary Anne into a taxi and instructed the driver to take her back to her hotel, as she was in no condition at this point to navigate her own way. I hoped she wouldn't recall any of our conversation, but, after she left, I wrote down as much of it as I could remember.

"Probably one of the questions I've not answered for you is how the Buchanans were murdered. I simply don't know. I believe they were shot, but all the details were instantly classified, and neither Piers nor I had access to them."

When Lesley had finished, Elspeth sat back and blew out her breath through her teeth. Lesley's narrative had been frank and open, and she seemed relieved at having shared it.

"I want to know how the Buchanans were killed," Elspeth said, "because there's no doubt in my mind that the murders of Malcolm and his parents are linked. Thank you, Lesley, for sharing so much. You have added to my determination to find out the truth."

Lesley addressed Elspeth plainly. "I'm not trained in detection, but two things stand out in my mind, particularly as I told you the story. The Tasmanian police were the first to investigate the crime in Rushmore. Would it be possible to find someone who was on the police force then who might be able to tell you more? A second idea might be to find out more about Mary Anne. Where is she now? Where is Maudy? Could either one shed more light on the items Mary Anne was given after such acrimonious exchanges with the security services."

Elspeth smiled at her guest. "Are you sure you don't want to become an investigator. Your instincts are right on the mark. I may have to go to Tasmania in the next few days for another reason, so a trip to the village of Rushmore seems to be looming on the horizon, but how, after all this time, could I find Mary Anne and Maudy?"

"Let me see if I can trace them. It may take a day or two. How can I stay in touch with you?"

"Lord Kennington insists I carry a satellite mobile phone at all times, even when I am 'off duty.' Without incurring any charges, you can email me, text message me, or simply leave a voice message on it. I'll chalk the charges off to expenses."

11

After talking to Lesley Urquhart, Elspeth thought how good it felt to be engaging her mind rather than her emotions. The lurid suggestions she heard in England from Jean Henderson and Victoria Symthe-Weldon Brewer rattled her sensibilities, but now Lesley had given her concrete evidence, something real to grasp, something to pursue other than skewed memories. Still, why did Malcolm never mention his parents' deaths? Had Mary Anne hidden them from her brother? If so, why?

Elspeth's thoughts raced on. A trip to Tasmania would not only help Lady Sarah but also allow Elspeth to make contact with the local police in hopes of finding someone who remembered the happenings in Rushmore in early nineteen sixty-nine. The search for Sarah's stepson might involve the police. If Elspeth judged correctly, when someone of title ventured into the smaller cities of the Commonwealth, people sat up and took notice, and therefore Elspeth decided she would accompany Sarah to Hobart.

Elspeth invited Sarah to join her for a glass of wine in the lounge bar, as they called it in Australia. Elspeth made her way down there, suddenly feeling tired and in need of a friend in whom to confide. Sarah appeared shortly afterwards.

"I will call Eric's office and have them make arrangements for us to stay in Hobart and hire a car for us. I'll ask for a driver as well. Eric should treat us properly," Elspeth said after they were seated and Elspeth told Sarah her plans.

Sarah laughed openly. "You're quite unexpected, Elspeth."

Elspeth was amused. "Am I? Why do you say so?"

"You take the privileges of the Kennington hotels as your due."

"I do," Elspeth said defiantly. "My job is highly stressful much of the time, and Eric has the resources to ease the way. He knows my worth."

Sarah chuckled. "I never have been able to stand up to him, although I've always been treated well when on assignment for him."

At the other end of the room a flowery woman was playing the piano and ended each stanza with an extended flourish. Elspeth suspected the selection of songs were chosen by London but wondered about the embellishments. They were out of character at a Kennington hotel.

Elspeth raised a glass of chilled wine to Sarah. "My motives are both pure and somewhat devious. For professional reasons, I want to make sure you find your stepson, as Eric commanded me to do, but for personal reasons I need to go to Tasmania. In the meantime, there's no reason why we shouldn't enjoy the evening, compliments of his lordship."

They dined together in Kennington style, and Elspeth billed it to her expense account at the Kennington Organisation. As dinner progressed, Elspeth knew she was forming a friend. She liked Sarah's straightforward manner. During the meal, however, Sarah trod on Elspeth's newly tender feelings toward Richard Munro.

"Do you have a man in your life, Elspeth? I see you don't wear a ring."

"I'm trying not to have one, but there is someone who would like to be."

"Is he respectable and not too young? Perhaps you shouldn't treat him so lightly and catch him while you can."

Elspeth felt herself flush and lamented the clearness of her Scottish skin. "Richard is, how shall I put it, far too respectable, and we have been friends since I was at school. He and I are not an item, and, no, I don't intend to marry him."

"Do you love him?"

"Sarah, if we are to be friends, which I hope we are becoming, I hope you'll not bring this topic up again."

"That bad?" said Sarah with a questioning look. "I hope I meet him someday."

The next morning Elspeth rang Pamela Crumm, who pressed Elspeth for what had transpired since they last talked. Elspeth related most of her initial conversation with Sarah Brixton but none of the information from Lesley Urquhart. Elspeth requested Pamela to make arrangements for them in Tasmania. Pamela promised to ring back within the hour.

Sarah and Elspeth took the evening Qantas flight to Hobart. Most of the way the skies were overcast with heavy summer clouds, but, as the plane approached its destination, the clouds opened to reveal a landscape of fields and hills, the fullness of the summer grasses and crops, and the deep green of the vineyards emphasized by the raked light of the sun.

Sarah turned to Elspeth and said, "It's rather like Shangri La, isn't it?"

Elspeth leaned over to the window and felt a pang of remorse that her reason for coming to Tasmania was a double murder and not the enjoyment of what seemed a place of magic and beauty.

Climbing down the steps from the plane, they scurried across the now darkening tarmac and into the boxy white terminal and were greeted by a rangy blond man wearing a nondescript uniform and bearing a hand-lettered sign saying "Kennington." He grinned at them with a smile filled with white teeth and showed them to a large saloon car at the curb outside.

As they swung into traffic, the daylight faded and a light shower began to fall. Traffic was only moderately heavy, and soon they crossed over a bridge that took them into the center of Hobart. They entered the hatch of streets of the central district, which was hillier than Elspeth had expected, and the driver pulled up at the doors of Harcourts Hotel, an historic edifice that Pamela said only escaped Lord Kennington's takeover plans because of its small size. The driver gave them his mobile number and, after relegating their cases to the hotel porter, slid into the twilight.

Sarah and Elspeth were delighted with the charming lobby, lounge, and elegant reception area of the hotel, all with beautifully proportioned moldings, high ceilings and cream-colored walls. The receptionist greeted them with typical Australian friendliness and assured them all had been made ready for them. He handed Elspeth a crisp white envelope with the hotel logo on the back.

"There were several messages so I put them together, particularly since one was from the police." The expression on the receptionist's face made it clear that Harcourts Hotel was not accustomed to having guests receive communications from the constabulary.

When she reached her suite, Elspeth opened the envelope, curious to see what the police might want and how they knew she was staying at the hotel. The commissioner of police had written a short note, explaining he had been contacted by the British high commissioner in Canberra and offered any support Elspeth might need. He gave his phone number and suggested Elspeth call in the morning after nine o'clock. At least, thought Elspeth, this was not Eric Kennington's doing but Lesley Urquhart's.

Elspeth was pleased to see the hotel had internet access in their guestrooms, and she would not have to deal with the microscopic keypad on her satellite phone. She took out her laptop and accessed her personal email account. Warmth filled her when she saw Richard had sent a message and both her children as well. She read her children's emails first, knowing they would be short, and then opened Richard's missive, which was briefer than usual.

> *My dearest Elspeth,*
>
> *Through channels I have followed you to Tasmania. Do you feel spied upon? No, please don't. I asked Andrew to keep in touch. He says Lesley Urquhart will not lead you astray as she is as solid as they come.*
>
> *Please keep me informed. My thoughts are always with you.*
>
> *Affectionately,*
> *Richard*

Dear Dickie, she thought with a smile, you are always the same.

A brief email from Pamela Crumm assumed Elspeth and Lady Sarah found their accommodations acceptable and indicated the Kennington Organisation wished for a speedy conclusion to the business at hand. It would be morning now in London, so Elspeth decided to call Pamela. Pamela picked up on her private line and said she had only a brief moment to talk because His High Lordship was in a rage in the next office about the non-delivery of flowers to the new Kennington Bermuda.

When Elspeth joined Sarah in the hotel restaurant, she could see Sarah was disturbed.

"Has something gone wrong?"

Sarah snapped her mobile closed. "I just had a frightful row with Clyde. I can't imagine why Marcus holds so much of his affection and concern. The boy is a lout and plays his father like a Stradivarius. Clyde is convinced Marcus is in great danger, a fear I assume most wealthy parents have, and thinks I ought to mobilize the entire Tasmanian police force to find him. For once, I'm on Marcus's side. What harm can come to him at a large rock concert other than a few recreational drugs and a slight loss of hearing. Marcus looks as disreputable as the rest of them. No one would suspect he has more money than God and can easily afford to buy a few joints and crash at a fancy local hotel with the other fans and a scantily clad girl."

As all travelers do, during dinner, they chatted leisurely about their trip. When they reached the end of the meal, Elspeth laid out a plan for the following morning.

She was open with Sarah. "I had a note from the commissioner of police in the envelope the receptionist gave me. It has to do with two murders that took place here in

Tasmania in nineteen sixty-nine. The victims were my fiancé's parents. Twelve weeks after their deaths, my fiancé was shot to death by a sniper in Cambridge, where we were students. No one was ever charged with either of the crimes. I've been a bit secretive about my reason for coming to Tasmania with you, but you undoubtedly will be brought into my personal affairs during the next few days, so I decided to share this with you. Actually, I could use your support, if you are willing to give it." Elspeth spoke as matter-of-factly as she could, but in the end her voice broke.

Sarah rested her chin on her hand and looked intently at Elspeth. "Is there a story here?"

"Yes, I think so, although it will probably be suppressed, but I also think there may be some danger."

"Why do you say that?"

"Because the authorities are still handling the murders secretly, even after all this time. Why would the commissioner of the Tasmania Police want to talk to me so soon after I arrived here, and why would the British high commissioner in Canberra ask him to? British high commissioners do not become involved in the investigation of a thirty-five year old mystery without reason, even for a friend."

"Elspeth, you are going to have to fill me in a bit more, particularly when you say there may be danger."

Elspeth sketched out the sequence of events that happened in nineteen sixty-nine. She was not certain why, but she carefully left out Mary Anne.

"One could hardly miss the link between the three murders, but why do you need to come back to this now?" Sarah asked.

"Because I've never forgotten what happened to Malcolm. It comes back to me again and again, in dreams, in memories, and at moments when least expected. Two people who are close to me suggested I take the time to find out why Malcolm was murdered, and, if I did find out why, my discovery might put his ghost to rest. That ghost is more haunting than I would like."

"Tell me about Malcolm."

"The memories are those of a besotted university student and will sound silly," Elspeth said.

"When I was at university, I definitely was silly about all of my men friends. Such silliness continued on for years afterwards, when I thought the passion of my body had nothing to do with my mind. It wasn't until I was married, when I was well into my forties, that I came to terms with it. Marriage destroys the myth of perfect bliss."

"I know. I was married for over twenty years. It's strange it's Malcolm and not my ex-husband who haunts me." Elspeth realized how easy it was to talk to Sarah. She rarely shared her feelings on an intimate level with other women, not even with Jean Henderson and especially not with Victoria Smythe-Welton.

Elspeth continued. "My time with Malcolm was perfect bliss. With him, everything became magical. When I was in Cambridge several weeks ago, I remembered so many of the conversations we had, all the laughter, and all the love. There was never anything else."

"Have you talked to anyone about Malcolm? People who knew him then?"

"I did talk to two other women who were at Girton with me."

"And what were their recollections of Malcolm?"

"Not as idyllic as mine. Neither one was complimentary toward him. Both saw him as a bit of a womanizer. That didn't strike true to me, however. We were together most of hours of the day. The only time we were really apart for any length of time was during the Christmas break. He wouldn't come to Scotland to meet my parents."

"Do you know why?"

"No, it still puzzles me. Perhaps it was that we'd only just met, but our mutual feelings were instant."

"Or so you thought?"

"No, Sarah, I was sure."

"Malcolm must have been a man of mystery, and a complex one at that, if he provoked such strong reactions in the other women."

As Sarah spoke, Elspeth felt a jab of pain. Had what Jean and Victoria said been the truth? Why hadn't Malcolm come to Scotland for Christmas? Were there parts of his life about which she knew nothing? What about his parents? Why hadn't he told her they were dead? And why was Richard so convinced she would uncover things that would hurt her?

Sarah smiled kindly at Elspeth. "I didn't mean to be so nosey."

"No, please, it's all right. My investigation seems to be stirring up more questions and emotions for me than answers, and talking about it with someone new helps."

Sarah sat quietly for a moment, thinking. Finally she asked, "What did you expect to find when you went to Cambridge recently?"

"More concrete information about Malcolm's death. I'd never before wanted to know the details, but so often the answers are in the details. It turned out the police were left baffled in the end."

"Are any of Malcolm's relatives still alive?"

"I'm trying to find out. I should know more in a day or two."

Suddenly Elspeth wanted to know where Mary Anne and Maudy were with such urgency that her stomach knotted. "I hope my meeting with the commissioner of police tomorrow will give me more information about Malcolm's parents' deaths."

They rose from the table, and Sarah suggested that they go into the lounge and order a brandy. Elspeth cried off, feeling a bit tipsy from the wine at dinner and needing to be alone. They made arrangements to meet for breakfast in the lobby at eight, and Elspeth took the lift to her rooms.

She lay in bed and thought about Mary Anne. Malcolm called her "the other MABB," since they both shared those initials—Mary Anne Buchanan Berkeley, pronounced the English way not like the Californian university. Malcolm spoke of her as a brother does of a sister, sometimes lovingly and some times with exasperation, but he never said much about her. Elspeth met her only once. She was tall and had fiery orange locks in contrast to Malcolm's sandy hair. Elspeth remembered Mary Anne's casual attitude toward her, as if Elspeth were of little importance. At the time Elspeth put this down to Mary Anne being distracted by her husband and child's concerns. In retrospect, however, Elspeth wondered if Malcolm had told Mary Anne anything about his relationship with Elspeth. Mary Anne was polite but distant, almost as if Elspeth had not been there. Later Elspeth broached this with Malcolm, whose only reply was, "That's MABB."

Lesley Urquhart said Mary Anne had come to Australia shortly after her parents' murders. Elspeth remembered Malcolm went to London about this time, mentioning casually that his "pater and mater" couldn't be pried from the Antipodes, but by that time they were dead. He must have known. Malcolm frequently spoke of the safe haven of Cambridge. A safe haven from what? Did he think he was in danger elsewhere? Why hadn't he explained his fear to her, particularly as soon afterwards he asked her to be his wife? With this hidden threat, what kind of marriage might they have had? Was the secrecy surrounding his parents so vital that he could not tell Elspeth, even if his life were in peril? Did he know about the secret his father mentioned to Mary Anne? Did Mary Anne ever learn what the secret was? Did she keep it from Malcolm?

Elspeth's mind went back to the dinner Lesley Urquhart gave Mary Anne. What had Mary Anne requested after her parents' deaths? Papers and other items Lesley had said. She also mentioned a key. Mary Anne's father had said, "Don't let them get the key." Later her mother dismissed this as the ramblings of an old man, but Mary Anne said her mother was frightened. Was the key one of the items given to Mary Anne Buchanan after her parents died? Did Malcolm know about it?

Most of all why had Malcolm never included Elspeth in his family affairs? What dark secret in their past could have been the motivation behind Malcolm and his parents' deaths? Was Mary Anne still alive? If so, how could Elspeth find her?

Elspeth wished she had taken Lady Sarah up on the brandy and then remembered she had a small packet of sleeping pills that she routinely took on trips when crossing time zones. She took twice the recommended dose and slept peacefully until her alarm went off at seven.

12

The phone rang in Elspeth's suite as she was finishing dressing. It was the police scheduling a meeting at ten with the commissioner because he was otherwise engaged until then. This gave Elspeth time to have a leisurely breakfast with Sarah, who shared with Elspeth she had slept badly as well.

"I hate rows with Clyde, especially about Marcus," Sarah said when she met Elspeth in the lobby. "I'm at such a disadvantage never having children of my own. I'm delighted you are here to offer me some diversion and perhaps advice. Did you know I was a photojournalist before I married Clyde? The more difficult the assignment, the better, although Mummy and Daddy were upset at my choice. Not the thing for a lady to do. I loved it. Perhaps marrying a widower with two brats for children was more of an assignment than I should have taken on. Since we have two hours to kill, let's go find a real Australian breakfast beyond the bounds of the cosseted environment here at the hotel and gorge ourselves on fat and salty food."

Elspeth liked Sarah increasingly and was delighted with her disjointed sentences and suggestion for breakfast. They asked at the reception desk about where to get breakfast outside of the hotel and were directed to Salamanca Square. The receptionist's tone, however, implied they might be more comfortable staying at Harcourts.

A Secret in Singapore

They stepped from the door of their hotel and met a wind filled with the morning heat of the Australian summer. It smothered them and made them hasten down Murray Street, past the mid-Victorian sandstone government buildings, and into the trendy shopping area of Salamanca Square. The stark stone buildings surrounding the square housed numerous boutiques and small restaurants. They found the one the receptionist had recommended and entered an interior of laminate topped tables, self-service coffee, and a made-to-order breakfasts featuring high fat, high carbohydrate breakfast foods normally eschewed by the diet conscious. They ordered eggs, rashers of thick cut bacon, toast made from artistically shaped loaves that came out of the oven only minutes before, and tomatoes filled with the richness of the early summer harvest.

They found a table in the corner, apart from the other diners, and sipped their hot coffee as they waited for their orders. They ate greedily, laughing at their sudden and uncharacteristic indulgence and were glad of the blast of conditioned air coming from a unit in the wall.

Elspeth sighed, put down her cup and looked at the others in the café. "I'm enjoying this much more than Harcourts, which is far too much like a Kennington hotel. I love watching the young people through the window. Speaking of young people, do you have a plan to find Marcus?"

"Last evening I asked the receptionist at Harcourts for assistance. The University of Tasmania campus near here in Sandy Bay is sponsoring the concert featuring the Tasmania Quolls and other punk rock groups tonight. I ordered us two tickets."

"And ear plugs, I hope."

"I always carry packets of them when I travel. Two pairs for each of us, if you like. I also emailed Clyde telling him I was on Marcus's trail. Am I being devious by not telling him I haven't the least idea whether Marcus will be at the concert or not?"

Elspeth chuckled. "Not in the least. I like your methods. Tell me more about the brat."

Sarah gritted her teeth. "I find him quite revolting, not as a person, but as a manipulator. Although he is physically attractive, particularly to girls his own age, his basic nature is perfidious. He will tell a lie when the truth will do. His brother keeps his distance from Clyde and me, but Marcus relishes needling us. Marcus was nine when his mother died. Clyde told me Marcus and his mother had a special bond and Marcus literally would not speak at all for weeks after she died. When he emerged from his silence, Marcus accused Clyde of killing Georgiana, Marcus's mother, that is. In despair, Clyde sent Marcus to numerous counselors. Marcus seemed to recover, at least until I came along. Clyde hid this from me until after we were married, because, as he said, he loved me and did not want me to run away because of what might be a difficult relationship with Marcus."

"Would you have?"

Sarah paused for a moment before replying. "I've often thought about that, but, no, I'm sure I would have considered myself capable of reaching out to Marcus. My optimism sometimes depresses me."

Elspeth laughed. "How do you deal with Marcus?"

"As little as possible. At first I tried but got nowhere. Finally I promised Clyde that I would continue to make efforts in Marcus's direction but expected nothing in return. So here I am in Tasmania, at the bottom of the world, trying to find Marcus. Life is cruel sometimes."

"If you truly consider yourself an optimist, Sarah, let's go to the concert tonight and consider we will have an interesting experience we would have missed had it not been for Marcus. Did you bring your cameras?"

"My digital ones only."

"Then let's go to the university and play at being journalists. That way we can talk to people, particularly if they think they'll have their pictures published in a newspaper or magazine in London."

"Who's being devious now?"

"Don't you still have connections in London who would publish a particularly good photograph of a rock concert at the bottom of the world as you call it? Besides, I'm expert at asking questions, an important skill in the security business. Deception is often the best way to get information one is looking for."

It was Sarah's turn to laugh. "I think we shall make a great team." Her enthusiasm infected them both.

After breakfast they walked to the police headquarters on Liverpool Street, where Commissioner Baines had left word for Elspeth to be shown to his office immediately upon her arrival. He stood as they entered and extended his hand. "Mrs. Duff and . . ." He obviously was not expecting two women.

Elspeth took his hand and introduced herself. "I'm Elspeth Duff, and this is Lady Sarah Brixton, a friend who has agreed to help me here in Tasmania."

Baines seemed confused. "Do you live here, Lady Sarah?"

Elspeth was relieved the commissioner had only a hint of an Australian accent because she sometimes had difficulty understanding broad ones and that he knew how to address Lady Sarah, which spoke of some breeding on his part. One never quite knew with the police if they knew proper forms of address. Elspeth thought of Richard, who would have amused by her unguarded snobbery.

"No," Sarah said without a flinch, "I'm following my stepson, who is a great fan of punk rock and has found Nirvana here."

"Ah, the concert tonight at the university," the commissioner said. "Quite a large contingent of my men will be out there, not because the students will do anything criminal, but because they are likely to become frenzied. Will you be going to the concert?"

"Yes, I hope to cover it for my London paper," Sarah said and sounded convincing.

"Are you a journalist?"

"Photojournalist."

"You will need a press pass. I can arrange to get you one. Remind me before you leave. Mrs. Duff, let's get back to you. Sir Andrew rang me from Canberra and asked that I give you any assistance you may require. He wasn't specific, but I've dealt with him before and know he wouldn't make the request if it weren't important."

Elspeth considered how to best approach the commissioner. She thought a version of the truth would be best. "I'm on leave from my job as one of the security advisors for the Kennington hotel chain, and when I was younger worked at Scotland Yard. I'm here to investigate a murder that took place in nineteen sixty-nine at the University of Cambridge in which I was personally involved. My investigation has opened up a Pandora's box and has led me here to investigate the murders of James and Anna Maria Buchanan in Rushmore that same year. They were the parents of Malcolm Buchanan, who was murdered in Cambridge.

I know any leads may be old, but I'm frustrated that I keep running into issues of secrecy around the Buchanans' deaths here in Tasmania. That's why I came here."

The commissioner, who was as tall and as long-faced as Richard, became stoic. "I see."

Sensing another roadblock, Elspeth went on. "Then you can't help me?"

The commissioner looked uncomfortable. "I can help only to some extent. The government sealed the files shortly after the murders were discovered. I can't open them without government authority, which I don't have. One of the policemen who went to the scene on the day of the murders, however, is still on the force. He was a young constable at the time, and he might at least be able to tell you what he saw when the bodies were discovered."

His words frustrated Elspeth. Had she come such a long way for so little?

As if reading her thoughts, the commissioner grinned, "I'm that constable, and recently Sir Andrew helped us enormously. A return favor is due. I don't think what I tell you will violate any official secrets act."

Elspeth felt hope return. "Anything you can tell me to help me find Malcolm's murderer would be appreciated, but I don't want to get you in trouble," she said. How far could she push him for information before he retreated into officialdom?

"I won't let you. In fact, I have to drive up to Rushmore, where the Buchanans were killed, on a personal matter tomorrow. Would you consider joining me? It shouldn't take more than six or seven hours there and back."

Elspeth had no idea if the commissioner was inventing a personal errand or not, but she accepted readily. "You're terribly kind, commissioner."

"Lady Sarah, will you join us?"

Sarah gave a large smile and nodded.

"Ladies, I'm afraid I must cut our interview short for the moment, but I'll pick you up at your hotel at nine in the morning. I think you'll find our trip along the River Derwent valley quite beautiful and Rushmore an enchanting village. Come prepared for the heat."

Sarah's mood changed subtly as the evening approached. The vivacity that accompanied their midday shopping excursion into the boutiques of Hobart changed to quietness as they entered Harcourts Hotel and took a seat in the lounge. They ordered tea and chatted desultorily. Finally Sarah seemed to come out of her torpor and spoke.

"What is it that Clyde wants? Am I to drag Marcus back to London? I wish Clyde had been more specific. If I ring him, I know there'll be another row, and I want to avoid that. What good does finding Marcus do? He won't change. Damn, I hate this."

Elspeth was surprised at the bitterness in Sarah's voice.

"I don't want to go to a punk rock concert, I don't want to find the brat, and I'm bloody well fed up with Clyde."

Her tirade was interrupted by the arrival of tea.

Sarah took control of herself. "I'm sorry. Sometimes it's so difficult to contain my despair. I married Clyde with such high hopes of fitting into his life, none of which has materialized."

"How long have you been married?"

"Five years, four too many."

"The dissatisfaction came that soon?"

"Yes, I suppose so. How long were you married?"

"Twenty plus years, perhaps five too many, but we had two children. At the end things were distant but never acrimonious."

"Marriage is hell." Lady Sarah took a long drink of tea and bit into a large piece of nut cake.

"Why don't we skip the concert?"

"Clyde would be furious."

"How will he know?"

"Marcus will tell him."

Elspeth reached over and conspiratorially put her hand on Sarah's. "We don't even know where Marcus is. What are the chances we could find him if we go to the concert? I suggest we have a quiet dinner here and share a bottle of good Tasmanian wine. You can lie like a trooper to Clyde, and I'll confirm we tried to find Marcus but were unsuccessful. When necessary, one can tell the truth but convey the wrong impression." Elspeth thought of Richard, who had frequently admonished her for this habit. "Are you up to it, Sarah?"

"I wish. Clyde would know I was lying."

"How?"

"By my voice."

"Let me see," Elspeth said biting her lip. "It's early in the morning in London now. Here, use my mobile. Let me get a piece of hotel stationery. I'll crumble it up by the receiver as you speak. My cousin Johnnie and I used to do that when I was a child and wanted to disguise our voices. Ring Clyde and then leave a message pleading bad reception. Tell him you'll try to ring again tomorrow evening, which gives us plenty of time to plan ahead. Surely there's a way we can find Marcus without having to endure the racket of punk rock bands. I expect we might enlist the help of the police commissioner tomorrow."

Sarah looked up at Elspeth and began laughing. "Elspeth, do you always think in this roundabout fashion?"

"Mmm. I suppose I do. I could always get around my parents, whom I love dearly but who sometimes had different ideas from mine. When I was in my teens, I had to keep pace with my cousin Johnnie and a friend of his from Oxford who visited in the summers. I try to curb these devious instincts, but when I hear about how you feel about Clyde and Marcus, I'm afraid my sense of mischief takes over."

"Was I so transparent?"

"A bit," Elspeth said with a twisted smile.

"I have a lifelong pattern, like yours. I never could keep anything from Mummy and Daddy, although I defied them often. I'm afraid I'm a bit the same way with Clyde. Here, give me the phone."

Elspeth lay back in her bath and contemplated the pleasures of a tub brimming with hot water and a large cake of delicately scented soap. Minutes before, she had returned to her room and found her email contained a charming note from Richard, wishing her success and hoping the high commissioner in Canberra was continuing to be helpful. Elspeth thought of Richard and chuckled, wondering how he might have reacted if he had seen Elspeth crinkling the paper as Sarah left a voice mail message for her husband. Elspeth remembered Richard once was in on a prank Elspeth and Johnnie were playing on Johnnie's sister Biddy. Richard disapproved at first, but he eventually joined in the fun. Richard later apologized to Biddy, although Johnnie and Elspeth did not. Elspeth wished she could go back to that time, before Malcolm, before her love for him consumed her, before the unending pain of his death. She tried to calm her thoughts and get back to that place of intellect that had sustained her since she had left London.

A brief email from Lesley Urquhart asked Elspeth to phone her in Canberra at nine-fifteen. It was now ten minutes past, which brought Elspeth out of her bath. She wrapped herself in a terrycloth robe, which she noted was less heavy than those provided in Kennington hotels but adequate for the temperate air in her room.

After Elspeth identified herself, Lesley said, "I hope I'm not keeping you from your sleep, but I've discovered a surprising fact about the Buchanans' murders that may be of help."

"No need to worry. I think I'm slowly becoming accustomed to this time zone, but it wouldn't matter anyway. Finding out about the Buchanans is more important. Tell me what you found."

"Incongruously, the woman killed in Rushmore may not have been Malcolm's real mother." Lesley said this without any emotion in her voice. "She may have been a decoy."

"Decoy? You mean a stand-in?"

"Possibly."

"Who identified the bodies?"

"Mary Anne Buchanan Berkeley, when she came to Australia five days after they were reported murdered."

"But surely she would know her own mother?"

"One would think she would."

"Lesley, you talked to her when she was in Melbourne. Do you mean she might have lied to you about her parents?"

"I don't think so, not to me anyway. All my life I've had an innate sense that recognizes when people aren't telling the truth, but I think she must have lied when she identified the bodies. I don't know why."

"Did she go to Tasmania to identify them?"

"Yes, Piers took her there. I didn't go because in those days women were considered too delicate to deal with the sordid physical evidence of a murder."

"Why then, after all this time, do you think the body of the woman who was murdered was not Anna Maria Buchanan?"

"Because I just went online and researched past issues of the newspapers around the time of the murders. I saw the photographs of the Buchanans in the files of *The Tasmanian*, the local Hobart newspaper. Anna Maria Buchanan was East Asian."

"East Asian? But that is impossible. Both Mary Anne and Malcolm were fair-skinned and definitely all Caucasian."

"I know, and Mary Anne was red-headed. She could not have been the child of an East Asian," Lesley said.

"Can you email me the website address where you found the photograph online?"

"I can, but it's a site where one needs a paid subscription. The high commission has one. Better yet, I will try to download the photograph and send it to you. Tell me if you agree with my assessment."

Elspeth shook her head in disbelief. Certainly Lesley Urquhart was mistaken. Elspeth tried to recall everything Malcolm had ever told her about his mother. He did not have pictures of his parents in his college rooms. Elspeth berated herself. Remember, remember, remember, but she could not. Who was mistaken? Lesley? Mary Anne? The newspaper? The last was the most likely. She would ask Police Commissioner Baines in the morning.

Elspeth did not have a peaceful night's sleep because she pondered these questions over and over again

13

Despite the gray and hot day, the trip from Hobart to Rushmore proved more scenic than Elspeth had expected. After picking up Elspeth and Sarah, Commissioner Leonard Baines turned his Jaguar out of Hobart and headed north on Route 1, following the ribbon of the River Derwent. Brief shafts of sunlight broke through the summer clouds and turned the river into a ribbon of white gold. Vineyards burgeoning with their fruit dotted the hills. The morning was steamy with the wetness from the rain the night before. Soon the hills gave way to flat grazing land, forming a basin between far-off jagged mountains. Occasional gum trees appeared along the roadside that pierced the flat land populated only by sheep just shorn of their wool.

The commissioner gave a running commentary on Tasmania's history, which delighted both Sarah and Elspeth. Sarah had her cameras with her and shamelessly asked that the commissioner to stop frequently. Their pace was sedate, the commissioner explaining that the consequences for speeding were severe all over Australia, even for policemen, particularly one on private business.

Elspeth consulted her map and sensed they would be approaching Rushmore soon. "Commissioner, I can't tell you how grateful I am you are doing this for me. The murder of the Buchanans is shrouded in so much mystery that any insight into what happened will be refreshing. Can you share with me anything that might help?"

"Let me tell you what I remember. I was new on the force, having done my training in London at Scotland Yard. I was born in Sydney, but my parents were originally from Tasmania. Their great grandparents came here as officials for the penal colony in Port Arthur and stayed on. I asked to be assigned here when I returned to Australia, and, because this was not a particularly sought after posting, my superiors were happy to comply with my request. I was assigned to a police station near Rushmore in Campbell Town. Most of the crimes in the region involved domestic violence and petty theft. When the call came in February about two murdered bodies in Rushmore, we assumed it was the result of a family fight. My superintendent requested I meet him in Rushmore, since at the time I was the only one on the force who had studied forensic pathology.

"We met at the town hall, where the amateur fisherman who had discovered the bodies was waiting for us. The bodies were hidden in the reeds about fifty yards from the bridge over the river on the road that went into the town. We'll cross it before we reach Rushmore."

"Did you actually see the bodies?"

"I did. They were lying just above the waterline. Both had been shot once in the temple and once in the chest. They were lying side by side, their faces turned to the sky, and their arms crossed over their chests. Mercifully someone had closed their eyelids."

Elspeth was jarred by Leonard Baines's words, which echoed those of Chief Inspector Llewellyn. Shot once in the head and once in the heart. Trying to regain her equilibrium, she said weakly, "Both of them side by side. That implies that they couldn't have killed one another."

"I agree. The only explanation was that they were shot elsewhere and carried down to the river. It was as if for some unknown reason they were laid peacefully to rest by the murderer. It might have been days before they were discovered. In the summer heat their bodies would have decomposed quickly and possibly even stripped by scavengers. The fishermen found them only hours after they were killed. Rigor mortis had set in, but there was no deterioration. Am I being too graphic?"

Part of Elspeth wanted to cry stop, but she knew she had to continue to seek out the detailed truth.

"No matter how hard to hear, I want to know everything. Thank you for being so sensitive to my feelings, but I didn't come here for niceties."

He turned from the wheel and nodded. "I thought not."

"May I ask you some more questions?"

"Of course."

"Where were the Buchanans living at the time?"

"In one of the cottages at the edge of town."

"Had they been there long?"

The commissioner turned his eyes briefly from the road and smiled at Elspeth. "I thought you would have a number of questions. Consequently I've asked the local historical society to arrange for you to talk to several of the people who were in Rushmore at the time. We should be there shortly."

"Commissioner, was Anna Maria Buchanan East Asian?"

"What gave you that idea? She had dark red hair and because of her skin coloring and name, I thought she might be Southern European. Why do you ask?"

"The photographs of her in the newspaper at the time showed an East Asian woman."

Leonard Baines looked perplexed. "How distinctly odd," he said quietly, almost to himself. "So it was her they were trying to protect, not him." Turning to Elspeth, he added, "Please forget I said that."

They turned off the main route and on to the straight stretch of a side road. It led to an ornate, low stone bridge and into a small village whose streets were lined with beech trees. Their dark green leaves rustled, causing shimmering in the sunlight. Despite the hot weather, a number of tourists wandered through the historic town square. The commissioner deposited Sarah and Elspeth in front of the small museum and historical society building, which sat up on a small rise to the south of the square.

Mrs. Angus Mack, a talkative woman filled with Tasmanian friendliness and enthusiasm, appeared to be in charge of the delegation of about ten women waiting for them. The commissioner joined them and introduced Elspeth and Lady Sarah, whose title elicited tittering sounds from Mrs. Mack and several of the other women.

An aging man, dressed in old-fashioned British tropical mufti, stood slightly to the side and gave a bemused look at the proceedings. Leonard Baines approached him. "Thanks for coming, Grant. Mrs. Duff was particularly anxious to speak to you. Mrs. Duff, this is Dr. Middleton. He served as the local coroner for the Campbell Town Police in nineteen sixty-nine."

Grant Middleton's handshake was firm. "I believe these ladies have arranged a luncheon for you, and so I'll leave you to their good care. When you are done here, come by my house. I live in the white cottage with all the bric-a-brac at the north end of the village square. You can't miss it." The doctor departed with Leonard Baines in tow and left Sarah and Elspeth to their exuberant hostesses.

Luncheon was set up in a function room off of the main gallery of the museum. The generous buffet included curried scallop pie, Cornish pasties, hot breads, a large green salad, some fresh mint peas and a large bowl of Doritos. An urn of strong coffee and a large pot of darkly brewed tea sat beside the food.

After they were seated at a long folding table covered with a checked polyester cloth, Mrs. Mack rose.

"We're delighted to be a part of your investigation," she announced. When Commissioner Baines rang me yesterday morning, I called together my troops." She waved her hand in a grand gesture at the other women. "As you can see from our sea of gray hair, many of us remember nineteen sixty-nine vividly." A collective suppressed chuckle went around the table.

"And we also remember that once the bodies were discovered, everything became very hush-hush. Security forces came in from Hobart and asked us numerous questions. They instructed us to keep what we knew about the murders to ourselves. Yet after all this time, I think all of us would finally like to say our bit. There can be no harm now, can there?"

Elspeth thought it was best to leave that question rhetorical.

Mrs. Mack continued with bravado. "I remember the morning well. Carl Weston came running to my parents' cottage and shouted that the police were all over the place, down by the river and at the Paisley cottage. The Buchanans had moved into the cottage about four or five months before,

I think, and they kept to themselves most of the time. Their maid shopped at the village shop, and once a week they hired a car to go into Launceston to get supplies not readily available here in Rushmore. As the months went on, Mr. Buchanan seemed to age quite rapidly. When they first arrived, he did some fishing and took walks with his wife every evening, but soon he didn't walk about at all. The village joke was that his wife was poisoning him, although we all felt badly about that after their bodies were discovered."

Another woman, who was younger than the rest, broke in. "She, Mrs. Buchanan, always treated us children with sweets from the shop. She would come out on the landing of the front door of the shop and toss them to us one by one. The others thought it great sport. I was eleven at the time and felt quite above catching sweets, so she would always save several for me and hand them to me in a most dignified manner, saying 'Patricia, I've saved these specially for you because I know they're the kind you particularly like.' I thought she was wonderful."

An older woman added her memories. "We always thought the Buchanans rather mysterious. He obviously was British—Scottish not English—because he had a bit of a burr, only a slight one. I lived in England during the war, working in communications, and was trained to distinguish people's accents. She spoke English as if she had been raised in England, but there was just a shade of the foreign in her words. Because of her given names we all supposed that she might be Italian or Spanish. But the thing that was strangest was that they did not speak English to each other or to their maid."

Elspeth suddenly could see her large handwriting on the grid paper. *My father was multi-lingual* she had written of

Malcolm's father. She tried to keep her voice neutral. "Do you know what language they were speaking?"

A woman seated near Elspeth said, "I thought it was Chinese, but my husband said it wasn't. He thought it might be Thai or Malay."

"Did the Buchanans speak this to each other most the time?"

"Yes, unless they saw one of us was around," the woman said.

Elspeth tucked this piece of information away and asked, "Can you describe the maid?"

Another member of the group said, "She was quite young, a teenager. I suspected she was Chinese, but in the summer she wore loose fitting sarongs like the kind they wear in Indonesia. My husband and I visited Bali once, and her clothing reminded me of the women we saw there, but her skin was not dark the way many Indonesian women's are. In fact, she looked rather like a young Madam Chiang Kai-shek. That's why I thought she was Chinese."

Elspeth tried to remember what Madame Chiang Kai-shek looked like, but no image came to mind.

Mrs. Mack could not remain silent for long. "Good heavens, I forgot all about the maid. She was called Ah-Sing or Ah-Ting, I think. When they called her by name, I always thought of music."

"What happened to the maid?" Elspeth ventured.

The women all looked at one another. No one had an answer. Finally one of the older women said, "She disappeared."

Elspeth looked at her with raised eyebrows. "Disappeared? When?"

The woman frowned as if trying to remember. "She wasn't here when the police arrived. The cottage was empty because I remember they had to break the door down to get in. We lived next door, and the arrival of the police brought us out of the house. My husband, God rest his soul, was often away, but we never locked our doors or had any fears before the murders. We came out and watched the police. At the time we had no idea why they were breaking into the Paisley cottage. Obviously the Buchanans did lock their doors. The cottage was let every summer, and the Buchanans were one of the many tenants over the years. We all said it was fortunate the murders did not take place in the cottage, because, of course, word would have gone around. The Paisleys would have a hard time letting it after that."

Sarah remained quiet during the women's reminiscences, but Elspeth sensed her growing interest. Finally Sarah could no longer contain herself. "Mrs. . . ." She paused waiting for a name.

"Mary Carter, Mrs. William Carter."

"Mrs. Carter, did the police talk to you after they broke in?"

"A young constable did come over to us and asked us if we had seen anything unusual in the last day or so. I remember this particularly because the night before we had heard a bit of a commotion coming from the Paisley cottage. We thought it was the Buchanans, because the argument was in the language they usually spoke. Since we believed we shouldn't be nosey-parkers, we closed our doors and windows on that side, although it was still hot outside even in the early evening."

Elspeth resumed her questions. "Did anyone else notice anything unusual around the time of the murders?"

Another older woman raised her hand shyly. "My fiancé and I were out walking the night before the murders. Rushmore, even then, attracted tourists during the day because of our beautiful bridge and our colorful history, but at night it usually is quiet. Ron and I were not taking particular notice where we were walking; we had other things on our minds. Suddenly a large car came rushing up the street and veered around us. We probably wouldn't have remembered it except for the murders the next day."

This news electrified Elspeth. "Did you see where the car was going?" she asked.

"To the end of the street, near the Paisley cottage. When it got there, it turned out its headlamps. We didn't pay particular attention because . . ." The faces of the other women all smiled at this unfinished statement, and the woman's face reddened.

"Any other recollections?" Elspeth asked. "Does anyone remember the weather?"

Mary Carter chimed back in. "It was hot, as I said, but later on there were thunderstorms. They cooled things down a bit. Always such a relief in late summer."

Elspeth was still trying to adjust her thinking about seasons in the southern hemisphere because she had lived north of the equator all of her life. February in Australia, of course, was late summer. She could imagine the summer evenings in Rushmore, filled with the aromas of the fields and flowers, perhaps the sounds of the flocks of sheep nearby, and the rush of the river, its noise traveling in the heavy night air. She wondered what the Buchanans heard that night. Would they have felt the peacefulness of late summer or were they filled with fear, not only from the impending thunderstorm but also from the unexpected appearance of an assassin whose arrival they might have anticipated for a long time?

Did the large car carry the murderer? Did it actually turn into the Paisley cottage? Did the thunder disguise the shots that killed the Buchanans? She must ask Dr. Middleton if he knew.

"Does anyone remember what time the storms came?"

Mary Carter again spoke up. "It was probably about nine o'clock and the sky was fading. I remember because, when I closed the windows, I said to Bill that it wouldn't be long before it would be cooler. I never like it when the days grow shorter, and I was aware that the summer nights were not as long as they had been in January."

"Did anyone else see the car?"

No one responded.

Sarah broke in. "Has Rushmore changed a great deal since nineteen sixty-nine?"

All agreed that it had changed little.

Elspeth wanted to return to the discovery of the bodies, but she sensed none of Mrs. Mack's "troops" participated in the actual event. She tried anyway.

"Were any of you involved the next morning?"

Collectively they shook their heads. Mrs. Mack, however, volunteered that her brother had been, but he was living in Sydney now.

"I shall be returning to Sydney shortly," Elspeth said. "Do you think I could entice him to a drink at the Kennington Sydney?" Elspeth said.

"I'll ring him and tell him of your interest. Where can I get in touch with you?" Her tone indicated the invitation would be accepted eagerly. Elspeth wondered if Mrs. Mack's brother had as much exuberance as she had.

"We'll be at Harcourts Hotel in Hobart this evening. You can reach me there or leave a message at the Kennington Sydney."

After finishing their meal, Elspeth asked the way to the women's room and, with a turning of the eyes, silently hinted to Sarah that they should excuse themselves simultaneously. Luckily the facility at the museum allowed for two women at the same time.

"Sarah, can you occupy 'the troops' for an hour or so? I don't want them to disperse before I talk to Dr. Middleton. I think the ladies may have more useful information if I only knew what to ask."

Sarah's eyes sparkled. "Of course, Elspeth. You know how much people love to be photographed, particularly by a press journalist. Leave them to me. They'll be convinced they will be featured on the front page of *The Sydney Morning Post* or even *The Daily Telegraph* in London by the time I get through with them."

"If you can, take as many pictures as possible. Also ask them if they have any photographs from the time of the murders. No, do that first. This is the historical society after all. Can you take digital images of what they show you and email them to me later?"

"Absolutely."

"Then see if they have a copy of the article in *The Tasmanian* the day after the murders. And anything else at all."

"Elspeth, you are returning me to my comfort zone. For the last hour I forgot totally about Marcus. What a blessing."

The troops were doing the dishes when Elspeth emerged from the women's room, slightly ahead of Sarah.

"Mrs. Mack, I want to thank you for all of your hospitality and help. I just spoke with Lady Sarah, and she would like to do a story on all of you. I'll leave you in her good hands. Can you direct me to Dr. Middleton's cottage?"

14

Elspeth followed Mrs. Mack's directions easily because the village of Rushmore was basically a crossroads. She found Dr. Middleton's cottage on the main square near the town hall and the church. Grant Middleton was tending his small garden and deadheading spent flowers from his rose bushes. His old yellow Labrador retriever sensed a guest and, with a gyrating tail, welcomed Elspeth to the garden.

"Don't mind Clemmie, yes, she's named after Lady Churchill. She considers it her lifelong duty to make all guests welcome. Not a very good watchdog, I'm afraid. Come into my surgery where we can talk privately, although Clemmie will insist on being there as well. Her presence is a great help to most of my patients, unless of course they're allergic to dogs or dislike them. Then she's banished and takes it all with ill grace."

They settled into his small consulting room, and Clemmie rested her head on Elspeth's knee.

"Lie down, Clemmie!"

Clemmie looked up and wagged the tip of her tail in disobedience.

"Please don't make her behave on my account. We had Labs at home in Scotland when I was a child. She must know."

Grant Middleton relented, and Clemmie lay down at Elspeth's feet.

A Secret in Singapore

The doctor broached the topic of the murders.

"Leonard Baines rang me yesterday and asked me to tell you as much as I could remember about the Buchanans and their murders. I had recently finished my medical training in London when it happened. My wife, who was born in Tasmania, convinced me this was the most wonderful place in the world. She proved right. I trained in general medicine and savored living in an old-fashioned village where I could be an important part of everyday life. When not tending to my patients, I would have time for a bit of gardening and farming. I'd grown up in London and loathed urban life. Through the Tasmanian Medical Association, I found an advertisement from a Dr. Archibald from Campbell Town who was looking for a young doctor to take his place as the general practitioner for this entire region. By the time of the murders, Dr. Archibald had retired, and I was struggling to take the place of a man who had held the trust of three generations of Tasmanians. I was slowly melting their already warm hearts and diligently attended to measles, flu, rheumatism, and childbirth. We bought this cottage and settled down to a comfortable and quiet life. When then-Constable Baines called me about the murders on that February morning, I was totally unprepared. I, of course, had courses in pathology at my medical college, but I never particularly liked the subject and had devoted little attention to it. Murder rarely occurs here in the countryside and, if it does, it usually involves members of a family."

"Yes, so Commissioner Baines said."

Dr. Middleton continued. "We knew the Buchanans, who lived down the street, but only slightly. They mainly kept to themselves. After several months here he apparently was ailing, but they never called me or sought my advice. Mr. Buchanan was attended by his wife, who was a robust woman, and by their Chinese servant. They arrived here at the end of October, and by Christmas time he seldom appeared outside of their cottage garden. I had seen drug addicted people during my training, and the similarity was marked. He often dozed in his chair, and his skin was yellowed, which made me suspect he was taking opium. Tricia, my wife, was particularly fascinated with their servant. Although Tricia was born in Tasmania, her parents bought a rubber plantation in Malaya before the war. Tricia and her mother were captured and spent four years in a Japanese camp. Her father went into the jungle and joined the resistance in the fight against the Japanese. Tricia was only a small child, but the effects of her captivity were profound. At the Japanese surrender, her family returned to their plantation but, until they died, both her father and mother held a profound hatred of the Japanese and a deep respect for the resistance forces, albeit their being communists, who had defied the Japanese for the entire period of the war. Tricia's family's plantation was not disturbed during the 'Emergency,' the communist rebellion in Malaya after the war, because he kept ties with his wartime comrades. He was criticized for this, but still he defended the communists' bravery and heroism. Tricia said her father re-fought the guerrilla warfare in his mind for the rest of his life. She remembered after the war people slipped in and out of the compound of their plantation during the night. Tricia was attracted to the Buchanans' servant because she recognized the sort of person who her parents sheltered during the Emergency. Tricia suspected the servant was a half-caste, not a politically correct term these days, the product of an Asian mother and a European father, a common happening in Malaya during colonial times."

Malaya again, thought Elspeth.

"One day Tricia found the servant alone in the garden of the Paisley cottage. She approached her and spoke in Malay. The woman reacted as if shot by a bullet and screamed, in Malay, for Tricia to leave on fear of death. Quite an overreaction. After that the woman avoided Tricia."

"How odd," Elspeth said, but a pattern was forming in her mind.

"Tricia decided to approach Mrs. Buchanan, who normally kept to herself. Tricia felt being straightforward had merits, so she asked Mrs. Buchanan if her servant was Malay or Chinese.

"'Would you know the difference?' Mrs. Buchanan asked.

"'Yes,' Tricia replied. 'I grew up in Malaya. My father had a rubber plantation there until his death ten years ago. He had connections with the communists because he fought behind the enemy lines with them during the war.'

"Mrs. Buchanan seemed startled and asked Tricia's father's name. When Tricia told her, Mrs. Buchanan thought for a moment and simply said, 'I didn't know him.' She sounded relieved Tricia told me later."

Dr. Middleton had more to add. "After that, both Mrs. Buchanan and the servant keep completely to themselves. By early February, Mr. Buchanan no longer came out in the garden. We hoped it was because of the hot weather. Many elderly people prefer the coolness of their homes to the heat of the summer days.

"The night before the Buchanans' bodies were found, Tricia and I were out strolling, when a large car came racing along the road. It pulled in by the Paisley cottage. We could hear the doors of the car slam, but later we agreed that we didn't hear anyone knock at the door of the cottage. When we got home, the car was still there. A bit later we had a thunderstorm, which cooled things down a bit. Afterwards

I wondered if this might have been the time the shots that killed the Buchanans were fired."

This confirmed what Elspeth suspected.

"Police Constable Baines, now the commissioner, rang me the next morning. He had received a phone call from Andy Coates, one of the young men in the village who was fishing near the bridge and came across the bodies. They were lying in the reeds about fifty meters from the bridge. Andy had the sense to leave the bodies as he found them, run home and ring the police directly. Constable Baines arrived from Campbell Town in about twenty minutes, and, because he had rung me first, I met him at the bridge. The bodies were not visible, tucked as they were in the vegetation. Andy led us to them. I did a cursory examination. Both bodies had been shot in the head and the chest, and both were quite cold. Rigor mortis had set in. I assumed they had been dead for about twelve hours. This set the murders at the time of the thunderstorm the night before.

"Leonard, that is the constable, and I looked for any sign of footprints but found none. There were broken reeds, but the rain must have washed away any other telltale signs of how the bodies came to be there.

"By the time we finished our examination, the police cars from Hobart had arrived. With them were non-uniformed men who directed us away from the scene and ordered, not asked, us to discuss what we had seen with no one. Mrs. Duff, you are the first person, other than Tricia, to whom I have told this after how many years, thirty-five? It feels good to share this with someone else now."

"You're very helpful," Elspeth said. "And afterwards?"

"*The Tasmanian* had a story about the murders the next day. I didn't see it, but I understand Mrs. Mack has a copy up at the historical society. I still don't know how the press got the story because the men from Hobart virtually locked down everything down. The story got around the village, of course, but soon people's attention was distracted by other news."

Dr. Middleton's words made the events come to life in great detail. Elspeth wondered if Mary Anne learned the same thing when she came to Tasmania after the deaths of her parents but doubted she had because of the silence the authorities imposed on everyone by the police. Elspeth wanted to find Mary Anne because she was the only person who might be able to shed light on the maid and what happened to her. Elspeth sensed the maid might not have been not killed the night of the Buchanans' murders but had no proof.

After finishing his narration, Dr. Middleton turned his attention back to the present. "Mrs. Duff, would you like to walk down by the river and see where it happened?"

"Very much. I would like Lady Sarah to come with us and take some photographs. I know any hint of the murders has long since been eradicated, but, as I proceed in my investigation, visual reminders may be helpful."

He nodded and rose from his chair. Clemmie jumped up, eager for a walk. "Let's go back up to the historical society and see how Lady Sarah is getting on," the doctor suggested. "We might also ask to see the newspaper article."

When they arrived, "the troops" were still intact and under Lady Sarah's command. Sarah covertly winked at Elspeth and looked innocently at the doctor. He obviously saw the exchange between the two women and grinned.

"Yes, indeed, we do have the article about the murder," Mrs. Mack assured them. "Lady Sarah already asked to see it, but I thought we would wait for you. It would be in the nineteen sixty-nine yearbook."

The back storage room proved to be the repository of the annals of Rushmore, and soon Mary Carter produced a dusty volume labeled nineteen sixty-nine in black India ink. Apparently no one had opened it for a long time. The archivist had been meticulous, and the entries under February contained a small clipping. It looked like a stop press. *Yesterday in Rushmore two bodies were found dead along the riverside. Local police have identified them as Mr. and Mrs. J.A.M. Buchanan of Rushmore and are investigating the cause of their deaths.* Unlike the typical stop press, a photograph of two people above the article was captioned *Mr. and Mrs. James Buchanan, in front of the school where they taught in Western Australia for thirty years.*

Elspeth asked Mrs. Mack for a magnifying glass, as the photograph was indistinct. Focusing in on the faces Elspeth concurred with Lesley Urquhart's assessment that the woman did look East Asian. Elspeth calculated that thirty years before nineteen sixty-nine was nineteen thirty-nine, the year the Buchanans reportedly began teaching in the Outback. The article was obviously wrong because the Buchanans were in Southeast Asia at that time. Why the deception?

Leaving the suffocating presence of Mrs. Mack and her troops, Sarah, Dr. Middleton and Elspeth made their way to the riverbank beyond the bridge. Reeds still grew there and revealed nothing of forensic interest. Sarah photographed the spot anyway.

Elspeth chose to ride in the rear of Commissioner Leonard Baines's car as they returned to Hobart. Sarah kept up an animated conversation with him for most of the way. Elspeth sat silently, preoccupied with what she had learned that day.

Malcolm's parents were shot in the head and the heart and laid out with arms crossed after death.

James Buchanan slowly deteriorated as if he were being drugged with opium. Was this true?

A large car had pulled up to the Buchanans' cottage before a thunderstorm that might have muffled the shots.

The Chinese or Malayan maid had disappeared. Did the people who came in the car abduct her? What was her name other than Ah-Sing or Ah-Ting? Was there a way to find out? And why was the maid so frightened when Tricia Middleton approached her?

Why was there a photograph in the Tasmanian newspaper that by implication falsified the information on James and Anna Maria Buchanan? A casual reader would assume that the James Buchanan and his wife in the photograph were the same people found along the riverbank. Obviously deception was the intent. There may have been a James Buchanan and his East Asian wife who had devoted thirty years of effort to teaching in Western Australia, but they were not the James and Anna Maria Buchanan who were murdered.

Why had non-uniformed policemen taken over the investigation?

Finally, why had Commissioner Baines mumbled, "So it was her they were trying to protect, not him."

Elspeth's head ached. The day had raised more questions than it had answered.

15

Although the accommodations at Harcourts Hotel were comfortable, Elspeth relished returning to the Kennington Sydney. Its surroundings offered the security of the familiar. Once in her room, she rang Pamela Crumm to tell her Lady Sarah's search for Marcus in Tasmania had proved fruitless and her own investigation was still unresolved. Pamela tutted. She said she would tell Lord Kennington about Sarah but not about Rushmore.

Elspeth took off her travelling clothes, wrapped herself in a luxious terrycloth robe and shamelessly used her Kennington Organisation satellite phone to ring Richard Munro. She wanted to talk to Richard, to hear his calm baritone voice, and to have him say something to settle her. His PA answered and told Elspeth he had been called to Brussels but would be returning to Malta on a flight at six that evening, early in the next morning in Sydney.

Next Elspeth rang Lesley Urquhart. "Lesley, will you be in Sydney anytime in the next few days. I'm scheduled to go back to London in two days' time but want to talk to you in person before I leave."

"I'll be there tomorrow morning. Can we meet for lunch?"

"Yes, I'll order lunch in my room so we can talk privately. Is one o'clock a good time?"

"Can we make it half past one?"

"I'll be waiting."

Elspeth took up the notes she made after the visit to Rushmore and realized she had promised Mrs. Mack to call her brother, who was present when the police examined the bodies. Elspeth made it a habit to write any contact information in her notes, and, reading through them, she found Dave Mack's phone number. She rang it and got a recording in a broad Australian accent. "This is Dive Mack. Leave your message unless it isn't important." Elspeth smiled and left a message for "Dive" to call her at the hotel before nine that evening or after eight in the morning.

She missed Sarah Brixton, who had stayed in Tasmania and whose company there filled the empty moments during which Elspeth might otherwise have resorted to self-pity. Elspeth decided to order dinner in her room and spend the evening trying to make sense of all she had learned in Rushmore.

Where should she start? She first thought about the time of Malcolm's death, but the events leading up to it really began with his birth. Therefore she decided to begin in nineteen forty-five, but she did not know the exact date Malcolm was born. She tried to remember if she had ever known. How odd she could not. Perhaps a better date would be when the Japanese took over Malaya. She logged on to a website that gave the timeline for the war in the Pacific. The dates given for the invasion were from December nineteen forty until January nineteen forty-two, so she began there.

She titled her document: KNOWN FACTS

1940-1941	*Japanese occupy Malaya*
January 1942	*Japanese take control of Singapore.*

1943	*Buchanans in jungle? Mary Anne born.*
August 1945	*Malcolm born in jungle before end of war?*
1952	*James Buchanan registers births in Singapore.*
1953	*Anna Marie brings children out of jungle.*
December 1968	*I meet Malcolm outside King's College Chapel*
Christmas 1968	*Malcolm is with MABB in London.*
January-May 1969	*Malcolm and I constantly together.*
23 Feb 1969	*Malcolm's parents murdered in Tasmania.*
18 May 1969	*Malcolm murdered in Cambridge.*
19 May 1969 - ?	*Insp Llewellyn investigates, Richard helps.*

A sudden pang of grief hit her; she pushed it away. Leave that until you have finished your investigation, her mind told her.

Elspeth returned to her time line and decided it did nothing for her, so she opened a blank document on her computer, saved it in the file containing her other notes on Malcolm's murder and titled it ONGOING QUESTIONS.

> *Where is Mary Anne today?*
> > *Can she shed more light on her parents' murders?*
> > *Where is Maudy and what is her real name?*

Why is the information on the Buchanans' murders still classified?

What happened to the Malayan/Chinese/mixed-race maid?

What were the leads Llewellyn said had dried up?

Would Richard's journal at the time reveal anything? He thought not, but why?

Hadn't he kept it in the event that I might have wanted to know?

Why didn't Malcolm tell me about his parents' deaths?

What was Malcolm's real relationship with Victoria?

Did Victoria's brother really know Mary Anne's husband? Where were both men now?

How could she find anyone who was in the jungles of Malaya during WW2?

(Sarah Brixton and her husband know all sorts of people. Could they help?)

Why was Mary Anne so insistent about getting her parents' effects?

What did they contain that was so important?

Did Malcolm know about this?

Could Lesley Urquhart provide any more information that might be helpful, particularly in regard to the Buchanan's stay in Rushmore?

Had the security forces found out who was in the car that came to Rushmore on the night of the murder?

More at hand, could Mrs. Mack's brother offer any information I do not already know?

The last question was the easiest, so she picked up the phone and called Dave Mack again. This time he was in. She set up an appointment with him for the next evening and then looked back over her list of questions. Unless Lesley Urquhart could provide some answers the next day, Elspeth considered her best course of action was to return to London and possibly to Cambridge.

Lesley Urquhart came up to Elspeth's room at one thirty precisely. Elspeth had ordered a simple lunch of freshly-made linguini tossed with broccoli spears, pine nuts and parmesan cheese, baby greens with slices of strawberries and fennel with a vinaigrette dressing, warm whole grain rolls, delicate lemon squares, iced sparkling water, and a bottle of New Zealand sauvignon blanc. Even simple meals like this one at Kennington hotels were served with a flourish and floral decoration.

Lesley accepted a chilled glass of wine and remarked on its quality. Her taste in wine seemed to have developed since serving cheap Australia wine to Mary Anne.

"I've accepted your invitation a bit under false pretenses," Lesley said. "I've found some information for you that might be useful, but my difficulty in uncovering anything more at all speaks more volumes than the information I was able to get."

"Lesley, I appreciate all the effort you've made. At this point anything new may be useful. The trail's gone cold."

Lesley explained. "In nineteen sixty-nine we didn't have a computer database, so I went into the archives in a dusty room in the high commission in Canberra to see if I could find anything. I've done this before because I'm writing a report on British immigration to Australia, so no one paid attention to me. I started in nineteen sixty-nine and went forward. In nineteen seventy I found a Mrs. Mary Anne Buchanan who moved to Sydney, where she lived at various addresses until nineteen eighty-two. The photograph in the file was missing, which isn't unusual as they were taped on in those days. After many years the tape deteriorates, so I couldn't determine if this Mary Anne was indeed Malcolm's sister. The interesting thing about the file was neither a next of kin nor any contact in the UK was listed. Next I went to the computer database, which was started in nineteen eighty-six. Mary Anne Buchanan's name, listing her birth date of nineteen forty-three and her birthplace as Malaya, was there, but there was no further information. The file read 'current whereabouts unknown.' The file had last been updated in two thousand and one. After that, I searched for other British immigrants to Australia with the names of Berkeley or Buchanan. There were several, as neither surname is unusual, but none with the same age or birthplace. I don't like dead ends, and so I searched further." She shook her head. "There was nothing."

Elspeth felt puzzled and said so. "Hmm. It appears that in two thousand and one Mary Anne still was in Australia."

"That was my thought as well. I remembered Mary Anne mentioned a daughter named Maudy, who was a year old in nineteen sixty-nine. That would put her birth date in nineteen sixty-seven or sixty-eight, probably in London. I searched that. No Maud Berkeley or Maud Buchanan came up. Maud, of course, is a common nickname for Mathilda, and so I put that name into the computer. No matches. Another failure."

"You're persistent."

"Absolutely. Now I really wanted to know more about Mary Anne, so I tried another tack. I went into the consular records of two thousand and one and the years following and looked under deaths of British citizens. Bingo!"

Elspeth laughed. "Lesley, you have the true Scottish determination."

"Try to," said the consul, her eyes sparkling. "Nothing in two and thousand and one or two thousand and two, but in January of two thousand and three, the consulate in Hobart recorded the death an M.A. Berkeley in Launceston in late December and burial in, of all places, the village of Rushmore."

Elspeth jumped at the news. "Where were the Buchanan parents buried?"

"Classified, but my bet is if you went to Rushmore you will find something recorded in the church records."

"I'm returning to London tomorrow afternoon, but I have a friend in Tasmania who is chasing her errant stepson. I know she will help. Lesley, you deserve a medal for this."

"Highly unlikely. A reprimand for digging where I shouldn't have is more likely."

"Why would Mary Anne be in Tasmania at the time of her death?"

"I have no idea. Perhaps if you find Maudy, she'll know."

Elspeth frowned. "If Mary Anne really is dead, there may be others who know something about this. Did you find out anything more about M.A. Berkeley's death?"

"Very little. She died at a local hospital, and the file indicated that her will specified she wished to be buried in Rushmore."

"Where would the will be filed?"

"I'm not sure. Probably in Launceston."

"Can you find out for me?"

"I can try. It's a bit out of my normal line of work, but Sir Andrew said. . ." Lesley let the sentence die. She sounded reluctant.

Elspeth felt she had overstepped her bounds and said so.

"No worry," Lesley said. "One thing we learn in the diplomatic service is to say no politely."

Before Lesley Urquhart took her departure, she assured Elspeth that, within her limited capacity, she was still willing to help. Elspeth gave profuse thanks.

It was now approaching three o'clock. Elspeth rang Harcourts Hotel and found Sarah in her room.

"Sarah, have you found Marcus?"

Sarah hooted with laughter. "Commissioner Baines was kind enough to let me know Marcus was taken into custody along with eighty or so other punk rock fans. No real harm was done, but the university authorities thought it best to round them up before any real trouble occurred. Marcus is with me now and much subdued." Then she whispered, "Serves him right."

Elspeth grinned. "When do you plan to leave Hobart, Sarah?"

"I'm putting Marcus on a plane in about an hour along with a detective, who will accompany Marcus back to London. Clyde's meeting him there."

"You aren't going with him?'

"Not on your life. I'm persona non grata with all concerned right now. I told Clyde I needed time and space away from Marcus. I've booked a private cottage at a lodge in the mountains here for four days of rest and recreation with my camera. I want to photograph the flora and fauna of Tasmania and have no intention of returning to London before the whole thing with Marcus blows over."

Elspeth laughed. "How I wish I could join you. But may I ask you a favor?"

"Ask away as long as it doesn't concern the brat."

"Would you stop in Rushmore on your way to the mountains?"

"I'd already planned to. I need to drop off prints of the photographs I took of the troops. Mrs. Mack has promised a quiet lunch at her home with just one or two others. How many do you suppose will be there?"

Elspeth chuckled. "Will you go by the church and find out if the Buchanans are buried in the cemetery there?" she asked.

"Do you think they are?"

"Possibly. If they are, this may be the first real clue I have about them after nineteen sixty-nine. Also find out if a M. A. Berkeley was buried there in early two thousand and three."

"Who is he?"

"She, not he. Malcolm's sister, Mary Anne."

"That would be interesting. I'll find out everything I can."

"Thank you, Sarah. You're a treasure."

"Will you tell Clyde that?"

"Of course. Ring me when you get back to London and let me know about your break in the mountains. I'm going back there tomorrow."

Elspeth gave Sarah the private phone number at her flat in Kensington.

Elspeth alerted the concierge staff about Dave Mack's arrival and booked a quiet table in a nook in the lounge bar at six o'clock. He was several minutes late and arrived with an apology about traffic. He was less aggressive than his sister and, like many Australian men, had hearty good looks and a cheerful manner.

"Your sister tells me you were on hand when the police constable was shown the bodies," Elspeth said after explaining briefly her mission to Tasmania.

"That I was. I was fishing with my mate when one of the blokes from the village came rushing up to us and told us he'd discovered the bodies upstream from the bridge. He was very upset, shaking terribly, so my mate and I helped him up from the bank. We hurried along to his home, and he rang the police. Afterwards, the constable came. We showed him where the bodies were. The odd thing was that they were lying there peacefully and, except for the bullet holes in their temples and chests, you would have thought that they were asleep."

"Was there any evidence of a struggle?"

"None. They were just lying there."

"Were the reeds around them broken?"

"A few. It was at the end of a footpath. Couples often went there to. . .well, you know, to do what they do." Dave Mack blushed, which seemed strangely old-fashioned but nonetheless charming.

"What happened to the bodies afterwards?"

"The doctor came to examine them, and later the coroner came from Hobart. The police took photographs. They tried to keep us away, but we knew where to hide to watch."

"When did they take the bodies away?"

"It was after the blokes in plainclothes arrived and told all the onlookers to stay away. A police ambulance arrived from Hobart, and the paramedics took away the bodies."

"Do you know if the bodies were eventually returned to Rushmore for burial?"

"Might have been. You'll have to ask Sally, my sister. She knows that kind of thing and has always been in thick with the padres."

"I left Rushmore without getting her number. Do you have it?"

David Mack obliged, and, after finishing his beer, he pleaded a dinner engagement and took his leave.

Elspeth was glad to be left alone and returned to her room to prepare for her flight the following afternoon. She opened

her email and found a long response to the message she had
sent earlier.

> *Elspeth, my dear,*
>
> *With apologies. Urgent business in Brussels has
> made me slight your earlier messages. I am sitting here
> in my study in Sliema and remembering the wonderful
> breakfasts we have shared on the balcony above, and
> now I am relishing replying more fully. I fear the last
> time you were here in Malta I was preoccupied with
> an urgent diplomatic crisis and could not give you the
> time I had hoped.*
>
> *Yes, I am still trying to find the journal I kept at
> the time of Inspector Llewellyn's investigation. I did
> intend it for you because I suspected someday you
> would want to know what happened after Malcolm's
> death. I fully understood at the time that your retreat
> to the Highlands was the only way you had to deal
> with the suddenness and brutality of the event, but
> eventually your good mind would want to know what
> did happen after you left Cambridge.*
>
> *I am trying to recall exactly where I put the
> journal. It is among my many books at my brother's
> home in Aberdeenshire. I cannot leave Malta until this
> affair with Brussels is settled, but that should only take
> another week or so. I have taken the liberty to alert my
> brother, whom you have not yet met, and asked him to
> search my belongings. Are you returning to the UK
> through the US or Singapore? Can you stop in Malta?*
> *Most affectionately,*
> *Richard*

Yes, Dickie, her heart told her, I will definitely try to come to Malta. Bah, you foolish woman, her mind said.

She tapped a short reply. *"Dickie, I am flying straight through to London. Can we meet later? Let me know a good time for you. Malta will be fine. E."*

16

On returning to her flat in Kensington, Elspeth opened her laptop. She found another message from Richard, which suggested a time for her trip to Malta. She next opened a large-sized email with a photograph from Sarah Brixton. The attachment was a close-up of a small headstone with crisply cut letters reading:

BUCHANAN
May God's Love Forgive Us All

Sarah's note was short. *I found this in a quiet corner of the cemetery of the Anglican church in Rushmore. I have an appointment with the priest on my way back down from Cradle Mountain on Tuesday next. —S.B.*

Elspeth downloaded the photograph from the attachment to Sarah's email and zoomed in to the headstone. No moss or lichen covered the stone, and the carving looked fresh. Either the stone was new or the cemetery well maintained. Weeds surrounded the stone, so Elspeth assumed the former was true. Elspeth rattled off a quick response to Sarah. *Brava! Can you find out who is under the stone, when it was put there, and who arranged for it? —Elspeth*

A Secret in Singapore

Elspeth put a printed copy of Sarah's email in the thickening folder containing her lists of questions and the notes she had taken in Australia. It was Friday in London, Saturday in Tasmania. She would have to wait until late Monday or early Tuesday to hear the results of Sarah's interview with the priest. She felt frustrated.

Elspeth decided to interview Jean Henderson again and rang her in Cambridge to invite her to lunch at the Kensington flat. Elspeth asked her to bring all of her drawings from their first year at Girton. Considering Jean's feelings at the time, how much of what she had drawn was true? Or were there only half-truths shown in the sketches? Elspeth knew perceived half-truths had value. She would have to look at the drawings again but did look forward to the experience.

Elspeth felt constrained with Jean as they ate their lunch. Elspeth had prepared the meal from a simple recipe given to her by a famous Hollywood actress who touted her cooking skills. Elspeth played on this because Jean was impressed when the actress's name was mentioned.

"Have you met her?" Jean asked.

"Several times. My ex-husband once choreographed her fight scene with the killers her movie-husband had hired. The scene was filmed over two days' time, and she spent the evening at our home in between shootings showing us her cooking skills, and she made this recipe. Despite her exaggerated looks on scene, she is quite domestic in real life."

"Your life must have been exciting in Hollywood," Jean said enviously.

"Actually rather dull. Shooting a film is a long and hard task, and most actors' lives are only glamorous in the press. I was very much on the sidelines, and my ex was, in the end, more in love with his work than me or the children."

"Do you ever see him, your ex-husband? I never see mine."

"Very seldom. Only when the children are involved in a family event."

"Have you ever considered marrying again?" Jean asked, as if with some purpose.

"I am much too middle-aged for that, and besides my job wouldn't allow it," Elspeth said.

Jean flushed and then smiled. "I have. In fact I'm seeing someone quite nice right now, someone I like a great deal."

Elspeth felt a small stab of envy at Jean's news.

"Jean, how delightful for you," Elspeth said and quickly changed the subject. "Would you like coffee now or later?"

"Later, please. What a marvelous meal. May I have the recipe?"

"As reward for showing me your drawings again, of course."

Jean brought out her portfolio and unfolded its sides. "I found several other ones I didn't show you earlier. I'm still astonished at my bitterness in those days. I know sharing these with you now may be important, so I ask you to excuse the unhappy heart behind my hand when I drew them." She laid them out on Elspeth's table.

The first one made Elspeth blanch. Jean's pen did not spare Elspeth this time. Elspeth was sitting bolt upright in a chair, her face catatonic. Tony Ketcham was showing a photograph of a broken bicycle to her, while Victoria and several other girls were peeking from behind a door and smirking.

Elspeth looked at the drawing for a long time, and finally said, "Was Victoria really so vicious? And was I really so unfeeling?"

Jean shook her head. "In retrospect, no, neither was true, but no one could understand why you did not cry, Elspeth.

That was what I was trying to show. As for Victoria, she was more sympathetic than I show her here. I hated her and put that animosity into the drawing. That's why I didn't show it to you earlier."

"I don't remember that DS Ketcham showed me a photograph," Elspeth said.

Jean looked puzzled. "I don't think I made that up. Perhaps I did, but I drew this only a short time after the policeman spoke to you. I wonder where I got the idea he showed you a photograph."

The second drawing depicted Garth Llewellyn, Richard Munro and Tony Ketcham, all recognizable. With highly suspicious demeanors, the three of them were holding large magnifying glasses and snooping through the handbags of girls lined up in front of Girton.

"Did they really search your belongings?" Elspeth asked.

"The inspector did come around and walk through our rooms. The other two were not with him, but they were waiting outside. One could only assume the inspector told them what he had found. My drawing was a flight of fancy about what might have been. I think we all felt a bit violated by the police enquiries."

Jean drew out another sheet. "Here is an earlier one, again not flattering."

The drawing clearly was of Malcolm and Elspeth in the Chinese restaurant. Malcolm was holding an open book, showing Elspeth a drawing in it, but his other hand was taking the tip off the adjoining table.

"You didn't like Malcolm, did you, Jean?"

"Frankly, no, because I thought he was being dishonest with you. You were one of the few people I liked at Girton. I didn't like to see you hurt."

"What made you think I would be hurt?" Elspeth asked.

"Because of what Victoria and others were saying about Malcolm."

Elspeth looked directly at Jean and asked, "Was it jealousy?"

Jean considered the question. "Perhaps. In those days, I delighted in others' misery."

"How did that relate to me?" Elspeth could hear the edge in her own voice.

"You were being deceived," Jean said matter-of-factly.

Elspeth felt herself redden. The lunch with Jean was proving more uncomfortable than she anticipated. "How?" she asked. Her voice broke.

"Malcolm Buchanan had a certain reputation. Didn't you know?"

"I only know that what we had between us was real." Elspeth hated that she sounded defensive.

Jean studied Elspeth and took time to answer. "Yes, I believe you're right. I believe it was real—for you both. I also think that Malcolm found this profoundly disturbing."

"Why?"

"Because you were the best thing that had ever happened to him. You represented what he wanted to become. I think that's why he proposed to you the night he died."

Elspeth found this new side of Malcolm mystifying, but she knew she had an ally in Jean. She continued questioning Jean even though she knew her answers might be hurtful.

"I seem to have been wildly naïve. I'd no idea Malcolm had a reputation. I never even thought to ask. What exactly was his reputation and perhaps more to the point, how did the girls at Girton know about it?"

Jean looked at Elspeth and sighed. "Once Victoria saw Malcolm and you were an item, she was quick to spread any gossip she could find. She traveled in a fast set, and Malcolm came and went to parties hosted by her chums. I was a terrible sneak in those days and often listened to conversations held behind closed doors. I simply took my tooth glass, held it to the door or the wall and put my ear to it, a spy's old trick. Victoria told her particular friends Malcolm was an easy catch for a night's entertainment and he had bizarre ideas about stealing things that didn't belong to him. That's why I drew him stealing the tip in the Chinese restaurant."

Jean's answer cut deep into Elspeth. She blanched. "Did Victoria give any more details?"

"She said she'd seen Malcolm steal money from the donation box at King's College Chapel and take things from various shops in town. She also said Malcolm described this as a thrill, to see if he could get away with it. He boasted of his cleverness because he never was caught."

Elspeth's throat parched, but she went on. "What else?"

Jean moved uncomfortably in her chair. "You don't know any of this do you, Elspeth?"

Elspeth shook her head. "No. I suppose love really is blind. The Malcolm I knew was charming, intelligent and gracious. I never saw him do anything vaguely dishonest."

"Then I'll stay with my assumption that Malcolm wanted to be what you thought him to be."

Elspeth nodded, although inside of her a light went out. Malcolm had presented himself as the perfect suitor. Yet she had recently discovered he had lied to her about his parents' deaths. No, not lied exactly, but simply omitted mentioning something that would be of vast significance in any person's life, not only one's parents' deaths but also the mode of them.

Needing to change the topic, Elspeth rose and brought the tray with the coffee pot and cups to the table. "Jean, why are so many of your drawings in the Chinese restaurant?"

Jean accepted her cup. "Because I was studying Chinese painting from the owner's mother-in-law. I went there once a week for lessons, and afterwards Mrs. Lu would treat me to a bowl of rice and a dish cooked especially for the two of us. We sat in a small room behind an ornate latticed screen with carved dragons and phoenixes, a room reserved for Chinese and their personal guests only. None of the students knew I was there, so I could watch them freely. Whenever I showed her my sketches, Mrs. Lu would say I had the eyes of a tiger and the fierceness of a dragon. I adored her old Chinese ways and visited her frequently, even after I left Girton."

"And you spied on Malcolm and me there." Elspeth said.

Jean nodded. "Malcolm came more frequently than you did. When you were not there, he usually sat with members of Victoria's crowd. They would order Chinese rice wine and after a while get very tipsy. I noticed Malcolm only ordered green tea when he was with you."

"Jean, you would have made a formidable detective." Elspeth hoped the sadness in her words was not apparent.

"I'm a detective in my work, but my pursuit is scholarly rather than forensic. I wouldn't like the danger of real detective work," Jean said.

Elspeth smiled. "More often than not, detective work is slogging and not dangerous. It's like working on a jigsaw."

"Am I supplying pieces that may help you with the puzzle of Malcolm's death? They're not pretty ones."

Elspeth tried to answer honestly. "I think you've provided me with pieces that show a changed picture of Malcolm."

A Secret in Singapore

After Jean Henderson left, Elspeth revisited these last words. Every time she was with Jean, she came away feeling more apprehensive about Malcolm. Was Jean still the bitter person she had been at Girton by her own admission? Or was she an acute observer? Eyes of a tiger or fierceness of a dragon? Or both?

After lunch with Jean, Elspeth considered how she might approach Victoria Smythe-Welton again. Elspeth retraced their conversation at the Tate Modern, trying to recall if Victoria had expressed the same kind of viciousness Jean had, but Victoria had not. She talked more as if Malcolm did the same sort of things the rest of her set did. Victoria did not condemn Malcolm other than saying he was unfaithful to Elspeth. Victoria's implications were that Elspeth was out of step with the morality of the late sixties, not that Malcolm was deceptive or evil.

Victoria bragged that she had several connections to Malcolm's family. Could Elspeth exploit these? Victoria said her father knew Malcolm's father during the war in Southeast Asia and her brother knew Malcolm's brother-in-law, Mary Anne's husband. Victoria suddenly became more interesting as a source of information than the snickering girl in the caricatures in Jean Henderson's drawings or Elspeth's recent gluttonous companion at lunch. Elspeth wanted to question Victoria again. Elspeth wished Sarah was in London and could initiate an invitation to her home, which Elspeth suspected was grand. Victoria, who had definitely come down in the world, might jump at an invitation from the wife of Clyde Brixton and the daughter of an earl.

Breaking open her computer, Elspeth sent an email to Sarah with this brief message: *When will you be back in London?*

Eagerly awaiting the results of your interview in Rushmore. I have a promising lead and need your help. –Elspeth.

Later that afternoon she had a reply. Sarah was returning within the week.

Elspeth had several days of unscheduled time before her departure for Malta. She considered visiting her daughter and her family in East Sussex but knew this might lead to questions as to why she was not on assignment for the Kennington Organisation. Elspeth had never told her children about Malcolm because to drag out an old romance seemed pointless.

She decided to walk in Kensington Gardens, which was near her flat in Gordon Mews, and used the time to formulate a plan to make the next few days productive. Several thoughts came to mind. She could explore in depth what happened in Malaya and Singapore under the Japanese occupation, but this seemed fruitless because Lesley Urquhart indicated the information on Malcolm's parents was still classified. She could try to find Maudy Berkeley, Mary Anne's daughter, but Victoria Smythe-Welton Brewer probably would divulge this information without Elspeth having to do any research. Elspeth stopped abruptly when she thought of her third option and was nearly run over by three youthful cyclists. She could go back and once again explore her time with Malcolm to see if she had any reason to believe Jean Henderson or Victoria Smythe-Welton's allegations were true. If she returned home to Loch Rannoch, she could try to bring back memories of her time spent there after Malcolm's death. She knew there would be heartache in doing this but maybe also a cleansing.

When she returned to her flat, she rang her family in Perthshire. Her mother answered after six rings and said, "I think pork would be more suitable."

"Mother, it's Elspeth."

Her mother seemed unfazed by her own odd greeting and replied, "Of course it is, my dear. I can't imagine anyone else having your voice."

Elspeth, despite herself, grinned at her mother's disjointedness and was filled with love. She wondered if Malcolm ever had this feeling toward his mother.

"May I come home for the next few days?"

"Of course, Elspeth. You always may. I thought you were in Malta, or was it Sydney?"

"Both and Tasmania as well."

"Are there truly devils there?"

"I didn't see any, but I will tell you all about it when I get home."

"When will you arrive?"

"I thought of motoring up in the morning. I should arrive for a late dinner."

"Your father will be delighted! Will pork do?"

Elspeth smiled at her mother's way of finally linking her non-sequiturs and assured her pork would be fine.

"I need to hole myself up and do a bit of writing."

"A new career? Much safer than careening around the world pursing unpleasant guests at Lord Kennington's hotels."

"Thanks, Mother. Say hello to Daddy. I love you both."

17

Although Elspeth would have preferred a quiet dinner with her parents, the pork roast was intended for a family gathering with various cousins, who shared with Elspeth news of their lives without enquiring about the details of hers. The effect was stabilizing. The following morning, after eschewing her mother's porridge for lighter fare, Elspeth felt centered enough to begin writing her recollections.

The Labs with which she had grown up had been replaced by a golden retriever, named Bounce, who was ready for a bracing morning walk. In her clothes cupboard Elspeth found an old kilt and pullover, garments she had not worn since her retreat to Loch Rannoch after Malcolm's death. If she put them on, she might be able to summon up the feelings she had in the late spring of nineteen sixty-nine. The kilt was a hand-me-down and had always been generously proportioned. Elspeth regretted that she now needed to loosen the buckles. She pulled on heavy woolen socks and warm boots and donned a boiled wool overcoat kept on the coat rack below.

Bounce was demanding and led Elspeth up to the braes above the Duff home. Elspeth took out a spiral bound notepad she had found in her room. Finding a place sheltered from the late winter wind and in the sun, she sat looking out over the snow-capped mountains beyond and began her notes.

A Secret in Singapore

I want to remember all the feelings I had in 1969.

Malcolm was everything for me, the centre, the core, the very essence of all I wanted to live for, and now he is dead. How can I go on living? The cold rain coming down when we first met ceased to exist the minute we entered King's College Chapel. The rising youthful voices, singing out the joy of Christmas, filled me with love, and it soon took control of my life. Aunt Mag had dressed me like a sophisticate, but how can an eighteen-year-old girl become a woman without knowing what it is like to love and be loved?

I wanted him to come to Perthshire for Christmas. I had no doubts he was the only man I would ever love, and I wanted my family to meet him. He didn't come, assuring me it was too soon and he had important work to do on his thesis. I couldn't imagine how the legalities of art theft could be more intoxicating than being with me, but I admired his maturity in saying it was too soon. I did not understand why our relationship needed time? It was a destiny that could not be denied. Why was spending Christmas with his sister, Mary Anne, in London more important. He kissed me and said when I was older I would understand.

I returned to Girton before Twelfth Night, and we celebrated with a meal in his rooms with other graduate students and some other girls from Girton. We all drank too much champagne. I don't know how I got back to Girton that night, but all of us returned safely. I'd never drunk too much before and vowed I never would again.

Despite the hiatus in seeing each other over the Christmas break, the magic of our relationship hadn't dimmed. When not in lectures, we studied together, ate together, laughed together and loved together. Perhaps Victoria assessed my primness correctly because we never slept together. That was for a later time. When Malcolm died, I was sorry that I had asked for this delay, but Malcolm once told me he loved me for doing this.

Because some of the events of 1969 have become so important in 2004, I want to address them.

The Chinese restaurant, Ming Palace, was a favourite haunt of the girls (we were girls in those days) and their dates because it was inexpensive and nearby. Malcolm and I went there frequently, lugging our books along, usually ordering a bowl of noodles because it was the most inexpensive thing on the menu, and, while sucking in the long strands, we laughed and exchanged the exciting things of the day, both intellectual and personal. Certainly there were other students around us, but I can't remember if they bothered us. Jean mentioned a waitress with whom Malcolm fought, but I have no recollection of her other than that she was shown in Jean's drawings.

Malcolm often went to London to do research on his thesis. He was excited by the trove of information he found at the British Museum on the subject of stolen art. (Isn't it ironic that so many of the treasures there were stolen originally? A 2004 perspective not a 1969 one.) When he returned from these trips, frequently taking several days, he was filled with such intensity that it was hard not to catch his enthusiasm.

Malcolm and I constantly talked about art theft. It was his field, and I was interested in matters of the law. He said to some people art was like any other commodity, to be traded and possessed, and for them it had no worth beyond its monetary value. But Malcolm disagreed. He contended what made art different was that the best pieces intoxicated people with their pure beauty. He trained me to see beauty. He took me to numerous exhibitions, both in Cambridge and London. He knew so much about art, and his knowledge encompassed not only European art but art from Asia, Africa, Australia and the Americas as well. He shared his deepest dream with me. He wanted to discover some stolen piece of art that not only had great historical significance but also was of extraordinary beauty. He told me that throughout history Asian art had been more subtly evocative of passion than that expressed in European art. I didn't believe him until he told me the story of Yang Kwei-fei, concubine of a Tang dynasty emperor in China, who had her chambers lined with exquisite pieces of jade, which she demanded as favours from her imperial lover. That story seemed to delight him, and he asked what I would do if I were an imperial concubine. As a sheltered Scottish lass, I found the whole notion that art could induce passion quite strange, and when I said so he laughed at me. I'm not sure why I remember this particularly. When we walked together through the British Museum, he would linger in the Chinese wing. He would admire the statues of Buddha and Kwan Yin, delight in the magnificent bronzes and marvel at the many pieces of jade.

He always evaded the subject of his sister, Mary Anne. He seemed content to spend Christmas with *her, but later the relationship seemed to cool. I asked him about this because we met Mary Anne one day in London, when we were touring some galleries in Chelsea. She invited us for tea, but the tension between them was obvious. I wanted to know her better, but Malcolm told me they had become estranged recently, but it really didn't matter because he now had me to love. As an only child, I wondered what it would be like to have a sibling. My various cousins were a lively bunch, but I felt a brother or sister would be different.*

Bounce presented a stick and nudged Elspeth to throw it for her. Elspeth obliged and moved slightly to stay in the sun. She went back to her musings.

What would life with Malcolm have been like if he had not been murdered? In 1969 I thought the universe revolved around him. He filled every cell of my body and all the emotions of my heart. He was the first man I loved, and I have never loved another one that way since. Did I think Alistair a substitute for this? He, like Malcolm, was a magical creature who would took me beyond myself, but I do not think I ever loved Alistair, even at first, the way I loved Malcolm.

Bounce brought back the stick with great pride and demanded another throw.

"Come, hound, let's walk farther up the hill. I find this spot disturbing," she said to the dog.

The retriever responded to Elspeth's demands with a furious wagging of her tail. If only people were as simple to please as dogs, Elspeth thought, wouldn't we all be happier?

Having begun using the old notepad, she continued writing in it when she returned home.

Why do I write so much about art? He made it come real for me, but for him it was something deeper. It obsessed him. He was fascinated with the possession of art, particularly collections in private hands. The ownership of art absorbed him. He especially hated what war did to art collecting, not only what was done by the Nazis, but also war throughout time. He ranted against collectors who bought art from refugees for a pittance. Art belong to the world, not to conquerors or unscrupulous financiers. When I asked him about patronage, he said all artists should be paid by the state and should have free rein to create their own masterpieces. We argued about this incessantly.

Once, when we were punting along the Cam, probably a week or two before he died, he said to me, "Elspeth, one day I will show you one of the most beautiful pieces of art ever created. It's been hidden away for many, many years, but I've found it. If its ownership were to be revealed, however, someone important, who stole it many years ago, could be in grave danger. So I must wait." He rubbed his hands with a certain amount of anticipatory glee, almost leaving the pole sticking in the mud out of reach.

I don't remember if Malcolm spent time with anyone but me during those months. As we wandered around Cambridge many people greeted him. He spoke highly of his tutor and of one of the curators at the British Museum, but other than that, his attitude toward people was flippant. He would tell amusing stories about his acquaintances, but he never mentioned any close friends. I would have been jealous if there were such friends. He sometimes spoke of a lonely childhood, and therefore I assumed he was a solitary person by nature.

I wonder now where Malcolm got his money. He frequently gave me small gifts, treated me to dinner and sent me flowers. He was forever purchasing expensive new art books. I never asked where his book collection went, but Mary Anne must have inherited it. She may have given it to the university. When Malcolm died, I didn't want to know what happened to his body or his effects. His spirit was gone, and nothing physical could bring him back. I did not even ask if there was a funeral for him.

During those first dark days I couldn't speak about Malcolm to anyone. Richard asked several times if I wanted to know about the investigation, but I didn't because every mention of Malcolm expanded the emptiness inside me. Richard kept a record of the investigation in case I ever wanted to know. I do now.

Malcolm's ghost, however, would not go away. I buried myself in my studies, but I would walk by places where we had been together and tears would fill me although I never wept. The excitement of working at Scotland Yard, my marriage to Alistair, the thrill of being involved even peripherally with the big stars of Hollywood, the joys of parenthood, and the arduous work for the Kennington Organisation could not replace the spiritual, intellectual, and emotional glory of those five months with Malcolm.

The rain outside began in earnest, and Elspeth had to deny Bounce another walk. Elspeth heard her mother in the kitchen, banging pots and pans the way she had a habit way of doing, and went to keep her company

Fiona Duff looked up at her daughter. "Elspeth, you look quite down in the mouth. Is Lord Kennington working you too hard? You are beginning to get to an age where you should slow down a bit. You really shouldn't run yourself ragged all the time. You look terrible. Where did you get that horrid kilt and jumper? Your father will be quite upset if he finds you dressed that way. He admires you so much when you come up from London or in from San Francisco or Paris or Hong Kong."

Fiona Duff rambled on until she looked up and saw the tears in her daughter's eyes, a happening so uncharacteristic that Fiona came and took Elspeth in her arms. No single gesture could have helped Elspeth more. Her mother stroked Elspeth's hair, now stylishly cut, in the same way she had stroked it when Elspeth was a child and her long hair was in tangles.

Fiona Duff was often accused of being dotty, but she had an uncanny ability to sense other's feelings, particularly her daughter's. "It's still Malcolm, isn't it?"

Elspeth nestled her head into her mother's shoulder and nodded.

"He had a mysterious hold on you, Elspeth. More than first loves usually do. I think it's because he died suddenly and the two of you never had a chance to come down from that place where young lovers go."

"Meeting Richard again brought it all back, Mother. When I recently was in Malta, Aunt Mag and Richard talked to me. They both suggested I come back to the UK and find Malcolm's murderer."

"After all this time? The police never could find the murderer. Won't your trying just make it worse for you?"

"Up on the braes today, I re-lived my time with Malcolm. I suppose now I should shed the tears that wouldn't flow when he died, but they won't come."

"A good cry does us all good," her mother said, but Elspeth wasn't sure. Fiona let her daughter go and offered her a piece of Victoria sponge and a cup of tea. Elspeth smiled up at her mother, who had not forgotten her favorite treat at teatime during her childhood.

"Mother, Daddy and you are so precious to me. I probably never told you that."

"Oh, you may not have, but of course we always have known."

"Malcolm, you know, was never close to his parents. I found out he was born in the Malayan jungle toward the end of the war." Elspeth poured out the story of Malcolm's early life as her mother busied herself around the kitchen.

"How sad," said Fiona Duff, as if she were not listening. "Parents and children need to get on with each other. No good ever comes when they don't."

Before her father returned from his office, Elspeth went and changed into the stylish clothes she had worn to see Inspector Llewellyn, substituting a stout pair of shoes because she knew her father liked to have a walk before tea. The rain had cleared and an ethereal mist rose from the loch. They kept to the road because of the wetness and proceeded hand-in-hand. Her father had walked with her like this in her childhood, and Elspeth felt warmed by the gesture.

"Did Mother tell you why I came home yesterday?"

James Duff picked up a stick and threw it for Bounce. "In her own way. She mentioned it had to do with your memories of Malcolm."

"They still haunt me, even after all this time. Richard Munro and Aunt Mag think if I find his murderer, the memories will be exorcised."

"Yes, he came last summer to ask about Malcolm. Did he tell you?"

Remembering how long it took Richard to confess this, Elspeth smiled. "He did."

They walked companionably, the early darkness of the winter evening holding them. After a comfortable silence James Duff spoke. "I had a case once of a woman who lost her first husband during the Second World War. He didn't die bravely but rather in a fight with another British soldier. Her husband's killer disappeared. The woman married twice after that, but she never was happy. She always wanted to know where her first husband's killer had gone. She spent much of her third husband's wealth to find him, because she couldn't let go of her memories."

Elspeth knew her father eventually would link this story to hers. "And did she?"

"Unfortunately, yes."

"Are you going to leave me dangling, Daddy?"

"No. After the fight, the man who was reported to have killed her husband enlisted in a regiment that went to India and, when he came back from the war, he settled in Canada. In the end the woman flew out to Vancouver and confronted him. He told her that he hadn't killed anyone, but that her husband had been having an affair with his wife. His wife, in a moment of passionate rage, had killed my client's husband, but the man had taken responsibility for it."

Elspeth and her father walked on, both knowing the road along the loch well enough that they needed no more than the failing light from the winter sky to guide them. Elspeth respected her father's wisdom. He frequently used examples from his law practice to illustrate a point for her. Since her years at Girton, Elspeth often wondered what her life would have been like had she fulfilled her original ambition and joined her father's firm of solicitors in Pitlochry. Would she now be as wise as he was? She had traveled all over the world. He had stayed near his boyhood home nearly all his life, but he seemed to know more of the human condition than she.

"Are you trying to tell me I shouldn't continue trying to find out who killed Malcolm?" Elspeth asked as they walked.

Her father hurled another stick for the dog, and then, with sadness in his eyes, turned and looked at his daughter. "No, I know you too well to suggest that. I think you must go on because you won't be satisfied until you can solve the case. Just don't be surprised if, in the end, you wish you hadn't discovered what actually happened."

18

Elspeth left Loch Rannoch the next day. Since she did not have to be in London immediately, she decided to take a leisurely drive through the places where she had grown up. The winter day was clear and biting, but the sunlight filled her with the hope her ordeal might soon be over. First she visited Blair School for Girls, now simply Blair School, where she had been a student. She got out of her car and wandered along the public paths among the copper beeches that divided the school from the castle. She heard the cheerful noises of the students below and smiled with warm remembrance of her childhood there.

Close to the school she discovered a small, shivering boy hiding behind a hedge. Elspeth did not want to alarm him, so she kicked at a stone in the path. He looked at her, clearly startled that anyone would find him.

"Are you running away, too?" she asked.

The boy cocked his head and gaped at her.

"Are you running away?" he asked.

"Yes, I suppose I am."

"Where are you running away to?"

"Singapore," she said, trying to make it sound mysterious.

"Is that far away?" he asked wide-eyed.

"Yes, all the way to Asia. But don't tell." She put a cautionary finger to her lips.

The boy forgot his shyness. "May I come with you?"

"Do you really want to?" she asked conspiratorially. "I'm chasing some dangerous criminals, murderers in fact." Elspeth hoped her expression showed how frightening her mission was.

"Are you with Scotland Yard?" he asked.

"I used to be, but now I'm on my own with no one to back me up. Can you fire a pistol?" She hoped he would not notice her amusement.

"No, my father keeps his guns locked up in a special cupboard. He says I'm not old enough to handle them."

"You have a very wise father. If you can't fire a pistol, I don't think you can come with me. Is that your school down there?"

"No," said the boy.

"Is the uniform a disguise? I used to wear one like it when I was a student at Blair."

The boy shook his head but cast down his eyes. "You're a private detective, aren't you?"

Elspeth looked seriously at him. "Yes, I am, but I only got to be one because I finished my schooling at Blair and went on to university."

"Was that a long time ago?" he asked innocently.

"A very long time ago. Now I travel all over the world chasing bad people."

"Do you like doing that?"

Elspeth considered the question. "No one ever asked me that before. Do you know, sometimes it's exciting, but sometimes it's scary. And I do know how to fire a pistol!"

"I'd like to be like you when I grow up."

"Then off you go back to school, and study hard. When you are older, get your father to teach you to use a gun properly."

The boy scuttled down the hill and waved at Elspeth, reminding her of her son when he was a child. She wondered if the young boy would look up Singapore on the map.

Next she followed the familiar roads to the family farm on Loch Tay. She found her cousin, Biddy Baillie Shaw, shooing several chickens from her vegetable garden. Biddy had been at dinner two nights before, but they had not talked privately together. Biddy greeted Elspeth with a wave. Elspeth parked her car and entered the steading surrounding the farmhouse. Biddy's husband, Ivor, had died suddenly the year before. Elspeth's entire family was surprised when afterwards Biddy took full charge of her life and the farm. Elspeth involved Biddy in the situation at the Kennington Stresa several months before and became closer to her then.

"Oh, 'Peth, I'm so glad you stopped by. Come have tea and tell me about Dickie and you. Has he proposed?"

"Of course not," Elspeth snapped. "Why would he?"

Biddy eyes met Elspeth's, "Have you given him the chance? No, I see you haven't. He loves you. You know that, don't you? Do come in and tell me why you are here."

Elspeth shared the reason for her visit but did not go into the details of her inner turmoil nor why she had not given Richard a chance.

Negotiating the motorways south, Elspeth considered these two chance meetings: the young boy, hiding from life, but so eager to be a part of it, and Biddy, whose life must have been torn apart when Ivor died, but who was getting on so well with living.

Elspeth found Scotland settling. Her writings there confirmed her feelings in nineteen sixty-nine, despite the new information from Jean. Elspeth arrived back in London with new hope she could put Malcolm's murder in perspective and would be able to carry on with her life in the way Biddy had done and the young boy wanted to do. Elspeth's optimism continued when she returned to her London flat and opened her laptop.

The email from Sarah Brixton was short; the one from Richard Munro longer. She saved the latter to enjoy at its own pace.

> *Elspeth,"* Sarah had written, *"I talked with Father Carter, the Anglican priest who takes the services at Rushmore, as well as several other churches in the area. He referred me to the sexton in Rushmore, who checked the records. A Mary Anne Berkeley bought a burial plot in 1969, and three sets of ashes were laid to rest there in the early winter of that year, although no one identified the ashes. In the summer of 2003, Mary Anne Buchanan's ashes were laid to rest there as well and the headstone was added. In neither instance was there a service. Hope this helps. I'll ring you when I get home. — SB*

Elspeth puzzled over the information in the email. Plainly Mary Anne bought the plot to bury her parents, and, because of the secrecy surrounding their deaths, their ashes would probably not have been released to Mary Anne until the winter after their deaths. But whose ashes were in the third box? She wondered if they were those of the Chinese servant who had disappeared.

Richard Munro's email was longer and more formal.

A Secret in Singapore

My dearest Elspeth,

My brother has indeed found the lost journal, not among my boxes but tucked away on his library shelf, where I asked him to put it many years ago. He tells me it is well preserved and, before I could ask him to save it for me, he said he had already sent it to the FCO to be put in the diplomatic bag for me. I expect it will arrive in Malta tomorrow.

I spoke to Magdalena Cassar about you coming to Malta, and she is as eager as I am to hear first-hand what progress you have made.

I have official duties this week but can get a bit of time off beginning this weekend. We can take my yacht to Gozo. Hopefully it will be a quiet trip and not stir up your insides. What a curse seasickness must be.

In the meantime, I shall carve out some time to read my journal and see if there is anything in it that will be useful to you.

I think of your progress every day, wondering not if you have found the murderer but if you are finding yourself.

With my deepest and warmest affection,
Richard

Elspeth was so used to relying on email that she had forgotten to call her Aunt Mag over the last three weeks. With a certain amount of guilt Elspeth picked up her phone and rang the converted farmhouse on Gozo. She wanted to talk to Aunt Mag before committing to Richard. She left a message for Aunt Mag to ring her back.

Delaying flying to Malta until Friday would hopefully give her time to arrange a lunch with Sarah Brixton and

Victoria Smythe-Welton, whose new surname perversely escaped Elspeth. Was it Distiller? She emailed Sarah back:

Dear Sarah,

What an interesting bit of news. I do hate the secrecy around Malcolm's parents, but I think you may have found out where Ah-sing or Ah-ting is now. No wonder she never surfaced, probably being buried in the churchyard in Rushmore the whole time.

Would lunch on Tuesday at your home be a possibility? I need to question one of my classmates at Girton, who has fallen at bit from her former respectability, but I think she will be impressed by an invitation for lunch from you rather than me. She may lead me to Mary Anne.

Am I being too forward?

Best regards,

Elspeth

Magdelena Cassar called back half an hour later and gushed forth an invitation for Friday. She chastised Elspeth for being out of touch. Her penance, Aunt Mag proclaimed, was to be a long visit in Gozo, when Elspeth was to share all. Of course, Richard was to be in attendance. Elspeth could not resist her aunt's loving enthusiasm and agreed to the visit but not to the length of stay. She explained Lord Kennington had coerced her to go to Singapore the following Tuesday to handle, "a small bit of business at his hotel there" as he put it. Elspeth acceded to his demand because she wanted some time in Singapore to trace the Buchanans.

Elspeth took out the tattered notebook from Scotland. She read it over once more. She had written for one purpose, but it might serve for another. In her attempt to describe Malcolm's lack of connection with others, she wrote that he had close ties to his tutor and a curator in the British Museum. Did she ever know their names? Would they still be alive after such a long time? She could contact King's College and get the name of the tutor, but the British Museum might prove more difficult. Rather than using the telephone, she decided to visit the museum the next day and find out if the curator still worked there.

Even thought it was well past seven in the evening, Elspeth rang Pamela Crumm, with hopes that her friend might still be at her desk. Pamela answered on the first ring.

"Pamela," said Elspeth without identifying herself, "who do you know at the British Museum?"

Pamela laughed. "Elspeth, I thought you were in Scotland. Why are you calling about the British Museum?"

"I need someone to talk to there. Someone old."

"It strikes me that most things in the British Museum are old, but I'm not too sure how many people are," Pamela said. Elspeth could imagine Pamela's grin.

"I want to talk to someone who was there in nineteen sixty-nine."

Pamela was still chuckling at her joke. "If you want to find someone old in the British Museum, I hope they aren't mummified."

"Pamela, you must have had a trying day, but do be serious. I want to find someone who might have known Malcolm and something about his research there."

"Eric was his usual self all day, without relief, worse luck. I am being a bit silly, but I think I can help you. Let me ring

Sir Christopher in the morning. He can open some doors, but the cost for my doing that is for you to give me an update."

Elspeth did so cautiously, leaving out the burials in Tasmania and the viciousness of Jean's drawings.

"Lady Sarah seems like a good resource. I'm glad you and she are getting on so well. I thought you would. Eric will be pleased."

"Are you going to tell him, Pamela? I hope not. I thought I had three months off, and now there are minor exceptions."

"Like a fully paid trip to Singapore? The possibility of extortion there is becoming a sore point for him."

"All right. You win that point, but I'd prefer you tell him the minimum you can get away with."

"I'll simply mention you are making progress and looking forward to your trip to Southeast Asia."

"You're a true friend, Pamela. Call me about Sir Christopher when you can. You might mention that I want to speak with someone who knew about the Chinese antiquities collection in the late sixties."

Sir Christopher provided a name of one of the curators emeritus, Amadeus Lynn. Pamela said she was assured Dr. Lynn loved talking about the past, both of Chinese antiquities and his career. Elspeth wondered if Lynn, or perhaps Lin, was an English or a Chinese surname. Sir Christopher had given Pamela Amadeus Lynn's home phone number, which she passed on. Elspeth phoned him after concocting a story as to the purpose of her call. The voice that answered was very much English.

"Mrs. Duff," he said in a most gentlemanly way, "Sir Christopher mentioned you might give me a call, and I will be delighted to see you. Would you mind coming round to my house rather than the museum? I've recently had knee surgery and still find it difficult to get around in the back rooms of the museum. Shall we say for tea? What day would be best for you?"

"Today? Tomorrow?"

"Let's do it today." Real delight filled Amadeus Lynn's voice. "Let me give you directions to my home."

The address he gave was in easy walking distance of Elspeth's flat. The fair weather continued, and she always enjoyed a stroll along the streets of London with their multiplicity of sights and sounds even in the exclusive neighborhoods of Kensington. Dr. Lynn's small house was tucked away at the end of a narrow cul-de-sac, hidden by larger houses visibly newly renovated and once again showing their historic origins. Elspeth found equal attention had been given to Dr. Lynn's home. Real estate in this part of London was as precious as that in urban California, she thought, although it appealed more to her aesthetic tastes.

Using the highly polished brass doorknocker, which was in the shape of an Asian lion, she rapped at the door. The door was heavy, and she could hear nothing behind it until it was opened, and an elderly Chinese woman leaned her head around the door.

"Come in," she said in perfect English but with a slight accent. "My cousin is expecting you."

The woman was dressed in a silk cheongsam, intricately embroidered in multi-colored patterns portraying exotic birds nestled among boughs of bamboo. It hung on her loosely and came to the ground, although the high slits in the skirt allowed her to move with ease. Elspeth was glad she had dressed with some care for tea, but her modern clothing paled before the classic beauty of the Chinese woman's dress.

"My name is Lin Ching-mei. Unlike my cousin, I did not take a Western name when I came to Britain many years ago. Amadeus, indeed. Do you know that means 'loves god'?"

Elspeth grinned at Lin Ching-mei's feistiness and suspected she was a bit of the proverbial dragon lady found in many Chinese tales.

Amadeus Lynn was an elderly Chinese gentleman, whose gracious manner and immaculate English tweeds and accent matched his eruditeness. Lin Ching-mei served green tea and Chinese sweet almond biscuits and then left the warm and sunny sitting room for other parts of the house. Faint birdsong trickled its way into the room through the windows closed to the winter chill.

"Mrs. Duff, ever since Sir Christopher called me and asked me if I was at the museum in nineteen sixty-nine, I've been trying to take myself back to that time. I came to the museum in nineteen sixty-five, when they were cataloguing a great number of works smuggled out of China and exported to Britain from Hong Kong. If you are a history buff, you know that the Cultural Revolution was in full swing in China at that time, and everyone was trying to rescue as many antiquities as possible. I studied Chinese art and history at Oxford and relished my new job. Am I to presume that you might be coming to ask about any of these objects?"

"Even in Scotland, where I grew up, we followed some of the worst atrocities of the Cultural Revolution. My search today isn't about an object, however, but about a person, a fellow student at Cambridge, who was doing his doctoral thesis on Asian art theft."

"A timely subject. What was his name?"

"Malcolm Buchanan."

Amadeus Lynn stiffened and then nodded mechanically. "I did know him, although only slightly. For several years he came to see my superior at the museum, but then he stopped coming. My superior told me he had died."

"He was murdered actually, and the gun that killed him was the kind the Chinese Communists used during their struggle for liberation."

"Are you suggesting he was killed by the communists?"

"Dr. Lynn, no one knows, and that's what I'm trying to find out."

"It's been many years since then. Is it still important?"

"Yes, for those who were close to him, it is. Is your superior still alive today?"

"Unfortunately he died at least twenty years ago."

"Did he ever talk to you about Malcolm?"

"Once or twice, maybe." Dr. Lynn said evasively.

"Do you remember what he said?"

Amadeus Lynn sat motionlessly and finally bowed his head. He offered Elspeth another cup of tea.

"Do you think those close to Malcolm Buchanan really want the truth after all this time?" he asked.

"I know they do."

"Then I'll tell you what I remember. My superior came to me one day and said he was helping a brilliant graduate student from Cambridge, whose specialty was Chinese art theft, particularly art objects from the Tang dynasty. My superior, whose field of study was jade from the Tang, brought out several pieces of jade from that era that had not yet been catalogued by the museum, and showed them to Malcolm Buchanan. He explained they all had been stolen in one way or another over the centuries. Malcolm asked their worth, which of course was priceless, but because they were in the possession of the British Museum they were unlikely ever to be sold. According to my superior, Malcolm pressed him on their worth to a private collector. Again my superior would not speculate. Malcolm laughed and thanked my superior for his help. Later my superior went to wrap up the treasured pieces of jade, and one was missing. It was a small piece, of minor significance, so my superior did not report the theft, thinking he might have been mistaken, but he did not welcome Malcolm back to the museum after that. We heard later he was dead. Is that what you wanted to hear?"

Elspeth steadied herself. "The people who have asked me to conduct this investigation might wish to doubt your words, but I'll pass on the information, of course," she said with as much composure as she could muster. "Is there anything else?"

"No. I've often thought how incongruous it was that a student whom my superior originally admired should have committed that theft."

The interview with Amadeus Lynn shook Elspeth. When she returned to her flat, she took out her notes from Scotland.

> *He shared his deepest dream with me. He wanted to discover some stolen piece of art that not only had great historical significance but also was of extraordinary beauty.*

Elspeth read the words she had written only days before in a new light. Were there other things hidden in her memoir? She opened the notebook and read it again. She had found Amadeus Lynn, and now she wanted to trace Malcolm's tutor. In all probability Inspector Llewellyn interviewed the tutor, and she hoped his name would appear in Richard's journal. She tried to envision the tutor, but no image came to mind. Had she actually met him? She could not remember. She decided to put this matter away until after her rendezvous in Malta with Richard and her trip to Singapore.

Most of all she wanted to talk to Maudy Berkeley. Through her family connections, Victoria Smythe-Welton might know where Maudy currently was. Elspeth was relying on Sarah Brixton to issue an invitation to Victoria as soon as she returned to London.

19

Elspeth had not been prepared to be impressed with the Park Lane home of Clyde and Sarah Brixton, but she was. Cleared by the doorman, Elspeth took the marble and mirrored lift to the tenth floor where Sarah, who was dressed as simply as she had been in Australia, greeted her. They entered a magnificent foyer with a full-length window that looked out over Hyde Park and the Serpentine. Winter sunlight filled the panorama of London beyond.

"Are you overawed with the view?" Sarah asked. "You're supposed to be. Clyde spent millions on this flat in order to impress his guests."

Sarah gave Elspeth a brief hug. Elspeth felt the same ease with her that they had shared in Australia, despite the opulence of their new surroundings.

"Sometimes I feel the money could have helped more people," Sarah said. "Mummy had liberal views, which she secretly passed on to me when Daddy wasn't around. Clyde insists on the bold statement, which of course has made him very successful and enormously rich."

"Sarah, I do appreciate your offering lunch here. We could have done it at the Kennington Mayfair, but this is much more impressive. I hope Victoria will be so overwhelmed at your invitation that she doesn't eat everything in sight. She's an aggressive eater, as you will see."

Sarah laughed heartily. "I don't need to tell the kitchen to make sure there is plenty; there always is."

A call from the reception desk below confirmed a Mrs. Brewer had arrived.

"The doorman isn't favorably disposed to our lunch guest," Sarah confided. "He put on the pompous voice that he uses when he disapproves. He liked you from his tone."

Elspeth smiled at the compliment. "Do you suppose it's because she is very large or because she's overdressed?"

"We will see."

Victoria swept off the lift. She was heavily made up and exhibiting too much bling and a wobbling cleavage. Elspeth made introductions, and Sarah escorted them into a sitting room, where a small luncheon table had been set for three.

"I thought we would be more comfortable in here because Clyde's grand dining room would engulf us," Sarah said. "Other than when we are entertaining royalty, I get indigestion thinking about the heavy draperies and overly polished hundred-foot long table."

Sarah's sparkling eyes made quick contact with Elspeth, who caught the jest. Victoria Brewer did not.

"This is charming," Victoria gushed. "I was so delighted when Elspeth rang me and said you would be asking me to come around for lunch, Lady Sarah. Elspeth assures me you are deep into the investigation of Malcolm's death, and I am as well. Too tragic. All of us at Girton grieved with Elspeth."

Liar, thought Elspeth, who had warned Lady Sarah about Victoria's effusiveness.

"All of you there must have done," Sarah said with a straight face. "Victoria, I understand you knew Malcolm's family."

The waiter who was attending the meal arrived at that moment with plates of artistically arranged, thinly sliced, and slightly rare lamb with sprigs of fresh mint, steamed herbed-flavored broad beans, and spring greens in a light olive oil dressing. The waiter displayed a bottle of pinot noir for Lady Sarah's approval, and, at her nod, decanted small amounts into the wine glasses provided.

Victoria looked greedily at her food and picked up her wine glass with a dainty gesture that her mother must have taught her. She sipped the wine demurely and then picked up her knife and fork with enthusiasm.

"My father was in Malaya during the war," she said between mouthfuls. "He was captured in Singapore and put into the prison with the other British soldiers. He never talked about it. I assume he must have known Malcolm's father. Only a small community of British soldiers made it through."

So much for a real connection there, thought Elspeth.

Sarah replied sympathetically. "How sad, but Elspeth tells me your brother knew Mary Anne Buchanan's husband."

Victoria's plate by this time was empty. Sarah nodded to the waiter to offer more.

"Edward Berkeley and my brother were at King's College together." Victoria didn't specify which university. "They kept in touch afterwards, and Robbie was an usher at the Berkeley's wedding. Mary Anne was so lovely and Edward so handsome." Consuming the copious amounts of food she had put on her plate, Victoria was beginning to warm up to her topic.

Sarah, with a reporter's instinct, pushed for more information. "Did your brother see them after the wedding?"

"They were all in the same set here in London."

Sarah apparently was not content with the answer. "Are they still?"

"Sadly no. Life is so filled with separations and divorces these days. Mary Anne and Edward went out to live in Australia shortly after Malcolm died. They divorced out there, and Edward came back to London. My brother and he sometimes meet, but he isn't the same without Mary Anne. Edward eventually remarried, I believe. My brother would know."

Elspeth listened in silence, enjoying the complex flavors of the meal, but she could no longer contain herself. "Victoria, are you saying that Edward Berkeley is here in London?"

"I'm extremely positive he is."

Elspeth wondered where Victoria learned this redundant English usage, hopefully not at Girton.

"Would your brother know how to contact him?" Elspeth asked.

"Absolutely."

The waiter's face did not show there was anything out of the ordinary in the haste with which Victoria was emptying her plate. Expressionless, he offered Victoria another round of food.

"Let me ring him," Victoria said before taking another large mouthful.

Victoria dug into her gold handbag and pulled out a neon blue mobile phone. She tapped in some numbers and waited. Finally she spoke, "Robbie, it's Vicki. Ring me on my mobile as soon as you can. I'm having a lovely lunch overlooking Hyde Park and have a question for you. 'Bye, 'bye." She snapped her phone shut, put it back in her bag and motioned to the waiter for another glass of wine.

After they had finished slices of a light lemon tart capped with perfect strawberries, the kind that are hard to find anywhere during the winter months, Sarah suggested that they withdraw to her study for coffee.

"This is my private space," she said, although anyone who knew her would not need to be told. It reminded Elspeth of the many libraries in the homes of her family's wealthier friends in Scotland—in comfortable disarray. Sarah had made no attempt to organize her projects, which were scattered around the room. "My darkroom is through there, although with digital photography I use it less and less and use my computer more and more. Do you do photography, Victoria?"

Victoria seemed less comfortable in this room than in the sitting room. Elspeth presumed Victoria did very little that was either productive or artistic.

"I leave picture taking to my husband, that is when he can get away from his business. He's so busy all the time." Conversation languished as coffee was served. Victoria added a substantial amount of cream and sugar to her cup and stirred it noisily.

To fill the void, Elspeth began talking about Australia. "Did you say Mary Anne and Edward Berkeley went out to Australia? To Sydney or to Tasmania?"

"Melbourne or Sydney, I don't remember which. Edward hated the countryside, as I remember, so I'm sure they wouldn't have gone to a place like Tasmania."

"Did they take Maudy with them?"

"Maudy?"

"Their daughter."

"Oh, you mean Mathilda. What a charming child. She was so excited about going to Australia and taking her first plane trip. She said one day she would be a world famous aviatrix, like Amelia Earhart, and fly all over the world."

Sarah joined in. "Did she? I mean become a pilot?" Sarah asked.

"I have no idea. I believe Mathilda stayed out in Australia with her mother when Edward returned here." Victoria by now had gained momentum. "Such a sad thing, the Berkeley's' divorce. Like you, Elspeth, Mary Anne never seemed to recover from Malcolm's death, or so Robbie said. He blamed the Berkeley's divorce on the murder. Isn't it amazing what a long-time effect the murder has had? I doubt we would be having lunch together today if it hadn't happened."

Elspeth agreed but did not say so. After getting the information she needed, she hoped never to see Victoria's elephantine body again.

"I suppose not," Elspeth said. "How different our worlds have become since Girton." She preferred not to take the comparison any further and turned to Sarah. "Will you show Victoria some of your work?"

They were looking through one of Sarah's portfolios when Victoria's gold bag let off saccharine musical tones. She had some difficulty leaning over and extracting her phone.

"Robbie. How delightful of you to ring back. I'm here with Lady Sarah Brixton, you know the tycoon Clyde Brixton's wife, having a delicious lunch in their Park Lane flat. Tenth floor and the view! I have a favor to ask. Do you know where Edward Berkeley is these days?"

After a silence, Victoria spoke again. "Another guest here is Elspeth Duff, who was a great friend of mine at Girton. She was Malcolm Buchanan's fiancée. She is trying to contact Edward Berkeley. I told her she might talk with you, or you could provide her with a number or an email address for him."

Another pause. "Let me put her on the line."

Elspeth motioned to Sarah to give her something on which to write. Carefully she took down the number that Robbie Smythe-Welton gave her.

A receptionist answered when Elspeth rang the number Victoria's brother had given to her. Elspeth recognized the name as that of an international brokerage firm of some renown.

"May I tell him who is calling?"

"My name is Elspeth Duff, D-U-double F. Robert Smythe-Welton recommended Mr. Berkeley to me. It has to do with Mary Anne."

After several moments delay Edward Berkeley came on the line. His voice was warm. "Hello, Elspeth. I remember you from the past, Malcolm and Mary Anne's past."

"You have a good memory, Mr. Berkeley."

"Edward."

"All right. Edward."

"Do you believe thoughts cross the airwaves? I do. I was thinking of Mary Anne this morning and the whole situation around Malcolm's death."

His tone was unemotional. Elspeth wondered what he was feeling.

"May I come and see you? I'd like to talk in private," she said.

"Have you had lunch?" he asked.

Elspeth thought of the sumptuous repast Lady Sarah had given them and admitted she had eaten.

"If you haven't eaten, may I join you at lunch and have a coffee instead? Drinking coffee all the time is a terrible habit I acquired in California during all the years I lived there," Elspeth said.

"A habit we all have these days. Can you meet me in my office in the City in the next hour?" He gave the address.

"Depending on traffic, I'll be there as soon as I can. Better still, I'll take the tube, much as I hate it."

Edward Berkeley's office was much less opulent than Lord Kennington's but the view was as good, which made Elspeth think Edward was well established in his firm. The coffee in the firm's dining room was up to Kennington hotel standards. She did not dilute it in the fashion of Victoria Brewer.

After the polite words that precede any serious discussion, Edward came directly to the point. "You have come looking for information about Malcolm, haven't you?"

"Yes, how perceptive of you. It's taken over a third of a century for me to face reality, but, yes, I've come to find out what happened to Malcolm and to Mary Anne."

"Mary Anne never recovered from Malcolm's death, you know. It haunted her to the point of obsession, and it finally ruined our marriage. After Malcolm died, she went out to Australia, taking our daughter Maudy with her. Did you know her parents died out there shortly before Malcolm was murdered?"

Elspeth nodded. "I've just learned that." She did not mention that she had gone to Tasmania or what she had discovered there.

Edward Berkeley continued. "Mary Anne spent six months out there and finally wrote saying she didn't want to come back to London. I loved her very much, and so I agreed to go out to Sydney. Our firm has a branch out there, which meant I was able to carry on with my job, but it didn't work in the end. Mary Anne became moody and distracted. Before Malcolm's death, she was so full of life, interested in the arts and all sorts of civic activities, but her life after the death narrowed and revolved only around Maudy and me. We couldn't have more children, so our one child was precious." Edward's voice broke. He looked down at his sandwich and adjusted the location of a perfectly placed gherkin beside it.

Elspeth looked away, not wanting to embarrass him. She waited as he gained his composure. She never had considered Mary Anne's husband before, but the man before her was handsome, kind, and feeling, and it struck Elspeth he was not the sort of man a woman would abandon.

Edward quickly recovered his composure. "I don't think of that part of my life often. I have another family now, who are bright and cheerful and fill me with so many good things that the grief of those days has mostly faded away." He put his sandwich aside and wiped his carefully barbered mustache. "Am I getting maudlin?"

Elspeth smiled at him and shook her head. "My own life has been full, and I have two wonderful children and twin grandsons, but, like Mary Anne and you, I've never been able to put Malcolm completely out of my mind. Do you think the Buchanans had some strange power that still afflicts us all?"

It was Edward's turn to smile. "Perhaps."

"Edward, do you stay in touch with Mathilda?"

He looked perplexed. "With whom?"

"Mathilda. Maudy."

"Maudy wasn't Mathilda. What made you think that? She was named Mary Anne after my wife, but we called her Maudy after a silly nursery peek-a-boo game we played with her. "Lawdy, lawdy, where is Maudy?" I haven't thought of that in years.

Elspeth lowered an eyebrow in a half frown, thinking of Victoria's insistence that Maudy was Mathilda. "How old was Maudy when Mary Anne and she went to Australia?"

"Let me see, she would have been not yet two."

Elspeth sipped her coffee slowly. "Do you see her often?"

Edward's face saddened. "When I remarried, Mary Anne cut me off completely and would not tell Maudy where I was. I had no contact with either one of them until Mary Anne died. At that time I had a call from Sydney, from Mary Anne's lawyer, telling me of her death. I asked about Maudy. The lawyer told me she had inherited everything from Mary Anne, but there really was very little other than family papers and memorabilia. I asked where Maudy was, but he would not tell me. I gave him my address and told him I would love to be in touch with her and I still considered Maudy to be a part of my family."

"Did she get in touch?"

"I'm forever optimistic, and therefore will say not yet." Grief returned to his face. "I think you're right. The Buchanan family continues to inflict pain even now. Although she may not want to accept it at this point, I just hope that one day Maudy will want to know about her father and come back to me." His face contorted, and he looked away. "Let me pour you some more coffee," he said.

20

Elspeth stood in the garden of Magdelena Cassar's home on Gozo, wrapped her exquisitely cut tweed overcoat more securely around herself and tamed her soft cashmere scarf. The rain had stopped shortly before she had stepped from the guest sitting room. The wind caught her hair, and the coolness of the air energized her. She looked lovingly around the garden. The caring hands of Giulio, Magdelena's houseman and gardener, had prepared the garden for winter. The flowerbeds were covered with straw, and the roses carefully deadheaded. One rosebush had produced two small white blooms, which Giulio had not removed. Their presence touched Elspeth with their persistence in blooming so late in the season. The vines on the enclosing walls were pruned back and the dry leaves except for a few stragglers had been removed. Elspeth had spent many hours of her life in this garden, at all seasons of the year, and it remained a special place for her. She had thought carefully before asking Richard to meet her here, and how best to guard herself from feelings that had grown in her over the last eight months at the times when she knew she would be with him. She also knew she continued to need Richard's help, and this would be the most private place in Malta to meet. His feelings were as apparent to her as it seemed they were to the rest of world, but he had never voiced them, other than to say he had selfish motives. She thought she knew what they were but was not ready to answer him if he spoke more clearly. This left her on unstable ground. Physically and emotionally she wanted to love him; intellectually she knew no way of doing so that would work for her. Perhaps she was using the search for Malcolm as an excuse to mask her indecision.

Her thoughts were interrupted by the opening of the French doors from the sitting room into the garden. At first she did not turn, but she knew Richard was standing there. His footsteps sounded on the gravel path as he approached.

"Elspeth," he said softly.

She turned and looked up at him. He stood eight inches taller than she, and, because she was wearing flat shoes, he towered over her. She made no bodily gesture to welcome him, fearing it might become too intimate, but instead smiled and said, "Thank you for coming, Dickie. Let's go inside. The wind has come up."

He returned Elspeth's smile, but she could see disappointment in his eyes.

She had laid a fire in the sitting room earlier, and, after they hung up their coats, she asked him to light it. She busied herself with the electric kettle and tea things.

"I've set up the table by the fire," she said, "so that we can lay out your journal, and I can take notes. I hope that's all right."

"Of course," he said expressionlessly.

She made the tea and poured it out for them. He offered her the chair closest to the fire, which was at right angles to the other one there. By design, this gave her some distance from him and made avoiding his eyes possible. He brought a small bound book from his jacket pocket and put it between them but did not open it. She touched its cover and then pushed it away.

"Let me tell you what happened in London after we last talked," she said, hoping to conceal her sudden aversion to the journal. She related the details of the luncheon with Victoria and Sarah, leaving out nothing. Richard seemed amused at Elspeth's description of Victoria and said one day he hoped to meet Lady Sarah. Elspeth also told him about Edward Berkeley.

Now that their first awkward moments together had passed, Elspeth felt on safer ground.

"The remarkable thing is that Victoria told so many lies. Or were they only half-truths? I don't remember that she was deceitful when we were at Girton, but Jean Henderson seemed to think so. I was beginning to be afraid my memories were faulty and Jean may be right, worse luck. It seems I was more trusting then than I am now. But Victoria did find Edward Berkeley for me and through him I may discover where Maudy is."

Richard set his teacup on the table. "Do you think if you do find Maudy, she can be of help?" he asked.

"I hope she will be. She's Malcolm's only living blood relative as far as I know," Elspeth said, fearful that even this lead might go cold. "Now, Dickie, I suppose you must show me your journal. Will it hurt?" she said with a wince.

He could not have missed her expression, but his face remained blank. "I think not. It's a straightforward recording of fact, nothing more. Met with so and so, no substantial new information, that sort of thing. I wish now I'd recorded more, because 'no substantial information' might now be substantial."

"I think I'm ready to read it; although I'm not completely sure I want to. It's easier looking for Maudy than facing those days after Malcolm died."

His eyes sought hers, but she evaded them and looked down at the book.

"Elspeth, let's read it together," he said. "You may not be able to read my scribble."

She touched the book and turned away from it again. With Richard next to her, could she keep her balance? She could create a physical distance between them but could she maintain a passionless one? Would Richard scold her again about her feelings for Malcolm? Or, would he become diplomatically polite, which she liked less because it could so coldly imply disapproval. Worse, would he look at her with the intensity of his hazel-green eyes, begging for some emotional feeling from her? She did not know how to anticipate his responses to her or prepare herself to deflect them. Yet she had come to Malta with the intention of seeing the journal, and now there was no turning back. She took it up and turned to the first page.

> I am recording these incidences because I believe that one day Elspeth will want to know what happened after she fled to Scotland. When she rang me after the murder, I knew she couldn't handle any more pain than Malcolm's death has already caused her. Therefore I have started this journal in case she ever wants to know what happened in Cambridge after she left.

Richard's handwriting was small and neat and, so far, decipherable. The next passages became more abbreviated.

> 21st May. Returned on train from Pitlochry after turning E over to her father. Met Insp Llewellyn at police station afterwards, introduced self. Some

*resistance. Explained family connections. Said I
was a confident of E's family, which seemed to
relax Insp L. At his request we started interviewed
G students.*

"G is Girton, L is Llewellyn and is E me?" she asked.
Richard nodded.

*Most know nothing. Victoria Smythe-Welton gushed
but added little. Jean SU implicated she knew more.*

"SU?"

"Surname unknown."

"That would be Jean Henderson. I'm glad you are here,
Dickie. How could I read this otherwise?"

"I planned it that way."

"What do you mean?"

"Writing in such a cryptic way thus giving me a chance
to sit near you thirty-five years later and interpret what I had
written." His voice was teasing.

"Oh, do be serious, Dickie." Elspeth's words were filled
with pleasure not annoyance, and then she regretted them.

*Insp L being assisted by chap named Tony Ketcham
from Scotland Yard. Not sure why he is involved but
seems pleasant enough. Said he had broken news to
E. Appt with MB's tutor, John Chisholm, this aft on
my own at L's request. JC knew nothing about MB's
death until police contacted him the next morn'g.
Surprised. MB hard at work on his thesis and promised
JC a discovery of significance. JC respected MB's*

*intelligence but hoped his enthusiasm didn't lead him
into sloppy academics. JC last saw MB the aft of his
death. Asked JC earlier if MB had a gun. JC thought
not. MB hated violence according to JC.*

Richard was sitting close enough to Elspeth to be able to
read along with her and therefore followed her next thought.

"He did hate war passionately," she said. "He railed
against the conflict in Vietnam and sympathized with the
protestors. We went to several rallies, which were serious
but also great fun, as we all went marching along, feeling
virtuous, singing loudly, and assuming our efforts would
have world repercussions."

"I never went to a rally."

Elspeth was surprised not at his words but at the regret
in them.

"I was so new at the FCO then that I didn't want to
espouse publicly any political views, particularly on a
matters of foreign policy. My friends from Oxford seemed to
understand, but I avoided any divisive discussion with my
colleagues at the FCO. Other new recruits were more vocal,
and they were given assignments in areas of the world far
from the conflict. I wanted to go to the Far East, as we called
it then, and kept my opinions to myself. I believe this led to
getting my first posting to Rangoon."

Elspeth tried not to think of Richard in Rangoon with
Lady Marjorie, as Elspeth knew they were married shortly
before Richard's posting there. What had life been like for
Richard and Marjorie in Burma? Had they been happy after
their wedding? Elspeth put away the thought and went back
to the journal.

"How old was John Chisholm?" she asked, trying to keep her mind steady.

"Probably in his early forties."

"Which would make him in his mid-seventies now. I suppose there's no hope of his still being at King's, but I wonder if he could be found."

"Could Jean Henderson help?"

"I'll ring her later and find out if there is a directory of tutors emeriti at the various colleges."

Elspeth picked up the journal again.

24th May. Several long days in London after my absence but went back in Cambridge this aft and found Insp L at the police station pouring over some notes. Nothing here, he complained, other than ballistics. Soviet automatic pistol, vintage, used in WW2 and during Chinese and other communist revolutions from late '40s into the '60s. Gun not found. During week Insp L interview'd some of the students at King's who had no further information.

Went around to Ming Palace, haunt of MB and his friends. Owners knew MB but could offer no info on murder. Waiters and cooks had nothing to add. All liked MB but said he liked the girls, particularly one toward the end—probably E. Insp L has appt with MABB on Mon. Asked to go with him. Will ring FCO to say I am ill. Won't add ill with concern for E.

"Dickie, what was that about?" she said raising an eyebrow and grinning, although she suspected she knew the answer.

He smiled at her but did not reply directly. "I think that is one of the rare times I lied to the FCO. I'd forgotten I did so. Thinking back, I'm amazed Llewellyn agreed for me to come along. Perhaps he wanted some 'gown versus town' reinforcement. He was a bit shy about his Welsh accent and painfully proper with the students, fellows, and other academics."

Elspeth could hear Richard's admiration for the policeman, something she felt as well after the interview in Hampshire.

> *26th May. Accompanied L to MABB's Chelsea flat. Quite fashionable. MABB appeared closed down and was upset when the murder was brought up. Indicated she knew nothing about a reason for murder or gun. When asked if any family reasons for the murder, she offered nothing. Insp L says he was taught that most murders were family affairs, but no evidence that is true here. MA said she was MB's only living relative, other than her daughter, and asked to be left alone in the future.*

Elspeth turned to Richard with concern. "Do you remember anything more about Mary Anne? Except for Lesley Urquhart's dinner with her and Edward Berkeley's description of family events in London and Sydney, Mary Anne seems amorphous."

"Mary Anne is not a person one forgets easily with her flaming red hair and pale, piercing blue eyes. Under different circumstances, one would have expected fire, intensity and passion."

"Like Malcolm," Elspeth said without thinking.

"From what you say, yes," Richard said dryly. Elspeth felt him withdraw slightly.

"What did Edward tell you about her?" he asked. "Was it that before the murder she was involved with the community as well as with her family, but all that changed afterwards? Certainly when Llewellyn and I interviewed her, it was as if she was making the motions of being alive, but life wasn't real for her anymore. Have you ever known anyone who felt like that?"

Elspeth remembered the days after Malcolm's death. "Yes," she said without explaining further. "Edward said she never recovered. That has to be unusual. We all recover enough to go on in the end." Elspeth was speaking about herself. Would Richard understand?

"During your interview with her, did she say anything about her parents' murders?" Elspeth asked. "In Hampshire, Inspector Llewellyn told me she simply mentioned they were dead. Malcolm did not tell me this."

"As I recall, Llewellyn didn't question her about her parents, but I did. You said Malcolm never spoke of his parents. I felt that if they were alive, they might be a comfort to you."

Elspeth suddenly was engulfed in a sea of deep sadness. Her own parents gave her so much love, but she felt Malcolm and Mary Anne's parents had not done the same for their children, nor would they have done so for her if they had been alive.

The next passage she read aloud.

> *30th May. Went down to Cambridge but Insp L not available. Went to see John Chisholm again. He greeted me sadly, saying the loss of Malcolm had put a pall on the college. Discussed Malcolm and his work. JC reiterated MB's brilliance, but also said he was uneasy*

about MB's lack of scholastic rigor. His words as closely as I can remember: 'Malcolm wanted to make a splash with his thesis. He thought it would assure him a place in the academic or museum world without the painstaking hours of research we all must go through. Malcolm was more impatient than most aspiring art historians. He also thought he could make money more readily than any of the others could. Before he died, I talked with him quite seriously about authentication, but he only laughed. "I'll surprise you all," he said.' I asked JC if Malcolm had been more specific. JC said Malcolm bragged he would unearth a stolen piece of Chinese art that would astound the world but won't say anything more about what it was. MB said it would make him rich and famous and then he would marry the love of his life. E may be pleased with that remark but I find it untenable.

She turned to Richard. "Dickie, why did you dislike Malcolm so? Your entry here exudes antipathy."

Richard looked back at her with challenging eyes. "From all you have said to me, I suspect you're beginning to see sides of Malcolm that weren't apparent to you when you were a student. I wanted you to see them, but you never believed me. You have a proclivity toward resisting the truth about Malcolm, Elspeth, even now."

The remark stung her. "I loved him, Dickie," she said defiantly. "I wanted to marry him and be a part of his whirlwind, crazy, high-flying intelligence. Every moment with him was an adventure. I've never met anyone like that before—or since for that matter." Elspeth blurted this out, knowing it might hurt Richard.

He did not reply, although his face tightened.

Regretting what she had said, she rose from the table. "I'm so sorry, Dickie. Let's not go into all that again. Will you have more tea?"

She switched on the electric kettle, waited for it to boil and refilled the teapot.

The moment passed, but the tension did not fully dissipate. Elspeth found her seat again and went back to the journal. "When you were interviewing John Chisholm, did you ask him anything else? I know you recorded the gist here, but it was a long time ago. Can you remember any more now?"

Richard covered Elspeth's hand as if in forgiveness. His touch was loving, which unsettled her further. "Memories are more impressions than actuality," he said. "You've always known I didn't like your relationship with Malcolm, but even now I can feel the magic of your feelings towards him. It wouldn't have lasted, Elspeth. Nothing that rarified ever does."

Elspeth withdrew her hand and steadied her voice. "Did John Chisholm say anything else?"

"He did, but I need to put it in context. In light of his murder, Malcolm's scholastic practices seemed irrelevant, but I've often thought of my conversation with John Chisholm. Malcolm wanted to dazzle him in the same way he dazzled you. Chisholm spoke of a change in Malcolm during the first part of the year, nineteen sixty-nine that is. Around that time Malcolm began to boast about this lost piece of art. Chisholm didn't specify exactly when 'the first part of the year' was, but I now wondered if there was any connection to Malcolm's parents' deaths. Did you ever read his thesis? It was supposed to contain this surprise," Richard said.

Elspeth shook her head. "Isn't that curious? I never did. Malcolm only spoke generally about his thesis, waxing eloquently about his passion for the topic of historical art theft, but I never read any of his drafts. He must have written a great deal of the thesis if his tutor had such despairing comments about it." Elspeth bit her lip and frowned. "Did Inspector Llewellyn tell you how Malcolm's personal effects were disposed of?" she asked. "I wonder where his research notes and draft thesis went?"

Richard confessed his lack of knowledge. "One can only assume Mary Anne took them, but I don't know. We were so focused on finding the killer or killers that things like his effects seemed unimportant. Llewellyn might know."

Elspeth sat silently, trying to understand the importance of what Richard had just told her. Could Malcolm's thesis and his parents' deaths be connected? Confusion and then revulsion toward the truth flooded her. She hoped it did not show. As neutrally as she could manage, she said, "Leslie Urquhart mentioned something about a key. What was that?" She took out her portfolio of notes, which she had left on the table, and shuffled through them. She read the ones recounting Lesley Urquhart's narrative.

> Mary Anne visited her parents, and her father drew her aside admonishing her to not let 'them' get the key, that it was a secret and worth a great deal of money and possibly someone's life. Mary Anne's mother dismissed this as being the ravings of an old man but was frightened, pleading with Mary Anne to leave it alone.

"Didn't Lesley tell you that Mary Anne made a great deal of fuss about getting her parents' personal effects?" Richard asked.

Elspeth had already made the connection. "I think we can assume the 'key' was among those effects. If only we could find it." For the first time that afternoon she felt energized.

Richard picked up her excitement. "You told me Malcolm visited his sister at Christmas. Would she have told him about the key at that time?"

Elspeth rubbed her fingers on her temples and frowned, as she often did when piecing things together. "I've no idea, but could the key have something to do with the lost piece of art and Malcolm's purported startling revelation to the art world? That would imply that the 'key' gave access to the artwork in some way. Dickie, I think we are on to something. What kind of key do you suppose it was: a code, or a key to a safety deposit box, or a locked closet, or a journal with information in it? There must be a way to find out. Give me time to work it out," Elspeth said. She rose and began to pace.

Richard's eyes followed her, although she could not guess what he was feeling.

He said, "Edward Berkeley mentioned a lawyer in Australia. Did he give you the name and address?"

"No, but I'm sure I could ask. Let me phone him now." Elspeth retrieved her mobile from her shoulder bag, which was hooked over a chair nearby. She called Edward's number and got a receptionist. "Tell him Elspeth Duff rang, and that I'll try later. I can be reached on my mobile." She gave the number. Two minutes later her phone rang. Edward Berkeley was returning her call.

"Edward, I'm sorry to disturb you again. I have a favor to ask."

The voice on the other end of the line was warm. "Ask away. Your visit brought back so many old haunting memories that I decided to try once again to find my daughter—Maudy, now called Mary Anne. I rang the lawyer in Sydney. He was guarded at first but did confirm that he'd kept in touch with Maudy. He said he'd let her know that I was trying to reach her. I told him about your possible interest, which I hope is all right with you. He said he'd tell Maudy, but he gave no indication of where she was or how frequently they had any communication."

Elspeth was pleased to have Edward as an ally. "I think, Edward, this means we're not totally cut off. I'm going out to Singapore next week on other business, but I can go on to Sydney to meet the lawyer. I don't know what I'll find out, but I'll keep in touch with you."

Edward Berkeley thanked her profusely. "Here's the lawyer's name and address. Shall I tell him you're coming?"

"You could mention it, but I don't yet know my schedule or how long I'll be detained in Singapore. Better yet, I think I'll go to Sydney first and then double back to Singapore. I'm supposed to be on leave from my job, but my employer is badgering me to do a bit of work for him in Singapore. Since I'm giving in to his demands, I can take a few days off for personal reasons beforehand."

"Is Lord Kennington such a hard task master?"

"How do you know I work for him?"

"The internet reveals many things, although unfortunately not the location of my daughter. Be in touch, Elspeth. Here's my private email address."

After her phone call, Elspeth returned to Richard. The wheels of her mind were turning rapidly. "Dickie, if I can speak to Maudy, I think we can find out about the key, particularly if the key is a physical thing. Do you think she would talk to me?"

He looked into her eyes for a long time and then smiled sadly. "Over the years, I've had to deal with people who have disappeared and are sought by their relatives," he said. "Such situations are complicated not because the people are untraceable but because people often want to disappear. Maudy seems to be this type. We've no idea what her mother told her about her father or what type of atmosphere she grew up in."

Elspeth sat back down alongside Richard and without thinking took his hand in hers. She did it as a gesture of thanks, but his caressing response filled her with physical warmth, which she had not anticipated.

"Shall we get back to the journal?" she asked, letting go of his hand as if she had been burnt.

He stiffened. "I thought I'd written a great deal more. I see there are only a few more notes. Let's get back to them."

The remaining notes recorded weekly updates from Llewellyn, who told of his continual failures.

The last entry read:

> Insp L becomes more and more frustrated each week. He tried to find out more about Mary Anne, but she left abruptly for Australia. There was nothing new about Malcolm's family. Finally his superiors made him declare the case closed. It was a great blow to him because he'd never been in charge of a murder investigation before.
>
> I contacted him about a year later and he told me that, although he was officially off the case, he occasionally made inquiries on his own time but had turned up nothing new.

"And thus endeth the reading," Elspeth said as she turned over the last page and shut the cover. She felt deflated. "We need to know so much more." She looked up at him but found his distant look had returned. Elspeth felt reading the journal had done more harm than good between them. She regretted she had been so outspoken about her love for Malcolm. She saw she had hurt Richard, but she did not withdraw her statement.

*

As Richard piloted his yacht back to its mooring in Ta'Xbiex in Malta that evening, he cursed Elspeth. "Damn you, Elspeth, damn you! You have such a handsome and sophisticated manner and such a fine mind, but why do you have such a willful nature and uncertain heart? And why, with all your infuriating ways, do I love you more than anyone else in the world? You erect such high barricades between us and don't recognize what's right in front of your face. There are other women who would have me in an instant, but I only want you."

Despite their delicious dinner together with Magdelena Cassar, he was miserable. Elspeth and he parted with distinct coldness, and he had no idea how to put things right.

21

As soon as she was back in her flat in London Elspeth rang Pamela Crumm. Pamela answered her private line almost before it rang.

"Elspeth, m'friend, have you found him?" Pamela said without saying hello.

"Found whom?"

"Malcolm's murderer, of course. Who else?"

"Not yet, but I'm determined I will," Elspeth said. "I have a favor to ask. If Eric wants me to keep doing jobs for him while I am on leave, I need something in return."

On the plane back from Malta, Elspeth had devised a plan she thought might work if she were to find Maudy, but first she needed the help of the Kennington Organisation.

From Pamela's reply Elspeth knew Lord Kennington had departed for the day. "I can try to shame him into it, if you like, but it may be hard. He's already given you a first class ticket to Singapore and free lodging and use of your expense account there. I'll approach him in the morning after he settles his latest arrangements at the hotel in Bruges. He should be in an excellent mood, since things are going well there so far. Now tell me what you want. I hope it isn't outrageous."

"I want two rooms at the Kennington Sydney. I can't say for how long or exactly when. I also want lunch reservations at the Kennington Mayfair for tomorrow or the next day, and I want Eric to pick up the tab."

"Are Sir Richard and you. . ."

Elspeth growled. She had not parted with Richard Munro on the best of terms. The ill feelings that rose between them when they looked at his journal disconcerted her. Afterwards they had dinner with Magdelena Cassar, who attempted to cheer them but did not. Richard left shortly after the meal was finished and cried off from listening to Magdelena play the Chopin prelude she promised him. He was polite when departing but made no gesture toward Elspeth. Elspeth listened to the Chopin, which she had heard many times before, but was unaware when Magdelena had stopped halfway through.

Elspeth's mind came back to London. "Pamela, stop pairing Richard and me. We are not an item. I'm trying to contact a lawyer in Sydney who may be able to put me in contact with Malcolm's niece. I may need the help of Malcolm's brother-in-law, her father. He's here in London now. I want to have lunch with him at the Mayfair hotel and give him some incentive to go out to Australia with me," she said. "Surely Eric cannot deny me this?"

"Leave it to me, ducks. He's lathering all over himself to have you back at work. I'll call you in the morning."

Could Elspeth really convince Edward to go with her to Sydney? She was not certain, but over the course of years she had developed persuasive ways few could resist. She planned to use every trick in her power to convince Edward. After some thought, she decided to dress in her most professional clothes, ones that she normally wore when working with the "very important people" who passed through the Kennington hotels. The dignity with which she wore these clothes and the manner she assumed while wearing them always impressed those around her, and she knew how to play this to her advantage. She hoped Edward Berkeley would not be immune.

Elspeth entered the hotel and sighed inwardly. She was back in her own milieu, and it made her feel competent and respected. Here she was not vulnerable to emotions she could not control. It crossed her mind that she could stop her search for Malcolm's murderer, turn away from Richard Munro and all the emotions he stirred in her and continue her career at the Kennington Organisation unencumbered. That would be the easy choice. Had she gone too far down the road of discovery to turn back? Would retreating now to where she was a year ago actually bring contentment? She could not answer those questions.

The manager of the Kennington Mayfair, with whom she had worked many times, welcomed Elspeth and thanked her for her past services to the hotel. Several of the staff greeted her as well. Two of the guests turned and acknowledged her presence. She recognized them with a nod and knew she had discovered secrets about them they were glad had gone no further. The manager confirmed Lord Kennington's office had arranged for the luncheon at the hotel's expense. Assuming Edward was busy at work, Elspeth asked the meal be served as quickly as the usual Kennington service would allow and acquiesced to the menu Pamela had chosen.

Several heads turned as Edward and she crossed the dining room to a secluded corner, and Elspeth knew she was already creating the right impression. She sat across from Edward and could see admiration in his eyes. Knowing her intense blue eyes could be arresting, she looked at him and smiled.

"You must wonder why I asked you here today," she said.

"I assume it has to do with Mary Anne and Malcolm," he said with a sad half grin.

"Yes, with both, but mainly with Mary Anne. Do you mind, Edward?"

His eyes met hers. "How could I deny you while you are providing me with such an excellent lunch?"

From his expression, she knew her tactics were working.

"As you know, I'll be going out to Sydney shortly," she said. "Will you join me there and help me find your daughter?"

Edward laughed. "You are direct, Elspeth."

"On many occasions I find directness works best," she said with an intentional smile. "You don't need to commit to the trip immediately. I'll approach Mary Anne's lawyer on my own, if necessary."

"Let me give it some thought," he said. "But why the interest in my daughter?"

"Because she might have a vital piece of information that will help me find Malcolm's murderer. If I find her, you may want to know where she is, and why she turned against you."

"I would like to know above all else and also to reconnect with her. Let me think about what you propose. I might be able to fly out over the New Year's weekend, or better still find some excuse to go to Sydney on business. When do you leave?"

"I leave London on Tuesday, arriving in Singapore on Wednesday, but my business there is loosely defined, and I can change my schedule to meet your convenience. Besides, I have arranged with Lord Kennington to offer you, at his expense, a room in the new Kennington Sydney."

"Does your job always give you these perks?"

Elspeth cocked an eyebrow, knowing the effect it usually had. "Only when he has asked me to do something he knows steps beyond the usual scope of my employment." She twinkled her eyes, and he laughed again.

"Elspeth, I'm sure you're very good at your job."

"Eric Kennington thinks so, and I try to keep it that way."

As they progressed through their meal, Elspeth once again broached the topic of Mary Anne.

"Edward, do you know much about Malcolm and Mary Anne's early years in Malaya?"

He stopped with his fork in midair.

"How do you know about that?" he asked. "She never talked about it. Did Malcolm?"

Elspeth shook her head. "The policeman in charge of the investigation into Malcolm's murder told me about it when I went to see him several weeks ago. I've spoken with several other people since then who confirmed it. And, no, Malcolm only mentioned he had been a boy in a hot climate. I never knew about his being in Malaya until Chief Inspector Llewellyn mentioned it."

Edward slowly wiped the corners of his mouth with his heavy linen napkin. "Something terrible happened when Mary Anne and Malcolm were young. I don't know what it was; Mary Anne would never say. Their mother brought them out of the jungle because of it."

"Do you know when that was?"

"In nineteen fifty-three, when Mary Anne was ten."

"Malcolm would have been eight. Did Mary Anne ever give a hint of what the problem was?"

Edward frowned as he answered. "I think it had to do with Malcolm. Something he did."

"What could a child of eight do that would cause his parents to send him away from them?"

"I have no idea. Mary Anne never told me other than that her mother shipped them to England to become 'civilized,' as Mary Anne put it."

"Do you know anything about Mary Anne and Malcolm's parents."

"Very little. I never met them. I think they were in some sort of undercover work. Mary Anne had not seen them for a long time before she went out to Tasmania for Christmas in nineteen sixty-eight."

Shock went through Elspeth. "Went out to Tasmania at Christmas in nineteen sixty-eight? Are you sure?"

"Quite sure. Maudy was only a year old, and Mary Anne said it would be the last time at Christmas she could leave Maudy. She said her father was ill, and she wanted to see him in case anything happened to him."

"Malcolm was not with you at Christmas?" Elspeth's voice was more constricted than she liked.

"No, whatever gave you that idea?"

Elspeth was not ready to tell Edward Berkeley that Malcolm had lied to her about his whereabouts that Christmas. "Did Malcolm go to Tasmania as well?" she asked instead.

"Not that I know of. Mary Anne did not say so."

"Might he have?"

"He might have, but I doubt it. Malcolm and Mary Anne were on uncomfortable terms then. I think his attachment to you made things worse."

"But why?"

"Because Mary Anne knew things about Malcolm she wouldn't share with anyone, even me. She only said he had a dark side that no one as fine as you should be exposed to."

Elspeth was taken aback and hoped Edward would not see it in her face, but he apparently had.

"Elspeth, the Buchanan family had secrets that you and I will never comprehend. You should let them lie."

Elspeth knew she could not, despite the seductiveness of letting her investigation into Malcolm's murder go, dismissing Richard from her life, and getting on with her career.

"Consider my offer, Edward, about Sydney."

"I will," he said. "I'd like to find out where Maudy is and who she has become."

Edward got in touch the next day. "Elspeth, please meet with Mary Anne's lawyer on my behalf as well as yours, and, if Maudy is receptive to meeting me, I'll come to Sydney," he said.

22

"Sarah, when are you booked to go to Singapore?" Elspeth said into her phone.

She forgot to identify herself in her haste to make arrangements to get to Sydney and back to Singapore before Sarah Brixton arrived. Pamela told Elspeth that Lord Kennington was sending Sarah to Singapore to help Elspeth, and her arrival would coincide with Elspeth's.

"Good evening, Elspeth," was the stoic response.

"I'm dreadfully sorry, I didn't introduce myself, did I? I'm rather in a rush."

Elspeth looked at her watch and saw it was well past nine in the evening.

"Luckily the butler told me who was on the line, although I'm quite good at voices." Sarah began to laugh. "Pamela Crumm has scheduled me for an afternoon flight a week or so after Boxing Day. On Tuesday I think, arriving in Singapore on Wednesday."

"Thank goodness, I think it will work."

"Elspeth, you must be clearer. What will work?"

"My side trip to Sydney."

"But you just got back from Australia."

"Yes, I know, but something new has turned up. Victoria Brewer talked a lot of self-aggrandizing rubbish at the lunch we had together, but she did get me in touch with Malcolm's brother-in-law, and he gave me the name of Mary Anne and her daughter's lawyer in Sydney."

Sarah sounded puzzled. "Is it so important that you can't let it wait until we both are done in Singapore?"

"I'm not sure how long we'll be in Singapore, and I feel I am so close to finding out something important that I don't want to wait. I'll see you on Wednesday next and will fill you in. Let's hope Morris Aldridge, the lawyer, doesn't take the Christmas holidays too seriously."

Ensconced comfortably in her first class seat to Singapore, and avoiding the often proffered alcoholic drinks, which she knew would cause jet lag, Elspeth thought back to the conversation that had taken place on her last day in Gozo. Richard's polite withdrawal still distressed her. Although he had sent a card, they had not spoken at Christmas, which saddened her despite the fact she had not told him where she would be. He had her mobile number. She suspected either he must be in Scotland with his brother's family or he had stayed in Malta, but she did not call him. Even now he continued to express his disapproval of her relationship with Malcolm and the effect it was having on her. Yet it was he who had encouraged her to go back and solve the case of Malcolm's murder. Did Richard think by always casting doubt on Malcolm's character he could turn her against Malcolm? This seemed absurd. Malcolm had been dead for thirty-five years. What right did Richard have to pass judgment then or now?

Before Elspeth left Gozo, Magdelena Cassar took Elspeth aside and put her strong arms around her in a gesture that was as old as their long and loving relationship. "Listen to Richard. He's a wise person," Aunt Mag said. "He speaks from both his head and his heart."

A Secret in Singapore

Damn and blast! Elspeth shouted inwardly. She did not need these complications any more.

During her years of employment with the Kennington Organisation, Elspeth had learned to get herself to sleep on long flights by thinking of fond memories, but that ability eluded her on the flight to Singapore. She tried to mesmerize herself by thinking of her Christmas at Lizzie and Denis's home in East Sussex and her infant twin grandsons, but she had been distracted by her own thoughts throughout the holidays. A man near her breathed heavily in his sleep, which annoyed her. Earlier she had avoided his attempts at conversation during dinner, and he had turned to his book and double whiskies instead. Elspeth's uncharacteristic self-pity irritated her as well.

Elspeth nodded off, but her dreams were uneasy. She was thankful for the dark eyeshades, but activity in the cabin only allowed her a few hours of fitful rest. When she finally gave up trying to sleep, rummaged through her hand luggage and found her notes.

In her longing for Malcolm over all these years, she had never considered what happened to his possessions after his death. Richard had speculated that Mary Anne took them. Mary Anne again. Lesley Urquhart told her Mary Anne died in late two thousand and two. She was buried in Tasmania with her parents and Ah-Ting, but where was Malcolm buried? Elspeth had never asked, although the question seemed an obvious one. Elspeth's parents had taught her the physical body meant nothing; the important thing was to keep a person's memory alive. It never crossed Elspeth's mind to ask where Malcolm's body was taken after his death or if there had been a funeral. She knew there was a post mortem, since both Richard and Inspector Llewellyn spoke about it and about the bullets that had killed Malcolm. The gun and shells were never found but the shape, type and individual characteristics of the bullets that killed Malcolm had been identified. Now it seemed unlikely the gun would ever be found. As Inspector Llewellyn said, the police had come to a dead end. Had she?

The steward offered her a choice of breakfasts, and she opted for the hearty Australian one. Suddenly she was hungry, and the tray with eggs, bacon, tomato, toast with butter and a selection of jams, fresh fruit and strong coffee seemed preferable to the one with French pastries and freshly squeezed orange juice. She declined champagne.

She considered the two options open to her. When she reached Sydney, she would try to find Maudy. Edward Berkeley doubted Elspeth would be successful, but she was not deterred by his pessimism. Maudy might not want to see her father, but she might relent to seeing her maternal uncle's one-time fiancée, who would not make any demands on her other than asking about her mother and Malcolm's parents. James and Anna Maria Buchanan lived their lives in the shadows, but others must have been there too. This led Elspeth's thoughts to Malaya during the war. The fact that both Mary Anne and Malcolm were born before the end of the war suggested either James or Anna Maria were part of the resistance forces that lived in the jungles, or, conversely, they were collaborators—or even double agents. How could she find out more about this? Lesley Urquhart said that the files were still sealed.

Other British people must have been in the jungles with the resistance. How could she contact them? Any veterans of the war would now be well into old age. Had any of them remained in Malaysia or Singapore? Could she find them?

A Secret in Singapore

Clyde Brixton was involved in mining, and, if Elspeth remembered correctly, Malaysia was at one time one of the top tin mining nations in the world and might still be. Would Clyde have contacts there? Should she email Sarah on her arrival in Sydney and ask?

They landed in Singapore on schedule, and Elspeth had an hour before her connecting fight to Sydney. Since she was now on her own, she took her place in the queue for economy class and tucked into the inadequate seat, knowing the flight would only be bearable if she was mentally able to block out the discomfort it provided. This second leg of her journey was claustrophobic but uneventful.

Although she arrived without a fixed appointment in the week between Christmas and New Year's, Elspeth was shown immediately into Mary Anne's lawyer's office. When she met him, she knew why.

An aging man with a hooked nose and gray hair combed back from his forehead rose from behind a clean desk and extended his hand.

"Mrs. Duff, I am Morris Aldridge. I retired from this firm two years ago, but come in every now and then because these offices are as much a home to me as anywhere else on earth. I didn't expect anyone to come and ask for me this morning. You are most welcome. What brings you here?"

"My father is a semi-retired lawyer in Scotland, and he, like you, still goes into his office. On Tuesdays and Thursdays. He says it gives him more purpose in life than staying home to tend the garden, and I think my mother is grateful for that. I appreciate your being here today. I only have two days in Sydney, and I had hoped to find you. I know it's the Christmas holiday season."

Morris Aldridge winked. "Then I'll see if I can clear my calendar in order to help you. What is it that you want to see me about?"

Elspeth could see the appointment book that lay in front of him was empty.

"Do you remember Mary Anne Buchanan or Mary Anne Berkeley? I'm not sure what name she might have used when seeing you. Her husband, now ex-husband, gave me your name."

The lawyer cleared his throat but said nothing. Elspeth continued. "Edward Berkeley told me Mary Anne requested you withhold any information on their daughter."

The lawyer nodded slightly but still remained silent. Elspeth had seen her father use the same technique to draw out information from someone while he revealed nothing. Elspeth was always amused by this tactic.

She continued. "I'm not here to help Edward find his daughter, although he still would like to. I really came about Mary Anne."

"Why is that?"

"I'm trying to solve a murder that happened in nineteen sixty-nine."

"Who was the victim?"

"Malcolm Buchanan, Mary Anne's brother. He also was my fiancé."

"Surely you would do better to go to the police."

"I've talked to the police on two continents, including the now retired Detective Inspector Llewellyn of the Cambridge Constabulary and Police Commissioner Leonard Baines in Hobart. I've also contacted a former colleague at Scotland Yard, who was involved in the murder investigation. Let me give you his name in case you need to verify my credentials."

"Other than being Malcolm Buchanan's fiancée, will you tell me who you are?"

Elspeth told the lawyer of her position with the Kennington hotels but that she was in Sydney on personal business. He took out a legal pad and made notes. Elspeth noted his hand shook slightly as he wrote.

"I know Mary Anne died at the end of two thousand and two in Launceston, and she is buried in Tasmania," Elspeth said.

He showed surprised. "How did you learn that?"

"The British high commissioner in Canberra had one of his assistants help me trace Mary Anne."

"Are you friends with Sir Andrew?"

"He is a friend of a friend. I've not met him," Elspeth conceded.

"You seem to have contacts in high places."

Elspeth began to wonder if she had come to Sydney on a fool's errand. So far, only a slight nod acknowledged the old lawyer had represented Mary Anne, a fact Elspeth already knew.

"Tell me, Mrs. Duff, what it is that you are looking for?"

"I think there may be clues to Malcolm's murderer among his effects. I wondered if these effects might still be. . .I was about to say intact, but after all this time that seems improbable. Hopefully some of the items belonging to Malcolm might still exist. I suspect Malcolm's things would have been given to Mary Anne as his next of kin."

"What things in particular were you looking for?"

"Malcolm was doing his thesis at King's College at Cambridge University. He was quite far along in his writing. I'd hoped to find his research notes or even a draft of his thesis, which his tutor said existed. Malcolm told his tutor the thesis would reveal the whereabouts of a long lost piece of stolen art, which would make Malcolm quite famous in his field. No one I can find knows what happened to Malcolm's notes or thesis. It could reveal the location of the piece of art that may have direct bearing on Malcolm's murder."

"How was Malcolm killed?"

Elspeth explained.

"Mrs. Duff, do you really believe that Malcolm was murdered over a piece of art? That seems highly unlikely."

"I have no idea. Unless I know what the piece of art was, I can't rule out the possibility."

The old lawyer rose and came around his desk. Elspeth took this as a sign that she was being dismissed, and therefore she was surprised at his words.

"Come back this afternoon at four," he said without any other explanation. "Also leave a number where I can reach you."

At two that afternoon Elspeth was roused from a deep sleep by the wakeup call she had requested. After dressing, she went down to the dining room of the Kennington Sydney. Had it only been just weeks before that she first met Leslie Urquhart here? For lunch, although it did not feel like lunchtime to her, she ordered a sandwich and a strong coffee. The food and drink did little to invigorate her.

At half past three Morris Aldridge still had not called to cancel their appointment, which filled her with some hope. His offices were not far from the hotel, and she decided a walk through the Domain, the public gardens in the middle of Sydney, would refresh her. The summer sun was still high in the sky, but a cool breeze blew off the harbor. The scent of the flowers and trees overpowered the smells of the busy city traffic, and birds Elspeth had never seen before darted by her. She was glad when she reached her destination, however, because it was warmer than she first presumed. When she was shown into Morris Aldridge's office, he had chilled lemonade waiting for her.

Elspeth handed her hat to a secretary, shook out her hair and straightened her tailored summer skirt, crafted both for coolness and unwrinkled sophistication. She took the seat she had occupied that morning.

"I've just come from winter in London and Malta and was not prepared for either the sun or the heat," she explained, hoping she did not look too flushed after her walk.

"Ah, Malta. I've visited there several times and find it so ancient in contrast to the newness of European civilization here in Australia." The old lawyer's attitude had changed, and now his voice was relaxed. He offered the lemonade, which he poured over ice. She took a long swallow, glad of its coldness.

"You must forgive my distance this morning. I needed to make sure who you were," he explained after they were settled.

"I assumed you would."

"You're well vouched for, Mrs. Duff. I also needed to make another call, actually a more important one."

Elspeth's curiosity was aroused. "Oh? To whom?"

"To Mary Anne Buchanan's daughter."

"Then you have contact with her?"

"Yes," he said, but he did not elaborate. "I wanted to ask her if she would see you."

Elspeth could feel her pulse quicken. "Will she?'

"She's considering it. She did allow me to tell you I represented her mother and now represent her here in Australia."

Elspeth puzzled over these last words. They implied Maudy might be somewhere else. Mimicking the lawyer that morning, she sat there and said nothing. The silence grew. She sipped her lemonade.

"My client, Mary Anne Berkeley Lee, spends some of her time here," Morris Aldridge said, as if reading her mind.

"Is she here now?" Elspeth asked.

"No," he said without further explanation.

"Then I won't be able to meet her."

Elspeth was disappointed. She could see he noticed.

"Mr. Aldridge, I still have two months before I return to my full-time job with the Kennington Organisation. Let me give you my satellite mobile phone number. You can reach me wherever I am and also leave a message. It's set up so that you won't incur any charges when you call. Please tell Mary Ann's daughter I'd like to meet her and talk to her about her mother and Malcolm."

"I'll tell her, but I warn you, she doesn't like to talk about her past. She did make one request, that you will guarantee in writing not to release her whereabouts to her father."

He pulled out a piece of paper, indicating where Elspeth should sign. The written contract surprised her, but she did as bade, hoping Edward would forgive her. Elspeth felt it important enough to speak with Mary Anne's daughter that she was willing to protect the younger woman's privacy. In exchange for Edward's help, Elspeth thought, perhaps I can soften Maudy's aversion to her father, but Elspeth did not hold out high hopes considering the formality of the document she had just signed.

23

She was just finishing packing for her trip to Singapore when her mobile rang. It was Morris Aldridge.

"I've set up an appointment for you with Mary Anne Berkeley Lee. I thought you might be pleased."

Elspeth felt both excitement and dismay. If she were to meet Maudy, would this change her flight plan? Where was Maudy? Would Elspeth miss connecting up with Sarah Brixton as arranged?

Morris Aldridge surprised her. "In Singapore tomorrow. I understand you're flying out this evening," he said. Elspeth imagined the lawyer's grin at his own cleverness.

How did he know he was on her way to Singapore? Elspeth tried to remember if she had mentioned it.

"Let me get a pencil. Tell me where and when."

"Mrs. Lee will meet you at Raffles Hotel in the Bar and Billiard Room at four o'clock for high tea. She'll book the table. Have you been to Singapore before? Even if not, you should have no trouble finding Raffles." His tone was ever so slightly condescending.

"I'm sure I'll have no difficulty, Mr. Aldridge," she said with some dignity and then added with a suppressed smile, "I'm quite used to finding my way around the world. But tell me, how will I recognize her?"

"Mrs. Duff, did you ever meet Mary Anne Buchanan?"

"Yes, once but many years ago." Elspeth pictured Malcolm's sister's fiery carrot-colored hair and her piercing pale blue eyes.

"You'll recognize Mrs. Lee. Although she is taller than her mother was, their coloring is the same, which is much more unusual in Singapore than I assume it is in Scotland."

Elspeth's curiosity was roused. "Can you tell me why she agreed to meet me?"

"I'll let her tell you herself," Morris Aldridge said and rang off.

Lord Kennington once shared with Elspeth that he never hoped to match the evocation of colonial times at Raffles Hotel, his chief competitor in Singapore. When he was first considering opening the Kennington Singapore, in light of this formidable rival, he chose to make his hotel distinctly different, a tropical garden experience rather than an evocation of the era of the Straits Settlements. He found a large home off Napier Road, close to the Botanic Gardens, and, to Elspeth's admiration, added to it without destroying the integrity of the British Colonial style of architecture of the original building. The transition was seamless. The grounds became a tropical garden, mirroring the Botanic Gardens beyond. A lush array of palms, banana trees, rain trees, and other tropical flora lined the drive as it approached the hotel. In the interior the hotel designers constructed a large atrium, cooled to a pleasant twenty-three degrees centigrade, seventy-four degrees Fahrenheit, at all times of the day for guests who were not acclimatized to the Singapore heat. Hundreds of orchids clung to the well-ordered plants and trees. Guests could stroll and sit among them without experiencing the heat and humidity of the exterior. Each of the several large conference rooms had a separate courtyard filled with local trees and flowering plants. In a bow to the weather, a swimming pool surrounded by palm-thatched cabañas and a drinks bar was added. Nothing was left to chance. Elspeth wondered how Eric Kennington was coerced into providing the pool. He normally eschewed them.

Because the hotel was a distance from downtown, luxuriously fitted Mercedes vans departed from the hotel at ten-minute intervals, delivering Kennington Singapore guests free of charge to any destination they requested. Elspeth took one of the vans into the city center to Raffles Hotel well before the appointed hour of her meeting with Maudy. Once there Elspeth used her time to compare Lord Kennington's effort with the famous hotel. She walked through its courtyards, climbed the stairs to the Long Bar, which was noted for its Singapore slings, and wandered through the pricey gift shop. Eric had made the right decision not to compete, Elspeth thought. At half past three she made her way into the main three-story lobby and sat cooling herself and thinking about the meeting ahead.

What would Maudy be like? Red hair was a certainty; but would she be recognizable otherwise? Maudy was an enigma. Why was she so carefully shielding herself from her father? And why was she so conveniently in Singapore when Elspeth happened to be traveling through? Did she live in Singapore or elsewhere? Perhaps this meeting would clear up some of Elspeth's many unanswered questions.

Morris Aldridge did not give Elspeth a number to reach Maudy, and therefore Elspeth had to rely on Maudy actually appearing as the lawyer promised. Just before four, she made her way to a corner of the hotel where she earlier had found the Bar and Billiard Room. She made herself known to the slender and beautiful young Asian woman, with her jet-black hair pulled into a tight bun, who stood by the door and greeted the guests, checking each booking on her computer. When Elspeth arrived, the young woman confirmed the time for tea and then called the maître d' who greeted Elspeth by name in a French accent.

"Mme. Duff," he said, "Mme. Lee has rung to say she will be late and has asked you proceed with your tea."

A smiling waitress, dressed in black trousers and waistcoat and a red shirt, led Elspeth to a secluded corner, and Elspeth accepted the napkin held out to her.

"Your tea is ordered," the waitress said, in the staccato English Elspeth had heard everywhere her during her short stay in Singapore. "You only have to choose which tea you like." Elspeth took the long slender menu, with its rope and tassel, and began reading down the list of possibilities, which filled at least a dozen pages and offered scores of choices of teas. She selected one of the many varieties of Darjeeling, one called Nurborg and described as a delicate and flowery tea, plucked from the Himalayas in the spring. Maudy, however, did not appear.

As she waited for tea, Elspeth looked about the room, wondering how many famous people had sipped tea and drinks here over the years. She was grateful for the conditioned air that filled the high space, although wooden-paddled fans rotated lazily on the ceiling, which added a touch of historic authenticity. The floor tiles of black, white, tan, and taupe and the dark wood bar reminded Elspeth of colonial grandeur, although the soft music played by a recorded piano and bass violin was definitely modern.

When the waitress brought her tea and a three-tiered tray of pastries and cut sandwiches, Mary Anne Lee had still not appeared. Elspeth was unsure if she should proceed with her tea but finally poured the pale liquid from the teapot and took a fruit tart from the tray. She ate slowly and looked out the window at the courtyard filled with wicker tables and chairs and a garden of banana trees beyond. Soon she sampled a sandwich and wondered when Mary Anne would come. Fifteen minutes passed. Elspeth poured herself another cup of the delicate tea, finished the last of the savories, and waited. The maître d' approached her several minutes later.

"Mme. Duff?" His tone was half way between a question and an acknowledgement of her presence. "I was asked to deliver this to you."

Elspeth nodded her thanks, waited until both the maître d' and waitress withdrew and only then tore open the heavy cream-colored envelope. Inside was a single sheet of paper, covered on one side with a tidy hand.

> *Dear Mrs. Duff,*
>
> *Please forgive my absence. Morris asked me to meet you today, and I had every intention to do so, but, when I arrived at the hotel, I knew I was not yet ready to talk to you about my family. I am aware of your relationship to Malcolm, and Morris explained it was primarily Malcolm you wanted to know about, but Malcolm is one of the vile pieces in the puzzle that is my family, and the wounds we have inflicted on each other over the years cannot be easily healed. Until Morris's call to me from Sydney, I have tried to forget as much as I possibly could. Morris, who has been my advisor for many years, even before my mother died, thought talking to you might dispel some of the*

*demons. I agreed until I saw you sitting at the table I
booked for us. There may be a time when I will be able
talk to you, but not now. Please leave information on
how to reach you with Morris. When I am ready, I will
contact you through him.*

With apologies,
Mary Anne Lee

Elspeth folded the letter and put it back in the envelope.
She signaled for the bill, but the waiter informed her that
it had already been settled. If Maudy was clever enough to
pay the bill, Elspeth knew that she had done so before the
note was delivered. Maudy must have left Raffles by now.
Although she was disappointed, Elspeth did not rush from
the tearoom and look for a redheaded woman. She knew the
effort would be pointless.

The interior courtyards at the Kennington Singapore
were interspersed with places for guests to sit, and the plants
grew in tidy beds. Orchids, bamboos, palms, and other native
plants were arranged geometrically in defiance of their
natural tendency to flow together, thereby creating British
order out of jungle chaos. The benches were covered with
heavy silk cushions. Elspeth suspected Lord Kennington's
directing hand.

Elspeth found Sarah Brixton in one of the courtyards. She
was sipping tea and nibbling coconut-flavored tea biscuits.

"Aaah, what a delight after such a long flight," Sarah
said. "No wonder Eric is so successful in far-flung parts
of the world. All the comforts of home found among the
richness of the East." She added in falsetto, "I will recommend
Kennington hotels to my closest friends."

Elspeth burst out laughing. "How nice to be with you again, Sarah. So many complicated things have happened since we last met. I need time to defuse and to talk to someone who is not emotionally involved."

"My ear is available at no extra charge," Sarah said grinning.

"In the past I've been able to talk to Richard about things, but we've had a frightful row. I'm totally knotted up about it. It's my fault. I should've known not to express my real feelings around him. They make him shut down and become stiffly polite."

Sarah screwed up her mouth. "How awful. You've made Richard sound so grounded and such a great support."

Elspeth lifted her chin in defiance in order to cover her hurt. "Grounded, perhaps, except on the subject of Malcolm."

Sarah looked bemused. "That bad? Wasn't Richard the one who urged you to start this investigation?"

Elspeth sighed before answering. "Yes, but now he's become terribly disapproving. I feel the way I did when I was at Girton. Even then Richard scolded me about Malcolm. It's only become worse; it's as if he needs to be proven right."

Sarah frowned. "Proven right about what?"

Elspeth blew out her breath. "That Malcolm was not fit to be in my life."

"But how can that be an issue any longer with Malcolm dead all these years?"

Elspeth stared straight ahead at a nearby spray of orchids, which she did not see. "I think Richard wants to prove to me that Malcolm was a bad lot."

"Can he do that?" Sarah asked.

"He's trying. In the last few weeks I've turned up a number of people in Malcolm's life who didn't like him.

Whenever I mentioned them to Richard, I could see the 'I told you so' look on his face. I'm afraid I was purposely unpleasant to him when we met in Malta several weeks ago. We parted on icy terms."

Elspeth did not share that since leaving Malta before Christmas she had not received any emails or phone calls from Richard, which was painful for her. She did not expect Sarah's next question.

Sarah held her biscuit in the air and examined it innocently. "What do you want from Richard?"

What did she want from Richard? Elspeth's knew her feelings were chaotic, and therefore she gave an answer to Sarah's question that was not completely true.

"Want from Richard? I want my old friend back, the one I can trust and rely on. I certainly don't want someone trying to prove me wrong." Or, she thought to herself, someone whose presence produces emotions I do not want to have.

Sarah stopped looking at her biscuit and took a bite from it. "I think something in you wants to prove him wrong, but I can't make out what difference it makes. It smacks of peevishness, which I don't expect from you, Elspeth. Malcolm is dead and Richard is alive. Why the struggle between the three of you? Surely you have some feelings for Richard you aren't admitting to right now. Are you merely hiding behind the unanswered questions about Malcolm's death in order to avoid what you feel for Richard? Forgive me for saying so, but your feelings are more transparent than you think they are."

Elspeth put her hand to her brow and rubbed two manicured fingers under her stylishly cut hair. She did not respond at first.

Sarah waited without offering solace.

"I think I don't want to go there, Sarah," Elspeth said curtly and felt miserable because she knew what Sarah said was true.

"My apologies, then. I shouldn't have jumped in where I'm not wanted," Sarah said. "It's rather a bad habit of mine—bluntness."

They sat in uncomfortable silence until a waiter appeared to offer Sarah more tea.

"Let's talk about our business here for Eric," Elspeth said, glad for the diversion created by the waiter dispensing more tea for Sarah and offering a cup to her. "But first I have a favor to ask you. Do you or Clyde know, or have access to, anyone in Singapore or Malaysia who was here during the war? With Clyde's mining interests, I thought he might have contacts."

Elspeth watched Sarah's face relax.

"Safe ground," Sarah said without further explanation. "I certainly can ask him. I'll text him when I get back to my room, or you can ask him yourself. He'll be here the day after tomorrow. I thought since, according to Lord Kennington's instructions, you were to pose as someone who was here for rest and recreation, and I was to be joining you as a friend, having Clyde along would add to our authenticity. I also thought a male presence might help us if we need to venture out beyond Singapore into Malaysia. Much of Malaysia is less safe for women than in Singapore."

"How clever of you, Sarah. I hope we won't bore him."

"Have no fear; he'll find some sort of pressing business to attend to if he wants to get away from us. Besides he admires handsome women like you."

Despite Eric's instructions for her to look as if she were on holiday, Elspeth seriously wondered if she could appear to relax. She picked up her cup of tea daintily, aping Victoria

Smythe-Welton Brewer, and said to Sarah, "Do I look like a lady of leisure?"

Sarah roared with laughter. "You can say you have been overworked recently and need a real break. That would explain any apparent tension."

"Let me try again. Lady Sarah, would you like another biscuit?" Elspeth picked up the plate of biscuits and served them the way her maternal grandmother did when she was not squandering away her husband's dwindling fortune. Elspeth found something soothing in the gesture.

"Let's think about where we might have dinner," Sarah said. She pulled out several guidebooks from her handbag and handed one to Elspeth. They began studying the restaurant sections, when a voice interrupted them.

"You must be Mrs. Duff and Mrs. Brixton," an immaculately dressed, middle-aged Asian man said to them in perfect English. "I am William Ling, the manager of the Kennington Singapore. I came to welcome you and ask if I can be of any assistance." Because of his mode of greeting, William Ling must not have known Elspeth and Sarah worked for Eric Kennington or of their assignment in Singapore.

Elspeth had seen Kennington managers all over the world greet guests in the same warm manner. She looked over at Sarah, who seemed pleased by the manager's lack of addressing her with her title; her incognito had held.

"Ellie and I were just deciding on where to have dinner," Sarah volunteered. Elspeth winced at the nickname assigned to her.

"To first time visitors to Singapore I often recommend Aux Fleurs, which is near here. Although you might want to save that for a night when you have had more time to rest after your trip out from London." He made several suggestions of restaurants in the center of the city easily accessible by hotel van and mentioned that visitors from Europe at first found venturing out into the heat and humidity daunting, even in the evening. He assured them that since they were staying for several weeks they would acclimatize. He must have read the registration information they had provided.

"We would like to hire a private car for our stay here," Elspeth said, laying the foundation of the assignment Lord Kennington had given them in Singapore.

William Ling suggested they should arrange for a car with the concierge in the morning. He then left them alone.

"Ellie? Where did that come from?" Elspeth said, screwing up her face.

"I thought it would show we are old friends. Do you have a nickname?" Sarah asked. "Shortened names are so much the rage these days."

"My cousins call me 'Peth, but I prefer my full name. My ex-husband wanted me to change my name to Elizabeth, particularly in America where few people have heard my name before, but I never did. Instead we named our daughter Elizabeth, although she soon became Lizzie. My family has all sorts of versions of Elizabeths in it, with an 's' and with a 'z' but I prefer my own Scottish version. And you?"

"I once had a Canadian colleague who called me Sally, but I hated it. No, I have always been Sarah, even to my nanny. The name makes me feel I should act more properly than I usually do. Do you think we passed the test with Mr. Ling?" Sarah said.

"We will see when we get our driver in the morning," Elspeth said.

The delight of Sarah's company at dinner put both Malcolm and Richard out of Elspeth's mind for several hours, which came as an enormous relief. They chose a Chinese restaurant specializing in tim sum, as it was called in Singapore and where Sarah practiced some elementary Mandarin, which she had picked up during an assignment in Beijing. Her attempts caused the waiters some confusion and a great deal of muffled merriment.

"I must have used the wrong tone," she said. "It's so hard to remember which tone is right and, if you get it wrong, you can say the most embarrassing things. Goodness knows what we will be served."

Everything the waiters brought, however, was delicious, and they headed back to the hotel well filled and well pleased. The night was closing in, and the sounds of the busy traffic in the city center soon gave way to the night sounds of the tropical landscape surrounding the Botanic Garden and the Kennington Singapore.

Elspeth bade Sarah goodnight but did not return to her room. Instead she found a bench in one of Lord Kennington's courtyards and ordered a brandy, although this was not her usual habit. Sipping the harshly smooth liquid, she fell into thought. The corner where she was sitting was dark, and few other people were in the garden. Several fireflies flickered, their light tenuous. Elspeth wondered if they represented her relationship with Malcolm—flitting against the darkness. Elspeth seldom sank into loneliness; she considered her life was too rich with her work and family. Tonight was an exception. She took another sip of the brandy. What of her relationships with Malcolm, Alistair and Richard? Died, divorced, survived, she thought, butchering the old mnemonic about Henry VIII's wives. Why couldn't she find happiness with a man? No, Elspeth, she admonished herself, such thinking will not do. Without finishing her brandy, as fine as it was, she left her glass behind, rose and went up to her room.

She sat bolt upright in her bed at three in the morning. Something was nagging at the back of her brain, something she knew might be important, but her sharp re-entry into reality chased it from her consciousness. Something someone said but viewed in a different context took on a new meaning. She knew she would not sleep until she remembered what it was.

She got out of bed and called room service for a pot of herbal tea. After it was delivered, she moved to the window, taking warmth from the hot cup in her hands, and looked out over the semi-darkness of the gardens below, which was dimly lit by the light of the half moon. The sealed window and hushed noise of the air conditioning blocked out the sounds of the jungle below, although Elspeth recalled them from their arrival after dinner.

Then she remembered. It was a contradiction, or was it? When Richard came to dinner at her flat in London, he said he still had contacts and friends in Singapore and Malaysia, but, surely, later he told her his contact in the high commission in Singapore (or was it Kuala Lumpur?), had moved on to the embassy in Djakarta. Were the friends and the contacts the same people? If not, then the friends might still be here in Singapore. Elspeth knew Richard and his late wife had friends all over the world. If such friends still lived here, that would mean they might be useful in Elspeth's search for the truth about Malcolm's parents, but asking about them would also mean she would have to repair her relationship with Richard. Damn! she thought. Why do I always come back to needing and wanting Richard Munro?

24

The late night tea did not calm Elspeth as much as much as she had hoped it would, and she could not get back to sleep. At half past four she got up, pulled out her laptop and opened the file labeled "In Search of Malcolm." It contained the notes from her interviews and also included the "To Do" and "Questions To Be Answered" lists begun back in London. She reviewed these now with an eye to consistency. Each list had a recurring theme—the link, if any, between Malcolm's parents' murders and Malcolm's own.

How could she use her visit to Singapore to discover any connection? Maudy might have helped, but she had balked. What was it that Victoria Smythe-Welton Brewer had assumed? That Malcolm's father was interned with the rest of the British who the Japanese captured in Singapore, but this might not be true. Elspeth needed to know more about the Japanese occupation of Malaya and Singapore and the Europeans there during the war. She would need to set aside time to find out. Would the British High Commission in Singapore have information? She might need Richard's assistance for this to happen. Bah! But she now had a new focus. She retired to bed and did not wake until nine.

Lord Kennington decided early in his career to make breakfast a centerpiece of each hotel, offering not only a superb British country manor breakfast but also fresh fruit, breads, jams, and specialty dishes traditional to the region where the hotel was located. He met the challenge of the multi-ethnicity of Singapore by having the kitchen prepare a table of Malay food, another of Chinese food, and a third of Indian food, along with the larger buffet of English and European continental selections. Most European guests who stayed for more than a few days gradually gravitated to the Asian tables to taste what was on them. Lord Kennington insisted that these foods be of the highest quality and authenticity, and he won many converts to the local food because of this.

Sarah and Elspeth agreed to meet at ten. Elspeth found Sarah in the breakfast room waiting for her. A waiter appeared and poured Elspeth a large cup of coffee from a silver pot emblazoned with the Kennington crest. Elspeth declined the proffered cream and sugar and sat back to wish her friend good morning. Sarah looked more rested than Elspeth felt. Elspeth did not mention her middle of the night activities. That would come later. Sarah served herself from all four buffets, but Elspeth limited herself to fresh papaya and lime and a buttery croissant, with some local guava jam made especially for the hotel. Both woman ate slowly and spoke mainly about the food and the opulent decor of the breakfast room.

Having at first eschewed a heavier meal, Elspeth took a second helping of papaya, of which she was extremely fond, several bits of fresh dragon fruit, its whiteness with black dots amusing her, and a slice of brown toast and jam. Sarah declared herself sated but ordered another cup of Lord Kennington's special Sri Lankan breakfast tea. They sat back, looked happily at each other and acknowledged they were enjoying the "Comfort and Service" bragged about on the Kennington Organisation crest.

When they finished their meal, Elspeth turned to Sarah. "Now that we have demonstrated we are ladies of leisure, I suppose we must earn our keep."

Sarah suggested they make arrangements for a car for a single day only and they use the car for sightseeing around the city. If the driver did not tell them what they were trying to discover, they could request another driver the following day. Their plans made, they approached the concierge's desk and accepted the offer of a mid-sized Toyota with a good air conditioning system and enough room for Sarah's camera equipment.

Abdul, their driver, spoke English rapidly, almost as if it were patter song. He took great care to settle them comfortably into the car. As he drove, Abdul spouted forth a vast quantity of information, some of which contradicted the guidebooks but made for an entertaining morning. Without offending him, Elspeth wondered how best to question him about his relationship with the hotel and if the hotel demanded back-handers. If he did have an understanding with the hotel that involved the management taking some of his profit, would he be willing to share that information with his passengers, particularly two middle-aged British women posing as tourists? Elspeth regretted that Eric told her to work undercover, which she seldom did for him.

They toured until lunchtime, particularly admiring the classical style British buildings, but Abdul was more effusive about the towering glass and steel skyscrapers that formed the backdrop to the city. At one, Elspeth suggested lunch, and Abdul took them to a famous hotel that once housed the old colonial administrative offices. The lunch was pricey but excellent, and the vast interior atrium cool and inviting.

Having finished a sparse and expensive lunch, Elspeth suggested Sarah and she find the ladies' room, where they might talk together without being overheard. They agreed Sarah would request they stop in Arab Street so that she could get some photographs of the fabrics and arts and crafts displayed there. Elspeth would stay in the car and get into a conversation with Abdul about how drivers were paid in other cities she had visited to see if she could pry any information from him about his relationship with the Kennington Singapore. If that did not work, she would have to ask him directly. She expected a denial.

Abdul was waiting for them outside the hotel and had kept the engine running to keep the car cool. They took their seats in the back and left Abdul to negotiate the mid-afternoon traffic, which was heavy but orderly.

When they reached Arab Street, Elspeth said the heat and noise were beginning to give her a headache, although in truth she was enjoying everything around her. Being a tourist did not seem like real work.

On cue, Sarah picked up her camera equipment and told Elspeth and Abdul she wanted an hour on her own to do her photography. Abdul found a parking spot along a yellow line on the street and offered to roll up the window between the driver's seat and the back seat so "the lady gets a very quiet time all for herself alone without trouble."

"No, Abdul. As long as I can stay cool, I'll be fine. Do you mind if I ask you some questions while we wait. I've traveled across the world many times, but I've never been to Southeast

Asia before. When I travel, I enjoy talking with people like you, because you can tell me so much about your country and your culture from a first-hand perspective. Do you mind?"

"No, missus, I am very glad to tell you all about everything in my country and how we live here."

"Did you grow up in Singapore?"

"No, outside in Malaysia about two hours by road from here. I am very lucky because my father has a very good and excellent business there. My brothers and I go to a very good school and learn very good English so we can now be in business here in Singapore."

"Do you have sisters as well?" Elspeth knew this strayed from the topic but she was fascinated to know how the female members of Abdul's family fared along side the males. "Yes, I have three sisters, who are all very very devout in the Islamic faith and very religious. They too learn English, but at home from my grandmother who teaches English to girls from very many of my family's friends. Now my sisters all have very good husbands who are prosperous here and in Malaysia."

Elspeth despaired the male dominance in Muslim culture even in cosmopolitan Singapore. She turned the conversation back to Abdul and his brothers.

"Do your brothers drive cars as well?" she asked.

"Yes. We have a very good business for all of us. We have five cars all together for three brothers. This lets us work every day, even if one or two of the cars are in the shop, so we keep them in very good repair."

"Do you drive often for the Kennington hotel?"

"Oh, yes, often, very often, almost everyday except for the holy days."

"I hope the hotel treats you well."

"Oh, yes. Very very well." Abdul bobbed his head up and down rapidly.

"I often stay at Kennington hotels and have met Lord Kennington. He always wants people working for the hotels to be happy."

Elspeth felt she was beginning to plant the right seeds for her enquiry when a merchant came out of his shop and interrupted them. He told Abdul to move on as the space was reserved for his customers. Elspeth doubted this because she knew they were illegally parked. Abdul left the car and confronted the merchant. Their conversation took place beyond Elspeth's earshot, but Elspeth saw some money pass between them. When Abdul returned to the car, he informed Elspeth the merchant had made a mistake. Elspeth was told not to tip Abdul, but she assumed their right to the parking space might have cost him several Singapore dollars. She wondered if she should make this up to him or of this was part of his business expenses.

"Abdul, I want to ask you a question about your family, if you will not be offended."

"No, I take no offense," he said, but he looked a little worried.

"Was your family in here during the Japanese occupation?"

Abdul looked up into the rear view mirror with a questioning expression on his face. "Yes, missus, but not in Singapore. They go back to our family's village. It is too small to concern the Japanese, but many bad things happen to them during the war."

Elspeth pushed him further. "Would that be in your grandparents' time?"

"Yes, and my grandparents' parents."

"Are any of them still alive?"

"Why do you ask, missus?"

"I'm trying to find information about someone who was in Malaya during the war, the father of a close friend of mine at university. Since arriving in Singapore, I've been asking a great many people about that time." The fabrication tripped easily off Elspeth's lips.

"My grandmother is still alive and sometimes she talks about the occupation. It is a bad time. Many innocent people are killed."

"Yes, I know, Malayans, Singaporeans and British, as well as many others."

Abdul swelled with pride and became talkative. "My grandfather is in the resistance against the Japanese, he calls them Nips, and later the British give him a medal in reward for information he give them and for his braveness."

"Was he in the jungle with the fighters there?"

"Oh, no, no. The people in the jungle are the communists. My family are devoted Muslims; we are not communists. Praise be to Allah! The Japanese do not like the Muslims. So my family works with the resistance. It is very very dangerous. My grandfather is very brave. Here is a photo of my family."

Abdul opened the glove box and brought out a black and white photograph that by its looks had been taken in a studio many years before. "This photo is from when my grandfather is seventy years old. You see he has his medal on his chest. He dies the next year and so this photo is very important to me."

Elspeth took the photograph, noting that all the members in the portrait were men. "Which one are you?"

Abdul pointed to a young man perhaps in his early teens. "I am very handsome, yes?"

"Yes, Abdul, you are, and your grandfather was as well. He must have been an impressive person. You said your grandmother is still alive. Does she live in Singapore?"

"No, she lives in our village in Malaysia." Abdul took out a map and showed Elspeth where.

Elspeth bit her lip. Abdul had not yet expressed any dissatisfaction with his arrangement with the hotel, but what would happen if she tried to hire him for a trip to see his grandmother? Would the hotel demand a percentage? First she needed to determine if Abdul's grandmother would see her.

"Do you think that your grandmother would be willing to talk with me about the resistance during the war?"

"I telephone her right away this very minute and ask," he said. He picked up a high-tech mobile phone and pressed a speed dial button. There was a long conversation in what Elspeth assumed was Malay.

Abdul turned to her. "My grandmother is very willing to talk to you about her husband's bravery if you come to her home tomorrow. I bring you there."

"Tell her I accept. Will you pick me up at the hotel at half past ten in the morning?" Now she was testing Abdul.

He spoke into the phone again, nodding rapidly as he spoke and then he rang off. "My grandmother asks you to share lunch with her. You are very honored, because she is not always willing to see strangers. She invites your friend as well."

"I'm grateful, Abdul. At half past then?"

"Yes, missus, but we meet at the Paragon, a very big shopping mall on Orchard Road, not at the hotel. I wait on the side of the mall by the clock near the taxi stand. I drive a black Mercedes. You can take a taxi to get there. It is not very far and only cost a few dollars."

"What will you charge me for the trip, Abdul?"

He gave a price, which Elspeth converted into sterling, and, although it was high, she accepted it. Sarah returned to the car at this point and was filled with the sights, colors, and textures of Arab Street. She asked to be taken around the corner to the Sultan Mosque. Elspeth joined her, and they spent the rest of the afternoon playing tourist. Elspeth did not get another chance to speak alone with Abdul. They returned to the Kennington hotel for tea. Payment for the day's taxi had been made earlier through the concierge, but Elspeth gave Abdul a generous tip to cover the cost of the merchant's demands on Arab Street.

"Thank you, missus. You are very very kind. About tomorrow, my grandmother is a very devout woman. She likes her guests to be careful in their dress. I see you beside the Paragon by the clock at half past ten."

When Elspeth shared with Sarah the gist of her conversation with Abdul, Sarah was delighted to be included in the trip to Malaysia but concerned.

"Clyde is due tomorrow and will be put out if I'm not here."

Elspeth smiled at Sarah. "Will it cause another row?"

"I'll text him and tell him I have a chance at a photo shoot that comes once in a lifetime. He'll be in a huff at first, but he's already told me that he has several business meetings here. I'm certain he can move them up. In our marriage the true love that absence inflames has long since been forgotten. Count me in. I have some headscarves that I always carry when I travel. We can wear them à la HM the Queen, or we can tuck them in at the corners the way the Muslim women do, making us properly dressed in their world. Tell me what color you are wearing, and I'll pick one out for you that matches."

A Secret in Singapore

Elspeth was not completely duplicitous when she told Abdul the heat bothered her. Actually it was more the humidity, to which she might become acclimatized to over time, but she was not sure she would. She thought of Richard and Lady Marjorie posted around the world and wondered if Marjorie managed to keep her cool demeanor in hot and humid climates. Elspeth was certain she did. During her visits to California with Richard, Marjorie never looked or acted less than a perfect lady and diplomat's wife. She probably, thought Elspeth, never perspired, most certainly her linen clothing never wrinkled, and undoubtedly she never found a scorpion in her shoe. Elspeth's thoughts were conflicted when it came to Lady Marjorie Munro. Elspeth assumed Richard married her for political advantage, but Elspeth never fully understood their relationship. Lady Marjorie was not the sort to show emotion in public, but Elspeth sensed Richard, for all his seriousness and reserve, was a passionate man underneath. How had Marjorie and he shared their affection in private? Had Marjorie satisfied him? Put these thoughts away, Elspeth said to herself. You don't need to know. But she wished she did.

After opening her email and finding nothing from Richard or her children, she lay down on her bed and succumbed to the ravages of international travel. She slept dreamlessly until dinnertime. She ordered a light supper from room service and slept on until morning.

The following day Elspeth met Sarah, who was dressed in pockets and carrying a large camera bag. Elspeth saw mischief in her eyes.

"Clyde has arrived and was annoyed at me, but I made it up to him," Sarah explained with a broad grin and a deep chuckle.

Elspeth tried to hide her amusement. "Where is Clyde now?"

"Upstairs. Thank God for the Kennington hotels' room arrangements. Clive was able to work late into the night in an adjoining room and was fast asleep when I got up this morning. I left him an affectionate note and told him we'd be back by dark. What time is dark, by the way?"

"Since we are so close to the equator, I would assume it is around six or seven all year long."

"We should be back by then. If we are late, I'll ring him on my mobile. Blessed be for modern technology."

25

As promised, Abdul was waiting for them by the clock at side of the Paragon shopping mall. He was dressed more casually than the day before, wearing a Hawaiian shirt patterned with garish hibiscus blooms. He boasted his brother had given it to him after a trip to the States.

"My grandmother likes this shirt, and I wear it when I go to see her."

Elspeth despaired that a woman would feel that way but would be offended if Sarah and she did not cover their hair or dress modestly.

Abdul opened the back door of a highly polished black Mercedes, a far more pretentious car than the one he driven the day before. When Sarah commented on this, he assured them this car was saved for special trips and occasions. He drove it when he was going home because his family would know his brothers and he were prospering in their livery business.

The air conditioning in the great car was welcome as the day was already hot and humid. They left the streets of Singapore and motored along the highway that crossed the border into Malaysia. The prosperity of Singapore soon faded behind them. They saw a new world, of a thoroughfare cut through jungle shaded by a large canopy of trees, of mud-spattered lorries hauling goods toward Singapore, and of cars carrying numerous passengers. The road was modern but, for the most part, the vehicles were not.

Abdul left the federal highway before they came to Melaka and turned up a narrow road. The road quickly turned into an asphalt track that barely allowed two cars to pass. It was lined by by local inhabitants in colorful Muslim garb and bull carts loaded with long logs. Soon the road narrowed again.

They approached a dirt drive with large metal gates and a high stone wall with pickets on top. Abdul tapped in a number on the keypad and drove through the slowly opening barrier.

"My grandmother meets you on the veranda of the women's quarters," Abdul told them as they approached the house, a large single-level thatched-roof building that was raised off the ground on wooden piers. An extensive veranda projected out from the back.

"You need to take off your shoes when you go inside. I go away now. You are very very honored my grandmother wants to speak to you. She speaks English very well because her father hires an English governess to teach both his sons and daughters, which is very progressive in the old days. She also goes to see relatives in England several times. My grandmother likes the traditional Malay ways now and stays in the women's quarters of our house, but she enjoys speaking English and watches English shows on the television."

A woman, obviously a servant, bowed to the two British women and led them into the interior of the house and back to the veranda.

"You are most welcome to my home," a woman's voice said from behind a screen. When she emerged onto the veranda, she was dressed like her servant in a traditional sarong, a brightly colored blouse, and flowered headscarf.

Her face was mapped with the fine wrinkles of old age, and her eyes were merry.

"I see my grandson brought you here in one piece, although I fear he drives too quickly. I have ordered lemonade and later a small lunch. Since you have come such a long way from Europe, I thought a light meal with fresh fruit and some of our local specialties might please you." She put up her hands as if in prayer and bowed her head to them in greeting. "My name is Safirah binti Ibrahim, Abdul's grandmother."

Elspeth was not expecting such openness but was delighted by it. She introduced herself in the same formal manner, "I am Elspeth Duff, and this is my friend, Lady Sarah Brixton."

The old Malay woman nodded in acknowledgement. "Mrs. Duff and Lady Sarah. Please sit down. You must be tired from your long journey."

The paddles of a slow turning overhead fan moved the air, and the space was pleasantly cool as they sat quietly and sipped the lemonade, which the servant poured from an ice-filled pitcher. Unfamiliar sounds of birds, frogs, and insects surrounded them and gave a sense of frenetic but friendly aliveness.

Elspeth sighed contentedly and spoke to her hostess. "There's a wonderful magic to this place. Has it always been this way?"

"Yes, as long as I have lived here—which is now over eighty years—even during the Japanese occupation. The British left us alone, but the Japanese did not. They killed many of us even here in this small and insignificant place. Mrs. Duff, my grandson tells me you want to talk about what happened during that time."

"Yes, although I realize the memories may be harsh. I'm trying to trace a British family who were in the jungle during that time."

"The Japanese soldiers rounded up the British and sent them to the camps," Safirah said. "Many of them died there. The Japanese had no mercy for them."

Elspeth tried another tack. "Your grandson tells me your husband was a hero in the war against the Japanese, and he was decorated afterwards by the British."

Safirah nodded her head. "Yes. That is so. He risked his life many times to get information out of the jungle and to the underground forces in Singapore. Later we learned some of this information reached Lord Mountbatten himself." Pride choked her voice.

"Did your husband work with the resistance forces in the jungle?" Elspeth asked.

"No. They were mainly Chinese and many of them communists. We are Malay. My husband knew many of the Chinese involved in the movement, but he was not a communist. He did get information from them at times, but he also traveled around the countryside selling vegetables and fruit, and, in the process, made notes and took secret photographs, which a friend developed. Every time he had information to take to Singapore I begged him not to go because I was afraid for his life. He was angry with me and said I was a weak woman. I know my place in a good Muslim household, but once he was taken ill and urged me to go to Singapore in his place. I have never done anything else in my life so frightening. I dressed in my husband's clothing and pulled a hat over my hair so it would not show. I took our old lorry filled with fruit for the markets in Melaka. My husband usually would trade these for things to take on to Singapore.

The Japanese gave him a small amount of petrol to do this. My husband gave me the names of the people to contact along the way. I was petrified, but he assured me if I spoke to no one but these contacts I would be safe. I asked him what to do if the *kempei-tai*, the Japanese security force, stopped me. 'Give them these' he said and handed me some papers, which he told me were official Japanese letters of transit, and also gave me some money."

Sarah broke in. "I would have been terrified. I've read what the Japanese soldiers did to so many of your countrymen during the war."

"The Japanese hated the Chinese but were more lenient toward the Malays," Safirah binti Ibrahim said.

"Tell us, did you have any trouble?" Elspeth asked.

"Not with the soldiers; I was very lucky in that, but with the lorry, yes. It broke down when I was half way between Melaka and Singapore. My husband knew how to keep the lorry running, but I did not. I left Melaka later than planned, and it was starting to get dark. I was afraid of breaking the curfew the Japanese imposed on the country, so I pulled the lorry, which was limping along, off the main road and into the drive of a deserted house. I thought I could spend the night there but did not know what I would to do in the morning. As I was facing this problem, I heard someone stirring in the back of the lorry. A young man crawled out from under the canvas that covered the items in the back. He was shabbily dressed and dirty and had not shaved for many days. My fright grew. He introduced himself to me in Malay, although I knew he was Chinese. He was able to get the old lorry going again. We arrived in Singapore when it was dark and joined a line of similar lorries that were waved on by the soldiers as we entered the city. When I reached the place my husband had told me to go, the Chinese man was no longer in the back. At that moment I knew my husband was very brave. He made trips to Singapore every month or two but always came home safely."

"Did you ever find out who the Chinese man was?" Sarah asked.

"Yes, several years later during the Emergency. That was the time when the communists tried to take control of Malaya in the late nineteen-forties. The man was called Hwa Lo-bing. Do you know who he was?"

Sarah recognized the name. "I interviewed a Hwa Lo-bing in Beijing about ten years ago. He was a vice-minister for cultural affairs in Deng Xiao-ping's government. Was he here in Malaysia during the Japanese Occupation?"

"I do not fully understand Chinese names, although I think that many people often have the same one. Hwa Lo-bing was one of the leaders of the Malayan Communist Party during the Emergency. He fled from Malaya before the British found him. He may have returned to China. I do not know. I only know he helped me on that night outside of Singapore, but I never saw him again. My husband might have told you more, but he died many years ago."

Elspeth was grateful for Safirah binti Ibrahim's information. Do you know if any British people were in the jungles with the anti-Japanese forces?" she asked.

"We heard rumors, but I do not know. My friend, Mrs. Koh, who is Chinese, might know. Would you like to talk to her? Her family was involved with the communists in the jungle, although I am not too sure when or how.

Elspeth tried to keep her voice steady to hide her eagerness. "I would like to meet her; do you think she would be willing to talk to me?"

"My friend likes to talk more than anything else. When I go to see her in Penang, she always tires me out." The old woman laughed, and her whole face radiated the rays of the sun that had warmed it for so many years. "Why are these things important to you. They happened so long ago that few people remember now."

"My fiancé and his sister, whose family was from Scotland, were born in the jungles of Malaya in nineteen forty-three and nineteen forty-five. I believe they lived in one of the communist camps. I'm trying to find out if anyone remembers them."

"My friend, Mrs. Koh, may know. I will telephone her."

Safirah turned to a lacquered box sitting on the bamboo table near her and pulled a satellite mobile phone from its depths. "My grandson Abdul gave me this and said I must join the twenty-first century. I am enjoying it but do not tell him so. If I do, he will only give me more things like email. Why should I have email? My friends like handwritten letters, and my sons and grandsons can call me on their mobile phones. I turn mine off when I do not want to hear from anyone."

After calling her friend, who extended an invitation to Elpseth, Safirah led them to a table at the side of the veranda. They found a colorful table setting with a platter of papaya, melon, guava, and pineapple and serving dishes of spicy noodles, skewered meat, savory green beans with bean curd, and curry puff pastries. "I hope you will enjoy an authentic Malayan meal. I thought you might not get an authentic one at your hotel in Singapore."

Elspeth was glad Lord Kennington did not hear this.

Elspeth and Sarah sampled each dish. The food was peppery and spread its fiery heat into their mouths and faces, but Elspeth travelled abroad enough that she was used to intensity in food. Sarah and she placated their palates with slices of cucumber and pieces of fruit and declared the food was excellent.

During the meal, Safirah talked about her children. She bragged about their successful livery business but was happy her eldest son had decided to stay home and care for their family. Her three daughters were married and had children of their own. One lived close by, and the two others were in Singapore, where Safirah visited often. She asked about both Elspeth's and Sarah's children but did not seem interested in their replies. They did not talk about the Japanese occupation again.

Abdul returned to the door to the veranda at two, and, after they gave their thanks and obtained Mrs. Koh's address, Elspeth and Sarah entered the chilled environment of the great Mercedes and settled in for the trip back to Singapore.

Elspeth hunted for a way to approach Abdul about his relationship with the Kennington hotel and thought she had found one. Sarah dozed off, and Elspeth now had another chance to chat one-on-one with him.

"Your grandmother is very proud of your success," she said. "Tell me, Abdul, how were you able to start your business?"

"My father wants his sons to become rich, so he says we go to Singapore. There is no good business in our village for us, and Singapore is very very rich. My brother Ahmad goes first and buys a taxi with money my father gives him. Ahmad at first he works in the financial district, but soon he sees the best way to make money is with the tourists. He writes to us and says we must study English very well and also learn Japanese, enough for a taxi driver, and also French and Mandarin. My father is not happy about the Japanese because of the things in World War Two, but he thinks perhaps the

Japanese are different now. My younger brother and I come to Singapore, live with my brother, and study very hard. We learn the streets of the city and soon all three of us take shifts with the taxi day and night. We save everything we can and soon we have two taxis. The second one is nicer than the first one. We buy a third nicer one. Now we have four and this Mercedes, for special events only."

"You are to be praised for your hard work. Tell me, Abdul, how were you able to get work with the Kennington hotel? Surely every taxi driver in Singapore would like that contract."

Elspeth could see Abdul's face in the rear view mirror and saw it contort. "This is very difficult. All the taxis must meet very highest standards, and we must always be prompt and fair in our prices."

"Does the hotel regulate you? Tourists like to know they are being treated honestly." Elspeth tried to sound conversational rather than inquisitive.

"The manager is the big boss," Abdul said noncommittally.

"Mr. Ling, yes, he is in charge. I have heard from others that sometimes he demands too much," she added hoping to elicit more information.

"A contract with the hotel is worth very much money to me and my brothers," Abdul said without taking Elspeth's bait.

"Abdul, why didn't you want to come to the hotel this morning?"

His eyes held hers in his mirror. "You go to see my grandmother. I not want to charge you extra for that."

"But we agreed on a price yesterday."

"That is not the price at the hotel. I give you the lower price because of my grandmother."

"Do you normally pay the hotel a commission?"

"We pay to have them call us. My brother tells me this is a very good business arrangement. We get many calls for taxis from the hotel and get many nice lady passengers like you and your friend."

By this time they were nearing the hotel in Singapore, and Lady Sarah woke up from her nap. With the increase in traffic, Abdul turned his attention to his driving and talked no more about his business. He dropped them at the taxi stand at the Botanic Gardens but out of sight of the hotel. Elspeth and Sarah decided to walk to the hotel, since the distance was short and they had been cooled by the air conditioning in Abdul's big car. Sarah had her camera out and did not notice Elspeth's preoccupation. Elspeth wondered how and to whom Abdul and his brothers make their payment. She hoped it was not directly to the hotel or to the manager, William Ling.

26

The atmosphere of the Kennington Singapore had a distinctly foreign overlay after their day with Abdul's grandmother in a Muslim household. Elspeth suspected Eric Kennington never ventured beyond Singapore when he was overseeing the renovation of the hotel buildings. Elspeth felt he had erred on the side of the imperial past and tried to recreate a reality that existed for only the small number of British colonials in the first part of the twentieth century in the Straits Settlements. Still the amenities of the hotel echoed the Kennington motto of "Comfort and Service," which was a relief after the long day on the road.

Elspeth was torn between her two missions in Singapore. One was personal and the other official Kennington Organisation business. She wanted to meet Mrs. Koh, but her conversation with Abdul reminded her she was in Singapore not just because she was searching for Malcolm's murderer but also because she was to ferret out any kickback schemes at the hotel.

Feeling hot after the short walk from the Botanic Gardens, Elspeth made arrangements to meet Clyde and Sarah Brixton for dinner and retreated to her room. Despite her earlier resolve not to be bothered if she did not find an email from Malta, she opened her laptop and logged in before shedding her wilted clothes and starting preparations for her bath. There was an email from her son, Peter, telling her he had made arrangements for repairs to the deck at her retreat north of San Francisco, and another from her daughter telling Elspeth one of the twins had fallen and scraped his knee so badly that it required three stitches. Elspeth wondered what her children would have thought of her day's activity, but she suspected they were too concerned with their own lives to care. She thought what life in the jungle was like for Malcolm and Mary Anne in contrast to the upbringing of her twin grandsons in East Sussex.

There was no message from Richard.

Elspeth expected Clyde Brixton to be a rugged man, who spent much of his times in the mines of the world, and therefore she was surprised when an ordinary looking British businessman rose from the table in the cocktail bar where Sarah was seated. He introduced himself as Sarah's husband. Of medium height and stature, with thick brown hair, and dressed in a conservative lightweight blazer and a typical open collared and pleated white shirt that Elspeth had seen Singaporean businessmen wearing, Clyde Brixton gave the appearance of being comfortable in the world of commerce in Southeast Asia. His handshake was strong, but his hands soft and well manicured.

He greeted her as if in mid-conversation. "So we are sitting here deciding on whether to fly or drive to Penang tomorrow. I have business there, and I understand you are on the track of a Mrs. Koh, who will answer all the questions you have about life in the wartime jungle. I've made arrangements for a private flight and hired a car there, but Sarah thinks we should hire Abdul to drive us, since his grandmother was so kind to the two of you. Doing that would extend our trip each way by several hours."

Elspeth saw why he was so successful in business. His warm manner did not hide the hard intelligence in his eyes. She did not expect to like Clyde Brixton, who seemed to have constant disagreements with his wife, but she did. She looked up at Sarah and sensed she was truly fond of her husband. Elspeth began to suspect the so-called rows were nothing more than the type of discussion that she had just interrupted regarding the mode of transportation for the trip to Penang in the morning.

Sarah turned to Elspeth. "Clyde thinks we should let you decide."

"That puts me in an awkward position," Elspeth laughed. "I have no preference. Perhaps we can compromise. We could fly and then ask Abdul if he can recommend a driver in Penang. He gave me his card with a twenty-four hour number."

"Are you always so diplomatic?" Clyde said. His lips twitched in a half grin.

"It comes with my job. I don't want to remember the number of times I've negotiated between warring guests. I try to see both sides, but I do have another reason for my choice. For the moment I want Abdul to think well of us because after we return from Penang I want to use other taxi drivers to see if they have the same arrangement with the hotel as Abdul and his brothers do. If we don't continue using Abdul, I'm afraid he might take offense at our abandoning his services, and I don't want to alienate him. You see, Mr. Brixton, Eric Kennington has asked me to investigate what agreements the hotel has with taxi drivers here. It appears someone in the hotel is making private arrangements that don't comply with the Kennington Organisation's official policy of no kickbacks."

"Please call me Clyde. 'Mr. Brixton' is far too stiff for friends. Sarah, can you live with Elspeth's decision?"

His wife happily nodded consent.

Clyde took control of the light plane once they had cleared the airport in Singapore. He told them that he had made this flight several times before and had filed a flight pattern that would take them over some of the scenic areas above the canopy of the rain forest between Singapore and Penang. They flew just above the tree line and were able to see the rivers and villages below. Elspeth unabashedly gawked out her window.

They arrived in Penang before ten, and the car Abdul ordered for them was waiting on outside the terminal. The driver, Yacob, told them he was Abdul's cousin and hoped to join Abdul and his brothers in Singapore once their business added several more cars. Clyde had promised his contacts in Penang that his wife would join them for lunch, so Elspeth deposited Clyde and Sarah at the offices where they were expected and had Yacob drive her beyond the city center into the suburbs where Mrs. Koh lived. Yacob said he was acquainted with her and regaled his passenger with a long discourse on his grandmother's friendship with Mrs. Koh.

"My grandmother is good friend with Mrs. Koh. She is very old like my grandmother. They are friends because they both work for the Red Crescent Society. Mrs. Koh is not a Muslim lady, but she and my grandmother like each other. When my grandmother come to Penang, she always go see Mrs. Koh. I think it is because Mrs. Koh live in a big house, which have air conditioning and is cool, and also Mrs. Koh have a good cook. My grandmother like Chinese food very much but not like to pay the high price in the Chinese restaurants. Mrs. Koh's family own large department store and give my grandmother discounts."

Elspeth was amused by these reasons for a friendship.

Mrs. Koh was waiting for Elspeth in her sitting room. Tea things were laid out, and Mrs. Koh graciously offered Elspeth a small, handleless cup filled with hot tea and sweet almond biscuits.

Elspeth relaxed with Mrs. Koh, who had been educated in England and often spent holidays with friends in Scotland. She once visited Loch Tay but had not ventured on to Loch Rannoch.

"Mrs. Duff, you have not come all the way to Penang to talk about Scotland. Safirah rang to say she enjoyed her lunch with Lady Sarah and you, and you were curious about the anti-Japanese forces in the jungles during the war. The Japanese usually tolerated the Malays during the war, which is one reason Safirah's family was spared, although her husband was deeply involved in black market activities. The Chinese, however, were treated with extreme hostility. Executions and imprisonment were common. I lost several of my own family during that time, but my husband's family suffered much more acutely. When Safirah said you were interested in the war here, I thought it best if you could talk to my husband. He has invited us to lunch today at his office but cannot get free until half past one. In the meantime, I thought you might like to see some photographs."

She brought out a large album, which was filled with black and white snapshots and a number of press clippings. Mrs. Koh explained these were from a local Chinese language newspaper.

They turned the pages together as Mrs. Koh pointed out things of interest. "My husband's family kept these photographs, even though many members of his family went into the jungle during the war, and some were killed by the Japanese. After Koh Tan Soo and I married, I met many of the ones who were still alive. Here is Auntie Plum Blossom, who was my favorite." She pointed to a small woman in traditional Chinese dress. "She was like a doll, even when she became old. What the Japanese did not know was that she went back and forth to the jungle disguised as a boy. The Japanese soldiers often gave her sweets and did not suspect she was carrying messages to the anti-Japanese forces. I was a young woman at the time and very timid, but I always admired her. She simply laughed when we said she was brave. She claimed she only wanted to see all the handsome men who were in the jungle."

"Were there any British men in the jungle with these handsome men?" Elspeth asked.

"Tan Soo would know better than I, but there were rumors at the time that some British soldiers had escaped into the jungle and joined the communists."

"You call them communists. Were all of them?"

Mrs. Koh knittted her brow. "We call them communists because after the war, during the Emergency, those who stayed in the jungle were openly allied with the communists in China, but during the occupation we considered them anti-Japanese patriots. My husband can tell you more about this."

They continued to leaf through the album. The few street scenes in Penang during the war showed light traffic, only the occasional car, and several Japanese war vehicles. In front of one was a European. This gave Elspeth an idea.

"Were there many Europeans here in Penang during the war?"

"I remember very few. Some high-ranking German army officers and one or two Italian ones as well. They wore handsome uniforms, which starkly contrasted with the drab uniforms of the Japanese."

Elspeth's head spun. *Bartolomeo is an unusual Scottish Christian name. Truth it is, sworn on the soul of my Italian grandfather.* Her conversation with Malcolm was as clear as it had been in nineteen sixty-nine. Malcolm's mother's name was Anna Maria, although Inspector Llewellyn said her nationality was not listed in the registration of Malcolm or Mary Anne's birth.

Elspeth drew in her breath and asked, "Were there many Italian civilians in Malaya during the war?"

"A few, but you must ask Tan Soo. Of course, the Italians were on the Japanese side."

Elspeth felt her hands grow cold. Was Anna Maria really an Italian, living here in Penang, perhaps with her family, and not in the jungle? If so, was James Buchanan with her? Was he working for the Axis powers or was he only posing as a collaborator? Damn, she thought, now I'm thinking like Richard Munro. Elspeth became aware Mrs. Koh was still turning the pages of the album and was chatting away about its contents. Slowly and painfully Elspeth brought her thoughts back to her hostess.

"You're fortunate to have these memories recorded here," Elspeth said.

"Perhaps, but they are not all happy. As one grows older, however, both happy and sad memories weave themselves together in a pattern of vague remembrance." She closed the album, and Elspeth saw misty tears in the old woman's eyes. "But Tan Soo will be waiting for us. I've asked my driver to come around. He'll take us into the center of town where our shop is."

Koh Tan Soo, like his wife, had all the grace of aging and the dignity that accompanies it. He had ordered a sumptuous Chinese luncheon, which was laid out on a round table in the board of director's dining room of the family's department store. As they ate, he described each dish with the accuracy of a waiter in a high-end restaurant.

"My husband wanted to be a chef, but he was the oldest son and expected to run the family business. When our cook is away, he always cooks meals for me, and he surpasses any cook I ever had," Mrs. Koh said.

"My wife is my greatest fan," Tan Soo responded with a pleased look on his face. "Everyone responds with gratitude to a well-prepared meal."

Elspeth could feel the deep love between these two old people who had lived together for a long time, much like the love between her parents, a kind of love Elspeth thought she never would have.

"Tan Soo, Mrs. Duff has come all the way from Scotland to ask us questions about the Japanese occupation. Soo Jin lives near Mrs. Duff's village there, and we did see the beautiful loch that surrounds her home."

Not exactly true, thought Elspeth, but close enough. It gave them a connection.

"What do you want to know, Mrs. Duff? As I grow older, the war comes closer to me. That time was very difficult for the Chinese in Malaya. Many of our family did not survive," Koh Tan Soo said.

"So your wife told me. Mr. Koh, I'm interested in the Europeans who remained in Malaya and were not interned.

I understand some British soldiers fought alongside the anti-Japanese forces."

"I visited the armies in the jungle many times during the war. Two of my older brothers joined the resistance. I saw at least two British soldiers there, and several Australian ones, living with the members of the resistance and sharing the same deprivations. I do not know their names."

"Were there other European civilians in or around Penang during that time? Perhaps Germans or Italians who supported the Japanese?"

"The Japanese needed Malayan rubber and tin for their war effort. I heard they recruited the help of some of the Europeans, possibly Italians, to run the rubber plantations and the tin mines. I don't know this first-hand, however."

"Do you know anyone who might confirm this?"

Koh Tan Soo took a morsel of spicy fish between his chopsticks, put it in his mouth and chewed slowly. Swallowing he said, "I will ask my cousin, who worked on one of the rubber plantations after the war."

Koh Tan Soo served Elspeth a morsel of bean curd in a red sauce, and she savored its delicate flavors until at the end its peppers came to bite her palate, which brought tears to her eyes.

Mr. Koh smiled. "Our food can catch you unaware. Do you like it?"

"I was surprised, but it's magnificent. I'm used to the Chinese food in California and London, but this is far superior and much spicier."

This seemed to please Koh Tan Soo. "How much longer will you be in Penang, Mrs. Duff?"

"I flew up this morning with friends and am returning to Singapore this evening."

"Where are you staying in Singapore?"

"At the Kennington hotel."

"A very expensive place."

"Actually I work for the Kennington hotel network and fortunately my room is paid for as part of my job."

"Will you be there long? I'll see if I can find out anything more."

"I expect to be in Singapore for at least another week. Here is my mobile number. Please ring me if there is anything else."

27

The day with Mrs. Koh in Penang left Elspeth's mind in disarray. Who previously had mentioned the Italians were on the Axis side? Was it Richard? She winced painfully at the thought of how she had left him. What if Anna Maria's parents had been running a rubber plantation or a tin mine for the Japanese? Would James Buchanan have been on the plantation or at the tin miner's home during the war, and would that mean he was cooperating with the Japanese? Until now Elspeth had assumed Malcolm's parents were hiding in the jungle, but it made more sense that they might be living together in the comfort of a rubber plantation or tin miner's home and starting a family there. Did that mean James Buchanan was a collaborator, or at best an undercover agent, as Lesley Urquhart had implied? Was this why there still was tight security around the details of his life? How could she find out?

She resolved to let the matter rest for a day while she tackled the problem of the taxi drivers called by the hotel. The late hour gave her an excuse to cry off from dinner with the Brixtons. She retreated to her room and ordered a simple meal of broiled chicken, new potatoes, and fresh green beans, a welcome antidote to the exotic foods served at Abdul's grandmother's house and by the Kohs.

She stretched out on the sofa in the seating area of her room and opened a best-selling novel she had bought at the airport. It soon lost her attention. Her mind went back in time.

Elspeth dipped her fingers into the Cam and stared up at Malcolm. He grinned boyishly at her and winked. Delight spread through her as she watched his strong arms pole the punt. He began to sing a song in Italian, obviously a love song. He had sung it to her before, and she hummed along, although she did not know the words. He guided the boat under a willow tree and waddled duck-like up to her. She laughed out loud and cuffed him lovingly on the upper arm when he took a seat beside her. He made snipping sounds as he kissed the ends of her hair as they blew in the wind, but his mind seldom stayed with the frivolities of lovemaking. He began talking about the sophistication of the Chinese language, the development of its pictograms, and the high art of its calligraphy. At the same time he drew out cucumber sandwiches from a picnic hamper and a bottle of cold wine, which he uncorked expertly. He poured out this libation into paper cups.

"I didn't think you knew Chinese, Malcolm," she said with surprise, and sipped the wine. It instantly went to her head. She giggled more girlishly than she would have liked, considering the seriousness of his conversation.

Malcolm bit exaggeratedly into a cucumber sandwich and said, "I spoke rather an infantile form of Chinese when I was a child, but I didn't learn the intricacies of the written language until I became fascinated with Chinese art. In Chinese characters, drawing and words meld into the highest form of art, which is seen everywhere in China, from cheaply printed newspapers to objects carved out of jade or other precious stones. Did you know most jade is not green?" Malcolm's mind characteristically leaped from topic to topic, making abstruse connections his listeners often found hard to follow. "And talking of green . . ." he said, filling her cup and offering her another sandwich. The conversation went off in another direction, which Elspeth did not recall.

At first the memory roused all her loving feelings for Malcolm, but now she looked at the incident coldly for the information it held and not the passion. If Malcolm spoke an infantile form of Chinese as a child, as both he and Victoria Smythe-Welton contended, he must have been in contact with some Chinese during his childhood. Malcolm was born the year the Second World War ended. What had Safirah binti Ibrahim said about the Emergency in Malaya after the war? Had the Buchanans and their children lived among the Chinese insurgents? Did they stay in Malaya after the Japanese left? Malcolm might have had a Chinese amah who spoke to him in Chinese, which seemed more likely. Malcolm did mention that he came to England when he was eight. Had Victoria told Elspeth Malcolm also spoke Malay? But most of Victoria's information had proven inaccurate.

Malcolm never spoke of the first eight years of his life, not even with the slightest allusion. He never mentioned a childhood prank or illness or pets or friends. He never talked of his early schooling or his parents' involvement in his early life. Why? Elspeth had no answer.

Elspeth wished she could talk to Richard and ask his help, but his silence spoke for itself. Resumption of their relationship seemed impossible after the hurtful and cold words they had last exchanged in Malta. She knew she could not retract what she had said because she had spoken the truth, but she wished she could find a way to make amends.

Elspeth rose early and breakfasted in her room, ordering only coffee, toast and fresh fruit. She dressed in a combination of clothes she felt made her look dowdy, left off her makeup, and pinned her hair back from her face in a way that emphasized the strength of her jaw and the sharpness of her nose in an unflattering way. Taking a big canvas bag and a floppy straw hat, both of which she had bought in the hotel gift shop, and adding several tourist brochures she found in the leather portfolio on the desk in her room, she ventured forth, hoping to avoid the Brixtons. They might question her unbecoming costume. She ordered a taxi from a concierge at the desk whom she had not seen before and specifically asked for someone other than Abdul, although she gave no reason for this. She hoped her request would not reflect badly on Abdul. She gave the concierge ten Singapore dollars, knowing the tip to be meager by Kennington hotel standards. She put her finger to her lips as if she was sharing a secret. The doorman at the front of the hotel spoke to the taxi driver and handed Elspeth into the back seat.

She decided to act the part of a middle-aged American tourist. When living in America, Elspeth was constantly annoyed at being asked if she were English. Rather than explaining the difference between being English and being Scottish, she learned to speak faultless Standard American

English. She could switch between her usual cultured British accent and her acquired American one without a thought. Her children often accused her of doing so in mid-conversation when she was talking to an American and someone from the UK at the same time as if she were a translator. Today her American accent would serve her well.

The driver of the small but new Honda introduced himself as Lok. Elspeth told him she wanted to see the some of the outer lying areas of Singapore.

Lok seemed to fancy himself a tour guide as well as a driver. He soon launched into the wonders of the areas of Singapore outside the city center. He drove her to the zoo, which she toured quickly and returned to the waiting car. They stopped for lunch at a Chinese restaurant that Elspeth assumed was run by one of Lok's relatives. It proved only average to a sophisticated palate, even one acquired in California.

After lunch Elspeth decided to approach to Lok. "Do you enjoy working with the Kennington hotels?" she asked. "I try to stay at one when I'm traveling."

"Yes, missus. They good to me."

"Do you have to pay them much to get passengers?" Elspeth loaded the question, although she hoped her voice sounded innocent.

"The hotel very particular," he said, stumbling a bit over the r and l sounds in the words. "I have contact, and I lucky to get connection. This is good business for me."

"You have a nice car."

"Yes, Kennington hotel insist."

"Do you know Abdul? He was my driver two days ago."

"You mean Abdul bin Hassan?"

Elspeth had never asked Abdul's surname and wasn't sure why it would be different from his grandmother's, so she nodded vaguely.

"He has better car and so pays more. It is good business."

"Who do you pay the hotel, Lok?"

"We pay. . ." At this point a goods van swerved over into their lane, and Lok did not finish his sentence in his effort to keep his car on the road and his passenger safe.

Elspeth would not let the subject rest, however. "My nephew," she lied, "drives a taxi in Los Angeles, mostly around Hollywood. He often drives film stars. For this he pays a large fee to a luxury hotel there. Some of the movie stars tip a large amount but some tip nothing. Do you suppose they think it is a privilege for my nephew to drive them?"

"I like go to Hollywood. Can nephew get job for me drive taxi there?"

Elspeth realized she had gone off on the wrong track and needed to return to his arrangements with the Kennington Singapore. She resorted once again to fabrication.

"My nephew pays the concierge at the Kennington Beverley Hills five hundred American dollars a month. This assures him he will get the best business there."

Elspeth waited for Lok to reply, but he did not. She hoped she looked naive. "Before I talked with my nephew, I never realized taxi drivers made these arrangements with hotels. I always thought the doorman simply flagged down a taxi from the street," she said.

"Not at Kennington hotel. Kennington guest get best taxi. Doorman make sure." Lok sounded incensed that any other arrangement would be acceptable.

"How do you know which doorman to pay?"

"We pay head man, Mr. Hangkow. Cash every month."

Elspeth knew enough about China to know that Hangkow was a city and not a surname. She must have heard wrongly.

"Just like Hollywood," she said and wondered why Lok said Mr. Hangkow was the headman. Wasn't the "headman" William Ling?

She took a long tour of the Japanese and Chinese gardens where Lok had driven her and had tea there. It was close to five o'clock when she returned to the hotel. She had done nothing during the day to repair her appearance. Her clothes were wrinkled from the heat and her hair in disarray. She was anxious to get to her room before anyone saw her. She scurried past the reception desk without looking up.

A far-too-familiar baritone voice behind her brought her up short.

"Elspeth, my dear, I hoped you would return soon, so I waited for you here in the lobby."

She turned, and her eyes met the long, aristocratic face of Richard Munro. Her heart bumped against her chest before she could take control of it.

"Dickie?" she gulped.

His attempt at a welcoming hug knocked her hat atilt, and her large bag swung around and hit him on the back. Elspeth seldom felt awkward, but in that moment she did. She disentangled herself from him and said, "Dickie, what on earth are you doing in Singapore?"

He held her at arms length, obviously puzzled at her costume. Finally he said, "Elspeth, we didn't part as friends in Malta before Christmas. I came to see if we could make things right."

Relief flooded through her, and she smiled at him with contrition. "I said things to you then I wish I hadn't. I've been regretting my words for weeks. Will you forgive me?"

"I have nothing to forgive, Elspeth," he said looking deeply into her eyes, which unsettled her, and taking both her hands, which she did not withdraw. "You and I have different opinions as to the worth of Malcolm. Your love for him, which you so passionately declared in Gozo, added nothing new to resolve our disagreement. I came because I've missed you. We should not have left things the way we did in Malta. I managed to get myself invited to a meeting in Hong Kong, although I really came to see you. I also have new information about Malcolm that may change either your opinion or mine."

Her eyes probed his, and she reddened at her reaction to them. "Oh, Dickie," she said, finally smiling, and then she touched his cheek. "I'm so glad you came. I do want to hear what you've found out. Can you give me a few minutes to freshen up, please? I've been out in a taxi all day, in an intentionally frumpy disguise, and. . ."

She did not need to finish; the love in his eyes told her what she wanted to know.

When she got back to her room, the phone rang.

"Elspeth, Sarah here. I saw you with Sir Richard Munro in the lobby. Is *he* your Richard?"

"He's not my anything!" Elspeth said fiercely.

"Quite a catch, Elspeth. You shouldn't treat him so lightly. Clyde and I knew him and. . ." Sarah paused, as if embarrassed, which was unlike her.

"Lady Marjorie?" asked Elspeth.

"Well, yes."

Elspeth laughed. "Sarah, have no fear about Marjorie. I've known Richard since I was at school. When he was at Oxford, he spent summers with my cousin Johnnie in Perthshire, long before Marjorie. I also met Marjorie several times over the course of their marriage," Elspeth said.

"There is quite a difference between you two," Sarah said bluntly.

"I'm sure Richard frequently makes the comparison," Elspeth said archly, "and I'm not sure I come up favorably." She did not elaborate.

It was Sarah's turn to laugh. "If I were you, I shouldn't make assumptions about his comparisons, Elspeth. You probably come out quite well." She said no more.

Good to her word, Elspeth joined Richard in the drinks bar twenty minutes later. His look told her he admired her quick transformation. She blushed with pleasure. He had already chosen a sauvignon blanc for them both. A waiter brought the chilled bottle, glasses, and assorted hot hors d'oeuvres to their table.

"Ms. Duff, will you lend me your evening?" Richard asked formally after she was seated.

"I give it to you freely, Sir Richard," she said, bowing her head to him. "But now tell me about the new information you have on Malcolm."

He took her hand. She lightly folded her fingers around his.

He motioned to the waiter to pour out the wine, and they toasted each other silently.

"I've found someone here who knew Jamie Buchanan during the war in the jungle. He's quite an old man now but, when I talked to him from Malta, he told me he remembers the time well. He's agreed to see us. I told him it would either be tonight or tomorrow morning since I have to fly on to Hong Kong tomorrow afternoon. He's expecting me to ring him after I've agreed on a time with you. He lives in a flat on the outskirts of Singapore and has invited us to his home."

Elspeth's excitement grew. "Tonight would be better. I don't think I can wait until tomorrow, now that this chance is so close. I've been unsuccessfully snooping around the Buchanan mater and pater's past ever since I left Malta. To find someone who actually knew one of them is a wonderful surprise. How did you ever manage it, Dickie?"

He looked pleased with himself. "As you remember, I served here in Singapore for four years. When I learned you were coming out here, I began making enquires among my FCO chums to find if they knew anyone who escaped internment in the terrible Japanese wartime camps and survived in the jungle. In the course of three days I had two names. The first was an ex-soldier living in Liverpool, but when I rang there, I was told he died last year. My call to Singapore proved more fruitful. Ex-Sergeant Gaylord Hall of the Australian Army lost touch with his regiment during the Japanese assault on Singapore in nineteen forty-two. He was injured but joined a group of other British and Australian forces who made their way into the jungle and were eventually picked up by the Chinese resistance forces who were hiding there. He was one of the few in his group who survived in the jungle, and he remembers the time clearly. After the war he remained in Malaya, and his knowledge of the wartime activities in the jungle proved invaluable to the British and

Malayan forces fighting the communist insurgency. Later he married a Malay woman, and they live here in Singapore on his pension and the largess of her family. He's delighted to talk to us, because he said his wife, children, grandchildren, and friends are tired of his stories, but they still hold a strange power over him. He likes retelling them."

Richard borrowed Elspeth's mobile and rang Gaylord Hall. They arranged to be at his home at half past seven.

"And now, Lady MacDuff, tell me where you have been and why you have stayed out of touch?" In addressing her, he used a name from their first acquaintance, in a voice he had usually affected when not quite approving of Elspeth or her cousin's antics during the summers long ago in Perthshire. Elspeth wasn't sure why he chose the name now. Was it meant to reprove her? But for what? His voice was jocular but edged on censure. She decided to recount her adventures in London, in Sydney, and recently in Singapore in as straightforward a manner as possible but was equivocal on how best to respond to the last part of his question.

He watched her as she spoke. She could not read his thoughts, nor did she offer any reason of her three-week silence, which had been as long as his. If he gave no explanation, why should she?

Having finished her narrative, she turned back to the moment. "Dickie, how did you know I was here in Singapore?"

"Pamela Crumm, of course."

"But she said she would not share anything I told her with anyone."

"She obviously does not consider me just anyone."

"Wait until I talk to her. So much for girlish confidences."
Although Elspeth laughed, she did not finish her conversation

with Richard comfortably and felt an uneasiness return between them.

*

Richard felt the tension too. His attempts at humor to soften their meeting seemed to leave her confused as to his message, possibly because he was not sure what to say to her. In Malta she had been rash, where by nature he preferred caution. He wanted to be sensitive to her feelings, but he was jarred when she expressed her love for Malcolm so vociferously. Richard often saw Elspeth's fondness for him in her eyes, but her heart always seemed to linger on those days with Malcolm at Cambridge. Richard did not expect this when he first urged her to take up the investigation of Malcolm's murder. Selfishly he thought she soon would see the futility of it and bring her life back to the present and to him. Now she seemed more interested in his finding someone who knew Malcolm's parents than in his own presence in Singapore. She seemed perplexed when he called her by a name he had used teasingly in their days together during their summers in the Highlands. He meant the name as an endearment, but he could see she did not react to it in that way. Most of all, he did not know how to deal with his own sadness that their misunderstanding continued. She did not say why she had not contacted him. Was it willfulness, to which she was prone, or simple disinterest in him? He did not know. He sensed she was struggling with her own emotions as well. They finished their wine in silence. By dinner, they had resumed a formal familiarity.

During the course of dinner Elspeth explained the mission Eric Kennington had assigned to her in Singapore and asked Richard if he would make a point of requesting Abdul take them to Gaylord Hall's home. She related briefly what she had learned from Lok that afternoon and explained she wanted to question Abdul about Mr. "Hangkow."

Abdul was waiting for them under the porte-cochère at the appointed time, but he averted his eyes when Elspeth greeted him. He must have heard about Lok.

"Abdul, this is my friend, Sir Richard Munro, who is the British high commissioner in Malta, and who also served as British high commissioner here in Singapore. I've told him how extremely helpful you've been to me and have recommended all of his friends and diplomatic colleagues ask for you when they come to Singapore."

Richard thought she was being a bit heavy-handed with the titles and connections, but Abdul immediately took the bait and smiled from ear to ear.

"My pleasure, yes, my very good pleasure, my lord," he said, bowing with respect.

Richard decided to join Elspeth's game. "Abdul, Ms. Duff has told me how important you've been during her stay here. While I'm in Singapore I'll make sure to ask for you. In fact, I would like to engage you exclusively until I leave tomorrow. Do I need to arrange this through Mr. Hangkow?" He purposely slurred the name.

Abdul looked nervous. "No, sir. I arrange it with Mr. Hancook myself."

"Then let me pay the extra so that you can tell Mr. Hancook I want you," Richard volunteered.

"Thank you, my lord," Abdul said.

Richard handed him a hundred Singapore dollar note, although he knew this was an overly generous tip, even for someone staying at a Kennington hotel.

28

The manner in which Sergeant Hall lived highlighted for Elspeth the disparity between the local lower middle-class population and the traveling wealthy in Singapore.

Abdul drove them to a multi-colored tower of high-rise buildings north of the city and explained that the flats inside were part of the Singaporean government's commitment to home ownership. The lobby to the lift was functional, extremely clean, bare and smelled of disinfectant. Richard pressed the button for the fifteenth floor. The hallway from the lift to Sergeant Hall's flat was sterile and softened only by windows at the end that looked out over the pinnacles of the other buildings of government-sponsored flats. Daylight was fading, and lights had begun to speckle in the windows of the buildings beyond. Home ownership may have been a worthy goal, but, having grown up in the sparsely populated Scottish Highlands, Elspeth shuddered at the proximity of so many close-by neighbors. Gaylord Hall's exuberant welcome, however, alleviated the starkness of the corridor and was warmer than that of any manager at a Kennington hotel.

Elspeth judged the Australian must be in his mid-eighties. Gravity and too much sun had taken its toll on his body. His hair was white, his face covered with brown spots, and his beard badly shaven. Yet his boyishness captivated both of his guests. His wife was an older round-faced Malaysia woman who had quiet, warm eyes and was dressed in a form-fitting patterned sarong and a blouse with three quarter length sleeves that Elspeth, with her love of clothes, had learned was called a *kebaya*. The woman greeted them respectfully, and her eyes gave an understanding and loving apology for her husband's boisterous enthusiasm.

"Com'in, com'in. Sir Richard, I welcome you and your lady to my home. This is my wife Maria," Sergeant Hall said and beckoned them in to his sitting room. He offered them sickeningly sweet rum cocktails made with pineapple, guava, coconut and brown sugar, his own specialty. They took seats on rattan chairs positioned around a large screen television.

"I love my sports," he shared with them, "and Maria likes the daytime talk shows from America." Maria hardly looked the type who would relish in stories of lurid life styles that appealed to American housewives, but she nodded in acknowledgment. "Oprah is my favorite," she said.

After they exchanged pleasantries and Richard and Elspeth commented diplomatically on the taste of the drinks, Sergeant Hall began to relate the story of his time in the jungles of Malaya from nineteen forty-two until he was repatriated to Singapore in nineteen forty-five.

"The jungle was both our enemy and our friend. It hid us from the Japanese forces, but the hardships were constantly there. We all had malaria because we had no quinine. Leeches, scorpions, and snakes made our lives hell every day. I can tell you many stories about the terrors we all faced. Few of us survived. Both the Japanese forces, the Nips, as we called them then, and their secret police, the *kempeitai*, stalked us relentlessly. We stayed on the move all the time. We were always hungry and often delirious with fever and infection. Those of us who survived lived day-to-day with one thought, to stay alive. For the first year or two we were on our own. The Chinese resistance forces and their sympathizers were our only friends. They brought us food when they could, but otherwise we scavenged what we could from the jungle and the deserted plantations and villages. Most of us were ill all the time, and all of us became skeletons and were scarred by the ravages of the jungle."

Elspeth shuddered, thinking of Malcolm's family.

"Sir Richard asked me to tell you about Jamie Buchanan, Mrs. Duff. As the war progressed, our group joined up with the resistance, who were mainly Chinese and who had set up their own camps. I think this saved our lives because they gave us some quinine when we were delirious from malaria, and they fed us. The portions were small, but we often had rice and meat from monkeys, wild boar, and an occasional bear. We caught fish when we could and added our catch to the community pot. One of our lot was an excellent shot, and he brought down game for our dinner as often as he killed the Japanese snipers who found our camps."

Elspeth looked around at Richard and found him watching her.

Gaylord Hall continued. "It is awfully hot and humid in the jungle and seasons are only defined by the coming of the rains. As best as I can make out the dates, during the autumn of nineteen forty-four three Brits who were equipped with radio equipment joined us. I think they came from a group of British intelligence officers who operated secretly out of the northern part of the country. One of them was Jamie Buchanan. Unlike the others, he was not in uniform and appeared to have no military rank. We all assumed he was a British planter or tin mine engineer who had been caught in the Nip's advance south across Malaya in nineteen forty-one, but he never said for sure. The other two Brits treated him distantly, as if something was not quite right about him, but he was by far the most skilled wireless operator among us and could fix the radio whenever it failed to work. The Brits stayed with our camp until the spring of nineteen forty-five, and we got to know them because we were the only ones in the camp who spoke English with any fluency. Jamie Buchanan spoke good Chinese and had a fair amount of Malay. He could understand Japanese, and when we encountered any of the Nips, usually when we were hiding in the undergrowth, he could translate what they said for us."

That explains why Malcolm said his father was multi-lingual, Elspeth thought.

"Jamie was more secretive about his past than the others. He mentioned he had a wife and a daughter, whom he hoped were safe. We all assumed they were living in one of the Japanese camps, but we heard many of the women and children died in the camps. Jamie slipped in and out of our camp, and we thought he had a way to meet his wife secretly."

Where? Elspeth asked herself.

"After a brief stay at home down under, I returned to Malaya in nineteen forty-seven to help fight during the Emergency. I never expected to hear of Jamie again. During the war the other Brits talked all the time about going home, to England that is, but Jamie always said when the war was over he would stay in Malaya. I heard more about him probably five or six years later after members of the Malayan Communist Party, the MCP, were driven deep into the jungle. The major commanding my group told the story of a Brit who had been in the jungle during the war and after the war had joined the MCP. The major said the Brit had risen in their ranks. The story went that he took his family into the jungle and lived with the insurgents. He became converted to their cause, turned against his own people and was trusted at the highest level by the MCP. When I asked the major who the man was, I was shocked to hear that his name was Jamie Buchanan. Jamie definitely was a strange one, but I didn't take him for a traitor. I asked the major if he thought Jamie might be with British intelligence, but the major doubted it. He told me that Jamie was responsible for the killing of several members of a British expeditionary force in the jungle, and the major doubted an intelligence officer would do such a thing. After that I never heard of Jamie Buchanan again, but I wondered how someone could turn like that against his own kind. I suppose I've always thought loyalty to one's country is an important thing.

"I've never told anyone this last part of the story, and I can't say for sure if it is true, but the major said it was. I don't know if he knew these things first-hand, but he was convinced the story was genuine. I'm sorry about the gory details, but I hope this is what you wanted to hear."

Richard and Elspeth sat silently as they listened to Gaylord Hall's story. At the end, Elspeth slowly drew in her breath. The story of the wartime horrors filled her with revulsion. She had heard of instances of soldiers turning coat in Europe and the Philippines from members of her parent's generation, but the story of Jamie Buchanan's treachery was different. Defections to the enemy in war happened, usually out of a sense of needing to survive, but out-and-out betrayal to one's country after the war shocked her. Was this why Malcolm was so reticent about his parents? Were his mother and sister in the camps during the war? Elspeth had read Agnes Keith's *Three Came Home,* which related the horrors in the camps for women and children in Indonesia, and suspected the conditions were similar in Malaya.

Elspeth knew little about the time of the communist insurgency in Malaya, but she thought Richard would know more. Would he be able to find other people who were still alive who remembered that time and Jamie Buchanan's betrayal? She was loath to ask him another favor, but Richard said he came to Singapore in order to see her and help her. There still was the mystery of where Anna Maria Buchanan had spent the war and where her children were born. Gaylord Hall assumed they were in one of the camps, but was this true? Elspeth felt that every time she stirred up information about the Buchanans they became less likeable. The Malcolm she knew seemed thoroughly British. She never considered him anything but a loyal British citizen and, if his parents' past was cloaked in mystery, Elspeth until now assumed they were involved in intelligence. Lesley Urquhart hinted that they were. Gaylord Hall's story blew that notion apart. He implied Jamie and Anna Maria Buchanan were traitors. That possibility existed for the generation that produced Burgess, MacLean, Philby, and Blunt, although their defections were to the Soviet Union and not to the Chinese-backed communists in Malaya. Why hadn't she asked Malcolm more about his family? And why didn't she heed Richard's advice all those years ago? Damn you, Dickie, she thought, are you going to be smug?

Abdul was waiting for them outside Gaylord Hall's tower of flats and took them back toward the hotel. He described the delights of Singapore at night but got no response from either of his passengers. He recommended they have a drink at one of the better modern hotels in the center of the city, but they said no. He dropped them at the Kennington hotel and assured Sir Richard he would be available at seven the next morning.

Richard led Elspeth into the lobby, and he suggested they retire to the garden to talk about what they had just heard.

"Why, Dickie? To prove you were right, that Malcolm's parents were not honorable people and I should have known." She walked from him with her head high in the air and her back rigid. She felt the same bitterness she had when Richard confronted her about Malcolm when she was at Cambridge.

"Please, Elspeth, I didn't come all this way to prove an old point," he said stiffly.

"Didn't you? Did you know what Sergeant Hall was going to tell us?" she challenged him.

"No, I didn't. I'd hoped what he told us would exonerate the Buchanans, not condemn them. Come, let's have a drink, and talk about where we are now. I don't know what you are feeling, but it seems Sergeant Hall's news is not sitting well with you."

"We don't even know if his story about the Buchanans is true. Now I suppose you will go digging up someone who will confirm it." Her anger surged and covered her inner dismay.

After ordering their drinks, Richard led Elspeth into the garden and sat down next to her on a silk cushion on one of the teak benches under a heavily flowered hibiscus bush. He did not touch her. Despite her anger, she missed his intimacy.

He did not look at her directly but talked to a jasmine bush across the white stone path at the foot of the bench. From the corner of her eye Elspeth could see the tautness of the muscles in his cheeks and cleanly shaven jaw.

"I do have one more person for us to talk to before I leave," he said. "When I suggested we meet Sergeant Hall, he said he was willing to tell his story, although I assure you I didn't know the extent of it. The person I want you to meet in the morning was less eager. I called in a past favor in order to get him to agree to meet us."

Elspeth folded her arms tightly across her chest and stared at the jasmine bush as well, as if it were their interpreter. "And I suppose he's on your side too?"

Richard turned directly to her and took her by the shoulders. "Elspeth, I didn't come to Singapore to fight with you. I came because I thought you wanted to know the truth about Malcolm and his family. I also wanted to see you for personal reasons that have nothing to do with Malcolm. If you want to give up the search now, I'll go no further and call off the appointment with Roger Black tomorrow morning." He obviously was provoked at her, although his tone was calm.

Elspeth's anger faded. "I always seem to be apologizing to you, don't I? Can't you understand? Nothing seems to be coming out the way I'd hoped. I'm afraid I'm taking it out on you. But who is Roger Black?"

Richard moved toward her and pushed back a piece of her hair with his long fingers. "Of course I forgive you, my dear." He looked lovingly into her eyes but she averted hers. "Sergeant Hall's story cannot have been easy for you," he said softly. "I hope Roger can clarify for you some of the things the sergeant told us."

"You've not said who Roger Black is," Elspeth said, glad of Richard's tenderness but still upset enough not to acknowledge it.

"He works with the Secret Intelligence Service," Richard said.

"A spy?"

"Not spy exactly. He is far above that; he is station chief here in Singapore."

Elspeth did not know the refinements of the British espionage system. "Station chief? You mean the head of British intelligence here?" she asked.

"Yes. I have worked with him in the past, although he wasn't here when I was high commissioner. When I rang him, he was reluctant to talk until I told him that you worked for Scotland Yard at one time. Eric Kennington vouched for you as well."

"Eric? Oh, no, Dickie, you didn't go to him?" Elspeth clenched her teeth, growled in a most unrefined way and turn away from him once again.

"I couldn't think of any other way. Lord Kennington is anxious to get you back under his wing, Elspeth. I believe he would go to great lengths to speed that process along."

Elspeth let out a groan. "This is suddenly a ghastly nightmare. Hopefully I'll wake up soon. Now, when do we meet this Roger Black?"

"Tomorrow at breakfast here at the hotel. I've arranged for a private room so that we can talk freely. Eric said he would pay for anything that would guarantee your speedy return to the fold."

"Is Roger Black going to destroy some more illusions of mine?" Elspeth demanded.

"I've no idea, my dearest. He did tell me he could shed some more light on Jamie Buchanan and his wife."

They parted coolly. Richard made his way into the interior of the hotel, and Elspeth took the lift to her room.

Elspeth expected Roger Black to steal through a back door and therefore was surprised the next morning when she arrived downstairs to find Richard sharing orange juice with him at the breakfast bar. Roger was a tall man, dressed in an opened-collared pleated dress shirt and neatly pressed khaki trousers. His face was tanned in the way of one who has spent much of his life in tropical climates. His hand took Elspeth's with a strong grip, and he smiled genuinely.

"Richard has been telling me you are a dogged investigator and will not rest until you get to the bottom of your case. I find that a bit alarming in such a lovely woman."

Elspeth smiled at the flattery, although she had dressed to make an impression. Her eyes held his steadily. Richard came up to her and took her arm. He motioned to a waiter, who escorted them to a private room off the main lounge. A typically elaborate Kennington hotel breakfast was waiting for them on the sideboard. The waiter unassumingly withdrew.

After they helped themselves to breakfast, Roger Black spoke. "And now, Ms. Duff, why do you want to know about Jamie Buchanan and his wife? This information has been classified for a good number of years. If Richard had not been so insistent, I would not have come this morning, even with the temptation of one of the Kennington Singapore's famous breakfasts."

"Richard has great powers of persuasion," she said, glancing at Richard, who raised his chin.

Roger Black looked over at Richard, whose face remained expressionless, and then turned his attention back to Elspeth.

"I told Richard I would take specific questions from you. That way I can tell you if each of your questions is one I can answer. I realize this is a convoluted process, but it allows me to help you without revealing more than needed. I hope these terms are agreeable."

Elspeth looked at him with admiration. She must remember this technique. "I'm grateful for any answers you can give me, Mr. Black, and will try to honor your need for confidentiality without asking why this secrecy is still a necessity. I trust Her Majesty's Government has its reasons."

"Exactly." He took a mouthful of his poached eggs à la Kennington topped with smoked salmon and fresh Hollandaise sauce and looked down at his plate appreciatively. "Shall we begin?"

Elspeth was too excited to pay attention to her meal. She had eaten too many Kennington breakfasts to be impressed by their opulence. She served herself sparingly and sipped her coffee. "Can you tell me if the Buchanan's daughter was born in the jungle?" she asked.

"No, Mary Anne Buchanan was born outside of a city called Ipoh, in western Malaya."

"Wasn't Ipoh under the control of the Japanese when she was born?"

"It was."

"How then was Anna Maria Buchanan safe from the Japanese?"

"Her father was the Italian ambassador to the Court of the Emperor of Japan in the early nineteen thirties. By command of the Japanese Imperial Government Mrs. Buchanan was spared internment, but, because her husband was British, she was kept under what amounted to house arrest in a villa of a tin mine owner outside Ipoh."

"Surely if their daughter was born in nineteen forty-three, Jamie Buchanan had some contact with his wife after the Japanese took control of Malaya."

"Only infrequently as far as we know. Obviously during two of those times his daughter and son were conceived."

"Was Jamie Buchanan in the jungle for the duration of the war?"

"I can't answer that."

From his tone, Elspeth was not sure whether he did not know or he did not want her to know.

"Was Jamie Buchanan in the British military?" Elspeth asked.

"He cooperated with the military, but, no, he was not."

"Their son Malcolm was born in nineteen forty-five. Was he born at the tin mine owner's home as well?"

"I believe so."

"Did Mrs. Buchanan's position make the men in the jungle distrust Jamie?"

"I don't know."

"I understand he later joined the Malayan Communist Party."

"He did. James Buchanan and his family went into the jungle after the Emergency began, but how do you know that?"

Elspeth skirted the question and asked another of her own. "At that time did he fight against the British, Indian and Malayan forces?"

"Unfortunately, yes."

Unfortunately? Elspeth wondered at the use of the word.

"Was he considered a traitor by His Majesty's Government? It's important I know this," Elspeth said.

Roger Black nodded almost imperceptibly but paused before he spoke. "Ms. Duff, we're on very sensitive ground here. What you must understand is that the British who fought in the jungle with the resistance during the Japanese conflict owed much of their survival to the Chinese there. Often strong bonds were formed. Most of the soldiers who survived were only too eager to return to their homelands immediately after the war, but Jamie Buchanan was different. Perhaps I'm telling more than I should, but you should understand that his seeming defection to the Malayan Communist Party was an understandable consequence of his loyalty to people who had protected him during the war."

Elspeth listened carefully, wondering if intelligence officers always spoke so obliquely.

"Seeming defection?"

Roger Black did not respond.

"Mr. Black, I'm not interested in Jamie or Anna Maria's political associations then, but I am curious about the lives of their children. Do you know anything about that?"

"Mrs. Buchanan brought her children out of the jungle in nineteen fifty-three and contacted the British authorities, asking that they arrange for her children's passage to England. She said the jungle was no longer a safe place for them. Because the children were British, the authorities agreed. The children were sent to Portsmouth in the company of a Chinese amah, who spoke passable English and was closely associated with them in the jungle. Once the amah delivered the children to their aunt, she returned to Malaya. We didn't keep track of her after that."

"Thank you for sharing that with me."

So Malcolm's statement that he learned rudimentary Chinese as a child was correct. At least he had not lied about that. One for you, Malcolm, she thought. She hated that she was now keeping score of his truths, his lies, and his omissions. The list she started in London was growing.

"I do have another concern, which you may or may not want to answer," she said. "Any information would be helpful in my investigation into Malcolm Buchanan's murder.

I know Jamie and Anna Maria Buchanan eventually retired to Tasmania. You've suggested in the nineteen fifties they may have betrayed the Crown. Malcolm's sister once said when Malcolm and she were children they occasionally visited their parents in various corners of the world. The only place I can remember is Lima. If my history is correct, Peru had an activist communist movement about then. Can you tell me if the Buchanans were in Peru as communists or as British agents?"

"I can't answer that."

Elspeth recalled the comments of the women in Rushmore. "All right then, did the Buchanan's ever teach in Western Australia?"

"Yes, for several years they did."

"Western Australia is a harsh place. Was their teaching there some sort of measure to repatriate them into the capitalist fold?"

"They requested the assignment."

"Can you tell me the terms?"

"No, that's classified."

Elspeth felt she had made some headway but was still not satisfied. She tried a new strategy. "When the Buchanans retired to Tasmania, did they have anything to fear from the communists who had been in the jungle?"

Roger Black looked at her, obviously considering his answer.

"No, I think not. Now, Ms. Duff, I must return to my office. Thank you both for a delicious breakfast."

He left Richard and Elspeth alone to finish their meal.

29

After breakfast, Richard and Elspeth retreated to the garden and found a quiet bench. Most of the hotel guests had departed for the morning, and Elspeth and Richard sat alone. The Kennington hotel gardens were designed for scent as well as color and geometry, and the sweet, almost cloying perfume from the surrounding waxy-leafed frangipani bushes filled the spot they chose.

Elspeth settled down on the bench beside Richard and turned to him. The anger she felt toward him the night before had melted away. She looked up at him with some embarrassment and found warmth in his hazel-green eyes. How could she express her confusion?

She decided to be honest about her reaction to the things they had learned in the last twenty-four hours. "I'm no longer certain why I took on this search, Dickie. Every turn brings new information that muddles me further. I'm beginning to doubt I can find a solution to Malcolm's murder. Everything seems to hinge on such small bits of information gleaned from people who remember the past in such different ways."

She looked up at Richard but could not read his reaction to her words, his face remaining unmoved. What about your heart, Dickie? she thought. She struggled to let the thought go and asked, "What did we actually learn from Roger Black?"

"May I interpret?" His tone suggested he knew he was on delicate terms with her. "I've dealt with many people in the intelligence service, and they often reveal more than they suspect."

"Please go on." She thought but did not add, "but don't chide me."

"I get the impression Jamie and Anna Maria Buchanan were not trusted by the British authorities," he said, "but that the intelligence service kept in touch with them from the time they went into the jungles after the war until they died. You were quite right in asking if the Buchanans went to teach in Western Australia as an act of, how shall I put it, contrition. The interior of Western Australia is a cruel place. I think we must presume the Buchanans were double agents, but no one except the Buchanans themselves knew where their real loyalties lay. In the end they may have wanted to come in from the proverbial cold."

Elspeth nodded her head as Richard spoke and wished his voice were tenderer. She had only herself to blame for that. "Yes, Roger Black gave me that feeling too. Where does that leave us? Obviously Malcolm's parents wanted to get their children away from the jungle in nineteen fifty-three. Can we assume, as Roger said, they were worried about the safety of their children? If the Buchanans were dedicated communists, why would they send their children to England and insist they be educated at good schools there? Was there some harm done to the children in the jungle?"

"It's a pity we can't speak to Mary Anne," Richard said. "She's probably the only person other than Malcolm and his parents who could have answered that question. Have you contacted Morris Aldridge to see if Maudy is willing to meet with you again?"

"No, but Maudy's fleeing from having tea with me at Raffle's must be significant. Let's hope I can get to the bottom of it."

Elspeth suddenly regretted Richard's impending departure. "When do you leave?" she asked.

"In about two hours. Abdul has been waiting for me since seven. I saw him from the lobby as we came out from our meeting with Roger Black."

"Before you leave, Dickie, will you do me a favor?"

"Of course," he said without adding any endearments.

"I want to be free to meet with Maudy whenever she is ready, but I need to wrap up my business for the Kennington Organisation here at the hotel. I plan to email Pamela and ask for the list of employees. Would you give Abdul a bit extra and tell him you want him to settle up with the hotel for his good service to you. I hope this will flush out the person taking the kickbacks."

"Why do you think that will help?"

"I'm sure Pamela can identify who our suspect is from the information I already have gathered, but I want to catch him in the act of accepting money."

Richard raised a conspiratorial eyebrow. "As you wish. I'll also tell Abdul to return to the hotel after dropping me off at the airport, as I promised his services to you for the rest of the day. I'll give him even more money than I already have, which was an outrageous amount."

"Let me know how much, and I'll make sure Eric reimburses you."

"Not to worry. Being with you these last few hours has been a reward in itself. The money is not important."

His words were more than mere pleasantries. She wished momentarily she were not so reactive. Why couldn't she just be straightforward with him?

She heard a rustle in the bushes behind her, but when she turned no one was there. Had someone been listening to their conversation and then slipped away? When Richard pleaded it was necessary for him to go to his room to get ready for his trip to Hong Kong, Elspeth felt a sense of loss. She wanted to make further amends with him before he left.

"Dickie, I'm sorry I'm being so beastly about Malcolm."

Richard looked at her and smiled sadly. "I think you are trying to recreate a dream, Elspeth, which may not be as idyllic as you think."

"So I'm finding out," she admitted.

"Do you remember where you came from when you went to Cambridge? You had loving home, with loving parents and a loving family. Unlike Malcolm, you did not endure the hardships of war, or the jungle, or hatred, or mental and physical harm. Most of our sort expect to trust our families and friends. We find it strange the rest of the world, and even parts of Britain for that matter, do not live that way."

"So it seems. Oh, Dickie," she said with sorrow and then stopped. "Just. . . . oh, Dickie."

He took her hand and held it for a long time but otherwise did not respond.

After receiving a perfunctory goodbye kiss on her cheek from Richard, Elspeth retired to her room. She was still distressed by her jumbled thoughts and chose to purge them by returning to the task Eric Kennington had given her. She checked the world clock on her laptop. The UK was eight hours behind Singapore, which would make it six in the morning in London. Elspeth knew Pamela Crumm well enough to know that she would be up and possibly would be at her desk.

As anticipated, the familiar voice answered her call. "Elspeth, I've been wondering what you are doing. Did Sir Richard surprise you?"

"I'll talk to you about that another time, Pamela."

"I can tell you're annoyed at me."

"Only mildly," Elspeth said, brushing Pamela's curiosity aside. "Eric sent me out here on an assignment, and I'm close to getting results. Can you check the employee list for the Kennington Singapore easily?"

Pamela chortled but responded to Elspeth's question without further comment. "At a click of my mouse. Who are you looking for?"

"I've tracked the taxi scheme down to a person whose name sounds like Hangkow to a Chinese and Hancook to a Malay. Can you find any match?"

"Hold on a minute. While I am scrolling down, tell me how things went with Richard." Pamela would not be waylaid.

"I was terribly irritated with both of you when he arrived, but he was very helpful finding contacts who gave me more information about Malcolm. So I have forgiven him. We parted on friendly terms."

"Parted? Only friendly? Elspeth, surely Richard and you. . ."

Elspeth interrupted Pamela's romantic musings. "Yes, he's gone on to Hong Kong to his meeting."

There was silence on the other end of the line until Pamela said, "Here we are. Hangkow or Hancook. How about Hancock? Wilmont Hancock, chief bookkeeper, Kennington Singapore."

"It could be. Do you have a photograph?"

"That will take a bit longer, but meanwhile you will have to tell me what new information there is on Malcolm."

"Pamela, you're shameless in your pursuit of thrills."

"That's one of the chief benefits of my job. So what did you find out?"

Elspeth omitted the information Roger Black had given her but told Pamela about the interviews with Safirah binti Ibrahim and Mrs. Koh and the narration of Sergeant Hall. Elspeth could hear Pamela pecking at the keys of her computer as they spoke.

"Here he is!" she exclaimed.

"Who?" Elspeth asked, having lost the thread of the conversation.

"Wilmont Hancock. I'm sending you his photograph as we speak. This will take a moment because I need to downsize the file." Pamela tapped at her keyboard. "Here it comes."

Elspeth hit one of the keys of her laptop to make the screen active and double clicked on Pamela's message. The picture filled the screen.

"But, he's the early morning doorman who. . ." she started to say.

She heard a sound behind her, but she did not feel the pain of the blow. It was too sudden. Blackness enveloped her.

*

On an impulse, which was unlike him, Richard decided to find Elspeth and say a final goodbye. He wanted them to part on more tender terms than they had shared in the garden, and he knew he might not see her again in the near future. He sent his cases down to the lobby and took the lift to Elspeth's floor. When he reached her room, he found the door ajar. He pushed it open and rushed forward to the chaos beyond. Her body slumped on the sofa beside her laptop computer. Its screen had been slashed savagely and the keyboard had been smashed brutally. He rushed to her and raised her in his arms, but she gave no response, not even a moan. He saw a small rivulet of blood seeping down her neck from the base of her skull.

30

Richard sat and held Elspeth's hand as he had for many hours and days since bringing her to St. Mary's Hospital in London. His emotions swung wildly, his concern for Elspeth's wellbeing, his love for her, his dismay at her stubbornness, and her avoidance at acknowledging how he felt about her or how she felt about him. She lay motionless, and the room was quiet save for the muffled roar of London traffic outside the window, the steady rhythm of her breathing, and the beeps of the heart monitor. He watched the machine's perpetually scrolling graph. He had long since memorized its peaks and valleys. Her pulse like her heart rate remained steady, which the doctors had told him meant her complete recovery was probable. It was only a matter of time.

He rose as the mid-January evening was crawling across London. He watched the streetlights coming on. People scurried along the streets, although it was still early for the end of the workday. He had watched the same pattern for the last fortnight. He returned to Elspeth's bed and took her warm but lifeless hand in his.

"Please wake up, my precious one," he whispered.

She stirred as if she had heard him and let out a short grunt. Richard gripped her hand more firmly and said, "Can you hear me, Elspeth?"

Her eyes slowly opened, but they did not focus. She turned her head toward him and blinked several times. He had waited a long time to see those startling blue eyes.

He leaned close to her and heard her faint whisper. He thought she said, "Is that you, Dickie?" Then her eyes closed, and she slid again into unawareness.

Not daring to leave lest she come back to consciousness, Richard pressed the call button. A nursing sister appeared immediately, concern filling her face.

"Sister," Richard cried out, "she just opened her eyes and spoke to me."

"Let me get the doctor," the nurse said.

The doctor came on a run. "Tell me exactly what happened," he said. The doctor's manner was coolly professional, but Richard sensed his excitement.

"She opened her eyes and spoke to me," Richard said, trying to contain his joy.

"What did she say?"

"She said 'Is that you, Dickie?' Or at least I think so."

The doctor looked at him. "Is that what she calls you, Sir Richard?"

"It was my sobriquet when I was at Oxford," he said with dignity. "That's when we first knew each other."

"Oh," the doctor said. "Then she recognized you."

Since Richard had found Elspeth lying unconscious in Singapore two weeks before, he rarely left her. Not knowing precisely who was her next of kin, he had phoned her father from Singapore, and explained his daughter had been injured and needed to be evacuated to London. Obtaining James Duff's authorization to act on behalf of Elspeth's family, Richard contacted Pamela Crumm and Lord Kennington, who arranged for Elspeth's airlift to London on Clyde Brixton's company plane. Once in London, Richard debated contacting Elspeth's children, not wanting to frighten them, but he was painfully aware he did not know how to reach them.

Throughout Elspeth lay in a coma.

Two days after Elspeth spoke to Richard, he stood once again at the window. Elspeth's steady monitors recorded no change, and her consciousness had not stirred since she had whispered to him. He turned to see a nurse enter the room.

"Sir Richard," she said, "there's a Mrs. Foxworthy outside who is asking to see Mrs. Duff."

Richard turned to the door as the woman entered, and his heart banged against his chest. He wanted to cry out. The woman who walked in the room was Elspeth the way she had been thirty years before. In his fatigue, Richard wondered if he was hallucinating. She had the same strong jaw, sharp nose, high cheekbones, the same light brown hair and the same handsomeness of all the Duff/Robertson women: Elspeth, her mother, and Biddy Baillie Shaw. The eyes, however, were different, dark chocolate brown, not cobalt blue, but they were filled with the same intelligence as Elspeth's.

"Sir Richard?" the woman said, as if she wasn't sure. "I am Elizabeth Craig Foxworthy."

Richard did not speak for fear of betraying his feelings. He wondered what this woman would have been like if she were Elspeth's and his daughter, not Elspeth and Alistair Craig's. Would she have his hazel-green eyes, rather than Alistair's brown ones, or would she have Elspeth's startling blue ones? When this child was conceived, did Alistair love Elspeth as much as Richard loved Elspeth now? He did not want to think of Elspeth and Alistair being together. What would it be like for Richard to have Lizzie Foxworthy as a daughter? He stiffened his face in order not to betray his thoughts.

Lizzie seemed puzzled at his sternness. She looked over at her mother and then back at him, her eyes large with fear. "Is she all right?" Lizzie said. "I'd not heard from Mummy since Christmas and was worried. Peter, my brother, knew nothing, so I called my grandfather in Perthshire. He said Mummy was hurt and here at St. Mary's in London. I would have come earlier if I'd known."

Richard was washed with selfishness, knowing he wanted to be alone with Elspeth until she was fully recovered. He had discussed with Elspeth's father the possibility of calling her children, and James Duff had agreed with Richard that Peter was too far away in San Francisco to help and Lizzie too involved with her young family. What could they do as their mother lay in a coma, her heart beating strongly but her mind oblivious? Richard now wished he had contacted Elspeth's children earlier.

He went around to where Lizzie was standing. He felt torn with the emotional shock of seeing someone who was so much a part of Elspeth, but whom he did not know except as a vague memory of Lizzie as a child when Marjorie and he had passed though California years before. The young woman who now stood in front of him looked so much like her mother that Richard could hardly speak.

"Your grandfather and I thought it best," he said, "to wait until your mother was out of her coma before we asked you to come see her." Richard felt his words were condescending, and he regretted them.

Elspeth stirred in her bed. "Dickie," she said clearly, and then she fell back into her own silent place.

Richard's eyes implored Lizzie's. He spoke to her as honestly as he could. "Your mother was severely injured, but the doctors say she will recover, but they don't know yet how long it will take."

"Sir Richard," Lizzie said with the stubbornly set jaw Richard recognized from her mother, "Grandfather and you shouldn't have kept this from Peter and me. We're her family, and we're no longer children."

Richard felt as if he had been slapped, although Lizzie's words were softly spoken. No, he was not family, but he loved Elspeth so deeply that he could not imagine they could care more than he. He wanted more than anything else in his life to be a part of the family, to have Elizabeth Craig Foxworthy as his daughter and not Alistair's. He could not say so because Elspeth always dodged his love and surely never spoke to her children of it.

He reverted to his accustomed position of authority, which he unexpectedly found overbearing. "Your mother needed someone who could be with her. Your grandfather gave me that responsibility since I helped air-evacuate her back from Singapore." The words sounded pompous, a quality Elspeth often accused him of having, and he regretted it.

Lizzie looked at him, the way her mother often did. "Then I must thank you," she said stiffly.

He could not read her mind in the same way he usually could not read her mother's. Their meeting was going badly, and he thought desperately how to change it. He did not expect Elspeth to help him but she did.

"Dickie," she said again from her bed.

Lizzie ran to her mother's bed, kneeling by it and taking the hand Richard had held for so many hours and days.

Elspeth responded to the touch and turned toward her daughter. "Lizzie," she said very clearly, "what are you doing in Singapore?" And then her blue eyes closed against the brown ones that mirrored hers.

Lizzie rose. Her dark eyes challenged Richard. "Will you tell me what happened to my mother? Why does she think we are in Singapore and not London? And why are you here?" she asked.

Richard thought how best to respond. How could he tell Lizzie what had occupied her mother's life or held his heart over the last several months?

"She was badly beaten at the back of the head at the Kennington hotel there," he said without further details. "I was in Singapore at the time and offered my services to Lord Kennington to bring her back here." He did not say why he was in Singapore.

"Sir Richard, I can hardly believe she was assaulted in a Kennington hotel. Outside perhaps but not in the hotel."

Richard remembered Elspeth often said she had two children, an American son, Peter, and a British daughter, Lizzie. Despite her birth in Los Angeles, at an early age Lizzie Craig chose boarding school in England and never returned to America except for brief visits to see her family. She was now comfortably settled in East Sussex with her husband, Denis, and their young twin boys. No one would have suspected Lizzie Foxworthy's place of birth from her address or appearance.

Richard responded more formally than he wished. "Your mother was in the process of uncovering some unpleasantness at the hotel. She was struck from behind. Since that time she has been unconscious, but we don't know the details of how it happened. We're hoping when she comes out of her coma she will tell us more. The doctors say she may not remember at first because of the trauma."

"How long has she been here?"

"Almost a fortnight," he said. "It took me two days to arrange for transport from Singapore before that."

Lizzie looked perplexed.

"Why are you still here, Sir Richard?"

He wanted to take Lizzie's shoulders and cry out, "Because I love your mother to distraction, because I cannot leave her, and because I need to know she eventually will be well." Instead he said, "I had a bit of leave coming and thought I could help. As a friend of the family." He hated what he said.

"She still thinks she is in Singapore," Lizzie said incredulously.

"She's slowly coming out her coma. She is only beginning to speak, but the doctors assure me her recognizing people is a positive sign. We'll tell her she is in London when she can comprehend it."

"We? Has anyone been here but you?"

"Pamela Crumm visits every day. Lord Kennington has been here twice."

"I suppose they are concerned because they are liable for my mother's unfortunate. . .it wasn't an accident, was it?"

"No, it was a deliberate attack, but Pamela and Eric Kennington came for personal concern for your mother, nothing more."

"And you, Sir Richard, I suppose you come and go as your time allows?" There was the same challenging fire in Lizzie's eyes he so often saw in Elspeth's.

"I'm fortunate to have the time to be here frequently," he said. "Elizabeth," he said formally, "I care. . .I care that your mother will recover."

She did not seem to hear the love in his voice.

"Yes, I'm sure," she said dismissively. "There seems little more I can do here until Mummy is fully conscious. Will you ask the staff to call me when she has come out of her coma."

"It will be my greatest pleasure to call you myself."

"Here is my number." She drew out a business card. "Again thank you for your help, Sir Richard. I'm sure if Mummy were awake she would be equally appreciative." As she left, Lizzie nodded with courtesy but not with warmth.

Elspeth came in and went out of consciousness for the next three days. The doctors were pleased at her progress. During that time she evoked Dickie's name most often, but once or twice asked for Lizzie, as if confused as to who was in the room.

Richard had arranged for a visitor's room nearby and slept there, always rushing to her side when the nurses told him she was awake.

On the fourth day, he entered her room, and she looked up at him with a smile of recognition. "Hello, Dickie," she said. "I seem to be in hospital and frightfully tied up in all this equipment."

"You do have a way of getting entangled in things," he said, his eyes filling with joy and tears.

"Did I dream that Lizzie was here in Singapore?" she asked. Then she said, "And why is my head shaved? I thought you were going to Hong Kong."

"Welcome back, oh my dearest one," he said, relishing the lack of logical flow in her words. "Welcome back to the living."

31

Loneliness wrapped Elspeth as she sat alone in her flat. Before the attack the space had been her retreat, her haven, but now she was confined here without respite until she was completely restored to health. She was allowed only one weekly parole to visit the clinic. The Kennington Organisation hired a male nurse to accompany her. Her inner sanctum became a cage. She was aware her mental faculties came and went and her memory was at best only partly there. She slept a great deal and occupied her time reading, looking at old films, and watching the inanity of most television programs. Often she would lose track of the plots in the middle of a film or show. She played music on her stereo, but there are only so many hours she could tolerate doing so. Her interest easily flagged.

Richard had insisted on a caregiver, who came every day, but, although the woman was attentive, she was vapid. Elspeth's housekeeper, Mrs. Brown, appeared every other day to cook meals for her and clean, but she did not offered any intelligent conversation. Stay quiet, the doctors admonished her, but solitude was driving Elspeth, whose normal daily life was so active, into a state of dark moodiness.

Lizzie visited several times but, despite her words of concern, was more involved with her husband, her young twins, and her job than with her mother. Elspeth's independent lifestyle had long contributed to a loving distance between them.

Richard sent affectionate emails at least once a day and usually more often. She had little to say in response but thanks for his concern. He had visited only once since bringing her home from the hospital and then fleetingly.

After a month, Elspeth was feeling slightly more lucid and decided to invite Pamela Crumm to dinner if she were willing to put up with Mrs. Brown's frozen dishes. Pamela came directly from the offices of the Kennington Organisation, dressed immaculately and eyes brimming with good will. On arrival Pamela was too true a friend to comment on Elspeth's cavernous appearance and closely cropped head. Instead she proffered flowers from Eric Kennington.

"Elspeth, ducks," she said, "his high lordship is champing at the bits for you to resume your job. He says he needs you back immediately."

Elspeth smiled sadly. "If only my brain would return to good repair. It comes and goes without any reasonable explanation as to why. Sometimes everything is there, and then the next moment I hardly recognize where I am. The doctors say the increasing length of my clear moments means eventually I'll be able to remember everything except perhaps the moment I was struck down. I may have lost that memory permanently. I hate being so dour. I even asked my housekeeper set the table so that I don't have to remember how to do so."

As they ate, Pamela talked of the latest happenings at the hotels. Elspeth listened but only understood parts of it. She could see Pamela watching her.

"You haven't heard everything I have said, have you?" her perceptive friend said.

"Pamela, I'm going crazy with the dullness of my existence. I never before have been so bored. I need something to get my mind around, but I don't trust it yet. The doctors say three to four months, but what am I to do in the meantime?" Her plea was genuine.

"How is the search for Malcolm's killer going? That has no deadlines," Pamela said.

Elspeth did not share the current delusions of her mind. Visions of Malcolm came and went. Sometimes his face morphed into that of Richard Munro, who was placing his hand on Victoria Smythe-Weldon's thick thigh. Sometimes Malcolm would be walking with Elspeth along the Backs, and all the love would return. Sometimes she saw Malcolm riding off on his bicycle for the last time with the Chinese waitress on his handlebars. These images confused her.

"I took an enormous amount of notes this last month," she said and then realized "this last month" was actually two months earlier. "I sent a backup to Peter in San Francisco when I was making these notes, and when he formatted my new laptop, he downloaded them all to it."

"Then perhaps you do have something to work on as you recover," Pamela said.

Elspeth focused in on her friend. "What a good idea."

"And Sir Richard?" Pamela asked. "Has he been attentive?"

"I hear from him now and again."

"And how often is now and again? Do not lie to me, Elspeth, m'friend."

"Why does everyone keep asking about Richard and me? There is no Richard and me."

Echoing Sarah Brixton, Pamela looked at Elspeth and said, "When are you going to recognize your feelings toward him?"

Elspeth bristled. "What feelings? He's an old friend, nothing more." She knew she was not telling the truth.

"Nothing more? Did 'nothing more' sit for a fortnight holding your hand and kissing your brow when you were in a coma at St. Mary's?"

"My father gave Richard responsibility for my welfare when I was in hospital. Daddy's too old to come to London."

"Elspeth, why are you lying to yourself?" Pamela said. "Why can't you face what you feel for him?"

"It seems as if everyone else in the world knows what I feel for Richard but me," Elspeth said defensively. "Now, Pamela, may we lay that subject to rest."

The next day the caregiver fussed about Elspeth, who did not take kindly to fussing.

"There, dear," the caregiver said. "All comfy?"

Elspeth inwardly growled. "My head hurts most of the time, but I make myself as comfortable as I can," she said.

The caregiver did not seem to notice Elspeth's sarcasm.

"Has Sir Richard come visiting again? Such a nice gentleman. He seems so fond of you. You make such a romantic couple."

"We are not a couple," Elspeth snarled.

"All right, madam," she said, seemingly offended.

When Richard phoned the next day, Elspeth was still feeling annoyed that others were constantly expressing their feelings as to her relationship with him.

Richard spoke kindly. "I'm finishing up meetings in Brussels and thought I'd come over to London. May I come and call on you?"

Elspeth ground her teeth.

"Why don't you just come out and say what you mean!" she said, angry at his politeness.

There was silence on the other end of the line.

"Dickie, I'm so sorry. That was so terribly rude. Please forgive me."

His voice became steely. "Politeness always serves me well with everyone but you, Elspeth. If you want frankness, which seems more your style than mine, then I will say what I mean. I want to come to London because I love you beyond all reason and want to see you above all other things in my life. I want to make love to you, but you continually push me away. I keep telling myself that if I am polite I won't offend your sensibilities and you will continue to tolerate my company. I tiptoe around you with politeness because I don't want to lose you from my life. I really want to say 'Please, I want you to love me, Elspeth,' but you probably don't. You draw away from me in the same the way you draw away from the truth about Malcolm. The most I can ask from you is that I may call on you and see how you are recovering from your injury. Is that frank enough?"

Elspeth winced. His angry words bit into the truth of her denial.

After a long silence, she whispered, "You never said you loved me before."

"Elspeth, you have such a fine mind, but is your heart trapped in a locked box? Much of the time I think so."

When he arrived, she still felt such contrition, that, as he entered, she put her fingers to his face and kissed him lightly on the lips, which she had never done before. Suddenly she shied away from him as if hit by an electric surge that carried down through her body. It was not from pain but pleasure. He looked at her with puzzlement.

"Elspeth?" he asked, as she drew away.

Confused by the strength of her emotion, she said, "This blasted head," and rubbed the stubble of her hair. She hoped he would assume her sudden body spasm was one brought on by her injury not by her heart.

Covering her feelings, she said, "Come in. Mrs. Brown brought in something special for dinner, and you can help me prepare it. Have some wine. I'm not allowed any, but you'll find a good white burgundy in the fridge."

As they fixed their meal, Elspeth went over to where Richard was chopping the vegetables for the salad.

"Dickie, perhaps I shouldn't say this when you have a knife in your hands, but I want to apologize once again for my rudeness on the phone. I've hated the last weeks here, going in and out of memory, with little to do but get irritated with the caregiver, with the housekeeper, with you, and mostly with myself. I need something to occupy my handicapped brain, something that will harm no one and keep me sane."

He selected a red pepper and cut it open to reveal the pulp and seeds. He looked at it and said, "This pepper is amazingly empty inside, but, Elspeth, despite your current loss of memory, you are not. Try to pull your memory back."

She bit her lip. "I want to. I'd thought to go back to the unfinished mystery of Malcolm's death. Pamela suggested I do so when she was here last week. In Singapore I felt I was closing in on understanding what had happened, but the solution evaded me there and does even more so now. My dear son has sent me a new laptop with copies of all my notes that I sent to him regarding my investigation into Malcolm's death. I thought if I went back to the files and saw what I wrote there, it would be a start."

Richard stopped chopping and put down his knife. He touched Elspeth's cheek, so slightly she later wondered if it had happened, and then resumed his chopping.

"I think that's a marvelous idea," he said.

The peppers for the salad were extremely finely diced, more than a master chef would have condoned. Neither Richard nor Elspeth commented on it.

Later, as they were having coffee, he said to her, "Elspeth, did you hear what I said on the telephone?"

She tensed. "Yes" was all she said.

"Do you have any response?" His eyes found hers and held them.

"I'm not ready to respond yet, Dickie."

"Will you ever be? I sometimes fear not."

She lowered her eyes and flushed. "I don't trust how I feel, but when I know for certain, I'll tell you. If I gave you any other response, it wouldn't be honest." She smiled at him wanly. "That's my second apology today, isn't it."

"Then I'll have to accept that," he said. He swallowed hard, and his face filled with sadness.

Elspeth opened her laptop the next morning, with hope it would help her open up her memory but feared it would not. Her notes began when she returned to Girton and met Jean Henderson, went on to her interview with Chief Inspector Llewellyn, then to Scotland, Australia, and Malta and finally to the interviews in Singapore. Only the last meeting with Roger Black was missing. She could recall only a few details of that breakfast. She must ask Richard how much he remembered. Reading over her notes, she sensed she had almost all of the information she needed to find her answer, but she still was not able to link everything together. She had felt this as well just before Richard found her lying unconscious in her hotel room. She read her last note to herself before going to breakfast with Roger Black. The note read: "Mary Anne, Mary Anne, why does it always come back to Mary Anne? What did she know that I do not?"

32

Focusing in and out as well as she could, Elspeth went over her notes again. That morning the doctors told her she had several more months before they thought she could function normally, but she had longer and longer periods of lucidity. When she did feel competent, she entered her thoughts into the computer. She attempted to make as many links as possible between the things she had learned in England, Malta, Australia and Singapore. At first the connections stymied her, but slowly she began to work them out. There were missing pieces. She wanted most of all to talk to Maudy. In the end she called Morris Aldridge.

His reply was courteous but short. "Mrs. Lee asked that she not be contacted other than through this office. You're welcome to call me at any time. I'll convey your messages to her."

Knowing that she might lose her concentration, Elspeth decided to write down everything that still puzzled her. She started with Malcolm and tried to keep her list chronological.

Why did Anna Maria Buchanan send Malcolm and Mary Anne to England? Edward Berkeley had said something terrible had happened in the jungle, but Mary Anne would never say what it was. The children reportedly were brought out of the jungle because they needed 'civilizing'.

If Malcolm was not with Mary Anne in London for Christmas in 1968, where was he? He must have gone to Australia as well. If Malcolm and Mary Anne did not get along, why would they both go to Tasmania? And why did Malcolm say MABB would not go to the 'Antipodes' although Edward Buchanan said she did?

Was Malcolm really in London at the end of February doing his research? He never said where he was staying. With a chum? Letters from him postmarked WC1 came every day to Girton.

What was the real relationship between Mary Anne and Malcolm? Why did Malcolm say it had cooled? Did Malcolm not want me to get to know Mary Anne for fear of what she might say about him? Did they fight at Christmas and, if so, over what?

Why didn't Malcolm say his parents were dead, or worse, murdered? Why would he cover up the murders? Did he fear I might react badly? Or something else?

What was Malcolm's relationship with his mother and father? He seldom spoke of them. Did Malcolm purposely hide his relationship with his parents? Why?

Edward said Mary Anne thought Malcolm had a dark side. Others, including Richard, did not like him.

What was Malcolm's relationship with the Chinese waitress? (Not sexual, but an 'evil sister'? Who had said that?) Did the waitress come from Malcolm's past and, if so, what was their true relationship?

At one time why did Malcolm say he didn't speak anything but Chinese baby talk, but then why did he contradict himself that day in the punt? Which story was true?

Where did Malcolm get his money? (Did he really pinch it as Victoria implied?) He never seemed to suffer from the lack of it, although now it seemed his family had little.

Why did Malcolm's tutor at King's think his research was sloppy? The tutor told Richard he regretted Malcolm's impatience.

What was it Malcolm thought he would discover that would make him instantly recognized in his field without the rigors of scholarship? And why would that make him rich?

Did Malcolm really steal the undocumented jade object at the British museum as Dr Lynn had implied? What was Malcolm's fascination with jade?

Was Malcolm really in Victoria's fast set?

If Malcolm was as unsavory as others implied, how could I have loved him so much? (Hurtful thought!)

Why did he propose to me?

Shaken, Elspeth wondered if Malcolm loved her as much as she had loved him. Her head began to pound.

Where is Malcolm buried and what happened to his belongings? Mary Anne would have known. Would Maudy?

Why are there so many unknowns, and why aren't all the pieces fitting together properly?

Elspeth abandoned her list, because she was no longer feeling equipped to deal with the emotions and doubts it evoked. She tried to divert her thoughts but could not. She rang Lizzie and asked about the twins, but she did not listen to the answer. It was the middle of the night in San Francisco, so she could not call her son, Peter. She phoned her hair stylist to arrange for him to come to the flat to deal with what Elspeth thought of as 'the stubble,' although it had grown out sufficiently to be fashionably styled in a short crop. She forgot to write the time down and had to ring back. Perhaps she should contact her parents, but she had nothing new to add about her health. She did not want to worry them. She thought Pamela would pressure her about her condition and when she would be able to return to her job. She knew Richard was in meetings in Brussels and would not want to be disturbed. The world was going on around her, and she remained a hopelessly homebound invalid. No, she thought, I won't give in to this. My brain may be impaired but my intelligence is not. She made a pot of coffee and returned to her lists, next considering Malcolm's parents.

Where were they during the war? Sergeant Hall said Jamie Buchanan came to the jungle camps but the men did not trust him. Why?

Was Anna Maria Buchanan's father really an Italian ambassador and what was his name other than Bartolomeo? What had life been like for Anna Maria during the war? How and where did Jamie Buchanan and she meet?

Why did Anna Maria bring the children out of the jungle in 1953? Had she brought something out from the jungle other than her two children?

Were Malcolm's parents communist sympathizers or Secret Intelligence? Or double agents? For which side?

Why in the Tasmanian newspaper was Anna Maria depicted as East Asian when her children obviously had no Asian blood?

Why were the murders of Malcolm's parents still classified?

What was the key Malcolm's father thought so important but his mother wanted to dismiss?

Why did Leonard Baines say, 'So it was her they wanted to protect and not him'?

Why was Malcolm laid out in the same way his parents were after they were shot?

Had they all three of them been shot with the same gun? (What a thought!) Where did the gun go after the murders?

What happened to the Malay, or was she Chinese, servant in Rushmore? Was it she who was buried with the Buchanans in the churchyard?

The questions about Malcolm's parents evoked less emotion than the ones about Malcolm, but Elspeth still could not grapple with the answers. There were too many things she might never know. She remembered her query to herself from Singapore. Why does it all come back to Mary Anne Buchanan Berkeley?

What exactly was Mary Anne's relationship with Malcolm—from the time they were children in the jungle until the last months of Malcolm's life?

Mary Anne wanted all her parents' effects. Did that include the elusive key?

Did Malcolm also want the key? Did it have something to do with the 'discovery' he wanted to use to launch his career?

Why was Mary Anne in Cambridge the day Malcolm was shot?

Why did Richard say Mary Anne seemed emotionally dead when Llewellyn and he had interviewed her after Malcolm's murder?

Why did Mary Anne divorce Edward in Australia?

What is the meaning of the inscription on the headstone in Rushmore and why did Mary Anne want to be buried there with the three others?

Why did Maudy balk at seeing her father, and why did she stand me up at tea at Raffles?

Elspeth despaired at answering all these questions, but, unless all her information dovetailed, she knew she would not be able to identify Malcolm's murderer. She had come too far for her to turn back now, although she wished she could.

Elspeth found the air stifling in her flat, and, despite her doctor's warnings not to go out alone, she took her tweed coat from the cupboard and walked out to Kensington Gardens. Pale February sunlight sent early afternoon shadows across the empty flowerbeds and the winter green lawns. The wind was biting, but it cleared Elspeth's mind. She walked on toward Kensington Palace and sat to rest on a freezing bench.

A young mother came up and sat at a bench across from hers. Her children played on the grass. The boy aimed and shot a toy gun at his mother, although she seemed unmoved by the attack. His older sister finally intervened and grabbed the young boy's gun. She pointed it at him and shouted. "There, you're dead." He fell down in a mockery of death, hands crossing his chest. Elspeth watched them, horrified.

"Are you all right, madam," a passer-by said as Elspeth gasped. Elspeth shook her head to clear it, but she was shaking.

"Yes, quite all right, thank you," Elspeth said, rising quickly. She fled back to her flat. She grasped her mobile and tapped in Richard's number, although she did not expect him to answer.

"Munro here," he said.

Elspeth's voice was quivering. Her words came spilling out. "Dickie, I know who shot Malcolm, and I know why!"

"Elspeth, is that you? Slow down, please. I don't think I understood."

"I know who shot Malcolm, and I know why," she said again more slowly.

"Who?" he asked. "And why?"

"I want to tell you in person. Can you come here as soon as possible, Dickie?"

"I can be there late this evening. Will you be all right until then?"

"Yes, quite all right," she said parroting her earlier words, although she didn't mean them. "Just come as soon as you can."

"I'll get the first flight out that has available seats," he said. "I'll ring you from the airport."

33

Although Richard had flown from Brussels to London many times, those flights never seemed as long as this one. They were delayed by heavy runway traffic and finally took off in the rain. They circled Gatwick for twenty minutes before landing. His window offered only the reflection of the wing's lights on the cloud cover, not the ground below. At last, this image was replaced by the brilliance of the landing lights, which gave hope of an imminent landing. Richard had called ahead to his club, which was on the way to Elspeth's flat, and asked his taxi driver to stop briefly there for him to drop off his hand luggage.

During the trip, Richard thought of his unresolved relationship with Elspeth. Her discovery might change this, but he had no idea how. It was he whom she had rung about her discovery and he whom she wanted to tell first. Not anyone else. Did that mean she was opening to him or simply that he was the prime mover of her search, and she felt she owed him an explanation? At best it would be both.

Richard did not arrive at Elspeth's Kensington flat until after eleven, but Elspeth was waiting up for him. She flung open the door at his knock.

He took her in his arms carefully for he could see she was in a fragile place. She leaned against him and let out short noises of hurt. Her body was shaking. He held her several minutes and then led her into the room. "Now tell me," he said gently. "Who was it?"

She laid her head on his shoulder, which still was wet from the rain. "It was Mary Anne," she whispered, "his sister. She killed him."

He drew back from her and saw her face, contorted with grief. "Why would she kill her brother?" he asked, touching her cheek.

Elspeth responded with a pleading look. "Here's where I need your support, Dickie. She killed him because . . ." Elspeth said, her voice garbled with pain, "because Malcolm killed their parents." Elspeth put her head back on Richard's shoulder and pressed her arms around him so tightly that he could hardly breathe. He stood silently, giving her time to calm herself.

"Are you sure?" he said into the soft crop of her hair.

"As sure as I can be without a confession," she said into his shoulder. "All the pieces fit."

He led her to the sofa in front of the gas fire and sat down next to her, his arm around her. Dark circles of grief ringed her eyes.

"Tell me from the beginning, my precious one," he said without disguising his feelings.

She looked at him, her eyes filled with heartache and pleading for solace. She took his free hand in both of hers and looked down to examine it, as if she could not face the moment of truth. She swallowed hard.

"Take your time. I'm here for as long as you need me," he said, hoping his words would comfort her. He knew he needed to give her space to explain her reasoning without his interposing his own feelings on her.

"I couldn't bear being imprisoned here for one more minute this afternoon," she said. "So I went out into the gardens, alone, without the caregiver or anyone else. It's been two months, Dickie, and my balance has been stable for at least the last two weeks. There could be no harm in it, and I couldn't stand these walls any longer. Real sunlight, even as feeble as it was, was better than staring at its reflection in the windows above the loft. I become damnably tired so quickly and needed to find a refuge. I sat on a bench across from a mother, who was dressed in a fashionable Burberry and stretch tights. Funny that I noticed. She looked uncomfortable in her role as childminder on what obviously was the nanny's afternoon off. Her son was shooting a toy gun at her, but she seemed to take no notice. The boy's sister came up, grabbed the gun from her brother and shot at him. Bang, bang, you're dead! My head swam. Bang, bang, Malcolm, you're dead because you shot Mummy and because you shot Daddy. This rang through my head like the peal of unrelenting church bells. Bang, bang, Malcolm, you're dead! It shook me all the way through because I knew it was true. A passer-by stopped and asked me if I was all right. I fled, assuring her that nothing was wrong. But everything was wrong, everything I ever assumed about Malcolm. Don't scold me, Dickie, please."

He said nothing but took his hand from hers and put his thumb to her face, wiping away the tears from her lashes.

"I've checked and double-checked the facts since I called you in Brussels. It's the only possible explanation. It began in Malaya during the war," she said, her voice almost expressionless as if she were narrating a documentary on television. "Both Mary Anne and Malcolm were conceived during that time, which would not have been possible had their parents been in the internment camps, which were segregated by gender. Roger Black told us Anna Maria was held in custody by the Japanese outside Ipoh. Did she bribe her guards to allow Jamie to see her? She could hardly disguise her pregnancies or the subsequent births of European children with reddish or sandy hair and blue eyes. Jamie's visits must have been tolerated. Sergeant Hall told us Jamie went to and from the jungle but was not trusted. Was this because he had reached some bargain with the Japanese over Anna Maria's confinement at the tin mine owner's villa? I think so."

Richard watched Elspeth as she spoke. As she launched into her explanation, he could see her mind overcome her emotions, a trait he often observed in her, usually to the detriment of their personal relationship. He let her continue. Her words seemed to calm her.

"Jamie and Anna Maria went into the jungles after the war with their two children. Why? Jamie must have been either with the Secret Service or a communist sympathizer. I suspect the former but cannot be sure. Sergeant Hall told us Jamie was an expert with radio equipment. During Anna Maria's house arrest during the war, she would have had at least limited access to the comings and goings of the Japanese in the Ipoh region. Jamie could have visited her and afterwards gone back into the jungles to relay his information to the Allied Southeast Asia Command. His controllers in New Delhi or London must have decided that Jamie had enough connections to the communist insurgents in the Malayan jungle to have him return there after the war. This would be consistent with his being a spy for the British."

Richard let her run her course.

"How would this affect Anna Maria?" she continued. "As a mother, I kept thinking about that. Why would she subject her children to the rigors of the life led by the insurgents during the Malayan Emergency? Did it have something to do with Jamie, or was she too a spy? I don't know, of course, but I can imagine growing up in the jungles in such harsh conditions would have a lasting effect on Mary Anne and Malcolm. You and I, as you said Dickie, grew up without war, protected from violence and hate. The Buchanan children did not. One can only imagine the horrors they saw and what effect it had on them."

Richard nodded, but he did not interrupt.

"Something happened to those children that must have warped them and, in the end, may explain why they acted the way they did," Elspeth said. "Edward Berkeley told me Mary Anne spoke of a dark side to Malcolm. I think this developed in the jungles when he was a child. I don't want to admit to this, but I no longer have any choice."

He took her hand, turned it over in his and kissed it lightly. She smiled weakly at him but did not otherwise respond to his gesture.

"Anna Maria Buchanan brought her children out of the jungle in nineteen fifty-three, but I think she brought out two other things. I'm stretching here, but I don't think I'm wrong."

"What did she bring?" he asked.

"I suspect something of great value, a piece of art, and. . ." Elspeth took a deep breath, "and an unborn child in her womb."

Richard frowned. Why would Elspeth think this?

"Their so-called servant in Tasmania, probably was her daughter and perhaps that of the Chinese leader of the cell of insurgents where they lived. The child later surfaced as the Chinese waitress at Ming Palace in Cambridge, where she was called Ah-sing or Ah-ting. Let me explain later."

"Please," he said. "I'm not following yet."

"Anna Maria brought Mary Anne and Malcolm out of the jungle and sent them here, to England, so that they would become 'civilized.' I find that an odd word. Neither Malcolm nor Mary Anne could have forgotten what happened on this trip to Singapore because Malcolm was eight and Mary Anne ten. I think, although I'm making a leap here, Anna Maria didn't want them to know she was pregnant with a child other than their father's. Mary Anne may have denied it, but Malcolm was cleverer than she or perhaps more devious and used this to his advantage. Grant Middleton in Rushmore told me his wife called the servant a 'half-caste.' Those are his wife's words not mine. Somehow Malcolm must have found out about his mother's relationship to Ah-ting, the child, and, probably in order to provoke Mary Anne as well as his mother, called Ah-ting his 'sister.' Victoria Smythe-Welton told me that the waitress said Malcolm was her 'evil brother.' It's hard for me to admit this about Malcolm, particularly to you Dickie, but it must be true."

"I understand," he said tenderly, never taking his eyes from her face, although she often looked away while speaking.

"I don't know the exact relationship between Anna Maria and her lover in the jungle, but I suspect Anna Maria was his lifeline to the West. Safirah binti Ibrahim mentioned a Hwa Lo-bing. I searched the web and found that after the Cultural Revolution ended in China he became a vice-minister for the arts there. Lady Sarah actually interviewed him. Could he have been Ah-ting's father? Did Anna Maria bring out to Singapore something precious that Hwa, or someone like him, had hidden or stolen earlier in his life? Hwa's Wikipedia biography stated his father had been a curator of art at one of the more prominent museums in Beijing before the Gang of Four destroyed its contents. The regime sent Hwa's father into the countryside during the Cultural Revolution. Even when he was in the jungle, Hwa must have worried about his future. Did Malcolm remember that his mother brought something belonging to Hwa, or her lover, to Singapore? I don't know but strange things were probably going on here."

"Do you think Jamie Buchanan knew about the true origins of the child?" Richard asked.

"Possibly," Elspeth said. "But Anna Maria's connections to her lover can't be ignored. She had an irrevocable grip on him. Anna Maria may have turned him into an agent for the British Secret Service. Leonard Baines let slip that the person being protected in Tasmania was Anna Maria and not Jamie, which might mean that she was the one with ties to the Chinese government through her ex-lover. Spies are different from you and me, Dickie. They must be willing to sacrifice personal relationships for what they call 'the good of one's country.' I couldn't live that way, but Malcolm's parents must have. A strong link to the Chinese Communist hierarchy couldn't be disregarded despite any personal animosity between Jamie and Anna Maria about the pregnancy and subsequent child."

"I'm glad I don't inhabit such a world," Richard said.

"I agree, but I had to consider that Mary Anne and Malcolm grew up in that world. The secrecy of their parents' lives could not have escaped their children. Mary Anne and Malcolm never lived with their parents again, but it is my guess that Ah-ting was raised by them, first under the guise of a foster child and later as a companion/servant."

"And the other thing she brought out from the jungle? What do you think it was?" Richard asked.

"I'm not exactly sure, but it might have been the piece of jade that Malcolm was going to 'discover.' It must have been large enough that Anna Maria couldn't conceal it from her children when they came out to Singapore from the jungle. This is a guess, but I can't be too far wrong."

"And where do you suppose it is now?" Richard asked.

"Somewhere in a safety deposit box, possibly in Australia or more likely in Singapore. If her lover gave the jade object to Anna Maria, I expect he wanted her to take it to safekeeping in case he ever needed to flee from China. Anna Maria must have kept the safety deposit box key for him. Remember, Lesley Urquhart told me how important the key was to Mary Anne after her parents' deaths, but it would be more important to Malcolm, since he was pinning his career on revealing the jade. Lesley told me Mary Anne last saw her parents alive in the summer of nineteen sixty-eight. I stupidly formed the misconception that summer was in July or August. Summer, of course in Australia is in December and January. Edward Berkeley told me later that Mary Anne went to Tasmania that December, and therefore Malcolm did not spend Christmas with her in London. I thought back. Malcolm told me was he was spending Christmas with Mary Anne. It was I who superimposed London on that conversation with Malcolm because I knew Mary Anne lived in Chelsea. If they did go out to Tasmania together, I expect Mary Anne learned how essential the key was to Malcolm, or rather how vital getting his hands on the jade was."

Richard nodded. Elspeth's intellect was clearly engaged but the emotional drain on her was beginning to show.

Elspeth set her jaw, inhaled deeply, let her breath out slowly and continued. "By February, Malcolm was being faulted by his tutor for his lack of scholastic rigor. What better way for Malcolm to alleviate this pressure than to produce the art object? He told me he was going to London in late February to do research but, in the space of that week, he could have flown to Tasmania and confronted his mother about the key. His daily postcards to me could have been pre-arranged."

"Easily," Richard said. "Any of his chums would have done it."

"If Malcolm did have a dark side, his mother would have known it. Do you recall my telling you one of Mrs. Mack's troop members mentioned the large car going to the Paisley cottage before the oncoming thunderstorm? Others confirmed it. Malcolm could have flown into Hobart and hired a car to go to Rushmore in order to confront his mother about the key. I suspect she wouldn't give it to him and an argument sprang up. Malcolm could have seized a gun that his parents brought out from the jungle and shot his mother. His father may have tried to defend Anna Maria, and Malcolm shot him as well. The shots would have been disguised by the thunderstorm."

"Of course," Richard said, "That makes sense, but why would Malcolm take the bodies of his parents and lay them out with their hands crossed on their chest?"

Elspeth rolled his hand over in hers and clung to it in order to prevent her hands from shaking. "That's how the warriors of old were carved in effigy on their stone coffins," she said. "Malcolm and I used to go to the chapels around Cambridge and London and look at these heroic knight's final resting places. Malcolm may have been paying a distorted final tribute to his parents as warriors, but I don't know if that's right. In the heat of the Australian summer he may have hoped that the two bodies would decompose quickly or even be eaten by scavengers so that they might never be recognized. Malcolm was seen in the village, or at least his car was. He didn't want the bodies discovered before he was safely away from the cottage and on his way back to England."

"Did Ah-ting come back with him?" Richard asked, now following Elspeth's thoughts.

"I think so. Ah-ting wasn't at Ming Palace when Malcolm and I first went there. She came later." Elspeth swallowed hard. "When Mary Anne went out to Tasmania after her parents' bodies were found, she must have been desperate to know if Malcolm had somehow managed to get the key. Lesley Urquhart told me what a fuss Mary Anne made about getting her parents' personal effects. The key must have still been among them."

"Meaning Malcolm was not successful in finding it," Dickie said.

Elspeth nodded. "Now I understand why Malcolm was silent on the subject of his parents' deaths. Mary Anne certainly would have told him about the murders when she got back from Tasmania, even if Malcolm and she were estranged. How could he tell me though? Mary Anne must have suspected Malcolm committed the murders, and she must have known why—to get the key and the jade."

"It must be a very precious piece," Richard said.

"Yes, extremely precious. Malcolm told me about it, not directly of course, so, until today, I didn't make the connection. I'm certain it was the piece Malcolm mentioned to me one day when we were punting on the Cam. It belonged to a concubine of the Chinese emperor; I think he said in the Tang Dynasty."

"Do you think it still exists?" Richard asked.

"Yes, I think Maudy has it or knows where it is."

"Isn't that dangerous for her?"

"She must think so. That may be why she doesn't want to talk to me."

Richard moved in his seat, because he knew she was approaching difficult ground for her—Malcolm's death. "Elspeth, I think I understand why Mary Anne killed Malcolm. She was avenging her parents' murderers, but how did she do it? Didn't Inspector Llewellyn say it must have been done by an expert marksman?"

Pain contorted Elspeth's face again. She slowly blew out her breath and shook her head as if to be rid of her feelings. "I stood a long time at the window after Malcolm pedaled away that last evening, long enough to have heard the shots if he actually was killed where his body was found." Her voice cracked. "I'm not sure why I never thought of that until now. I'm now certain Malcolm was not killed riding on his bicycle just south of Girton. I suspect Mary Anne confronted him elsewhere and shot him when he was standing near her, first in the heart and then in the head, just as her parents had been. The shots were too accurate to hit someone on a bicycle. After killing him she brought his body back toward Girton and dragged it and the bicycle into the bushes. In a final act of revenge she crossed his hands across his body, the way he had done with their parents. The authorities must have told her how her parents were found. It hurts me to admit this about Malcolm, but I can think of no other reason. No one else in Cambridge that day would have known."

"Where did she get the gun?" Richard asked in puzzlement.

"Chief Inspector Llewellyn told me how. He said it in passing, so I hardly took notice. He said Mary Anne was in Cambridge the day Malcolm died, and she waited for Malcolm in his rooms at King's College. When Llewellyn first talked to Mary Anne, she suggested Malcolm had gone to Girton to see me and therefore she never saw him. She couldn't deny she had been at the college because the porter saw her. That's how Llewellyn first knew about me and why he passed that information on to Tony Ketcham. I presume while Mary Anne waited, she searched Malcolm's rooms and found the gun, which he must have brought back from Tasmania and hid among his belongings. Airport security was not so strict in those days. She must have driven out toward Girton, seen Malcolm on his bicycle and flagged him down in order to confront him about the gun. She may have had doubts before then, but the gun confirmed what she already suspected."

"Then she shot Malcolm on the spur of the moment," he said.

"No, I think she had waited for a long time to kill him but hadn't found the means to do so until she found the gun. That would explain why such an unusual gun to be found in Britain was the murder weapon, and why Special Branch—in the person of Tony Ketcham—was brought in."

Elspeth took her hands from Dickie's and covered her face. He waited without moving. Once again she regained her composure, but he saw how damaging her revelations were to her.

"And in the end," Elspeth said hoarsely, "by having committed murder Mary Anne destroyed her own life. She had a child to raise, but she could not decently stay married to Edward Berkeley while knowing what she had done. I don't know if Maudy ever learned the truth, but she could not ignore her mother's depression. After Mary Anne learned she had cancer she made arrangements to be buried in Rushmore, with her parents and. . .and also with Malcolm, the third person to be interred there in nineteen sixty-nine. Mary Anne must have arranged it."

Elspeth was shivering. Richard drew her up from the sofa and led her toward the gas fire. He put his arms around her and said, "How are you feeling now, my dearest."

She leaned against him, and he could feel her heavy breathing.

"Numb," she said, "and terribly sad. In some way I feel I was used by Malcolm, and he may have proposed to me in case I would ever find out the truth. As his wife, I couldn't testify against him."

Richard held her closer and hoped he could warm her. "For all that Malcolm was, I think he loved you. Since we are conjecturing here, I also suspect he knew he had gone too far toward evil to be a good husband to you. Your marriage wouldn't have lasted and, in the end, have given you more dismay than his murder did."

She put her face into Richard's shoulder, and the sobs came, deep tearless ones that had been buried there since the day Detective Sergeant Tony Ketcham had come to Girton to tell her his news. Richard held her and let the convulsions of her body take their course. It took a long time, but he did not let go of her.

Finally she drew away him and said, "Thank you, Dickie, for not saying I was a fool."

"You're not a fool, Elspeth, and never have been."

"But I'm foolish in the ways of the heart," she said and leaned into his chest again.

He turned her face up toward his and kissed her on the lips. For the first time she did not resist. Many months later she told him in that moment she fell completely in love with him. She said it was the only touch of happiness for her that evening. She also told him about the rivers of comfort and pleasure his kisses gave her, how warmth rushed through her body, and how she found both solace and wonder in them.

Epilogue

By late May Elspeth no longer had moments of forgetfulness and felt ready to re-join the world of her workplace. To Lord Kennington's delight, she resumed her duties with the Kennington Organisation, but she was given only short assignments. She continued her weekly visits to the trauma clinic and was pronounced almost completely recovered by the onset of summer. At the middle of July the summons came. She was asked to appear in the trial of Wilmont Hancock in Singapore in early August. Pamela Crumm hired a lawyer from Singapore to coach Elspeth on her testimony at the trial and made arrangements for her first class air travel and a room at the Kennington Singapore. Saying she needed to ease Elspeth's feelings about returning to the place where she was so frightfully beaten, Pamela had given Elspeth one of the more desirable rooms with a view out over the Botanic Gardens.

At her employer's command, Elspeth visited the Kennington Organisation offices in the City of London before her departure. Eric Kennington was waiting for her. He stood behind his Chippendale desk and appeared to be contemplating the traffic twenty floors below when Elspeth entered. As always, his admiring eyes greeted her. Her pallor had lessened, and her hair had grown out to the stage where it could be considered stylish, although it was not as becoming as her usually longer coif. Pamela Crumm was not in attendance. Elspeth felt this must be by design.

After Elspeth took a chair and a minion whom she did not recognize brought coffee, Eric spoke about his concern for her and for the reputation of the Kennington Singapore at the trial in Singapore.

"Despite the concerted efforts of my lawyers in Singapore, I haven't been able to have the trial held *in camera*, but I've been able to keep it from appearing in the press so far. You should know I had the extortion charges dropped against Hancock. We found three hundred thousand pounds in a bank account in Manchester in his deceased mother's name, but he agreed to return it to us in exchange for our not pressing our own charges against him. We'll use the money to pay back the taxi drivers and tour guides. The rest will be put in a fund for their health care and retirement. The judicial authorities in Singapore wouldn't allow us to bargain away the assault charges. I'm sorry you have to endure the ordeal of testifying against Hancock, but we will try to make your stay as pleasant as possible, considering how you must feel about returning to Singapore. There's one condition, however."

Elspeth had worked for Eric Kennington long enough to guess it had something to do with the wellbeing of his hotel. She was right.

"I want you to make every effort to divert attention away from the hotel during the trial. Sir Richard will be staying at the hotel as well, but I think it best you limit your contact with him. If anyone gets the sense that the two of you are more than acquaintances, it might be used against us somehow. An employee cannot be seen consorting with a guest, particularly a distinguished one."

Elspeth hoped she looked incensed. "Heavens, Eric, what gives you the impression that Richard and I are more than old friends. I certainly hope Pamela has not been imposing on you her romantic ideas of my relationship with him."

Eric Kennington looked askance at Elspeth. "I generally don't meddle in the love lives of my employees; I leave that to Pamela. But even I can't be blind to the change that has come over you since the unfortunate incident in Singapore and Sir Richard's obvious affection for you. You have softened, and it becomes you. My only hope is that your friendship, as you call it, with him will not take you away from your employment here."

"I have no intention of leaving my job, Eric. It's the core of my life." Elspeth hoped that her tone was ardent rather than defiant, but she was not certain how Eric Kennington read it.

He raised his heavy eyebrows. "Is it still? I'm not sure."

"You needn't worry, Eric. I promise you if there are any changes in my feelings toward my job, I'll let you know directly. When I return from Singapore, will I be given an assignment abroad, a real one? The doctors say I'm quite ready."

Eric seemed satisfied, at least momentarily. "There're several possibilities. I'll discuss them with you when you return."

"Thank you. I must admit I'm eager to get out of London, particularly during the summer when it is so crowded."

She shook Eric's hand as she left his office, thanked him and smiled her most engaging smile. She was not sure he trusted its sincerity.

Elspeth knew she had changed. She could no longer ignore that her feelings for Richard Munro went well beyond friendship, although she also knew she was still not ready to commit to him and all the complexities that commitment would entail. When he came to London, she awaited his arrival with anticipation and was no longer averse to his loving attention. She did not draw back when he touched her with fondness, and she found pleasure in his embraces. He did not ask her for more, although she suspected he wished for it.

From her flat that evening she rang Richard in Malta to ask him about his travel arrangements to Singapore. She was disappointed with his answer.

"Unfortunately my stay will be a short one, as this is an extraordinarily inconvenient time for me to be away from my duties in Malta and Brussels," he said. "I'll stay as long as I'm needed but can linger no longer, as much as I will love being there with you. Pamela Crumm has already booked my room at the Kennington Singapore. She said you will be staying there too."

"Dickie, beware of Pamela's matchmaking. Eric instructed me that we must show no more than mere acquaintanceship when we are there, at least in public. He doesn't want to raise any flags that might attract the press or effect the outcome of the trial."

"I'll be the model of rectitude," he said, "at least in public."

She said, suddenly serious, "If I'm going back to the Singapore, I want to see if I can make contact with Maudy. I want to know if the jade object really exists. I've decided to try to reach her through Morris Aldridge once again. I can't be sure how much Maudy knows about her mother and her uncle, but, if the jade does exist, it must belong to Maudy or at least she must know its whereabouts. I thought of asking Morris Aldridge if he would forward a letter to her from me, and in it I'll simply ask to see the jade and nothing more. Help me write it. I've some ideas, but they need some polishing and some diplomatic touches. Let me email you what I have in mind."

Together they worked on the draft of the letter, and she dispatched it by overnight express to Sydney a week before leaving for Singapore. She expected no reply and was surprised when a letter, posted in Singapore and bearing Maudy's name and a Singapore address in one of the better residential areas, was waiting for her when she arrived at the Kennington hotel there.

She tore open the letter and read over its short contents several times, her emotions in disarray.

> *Dear Mrs Duff,*
>
> *First I must apologize for running away from meeting you at the Raffles last December. I thought I would be able to speak to you then, but when I saw you, I knew I couldn't. I didn't want to talk about my mother, which you had requested we do. The simplicity of your current request puts my mind at ease. Yes, I will honour your request, but nothing more. Call me at the number above and we can set up a time.*
>
> *Again with apologies,*
> *Mary Anne Berkeley Lee.*

Elspeth could not contain the excitement she was feeling, but also knew that with this last piece of information she had no way to deny what she believed to be true. With Richard's support, she had endured the first few days of despair after discovering the only possible truth about Malcolm's murder. Until reading Maudy's letter Elspeth thought she had come to terms with it. Now she dreaded confirmation but accepted that it represented closure.

She turned to the receptionist. "Has Sir Richard Munro checked in yet?" she asked.

"No, Ms. Duff," the receptionist said.

"When he does arrive, please give him my room number and ask him to ring me," Elspeth said. She proceeded to her room, where Lord Kennington had special flowers waiting for her. A personal note lay by them. *Elspeth, Good luck and stay under the media's radar. E.K.*

Richard's did not ring until just before dinnertime. Elspeth could hear fatigue in his voice. "I'll let you rest, Dickie, but not before telling you Maudy has agreed." As an afterthought she added, "Do you want to come with me when I go to see the object?"

"No, dear one," he replied. "I think this will be the time you bid your final goodbye to Malcolm. You should do that alone or only with his niece. Later you can tell me what you saw."

They dined quietly in the terrace dining room and without any show of affection. When they were finished eating, he pleaded an early night. He left her at the door of her room, which Pamela had carefully located on the floor above his. Since there was no one in the hallway, he kissed Elspeth. She responded with a warm caress but she did not invite him in.

The next morning Elspeth rang Mary Ann Lee. Since the trial was to begin immediately, Elspeth put off their meeting until she had given testimony. The Kennington Organisation's solicitor instructed Elspeth that her testimony as well as Richard's should be short and factual. Their time in the witness stand lasted only a few hours, although the trial lasted longer. Wilmont Hancock was sentenced to twenty years in prison for assault with a deadly weapon with intent to kill. Elspeth and Richard did not return to the courtroom and did not hear the sentencing. They were standing in her room looking out over the Botanic Gardens when the call came from the lawyers, who told her the outcome and said Sir Richard and she were free to return to Europe.

"This is always the hardest part of my job," Elspeth told Richard. "Although people who commit crimes deserve what is meted out to them, I hate to be part of it, particularly since I'm not a member of the police and my job is not to bring justice. As Eric frequently tells me, I'm here to protect the security of the hotel and its guests. Unfortunately, there frequently are consequences beyond that."

"It must be difficult for you," he said.

Elspeth sighed. "I don't want to think about what awaits Wilmont. It will break him, as is intended, but I'm sorry I was a part of it, both because of my injuries and the punishment now to be inflicted on him. Now, I suppose, it's my time to face reality. I have an appointment with Maudy at three at the OCBC bank building. Will you be here when I get back or do you need to return to Malta immediately?"

"My flights to Rome and on to Malta aren't until late this evening." He put his hand to her face. She knew he could feel her tension. "What do you fear in this meeting?" he asked.

"The truth," she said.

"But you know that already."

She shook her head. "I've never had proof, only my own suppositions, but now I'll know the truth, or at least a bit of it. There's still a small part of me that wants it all to go away."

"I understand, Elspeth," he said almost in a whisper, and she knew he did.

A Secret in Singapore

Mary Ann Berkeley Lee looked up in recognition as Elspeth came through the glass doors of the bank. Morris Aldridge was right. Maudy's flaming hair and tall stature made her stand out from the Asian customers.

"Thank you, Mrs. Lee, for doing this for me," Elspeth said to her once they introduced themselves to each other.

Maudy's eyes held Elspeth's for a moment. "What you are about to see, Mrs. Duff, has caused my family untold misery. I only consented to let you see it because my mother asked me to do so before she died. She made me promise if you ever came and specifically asked to see what has been locked up here in the bank since nineteen fifty-three, I would let you do so. She also requested you be alone when you open the safety deposit box and examine what is in it. She said you were as harmed by the box's contents as my family was, but you were the only innocent one. Does that make sense to you?"

Elspeth closed her eyes, swallowed and nodded. "Yes," she said simply. "Is the jade very beautiful?"

"It destroyed my family," Maudy said. "I've never seen it and never want to. I've instructed the bank manager to take you to the vaults. I'll say goodbye now."

Then Maudy was gone.

With unsteady hands Elspeth unwrapped the coarse pieces of cloth and drew a statue from them. Its beauty was so breathtaking that Elspeth gasped. Stroking it, she felt the jade's coolness after its long burial in the vaults. She touched the delicate folds of the statue's long robes. Kwan Yin, the goddess of compassion, carved in rose-colored jade with a refinement fit for an emperor and his favorite concubine, looked lifelessly back at Elspeth. The goddess's power was indisputable even to someone with only a passing knowledge of Chinese art. Elspeth traced her fingers down the goddess's form and finally took up the rags in order to wrap the statue back in its shroud. Underneath the cloth was a letter addressed in a tidy hand. "This letter is for Elspeth Duff of Perthshire, Scotland, if she ever comes to find it."

Elspeth broke the seal on the envelope and read Mary Ann Buchanan's confession, which was dated in two thousand and two, six months before her death. Elspeth was essentially correct about what had happened, although the details differed in some instances. She still had unanswered questions. Where was Ah-ting now and was she really Anna Maria's daughter? Why wouldn't Maudy speak to her father? But these questions were not significant in light of the bigger truth. Elspeth read the letter several times over. It was four pages long and told her what she already suspected. She put it in her handbag. Then she reverently replaced the carving of the goddess in its wrappings and cradled it where she had found it. Taking up her bag, she called the attendant to let her out of the vault.

"Do you have a shredder?" she asked him.

"Yes, madam. There's one in the manager's office. He asked to see you before you leave, as he will need Mrs. Lee's key."

Elspeth returned the key and asked the manager if he would shred the letter. She watched it being cut into a thousand minuscule diamonds and with it her youthful delusions.

Richard was waiting for her in the main lounge when she returned to the hotel. He looked at her as if seeing into her heart. She took his arm and led him to the privacy of her room.

A Secret in Singapore

"Almost all of what I thought might be true was indeed so, at least according to Mary Anne," she said after telling him what had happened at the bank.

What Elspeth did not tell Richard, however, were about the two paragraphs that she felt belonged in a place that only Mary Anne and she could share.

> *I truly believe that Malcolm loved you, but by the time you two met, he was so far down the evil path that he chose for his life that I doubt he could have reformed sufficiently to make you a good husband. Before you, Malcolm never had a relationship with anyone whom he did not plan to manipulate to his own advantage, but I think you were different. For the sake of my parents, I kept in touch with him after their deaths, although often it was a struggle to remain even slightly polite.*

And then:

> *Malcolm was an unruly child. He liked to kill snakes and spiders and frighten the women in the camp. He frequently got in fights with the few other children there, and when he was eight years old he battered in the head of one of the other boys. The boy later died. My parents, particularly my mother, were horrified, and they agreed that Malcolm and I should be sent back to England, where it was hoped Malcolm 'would become civilized'. The leader of the camp made arrangements for our passage to Singapore. As we were leaving, I heard him ask my mother to take an object tightly wrapped in heavy padding and a burlap cloth and deposit it in a safety deposit box in Singapore as*

*quickly as she could. My mother would not tell us what
was in the packet. The leader swore her to secrecy,
because he said, if he were found with this object, the
government back in China would execute him when
he returned there. Although I was not supposed to
see, when he gave the packet to my mother, he kissed
her on the lips, touched her belly, and told her what
was between them would never be forgotten. I always
suspected that there was a special relationship between
my mother and the leader because he spent long hours
alone with her when my father was not present."*

After she finished telling Richard what the rest of the
letter said, he bowed his head and took Elspeth's hands in his
own. She looked up at him.

"In the end, Mary Anne's words on the tombstone in
Rushmore reflected the tragedy that filled the lives of her
family. 'May God's Love Forgive Us All.' All four of them—
Jamie, Anna Maria, Mary Anne, and Malcolm—are buried
under those words. May the compassion Kwan Yin bless us
and allow those of us who are still alive to find forgiveness
and peace," Elspeth said.

"You were right to destroy the letter. No one else needs to
know," Richard replied.

She touched his face with the tips of her fingers. "No, no
one else needs to know. Thank you, Dickie, for being here and
living through this with me."

"Elspeth," he said softly and nothing more. She did not
need him to do so.

Author's Appreciation

My gratitude goes to the many people who provided information for this book. Kate Perry, archivist at Girton College at the University of Cambridge, sent me extensive notes on the college and introduced me to Hilary Goy, who was at Girton at the time Elspeth would have been there. Hilary gave me an extensive tour of the college and explained to me what life was like at Girton in the late nineteen-sixties. My friend Judith Horstman and I went to Australia together, and the scenes in Sydney and Tasmania sprang from that trip. Ian and Gim Crew met me in Singapore, and they accompanied me to many of the places in the book. I developed the scenes in Malta, Scotland and London from my many visits to those places.

The staff of the Bar and Billiards Room at Raffles Hotel were especially kind when I told them I was writing a book, part of which would take place there.

Special thanks go to my editor, Rachel Marsh, M.Phil., in Dundee, Scotland for correcting my numerous mistakes. Any faults that remain are my own. As always, I deeply appreciate the help Jocelyn Jenner has given me.

Read on for an excerpt from *A Crisis in Cyprus*, the fourth Elspeth Duff mystery.

From *A Crisis in Cyprus:*

Philippa Allard-Thorpe strove for perfection in all the things she did. A child of obese parents, she became anorexic in her teenage years in order to achieve what she considered the perfect figure. She said she had graduated summa cum laude from her American university, and, occasionally when travelling in America or entertaining American guests, she displayed a Phi Beta Kappa key in her lapel, although no proof existed of either of these accomplishments. In marriage she wanted a perfect husband and perfect children. When Ernest Thorpe proved human, she divorced him. When her first child died, her second child became an imperfect replacement. Now, in mid-life, her immaculately clothed and slender figure, classic high cheekbones, and unnaturally straight white teeth disarmed all who met her. Yet, if one looked closely, nothing could hide the rigidity of her soul.

As the new manager of the Kennington Nicosia hotel, she insisted there be no errors in the comfort or service provided to the guests. A mistake by any member of her staff meant instant dismissal. Guests were charmed and became relaxed; the staff grumbled but benefited from being employed by the hotel at above average wages.

The one thing Philippa could not control was the manner of her death. When her murderer confronted her, she could find no perfect way to save herself. She could not make her transition from life to death into a perfect affair, although in the end she was perfectly dead.

Ann Crew is a former architect and now full time mystery writer who travels the world gathering material for future Elspeth Duff mysteries. Visit *anncrew.com*.

70574162R00207

Made in the USA
Columbia, SC
22 August 2019